BRAT

and the

Kids of Warriors

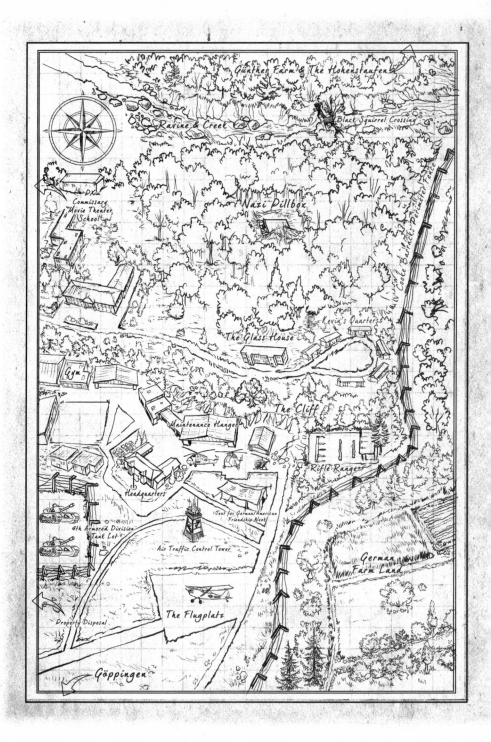

BRAT

and the
Kids of Warriors

Michael Joseph Lyons

BRAVUR
MEDIA

Chicago, Illinois

Library of Congress Control Number: 2017907817
Hardcover ISBN 978-1-946957-02-3
Paperback ISBN 978-1-946957-00-9
Ebook ISBN 978-1-946957-01-6

www.MichaelJosephLyons.com
www.facebook.com/michaeljosephlyons/

Publisher's Cataloging-in-Publication Data

Names: Lyons, Michael Joseph.
Title: BRAT and the kids of warriors / Michael Joseph Lyons.
Description: Chicago : Bravur Media, 2017. | Summary: Military brats lead a life
    of adventure, spies, making new friends, and dealing with their own set of
    enemies.
Identifiers: LCCN 2017907817 | ISBN 978-1-946957-02-3 (hardcover) | ISBN
    978-1-94657-00-9 (pbk.) | ISBN 978-1-946957-01-6 (Kindle ebook)
Subjects: CYAC: Children of military personnel—Fiction. | Brothers and sisters—
    Fiction. | Cold War—Fiction. | Self-reliance—Fiction. | Adventure and
    adventurers—Fiction. | Historical fiction. | BISAC: YOUNG ADULT
    FICTION / Action & Adventure / General. | YOUNG ADULT FICTION /
    Historical / Military & Wars. | YOUNG ADULT FICTION / Social Themes /
    Self-Esteem & Self-Reliance.
Classification: LCC PZ7.1.L96 Br 2017 (print) | LCC PZ7.1.L96 (ebook) | DDC
    [Fic]—dc23.

Printed in the USA
First Edition, June 2017

This book is dedicated to
my children,
who always begged for *just one more brat story*,
long after they should have been sound asleep

&

all those children of our military personnel,
you kids who so proudly call yourselves military brats,
for all the times you had to move,
for all the friends you left behind,
for those long weeks, and months, and years when your military parent
couldn't be there,
and
for your fabulous and adventurous lives.

Contents

BRAT

and the
Kids of Warriors

Part I

The USS *Upshur*

1

Spittin' Contest

One slip and you'd go crashing five stories down into the cold, foamy water. And you'd keep going down, down, down—five thousand feet down—all the way to the bottom of that ever darker ocean, never to be found. But did that bother the three children leaning out over the ship's rail? Not one bit. They were in the middle of a serious spittin' contest. Riding the rail, as the waves smashed up against the ship, heaving it from side to side, was a bit like riding the rollercoaster back on Coney Island.

"I can't see my spit by the time it hits the water," groaned Rabbit. Rabbit's real name was Kirsten. She was seven, and in every way the youngest of the three McMasters kids. Even her parents called her Rabbit because she ran around like a half-crazed jackrabbit. She was all fun and, most of the time, totally out of control. "We need something big to throw!" She was stretched way out over the edge of the gunnel, what they'd called the railing before knowing better.

"Yeah, like what?" asked her brother. Nobody ever called him anything but Jack. He was the only boy in the family, a fact that didn't please him.

Rabbit reached in her pocket for an orange she'd swiped from lunch.

"Oh no you don't!" yelled Laura. The others called her Queenie behind her back, because even though she was only a year older than Jack, she thought she was the boss of everything. Everyone knew better than to say it to her face.

But even Jack knew Rabbit needed a boss. When *she* got in trouble, *they* got in trouble. And there were plenty of ways to find trouble on their ship.

Well, it wasn't really theirs, of course; it belonged to the United States Navy. They'd been at sea for three days. Not out-to-sea like some fabulous Caribbean cruise, with blue skies, warm sun, and tranquil, turquoise water. The USS *Upshur* was fighting twenty-five-foot swells, freezing waters, and high winds under dark-gray skies. The massive, gray ship was a nonstop rocking-horse ride through the vast North Atlantic, headed for Bremerhaven, Germany.

It was late in 1957, and World War II was fresh in everyone's mind. The US military was still shipping soldiers to Germany, including over two thousand on this particular troop transport ship, plus some of their families. The one thing they all had in common was—puking. They were mostly a miserable, seasick bunch. But these three kids were convinced they were on the greatest cruise that ever sailed. They were determined to make the most of every minute . . . without getting caught by their mom or the United States Navy.

Rabbit, quick as lightning, jumped back up onto the bobbing gunnel, drew back her arm, and yelled, "Bombs away!" She threw the orange overboard. The three could see it all the way down. When it hit the water, it made a satisfying splash and disappeared forever.

Rabbit jumped back down onto the deck, dancing around with arms raised high in triumph. She sprinted off, yelling over her shoulder, "We gotta get more stuff to throw. Come on!"

"No!" Queenie made a grab for her, but not fast enough.

Rabbit shot past her. With her ponytail flying and her open coat flaring out behind her, she looked like a superhero off on a mission.

Jack and Queenie went tearing after her, but Rabbit was rabbit fast. She pushed open the ship's heavy outer door and disappeared. Coming to a narrow, metal stairwell, she grabbed the railings, one hand on either side. Her feet never touched a single step all the way down. The children had learned that trick from the sailors their first day out.

Jack and Queenie could no longer see her, but once inside the stairwell, they could hear her feet clanging on the metal floor below. They figured she was headed for the dining facility.

By the time they got there, Rabbit was on her way out, a big apple in each hand. She'd just about made it when a sailor grabbed her arm. "Hey, kid. What d'ya think you're doing in here?"

Queenie caught Jack's shirt to hold him back. The guy hadn't seen them yet. She shook her head and mouthed, "She's gonna get creamed—and Mom'll kill us, too."

Jack felt his stomach tighten. Rabbit was always pushing it one step too far. And *fair* was not the word that came to mind when dealing with his mom and dad. Jack and Queenie could be a hundred miles away, but if Rabbit got in trouble, *they* should have stopped her. They were having a great time on this ship, and he didn't need his little sister messing it up.

They inched close enough to see Rabbit without being seen.

Rabbit smiled at the scowling Navy guy. "Hi," she said. "My name's Rabbit. Who are you?"

"I'm the mess steward. I'm in charge of the mess facility. And you, young lady, are in serious trouble." He pointed at the apples in her hands. "That's stealing."

Rabbit ignored his comment and looked up at him, an innocent, confused expression on her face. "Mess facility? But I didn't make any mess. Do they call it that 'cause people spill stuff when they eat?"

Jack was sure she'd done it now.

But the mess steward didn't get angry. He laughed. "Kid, I think you just might have something there. That's the best description of this place I've heard yet. I'm the head guy in charge of cleaning up the mess."

Rabbit said, "I still don't get it. Why *do* they call a dining room a *mess facility*?"

He pulled out the nearest chair at a round dining table and sat down so he could look the little girl in the eye. "Rabbit, I—like—you! My name's Ernie."

Rabbit's hand shot out to shake his. "Nice to meet ya, Ernie."

Ernie took it. "Likewise, Rabbit."

She plopped down in the seat next to his. "So, do you actually get this whole mess facility thing?"

"Are you kidding? Nobody *gets* it. But I can *explain* it. The Navy changes the names of everything, just 'cause that's how the Navy does things. They say *mess facility* for dining room. To them, a torpedo is a *fish*, a bed is a *rack*, a window is a *porthole*, a rope is a *line*. When the ship is rocking back and forth, making people seasick, the Navy says the ship is *rollin'*. See what I mean? They change the names of everything."

"*Rollin'*? That makes no sense. *Rollin'* sounds like the ship will roll over and we'll all drown."

"Exactly," he said. Then his face turned quizzical. "Rabbit, you're not Navy, are you? What kind of brat are you, anyway?"

"I'm an Army brat," she said, as if stating the obvious. Children in military families are often called *brats*, and, like most of them, Rabbit embraced the label with great pride.

"That explains a lot," he chuckled.

"What else does the Navy say?"

"You know when you went to the Abandon Ship Station for the abandon-ship drills? The Navy calls those *whaleboats*. But the captain's is called the *captain's gig*. And when you go out on deck, you're not going outside, you're going *topside*. Sailors working topside are *deck apes*. All sailors are *swab jockeys*."

Rabbit's eyes grew wide. "There are *ponies*?"

"No, Rabbit. Not one. *Swabbing* is mopping, and sailors do a lot of it."

Rabbit spread her arms in amazement. "That's a whole nother language."

"The Navy is a world unto itself. You know what the Navy calls a bathroom?"

"What?"

"The *head*."

"Well, that one makes sense," said Rabbit. "My mom's had her head in the head since she got on this boat."

"It's a *ship*, Rabbit. A *ship*." He sounded stern but his twinkling eyes ruined it.

Jack began to breathe again. The situation was going their way, but it could change at any minute; Rabbit was definitely a loose cannon.

Jack felt Queenie let out her breath. They were no strangers to these tense situations. After all, this was really just one more episode in a string of grand adventures.

It started the day they left New York City. The ship was hardly out of the harbor when their mother started getting seasick. From the moment they left the dock, she hadn't been her normal self. Mrs. McMasters was a tall, attractive woman, smart and self-assured. People just naturally listened to her, respected her, and followed her lead. But Mrs. McMasters and ships, not to mention oceans, did not get along. So, right from the beginning, if she wasn't bolting for the bathroom to throw up, she was lying in bed, miserable. She'd simply told the kids to be good and go play.

To Jack, Rabbit, and Queenie, "Go play" meant roaming the *Upshur*, a place unlike anywhere they'd ever been. Its only color seemed to be gray, and the air was filled with the sounds of clanking metal, loud bells, and blasting horns sounding for no apparent reason. The minute their mother let them leave their quarters, they knew their mission: Explore every inch of the ship.

They ran along an upper deck, weaving their way through a cluster of US Army soldiers. Jack suddenly wondered, *Why are our Army guys still in Germany, anyway? Who do they need to fight?* Not for the first time since his dad left for Germany, Jack's thoughts turned serious. *Are we moving to a war zone?*

"Hurry up, Jack. We have places to go," Queenie yelled.

He'd slowed down to study the soldiers. *Shake it off, man.* He snapped his head from side to side to clear it. *You can worry about that later. For now, just enjoy the ship — as much as you can with two girls.*

The three of them actually made a great team, perhaps because they were so different.

Queenie and Rabbit were opposites. Queenie always looked well put together. She stood up straight and sat up straight. Her dark brown hair looked right out of a beauty salon. Her clothes repelled wrinkles and dirt. Her socks never slouched. She always said the right-and-proper thing. Well, almost always. Queenie was in training to be a lady.

On the other hand, Rabbit and her socks were always slouched. Looking correct was not Rabbit's priority. Her blond hair never stayed combed, which was why her mom put it in a ponytail most of the time. A ponytail that sprouted golden tufts within half an hour. Rabbit was the kind of kid who would walk out the front door in spanking clean clothes, and within ten minutes they'd be a wreck — wrinkled, dirty, and, all too often, growing holes. As for keeping her shoes unscuffed — impossible! There was just something about Rabbit that made her shoes scuff. Worst of all, she was The Mouth of the South. You never knew what she would say. Absolutely anything could and would come out of that mouth. Rabbit was in training to be a Wild Child.

Jack, well, Jack was actually like both his sisters. How could one person achieve that? When adults were *not* around, he was much more like Rabbit. Oh, his shoes looked fine, but in those shoes he ran his own agenda. No kid ever accused him of being too proper or correct. However, with adults, he was a model citizen. Like Queenie, he stood up straight, always said the right things, and always looked correct. Adults saw Jack as a well-put-to-gether young man.

Unlike his sisters, Jack was the perfect chameleon. Queenie was always Perfect Child Queenie who could never be like Rabbit. Free Spirit Rabbit simply didn't have it in her to think or act like a Queenie. Jack, on the other hand, could go from Wild Child to Mr. Perfect as quickly as you could turn on or off a light switch. And Jack had the brat-radar needed to detect the presence of adults. The minute his adult-detector went off, he'd flip the switch from wild to perfect child. Jack got away with more than most kids because he was a true chameleon who could read adults, under-stand what they'd want, and know how to provide it. Jack just naturally understood that if you give people what they want or at least what they expect they can have, you tended to stay out of trouble. You remained in people's good graces.

So this excellent team quickly figured out all the basics of the ship. Not only could they find the big dining room, they knew all the snack bars, too. One of the sweetest things about this ship was that everything seemed to be free. You could order a cheeseburger and fries at one of the snack bars and all you did was say your cabin number—yup, free food. To Jack, that was heaven, because Jack's single most defining characteristic was hunger! Jack McMasters only came one way: hungry.

By the end of the first day, they had explored all the decks of the ship and been to the kids' play area. That area was okay because it had an indoor jungle gym and games. But a few hours of that was enough. They moved on.

By the second day, they had learned all the ins and outs of the nursery. Necessary information, because their mom had sentenced Rabbit to time there for running her mouth at dinner the night before. Jack and Queenie came to her rescue. It didn't take them long to gather intel on the nursery and how it operated. *Intel* was one of those Army words Jack loved. It meant intelligence, as in gathering valuable information by spying. Jack and Queenie figured they were naturally gifted spies. In this case, they decided their best bet was a fake note asking the nursery to release Rab-bit. Being experts in deception as well, in the note they forged from their mom, they were careful to refer to their sister as *Kirsten McMasters,* not *Rabbit.* It said to release Kirsten into the care of her sister, Laura McMas-ters, who would return her to Mrs. McMasters's cabin.

The note, written in Queenie's best cursive, did the trick. It also got them introduced to the head of the nursery, Miss Ritter. She handed

Queenie her log book where all kids had to be signed in and signed out. Vital intel, since they used the book method to spring Rabbit the next day, too, without bothering with a note. Queenie walked in with her very superior attitude and said to Miss Ritter, "Is Kirsten here?" Then she just signed her out. It worked like a charm.

That is, until Mrs. McMasters somehow managed to get out of bed and showed up early to get Rabbit. That's when she learned that Queenie had signed her out an hour and a half earlier. Woops—big trouble for the three brats! That evening it was straight to bed—all movie privileges canceled.

Until then, they had managed to see every movie aboard the ship twice—in the passengers' theater and in the sailors' theater, too.

Sure, they'd been caught—and kicked out—of the sailors' theater. But ever-persistent, they'd managed to get in—and stay in—the sailors' theater twice. They had figured out to show up at least twenty minutes early and, when no one was around, try the back door of the theater, and if it was unlocked, slip in and hide inside the crawlspace under the stage till all the sailors had arrived. If they crept out of hiding after the lights were off and the previews were playing, they could sneak into the front row. The sailors never sat in the front row. Go figure.

They soon realized that the movie projectionists traded the films between the two theaters, so they'd seen them already. But they also realized that *The Forbidden Planet* was far more exciting when it was forbidden, or at least playing in a forbidden zone.

The McMasters kids were like all respectable brats. For them, a "Naval Personnel Only" sign waved like a red cape in front of a bull. The kids reasoned that the best way to find those signs was to follow the sailors doing their duties. The trick was to act naturally and follow from a distance so the sailors never knew they were leading them to the "Naval Personnel Only" places on the ship.

That technique led the brats to the sailors' bunk rooms filled with beds stacked five high. The bunks had no mattresses, just crisscrossed bands of gray canvas hung from gray metal poles, with nothing but a gray blanket. No closets either, just each sailor's single gray footlocker lined up under the bottom bunks.

Anyway, before they'd gotten very far exploring the bunk room, Rabbit scrambled up the bed polls like a monkey and dove into a top bunk. Unfortunately, she did it in typical Rabbit fashion—without looking to see where she'd land. The bundle of gray blankets contained a sleeping sailor who didn't stay sleeping for long. Rabbit's body came flying off that bunk like a dive bomber, flattening Jack and Queenie. The sailor's shouts woke other sailors scattered throughout the room. The pile of twisted arms and legs on the floor managed to untangle before Rabbit's victim could climb down.

Just steps ahead of the angry sailors, the brats flew beyond the "Naval Personnel Only" restricted area and out where a bunch of kids were crowded around on deck. They pretended not to notice the sailors who came flying out the same door to hunt them down. The sailors couldn't figure out which kids had been in their bunk room, and they were smart enough not to accuse innocent children whose fathers might be officers.

The McMasters kids knew they'd cut that one just a little too close. So being the wise children they were, they lay low for the rest of that day.

When the ship first left New York Harbor, they watched the great city's skyline get smaller and smaller. The next day they walked the decks on both sides of the ship but couldn't see land in any direction—only endless ocean. The third morning they strained to see Germany, but only ocean lay ahead.

Rabbit was almost jumping out of her skin. "I can't wait to get there!"

Queenie rolled her eyes and edged away.

Jack looked down at his little sister and said, mostly to himself, "Don't be so anxious to get there. We should just enjoy this ship while we can. Once we're there, we're right back to square one—with nothing. Our friends are gone. Everything and everyone we know is gone. We don't know a thing about the place we're headed. We don't know where we'll live or where we'll go to school, or what that will be like. Except for Mom and Dad, we won't know a single soul. Who knows if we'll even make friends?"

But Rabbit wasn't listening; she was bouncing up and down on her toes, grinning. Queenie must have heard him, though, because she said, "Don't make yourself crazy, Jack. We'll manage."

He nodded grimly, shaking it off. "You're right. I'll worry about that later. For now, we've got the *Upshur* to explore."

Within an hour, they'd discovered the gym. They hadn't known the ship even had one, but finding it was no accident. Once again they ran across a

"Naval Personnel Only" sign. This time it was fastened onto a set of gray double doors. So, naturally, they went straight through them. The gym had barbells and weights to lift, as well as parallel bars and a full basketball court. There they found a wire rack of basketballs. Perfect. They each grabbed a ball and started taking practice shots. But before they were even warmed up, the bouncing balls and Rabbit's big mouth made a tough-looking sailor rush in and yell, "Hey, brats aren't allowed in here! Ship out right now or I'll report you."

They left one step ahead of the authorities.

No great loss, thought Jack. Basketball wasn't exactly his game. He was never sure how far away things were. Which made it tough to shoot baskets. Actually, shooting the ball was no problem; the tough part was getting it near the hoop. He blamed his eyes—he hated his eyes. But there was nothing he could do to fix them. He'd had eye surgery when he was three years old, at Walter Reed Army Hospital in Washington, DC. But the surgery couldn't have gone all that well, because his parents had been dragging him to eye doctors ever since. They kept talking about something called depth perception and how he didn't have it. One doctor said that everyone else could see life in 3D, but Jack had to learn to manage with only seeing 2D.

Their best adventure that day began when Queenie's superior nose led them off a main corridor to where ten big, canvas pushcarts were piled with towels, sheets, and dirty clothes. She said, "These doors lead to the laundry. They *have* to have one. How else could they clean up all the puke?"

Jack nodded. "We should see that operation."

They decided to back off and get comfortable so they could gather intel from a position where they could see but not be seen. About every half hour someone came out of the door, got a few big carts of dirty laundry, and wheeled them in.

Jack said, "Let's get in a cart. It's our best bet."

They picked the cart closest to the door. Queenie held it steady while Rabbit and Jack climbed in. She covered them up with dirty laundry. Once they were hidden, she looked in a couple of carts for a sheet much cleaner than the ones she'd stuffed on top of Jack and Rabbit. She smoothed half of the sheet on top of the cart. Then grabbing hold of the farthest side of the cart, she pulled herself up, almost toppling the cart as she flopped in. She landed on top of the other two, causing a lot of shouts and wiggling, and then she pulled the other half of the almost-clean sheet over herself.

Rabbit's voice came up from the bottom of the cart. "Smells like somebody took a dump."

That time, even Queenie started giggling.

Jack sang in a muffled voice, "Diarrhea, jolly diarrhea . . ."

No matter how hard they tried, they just couldn't stop laughing.

Suddenly, the door banged open. The kids froze mid-giggle. The cart began to move. Their plan might have worked, but as the cart bounced over the threshold, the door swung back, hitting the side of the cart. Rabbit put out a hand to steady herself and felt it sinking into a puddle of barf. She let out a deafening screech. The startled sailor jerked the cart to a halt. Everyone's weight shifted, the cart fell over, and the dirty laundry and three kids came flying out.

Every worker in the place looked their way. Jack jumped up first and grinned. "Rats, busted again! Hi, everyone. Could we have a tour? We were willing to sit in puke to get one."

That got the sailors laughing. Soon, Jack had them nodding that the play area did indeed sound boring and that learning about the ship was a much better use of their time. The sailors seemed to get a kick out of outrageous Jack and his creative approach to getting into the laundry, the first kids ever to stow away in upchuck.

So the brats got their tour of how everything worked.

Jack couldn't believe how many carts were lined up inside the laundry. He asked, "Who has the dirtiest stuff? The kitchen or the engine room?"

"Are you kidding?" said the sailor who discovered them. "There ain't no puke in the engine room."

That got everyone laughing.

"Navy personnel are the best; they don't get seasick. The Air Force on the other hand . . . very weak stomachs. But the Army—worst of all. They're a bunch of serious pukers!"

"Hey, we haven't puked once and *we're* Army!" Rabbit shouted.

That pretty much ended the tour. They were escorted out to the sound of sailors shouting, "Get outta here, ya little Army brats!"

But Jack could tell they were amused, not mad. They had made some decent friends that day.

And here was Rabbit making another buddy, this time out of Ernie, the guy who just caught her stealing apples.

Jack and Queenie tried to look casual as they lounged outside of the dining room, just in case Ernie caught a glimpse of them. Or Rabbit did. She couldn't be trusted not to give them away.

"Hey, what kinda name is Rabbit, anyway?" asked Ernie.

"Ah, that's just what everyone calls me. My real name is Kirsten."

"Well, I think I like Rabbit better than Kirsten. Why do they call you Rabbit?"

"I don't know. They say stuff like I'm always running around like a jackrabbit."

"And are you always runnin' around like a jackrabbit?"

"On this ship I sure am. It's great here. We've been all over the place. This ship's one of our best adventures!"

"Yeah? Been all over the ship, huh? And do your mom and dad know you're running all over the ship?"

"Are you kidding?"

The corners of Ernie's lips pulled up in a quick smile. "So where are they?"

"My mom's in our cabin with her head in the toilet, and my dad is already in Germany. That's where we're gonna live."

Ernie looked down at the apples that Rabbit had nicked. "So what's with the apples? Don't we feed you enough?"

"We get stuffed at every meal. They're for one of our projects."

Ernie tilted his head. "Projects?"

Rabbit moved in a little closer and whispered, "See, we were leaning over the rail of the ship, and . . ." She paused.

"And?" Ernie asked.

"We were having this kind of spittin' contest. But we were so high up and the waves were so rough and it was so windy that we couldn't see our spit hit the ocean. I mean, that was a big problem, 'cause we couldn't tell who was winning."

With a little gap-toothed grin, Ernie said, "I can see that would be hard, being it was a good spittin' contest and all. But I still don't get it. Why'd you want the apples?"

"See, we couldn't see our spit hit the ocean and, you know, we wanted to see *something* hit the water. So I had this orange from lunch and I chucked it overboard. Boy oh boy, did *that* one hit. I mean we could *see* it. It was so great we wanted more stuff to throw."

"So you figured some more fruit from the mess facility would do the trick?"

Raising her shoulders in a big shrug, she gave Ernie a look that said, "Well, what do *you* think?"

Ernie *did* think. "Apples would be okay, I guess. But if you want to be the best bombardier ever, I know just the thing to do. And you won't be wasting Uncle Sam's good food doing it."

At this point, Jack and Queenie weren't about to be left out. They moseyed around the corner, acting all surprised to find Rabbit.

"So there you are!" said Queenie.

Ernie and Rabbit looked up, and Ernie said, "Rabbit, are these your cohorts in crime?"

"I'm not sure what *cohorts* is, but that's my brother, Jack, and this is my sister, Laura."

"Nice to meet you," said Ernie, and everyone shook hands. The military's pretty big on shaking hands.

Queenie looked right at Ernie. "So what would make us the best bombardiers?"

Ernie glanced over at Rabbit, who rolled her eyes back at him and said, "They call *me* Rabbit, but she has the really big ears. You can let them in on it."

Ernie flashed a smile. "Okay, ladies and gentlemen, step right this way."

For the first time since boarding the ship, the three kids were shown the inner sanctum of the mess facility. Until that moment, they'd never figured a way into the ship's kitchen. Ernie, of course, squared them away, telling them that in Navy-speak, the kitchen is called *the galley*.

Jack was amazed how cramped everything was. Work tables, rows of stoves and ovens, and a small army of cooks took up every inch.

They walked by people chopping vegetables, cooking at stoves, and kneading bread. Over in a back corner, Jack noticed a couple of very grungy sailors in filthy T-shirts washing dishes in a tight, little sink area, sweat running down their faces.

"And we think *we* have it bad, having to wash the dinner dishes every night at home," said Queenie, glancing at her brother.

Ernie said, "We call it *the scullery*. If you're unlucky enough to catch dish-washing duty . . . it's so hot in there you sweat like a pig. It's the ultimate crap job."

"I shall never complain again," said Queenie.

Rabbit whispered to Ernie, "Don't believe her."

In another small area they spotted a guy in a tall, white chef's hat, frosting an enormous chocolate cake.

Starring at that luscious cake, Jack groaned, "This is the kinda place that makes a kid really hungry."

Ignoring Jack's veiled attempt to get food, Ernie stopped to introduce the kids to Chef Porteaux, lord of the galley. He gave Ernie a questioning look that clearly communicated, "Why are these little brats in my kitchen?"

Ernie quickly explained they were going to be on K.P. (Navy-speak for *Kitchen Patrol*). Without giving Chef Porteaux any time to think about that, Ernie hustled the kids to the back door, into a room stacked with food from floor to ceiling and where even more sailors were working.

But they kept moving through the narrow storeroom and out the rear, into a small, dark passageway lined with garbage cans and over to a set of heavy metal doors. Once through, they found themselves out in the cold on an open deck overlooking the rear of the ship. It was like a big, private balcony, rocking up and down, back and forth, where massive waves banged against the ship.

As Queenie crossed the balcony, her feet slipped on the wet deck and she caught her toe in one of the small holes running along the bottom of the gunnel. "Oowww!" she cried, grabbing her foot. "Why do they have those stupid holes? Don't they know they're dangerous?"

Ernie said, "You wouldn't call them stupid if the sea was high. The waves come crashin' right over these decks and flood 'em. Those there scuppers let the water drain back into the ocean. But you're right about catching your toe in 'em. That's why we changed *scuppers* to *scuffers*. They sure ruin a good shoeshine. But with no scuppers, there's no place for water to go. Get it?"

"Do waves really get so big they crash onto the decks?" Rabbit was amazed.

Ernie nodded. "You ain't seen nothin'. I've been in plenty of rough seas. Especially up closer to the North Pole."

"You went to the North Pole?" exclaimed Rabbit. "Did you see Santa?"

"Sure did. In fact, his sleigh and all eight reindeer flew right over our ship."

"Was it Christmas?" Rabbit's eyes were as big as fifty-cent pieces.

Ernie gave her a long, reluctant look, and finally said, "No, it was summertime, and instead of wearing his big, red coat, he was in a red T-shirt."

Jack laughed. But Queenie scoffed, "What was he doing out there if it wasn't Christmas?"

"No clue. Prob'ly just training his reindeer." Ernie smoothly switched topics. "Rabbit, check out the view from back here."

They leaned over the back gunnel. This deck was much closer to the ocean than where they'd been during the spittin' contest.

The ocean was still rough, but the wind seemed to have died down. Actually, the wind was just as bad as before, but because they were aft, the ship blocked much of it. The giant propellers were churning the freezing, gray water, creating a huge wake that stretched out in a long path behind the ship. A sizable flock of seabirds followed the ship—the first birds the kids had seen on the voyage.

"Wow, how did those birds fly this far out into the ocean? How do they survive?" asked Jack.

"Oh, you'll see in just a second," said Ernie, "but first, Rabbit, let's give your apples a go."

Rabbit gave Jack one apple and kept the other for herself. Queenie, having no apple to throw, looked rather put off, but for once she didn't make a big stink. Rabbit chucked her apple over the side. This time it was easy to see it plunk into the water. Not bad. But with all the propeller churn it didn't make that big a splash. Jack launched his, producing the same result.

Queenie said, "It's no good. We need something bigger."

Jack thought, *You delight in pointing out what everyone else does wrong.*

Ernie didn't seem to mind. "Right you are, Laura. Follow me!" He led them back into the dark corridor and grabbed a garbage can of food scraps. "How's this for bigger?"

The kids just stared.

"Don't you see? You'll be some of the greatest bombardiers of all time."

Ernie had Jack and Queenie each take a handle and carry the big can to the back rail of the ship. He put Rabbit in charge of counting to three, and they dumped its contents over the side. It did, indeed, make one spectacular splash.

Everyone cheered.

Then something very surprising happened. Instead of sinking out of sight, some of the garbage popped back up to the surface as a floating smorgasbord of cans, bottles, paper, lettuce leaves, crusty rolls, and a huge fish bone with the head and tail still attached. That's when all the birds started dive bombing.

"Lunch time, little birdies," yelled Rabbit with delight.

"Okay, it's getting close to dinner time, and I need to get back to work. So I better wrap this up before Chef Porteaux gets cranky," said Ernie. "Try to stay out of trouble, will ya?"

"Okay, Ernie. But can we be bombardiers tomorrow?" asked Rabbit.

"Sure, come to the kitchen door any morning, about nine hundred hours. That's when we do the garbage dump."

Jack knew Ernie had things to do, but he called Ernie over to the rail for one quick question. "By watching the garbage, you can tell just how fast this ship is moving. Lots faster than I thought."

"Oh, yeah, this old rust bucket can really haul, Jack. In fact, she's probably doing about nineteen knots. Now you gotta get out of here before I get in trouble."

"Nineteen knots?"

Ernie smirked. "Okay, kid, I'll translate it into simple Army terms. Nineteen knots is just under twenty-two miles per hour. Got it?"

"Got it," said Jack.

Ernie led them back through the kitchen, careful to keep a safe distance between Rabbit and Chef Porteaux.

Once they were back in the corridor, Rabbit hugged Ernie and then bolted for who knows where.

Jack said, "Any idea how we could get onto the bridge for a look around?"

"Ah, Jack-me-boy, that's a tough one. Very few people get invited to the captain's domain. But let me give it some thought."

Before Jack could say thanks, Queenie snarled, "Move it, Jack. It's almost six."

Jack rolled his eyes, as if to say, *Sisters*. "See ya 'round, Ernie."

"See ya 'round, Jack."

2

Look Sharp, Act Sharp, Be Sharp

The McMasters family had two simple ground rules.

Rule #1: "Be home by 6:00 p.m. for dinner or get killed." The kids knew their mom meant business. She didn't much mind where they went during the day, as long as they were home at six sharp. Family dinners were very, very serious business in the McMasters household.

Rule #2: "Don't get in trouble." This was mainly their dad's rule. And he never let up on it. But the kids knew it really meant, "Don't get caught." If you *did*, Dad *would* kill you.

Rule #1 propelled Jack and Queenie down the narrow corridor toward their cabin, Queenie fuming, "She's going to get us all in trouble."

But, as if by magic, Rabbit skipped around the corner, reaching their cabin door first. It was exactly one minute to six.

Queenie said, "Where have *you* been?"

"Nowhere." Rabbit was the model of innocence.

Mrs. McMasters was sitting at a small vanity table, putting on her face—her way of saying putting on her makeup. Their mother never went out in public unless she was beautifully dressed and her makeup was perfect.

"Right on time," she said, looking up with a smile. She seemed a little less seasick. "Where have you kids been?"

"Nowhere," all three said casually.

"Did you have a nice day?"

"Yes, Mom."

"What did you find to do?"

"Nothing," they said with one voice. Revealing a day's grand adventures was the surest way to never have another.

"Wash up, get changed, and be ready to leave for dinner in five."

So in five minutes flat the girls were in dresses, and Jack was in slacks, a clean shirt, and a sweater. They all wore shoes polished to a shine.

Shining shoes was one of Jack's daily chores, and it had to be done before any shoe left their quarters. No McMasters ever stepped outside in scuffed shoes. That meant the family never went anywhere in this whole, wide world without a shoeshine kit. In it were brushes, old rags, and cans of Kiwi polish (the only brand they'd ever dream of using). Jack's toughest job was making sure the colonel's Corcoran jump boots were properly spit shined. If the colonel couldn't see his own reflection in the toes of those boots, well, let's just say Jack's day would start off poorly. That spit-shine step required tools most civilians wouldn't think to use. Things like a book of matches for melting some of the Kiwi wax, a small bottle of alcohol to use sometimes instead of spit to get a perfect shine, and one of Mrs. McMasters's torn silk stockings—the greatest buffing device on the planet.

But with the colonel already in Germany, Jack's job was pretty much a breeze.

Life on board ship definitely was different from life on base. On board, they went out to dinner every night. The ship's dining room was more like a restaurant than a mess hall. On base, they rarely went to restaurants, because Mrs. McMasters was a legendary cook. She made a better-than-any-restaurant dinner every single night.

Even so, the kids liked these shipboard dinners because they could order anything they wanted. Their mom, on the other hand, was too seasick to enjoy the food. She only left the cabin to be at dinner with her children. But each time, she seemed about to throw up.

However, not even seasickness kept Mrs. McMasters from delivering her pre-dinner lecture. As they walked toward the dining room, she began, "I want you children to *behave* at dinner tonight. Remember your *pleases* and *thank-yous*. And always say, 'Yes, ma'am' and 'Yes, sir.' Do you understand me?" Without pausing even a second to let them respond, she pushed on. "And another thing: Remember that children are to be seen and not heard. Got it? You sit up straight and remember your manners. Rabbit, use your fork and knife the proper way, and keep your napkin in your lap. I don't want to have to keep reminding you. You know how to do it correctly. Make me proud of you tonight, children."

Pretending to listen was good enough. Everything she said was covered under her motto: "Look sharp, act sharp, be sharp."

At the door, they waited for a steward to seat them with other passengers at one of the tables for eight. Tonight's steward gave the kids a sly wink, silently mouthing, "Hi, Rabbit."

Rabbit grinned, mouthing back, "Hi, Ernie!"

He led them to a table of ship's officers who were decked out in crisp, white uniforms trimmed in gold. As Mrs. McMasters approached, all the officers got to their feet and stayed standing until everyone had been introduced and Mrs. McMasters was properly seated. She was next to a good-looking officer named Commander Allen. When Jack heard he was the XO, he stopped daydreaming. The XO might not be the captain, but he is the executive officer, the second in command who runs most of the day-to-day operations on the ship. Jack soon learned that Commander Allen had been in the Navy since World War II and had been on a ship in the D-day invasion. Jack and his sisters, like all military brats, had been raised on the stories of World War II. Their father and uncles had all been in the war.

"Where is your husband, Mrs. McMasters?" asked Commander Allen.

"Lieutenant Colonel McMasters is already in Germany. He's part of 4th Armored Division, stationed in Göppingen."

Commander Allen nodded. "That's about half an hour outside the city of Stuttgart."

Mrs. McMasters smiled. "So I hear. We are rotating to Germany from Fort Hood, Texas, as part of Operation Gyroscope, replacing 8th Infantry Division at Cooke Barracks. They are part of 7th Corp."

He smiled back. "I might not be Army, but I know 7th Corp defends the entire southern third of Germany. Your husband is a tanker?"

"That's right," she said, allowing just a hint of pride.

Jack realized Commander Allen might be his best bet for getting onto the ship's bridge. Very casually, he said, "Commander, you must know a lot about how this ship operates."

Commander Allen smiled a bit dismissively at Jack before saying to Mrs. McMasters, "I suppose I might know one or two small things."

"I've been trying to figure out just how fast this ship is going," Jack said. "Could you help me?"

Jack's mom gave him "the look" that he wasn't just being seen.

Jack knew he was pushing his luck and was glad his dad was safely in Germany. You could get the "kill look" from the colonel for almost anything. And what came after that was never fun. But with his dad gone, Jack risked another comment. "I mean, with all the big waves and wind, it's kind of hard to tell if we're moving very fast." Then, he wisely went silent, giving Commander Allen his best unflinching stare. Jack could see the moment when it became clear to the commander that Jack was not going to go quietly into the night, so he might as well talk to him, even if he'd rather be chatting with Mrs. McMasters.

"Jack, the weather has been a bit rough, but that doesn't slow us down. We are burning a bit more fuel, but we've still been able to keep a steady nineteen knots."

"Um, nineteen knots," said Jack. "That seems pretty fast. But, I don't really get the difference between knots and miles. I mean, how does that translate into miles per hour?"

"Ah, Jack, I can tell you're not a sailor. More of a land lover and aspiring tanker, are you? Here's how it works: Both a mile and a knot measure distance. When we say a *knot,* we mean a *nautical mile*. The difference between a nautical mile and a regular mile is that a knot is about fifteen percent longer."

Jack paused for a few seconds, looking as if he were doing heavy mathematical calculations. Finally he said, "So that means the ship is going faster than nineteen miles per hour. In fact, that means it's going almost twenty-two miles per hour. Do I have that right?"

Now it was Commander Allen's turn to do some fast math. He seemed to see Jack for the first time. "You might not be a sailor *now*, but you certainly could be, with a little training. You're correct. The ship is making about twenty-two miles per hour."

Perhaps it was something in Commander Allen's voice, but the other officers started paying attention to the conversation.

Jack *was* pretty good at math, but he was even better at making good impressions. After his talk with Ernie, Jack had done the calculations that would help him make a good one now. "So, since New York to Bremerhaven is about 3,400 miles, and if we're making twenty-two miles per hour, that means it will take us . . . let's see," he said, pausing for effect, "seven days to get there. That means we have about two-and-a-half days left. Right?"

"Gentlemen," said Commander Allen to the officers around him, "it looks like we've found ourselves a new prospective sailor. What say we show him around the bridge tomorrow and give him a better feel for how things work?"

The men all nodded their approval.

Quick to capitalize on his win, Jack asked if he could bring his sisters along.

Commander Allen said, "Feel free to bring them and your mom, if you like, but be there at ten hundred hours sharp."

Ten o'clock was fine with him! Jack glanced over at his mom to see if she was okay with all this. Mrs. McMasters seemed quite pleased. And Jack, knowing it was high time to resume his model-child act, was seen and not heard for the rest of dinner.

As everyone was getting up to leave the table, Queenie asked their mom if they could go off to the movies. Mrs. McMasters said it was fine, if they returned to the cabin right after the show. The McMasters children politely shook hands with each of the officers and got out of there fast.

In the corridor just outside the dining room, Jack saw Ernie heading for the kitchen. In a quiet voice he called after him, "Hey, Ernie. Thanks."

"What for?"

"For seating us with Commander Allen. You got us invited to the bridge tomorrow."

"Just what you wanted. Nice work."

"Thanks to you." Jack beamed. "See ya, Ernie."

"See ya, Jack."

3

The Bridge

The next morning Mrs. McMasters was again looking a little green. Clearly she wasn't getting out of bed anytime soon. So after breezing through their chores, the kids were up and out, roaming the gangways, corridors, and decks.

As they did each day, they went topside, racing to the front of the ship to try to spot Germany. No land in sight yet.

Rabbit yelled, "Pancakes!" She bolted for the stairs.

Queenie and Jack sprinted after her. Jack was sure he could smell bacon.

Ever hungry, Jack was in heaven. He lightly buttered his large stack of pancakes before pouring on so much syrup that the stack was floating on a lake. Rabbit, on the other hand, painted each pancake with massive quantities of butter before adding just a little syrup. Rabbit was a butter girl. Queenie once caught her taking a big bite right out of a stick of butter. Rabbit would have eaten the whole thing if Queenie hadn't snatched it away.

All facts considered, this was one of their more civilized breakfasts. They only ordered three extra portions of bacon.

By the end, they were all so lead-bellied they didn't want to get up from the table. Sitting there in a pancake-induced coma, Jack's thoughts drifted to his mom. And since Jack believed that most problems could be solved with food, he ordered her some toast and poached eggs. Queenie began to order her coffee. But, for once, Jack was able to correct his older sister, pointing out that while their mom normally drank coffee, when she was sick, she always drank tea.

Queenie carried the food on a large, silver tray. Jack followed with the pot of tea and a cup. Rabbit was left following along with nothing to bring her mom. Until she thought to swipe a flower out of the big vase just inside the dining room. The children marched off in a grand procession to care for their mother.

Queenie placed the tray next to her on the bed. While Jack poured the tea just like the waiters at dinner, Rabbit filled a glass with water before plopping the flower in the glass.

Mrs. McMasters smiled weakly at each new proof of their care, before turning a little greener as she studied the eggs. "Thank you, children. I'll taste these wonderful eggs after you're on your way. Give my apologies to Commander Allen. Tell him I am feeling a little under the weather. But do thank him for me."

"Mom, you aren't under the weather, you're sick," said Rabbit.

Queenie just said, "Rabbit, I'll explain it to you later. Let's go."

As they headed out the door, their mom called weakly, "Mind your manners."

The one thing no one had bothered to explain was how to find the bridge. They knew its general location from all of their exploring, but once they got close, no sailor would say more than, "No kids on the bridge. Get out of here."

Jack felt his insides start to tighten. *What if we don't find it in time? Commander Allen expects us there at ten hundred on the dot. Mom won't take any lame excuses.*

He tried saying they were supposed to meet Commander Allen at ten hundred hours. The sailors seemed even more doubtful, until one finally dragged them off to a junior officer buried in paperwork outside a big set of doors.

"Expected on the bridge? What's this all about?" demanded the officer, obviously put off at having to deal with a bunch of brats.

Queenie looked the young officer right in the eye and said with real command presence, "That is correct, sir. My name is Laura McMasters, and this is my brother, Jack, and my sister, Rabb . . . uh . . . Kirsten. I am *sure* if you contact Commander Allen, he will be pleased to see us."

He gave her a hard look, but Queenie locked eyes with him.

Finally, sounding impatient and skeptical, he said, "Just a minute." Picking up a phone, he began relaying the story to someone on the other end of the line. There was a short pause. Then his eyes widened just enough for Queenie to know they were in. She tried not to gloat.

He gestured for them to stand over by the doors. "Someone will come for you. Stay right there—and don't move."

Jack stood staring at mahogany doors so glossy they must have been polished every day. The big, brass doorknobs shined like pure gold. He figured they led onto the ship's bridge.

Suddenly, one of those doors swung open, and a lieutenant from dinner the night before came out. "Ah. The McMasterses, and right on time. The commander will see you now." Queenie glanced back at the amazed desk officer, flashing him her superior smile.

They walked into a conference room with maps and charts on every wall. From there, they were shown up a small set of metal stairs, across a narrow catwalk, and onto the bridge.

The first time on the bridge of a United States naval ship never fails to impress and amaze. It certainly impressed the McMasters kids. Sitting in one of two big swivel seats was Commander Allen. On the back of his chair was a handwritten sign that said, *BOSS*. It made things really clear. He was in charge.

Windows circled half the room, giving them a perfect view forward. Obviously, this was the highest point on the ship.

Jack stared out, fascinated. He watched a bunch of deck apes working topside on painting detail. The Navy painted its ships nonstop, and always haze gray. A sailor had told Jack, "If you don't salute it, paint it." Jack thought, *A sailor's life is seriously gray: gray skies, gray ocean, and a ship painted nothing but gray.*

Commander Allen's chair squeaked as it swiveled around, bringing Jack back to full attention.

The commander said, "Jack, and ladies, how are you today? Doesn't look like your mother made it up here with you."

Leave it to Rabbit to blurt out, "Nope—she's still barfin'."

And leave it to Queenie to intervene smoothly. "Actually, Commander Allen, she would have loved to have been here. She asked me to pass on her regrets. What Kristen was trying to say, sir, is that Mom is a bit under the weather."

"Tell her I hope she feels better and we see her at dinner tonight." Then, looking right at Jack, he said, "Let me introduce you to Master Chief Petty Officer Cramer. He is my AB, which, by the way, means Able Bodied Seaman. He is my lookout."

The kids all shook hands with Chief Cramer.

He studied Jack. "You're pretty good at math if you figured out how to convert knots to miles per hour. One day maybe you'll be sitting in a chair like this. Would you like to be a boat driver?"

"It certainly looks fascinating, and, well, a bit complicated," said Jack, studying all the electronics, switches, levers, and scopes.

Footsteps sounded on the metal catwalk.

Commander Allen glanced around and said, "Jack, let me introduce you to Alexander Knox. His dad is Commander Knox. He and his family are also being transferred to Germany. Commander Knox is an old friend of mine, and I wanted you boys to meet."

Everyone nodded hello. The kid looked just a little older than Jack.

"Alex, we were just starting to talk about how things work around here. And, yes, Jack, it does take a lot of training," said Allen. "Here's how we operate. I'm called the OOW, which means the *Officer of the Watch*. From this seat I have tactical command of the ship. I drive and the chief, as I said, is my lookout."

"Are you the captain of the ship?" asked Rabbit.

"No," said Commander Allen, with a bit of a smile, "but as OOW, it is usually my duty to sit in the captain's chair to drive the ship. There are times when the captain takes the seat to drive during critical maneuvers. At other times he is up here on the bridge to observe us as we do our jobs."

"What's an example of a critical maneuver?" Jack asked.

"When we come into the port of Bremerhaven. The captain will make sure we safely navigate around other ships in the channel. We'll slow down as we get close to port. When we're about a mile out, a small boat will come alongside and a pilot will come on board."

"An airline pilot?" asked Rabbit. Queenie's glare communicated, *You're too young for this conversation, so keep your big trap shut.*

"No, not an airline pilot," said Allen, again smiling at Rabbit. "He'll be a harbor pilot. We'll lower a long, narrow set of stairs called the *accommodation ladder*, which is suspended over the side of the ship. It allows someone to board the *Upshur* from another boat. Have you seen the metal staircase hanging off the starboard side of the ship?"

The three McMasterses nodded yes.

Jack noticed that Alex didn't bother nodding, but his expression said he'd seen it a million times. Probably because his dad was Navy and he'd been around ships his whole life. Not like Jack, who was just figuring out that sailors called narrow staircases *ladders*.

"The pilot will jump from his boat onto those stairs and come aboard the *Upshur*. Once on the bridge, he'll help the captain get the ship safely navigated through the harbor. Ports like Bremerhaven are very big and crowded. The pilot spends his whole life getting everything from large naval ships, to cargo ships, to small boats, safely in and out of the harbor. It's his job to get us safely docked up. That, Jack, is what we call a critical maneuver."

"I see, sir," Jack said.

"If you want to be an OOW or AB, you need to understand not only all this equipment, but how it relates to the inner workings of the engine room, as well as everything else on the ship. Our steam-turbine engines crank one giant shaft, which turns the two propellers that drive this ship. But they really have to crank, because this ship is 533 feet long, and she weighs over 11,200 tons. If we want to make nineteen knots, the engines have to generate 13,500 horsepower. Understanding how everything works on this ship takes years of training."

Looking around, Jack said, "I don't see any gas pedal, or break, like in a car. So how do you speed up or stop?"

"For that, we communicate with the engine room," said Commander Allen.

"With a telephone?"

"No. We certainly have a telephone as well as a speaker system that we can broadcast over, but for controlling the ship we use the engine telegraph. This round device with the big levers lets us communicate the speed we want: stop, stand-by, slow, half, full, etc. We use it to transfer precise orders from this bridge to the engine control room to change speed or direction."

"Keen-o," Jack said, loving its precision.

Alex pointed to an electronic screen. "Is this the radar scope?"

The commander nodded. To Jack he said, "Do you see how the green line circles around the scope? That's the electronic read coming in from that radar tower over there." He pointed out the window to a pole coming up out of the ship with a rectangular panel spinning on top of it. "This gives us a view of anything in the skies around us. See that little green blip on the screen? That tells us that there's an aircraft flying off our starboard side."

Everyone stared out the windows looking for the plane.

"But I don't see a plane," said Queenie, confused.

"No, you wouldn't," said the commander. "Look at the screen and the rings coming out from the center of the scope. The green blip is out just beyond the fourth ring. Each ring is a mile. That plane is more than four miles out from us. The human eye can't see that far, but the radar can see fifty miles in any direction, even in fog. It's our eyes in the skies."

Alex walked over to the other scope. "So this one's the sonar?"

"Sure is. Think of it as a radar scope, but instead of being our eyes in the skies, it's our eyes under the water. You still have the green line going around, refreshing the images on the screen. And you still have rings going out, telling us how far away things are. For example, this sonar would let us know if a submarine were tracking us. Not something we worry much about today, so most transport ships don't have sonar, but this one does."

"Commander, you might want to have a look at this," Chief Cramer interrupted. He pointed to the sonar screen. Quite near the ship were three small, very faint blips.

Commander Allen mused, "They're too small to be ships of any real size and they're not showing up very brightly on the screen." He sounded casual, but his eyes never left the scope; the three blips became five blips and seemed to be closing in on the ship.

"Interesting." The chief sounded more intrigued than worried. "It's unlikely a seagoing vessel that small would be out this far. If I am not mistaken, they're whales. Given our current location, I'd guess we have right whales off our port side."

The kids hurried to the window but couldn't make them out.

"What's a right whale?" Alex asked.

Everyone looked at the chief, who seemed to know the most.

"Let's see. They're definitely large whales, and it seems to me they're normally black, with whitish patches on their heads and bellies. Anyway, sightings of them are getting rare these days, because whalers hunted them almost to extinction. But sometimes you can still spot them in the North Atlantic."

"Why do they call them *right whales*?" Queenie asked.

The chief rubbed his chin. "If I remember correctly, they got their name from the whalers who figured they were the 'right' whales to hunt. You see, when killed, instead of sinking to the bottom of the ocean, they remain afloat. Also, they would come close to boats, because they're naturally curious and friendly. You know, today might just be your lucky day to spot them."

"Let's get down on deck and see 'em!" exploded Rabbit.

It was pretty clear Rabbit was getting ready to bolt, and that the other kids were eager to whale watch. Commander Allen obviously knew when he was upstaged. "Excellent idea. Go check it out, and let me know if you spot any. I'll see you all at dinner tonight."

They hurriedly thanked the commander for showing them the bridge and were out of there in a flash. Rabbit, as usual, was in the lead, screaming, "Which one's the port side? Which way do we go?"

Jack was trying to remember port from starboard when Alex streaked by, yelling, "This way—follow me!"

They bounded out onto the deck where they'd had their spittin' contest. This time, four kids leaned over the rail of the rolling ship. The swells were a pleasant five or six feet, and the sky, though gray, was clear of rain. They all stared over the gunnel. Nothing but ocean.

"This is Nowheresville," Queenie said.

"Be patient," Jack said. "I have this odd feeling they'll show up."

So they stared out into the gray for the longest time. No whales.

Finally Alex offered up, "My dad says that sometimes when you see everything, you see nothing."

"What does *that* mean?" Queenie demanded. You'd think it was the dumbest thing she'd ever heard.

But Alex didn't seem the least put off by her, perhaps because they were about the same age. He just went on explaining some expert advice that might help in the situation, without seeming to care if she thought he was crazy. In that respect, he was a lot like Jack.

"We're looking out at this big ocean, and we don't see anything. Right?" he asked.

"Yeah," said Jack.

"My dad says if you try and do that, you're likely to miss what you're looking for. The Navy uses a trick called *grid search*. You imagine the ocean has crisscrossed lines on it, like a bunch of tic-tac-toe lines. Then you search one little section of the grid at a time. Get it?"

"Yeah, I guess so," said Jack. "Break it down into squares and look for the whales in one square at a time. Right?"

"You got it."

They all tried that for a while. Still nothing.

Jack mused, "The bridge of the *Upshur* was pretty righteous."

"Definitely," said Alex.

Queenie started chanting, "*Upshur, Upshur, Upshur, Upshur*. Ever notice that the longer you repeat a word, the stranger it sounds?" She resumed, "*Upshur, Upshur, Upshur . . .*"

They all started saying it.

"*Upshur, Upshur, Upshur . . .*

"*Upshur, Upshur, Upshur, Upshur . . .*

"*Upshur, Upshur . . .*"

They started laughing as it began to sound more and more bizarre.

"*Upshur, UPSHUR, U-P-S-H-U-R, Up Shur . . .*"

"What a crazy name," said Queenie. "What in the world does it mean?"

Alex said, "Maybe *upchuck*, like in *barf, puke, ralph, upchuck*. I mean, think about it. What do most people do on this ship? They upchuck. And it sounds like *Upshuuuurrrrrr*—you know *shuuuurrrrrr*, like the noise you make when you're puking."

Jack jumped in. "The Navy started out with the *USS YOU'RE FOR SURE GONNA PUKE*, but figured that name was too long, so they shortened it to *Upshuuu...rrrrrr*."

Queenie nodded. "That's probably what happened. Except the name was still too long, so they settled on the code word *Upshur*. That way passengers would come aboard not knowing they were on the greatest puke machine ever invented."

"So the *USS Puke* became the *USS Upshur*," Alex said. They all started chanting, "*Upshur, Upshur, Upshur . . .*"

Jack waved his arms to cut off the symphony. "We're wrong. Here's the real story: The ship rocks so much, the first crew thought the ship would roll right over and drown 'em, so the Navy renamed it *Upforsure* to convince them they weren't gonna die."

Laughing, they changed their chant to "*Up? Sure! . . . Up? Sure! . . . Up? Sure! . . .*"

Eventually, the cold North Atlantic wind pushed them along the deck toward the rear of the ship. At that point, the girls complained they were frozen and went inside, but Jack and Alex decided on one more grid search. Just as they'd made up their minds to quit, it happened. Jack was on his third-to-last grid square when, for just an instant, he saw a massive tail flip above the surface of the water. Then it disappeared.

Jack shouted, "Did you see that?"

"Where?"

"Right over there," pointed Jack. Tracing the grid with both arms, he showed Alex how to find the spot. "It's about three grid squares—"

"I see him!" Alex yelled. "Honest to God, I just saw him! Did ya see the size of that tail?"

Just as quickly as the whale had appeared, any chance of its return seemed to vanish. But both boys knew it was headed for the rear of the ship.

"We've gotta find a way to see astern," said Alex. "How, I don't know."

"Astern?" Jack asked.

"Behind the ship. We need a way to see out of the rear of this ship."

"I know one," screamed Jack, and he took off running. "Follow me!"

With Alex on his heels, Jack re-entered the ship. Grabbing onto the ladder railings, he slid down on his hands, feet never touching a stair.

Jack yelled over his shoulder, "That grid-search stuff really works!" Two more quick turns and he raced into the mess facility.

Alex still had no idea where they were headed. He just made it his business to keep up.

Jack raced across the dining area and through the double doors into the galley. Halfway across the kitchen, in the midst of all the clatter and chaos of Navy cooks putting the final touches on lunch, he ran right into Chef Porteaux. Wrong time for kids to show up; the lunch crowd would be there in fifteen, and he still had a lot to do.

"Chef Porteaux, there's a school of whales astern and we're headed out there to see them."

It was obvious the chef was not buying their story and was about to throw them out.

"I'll go with them and check it out, Chef," said a voice from behind them. Ernie.

Rolling his eyes as if in no mood to deal with this, the chef nodded his okay to Ernie. They headed for the rear of the galley.

Within seconds, Chef Porteaux yelled, "Hold up!"

Jack's heart stopped. He was sure if they didn't get there soon they'd miss the whales entirely.

But instead of changing his orders, Chef Porteaux simply said, "Chief Steward, I seriously doubt there are whales in these waters, but just in case there are, come and get me."

Ernie saluted.

The three trekked through the galley, the store, and the garbage corridor to get out onto the back deck.

As they hurried, Jack said, "Ernie, this is my friend, Alex."

"Nice to meet ya, Alex. Any friend of Jack's is a friend of mine."

"So what's the real story, Jack?" Ernie asked, once outside, looking at the empty ocean.

Jack just stood there, staring out at the big Atlantic. "Faith, Ernie. Have a little faith."

Sure enough, a couple moments later, Ernie saw a massive, black whale pop his head out of the water. The giant beast couldn't have been any farther away than a pitcher is from home plate. His head immediately vanished, but his back rolled up above the churning water of the ship's wake, as he blew twin streams of water. They seemed to come from two different spouts on top of his head.

Ernie looked stunned. "I think I better go get Chef."

As if out of nowhere, not one, but five right whales surfaced off the rear of the ship. The boys could only stare.

It didn't take long before they were joined by Chef Porteaux and a bunch of the mess cooks, who shared their awe of this fabulous display of nature. Jack was relieved the whales weren't in any hurry to leave. They seemed to know they'd drawn a crowd. And they certainly seemed to like playing in the ship's wake.

It dawned on Jack that he needed to notify Commander Allen. He leaned over to Alex and said, "I'll be right back."

"Where you going?"

"I gotta get back up to the bridge and let them know we've spotted the whales."

"That will take forever and they may be gone by then. Let's see if Chef Porteaux can call up to the bridge."

Jack was both surprised and pleased when Chef Porteaux agreed to let the commander know. Somehow, even the girls managed to get the word where to come. Minutes after they showed up, Commander Allen arrived with a very special spectator, the ship's captain, who studied the whales intently. Turning, the captain smiled down at Jack and Alex. "Commander Allen tells me you two are the sharp-eyed boys who first spotted these whales."

They both said, "Yes, sir."

"Nice to meet you," said the captain, shaking hands with Jack and Alex. "And nice find, boys. I don't know if you realize it, but this is a rare sight. This is the first time I've seen the right whales in more than twenty transatlantic crossings."

"You bring all the soldiers to Germany?" asked Rabbit, eyes wide.

"No, young lady." The captain smiled down at her. "One ship could never transport all the troops needed in Germany. We have over fifty Army, Navy, and Air Force bases there, with more troops than anywhere else in the world. You're going to a very exciting place."

Jack and Alex eyed each other.

The captain turned to Chef Porteaux and said, "Why don't you have someone bring us some roast-beef sandwiches and Cokes, so we can have a little lunch out here, while we watch."

And that's how the kids came to have lunch with the captain of the ship.

Everyone was mesmerized by the whales playing in the foam.

"Hey, that's funny. That one over there has a giant mustache in his mouth," blurted Rabbit.

"Holy cow, you're right!" admitted Queenie, shocked when she saw a whale's head come launching out of the foam, with his giant mouth wide open.

The captain leaned down on the gunnel next to the girls. "Instead of teeth, the right whale has that mustache-looking thing, which he uses to strain tiny fish and other sea life from the water for his food."

"Amazing—and they have no teeth?" asked Queenie.

"None. They swallow the tiny sea life whole."

Rabbit tugged on one of the captain's sleeves, intent on getting his attention away from Queenie.

Turning, he looked down at the little wreck of a girl, hair flying every which way, blouse un-tucked, socks falling down. Lord only knows what he thought of that ragamuffin. She innocently looked up at him and asked, "Why do they call this ship the *Upshur*? Is it like *up sure*? I mean like being *sure* to keep this ship *up* so we don't drown?"

Jack looked at Alex and Queenie, horrified, wordlessly shouting, "Doesn't she know how disrespectful that sounds?

Jack cautiously tried to get a read off the captain's face, desperate to know how he'd react. He'd never thought she'd blab to an adult how they'd made fun of the name, much less to the captain of the ship. The longer the captain didn't react, the more panicked he became. The last thing they needed was to be reported by the captain for having inappropriate behavior.

Fortunately for Rabbit, and for them, the captain started to laugh. Only Rabbit could have gotten away with a question like that.

He leaned down in his crisp, ultra-white uniform, with all its gold braiding and ribbons, and in a kind, tolerant voice, said to Rabbit, "Young lady, that's a pretty interesting way to think about this ship's name. Because, you know, we do work pretty hard to make sure she stays upright."

He looked at all the kids, and asked, "Do any of you know why we call her the *Upshur*?"

When it became obvious no one knew the reason or would venture one, the captain said, "I'll tell you the story of how this ship got her name. Shall I do that?"

"Yes, please," said Rabbit, eyes full of curiosity.

"Well, she's named in honor of a war hero and winner of the Congressional Medal of Honor."

All the captain had to do was mention the words *Medal of Honor* and everyone within earshot halted their conversations and began to listen. The Medal of Honor is the highest award any American soldier, sailor, or airman can receive. And everyone on deck knew the words, *"at risk to his own life, above and beyond the call of duty."*

"The ship is named for Major General William P. Upshur, United States Marine Corp. You see, in October of 1915, just before we entered World War I, the US Armed Forces were involved in a conflict down on the island of Haiti. The problem was with Haitian rebels who were called the Cacos. At the time, Upshur was a young captain with 15th Company of Marines. Here's what happened: He and his men took off on a six-day reconnaissance patrol from Fort-Liberté. That means they were out on horseback, scouting for the Cacos rebels.

"And let me tell you, it took some doing, but they finally ran into them. After dark on the evening of the twenty-fourth, his detachment of Marines were crossing a river in a deep ravine and suddenly were attacked on three sides by over four hundred Cacos. They shot up the Marines badly, but Captain Upshur and what men he had left fought their way forward toward the enemy. They finally managed to cross the river and get onto higher ground, where they dug in.

"The Cacos fired on them all night long. At daybreak, instead of staying pinned down by enemy fire, Captain Upshur attacked with the three squads he had left. And he attacked not just in one, but three, different directions. He and his few Marines, in a hail of gunfire, with people being killed all around them, managed to surprise and scatter the Cacos. That became known as the Battle of Grande Riviere. And Captain Upshur and his men didn't stop there. Pushing on, they successfully aided in the capture of the nearby Fort Dipitie."

The captain paused for his listeners to reflect on the story. "We named this ship after Upshur because he showed us what it means to never give up, never retreat, and never stop attacking."

When he was finished, the kids were far from laughing at the ship's name, and they probably never would again. It had become a name of honor.

With a quiet smile, the captain said, "So, how are those whales doing?"

The kids moved back to the rail for another look. The whales were following even closer, as if they, too, had been listening to the story. The captain thanked Jack and Alex for spotting the great whales. Leaving, he said he'd let others know to come out and see their amazing find.

It didn't take long for more sailors, and even passengers, to start appearing on the ship's small rear deck. As the crowds grew, Jack and Alex decided it was time to ditch the girls and scram.

With nothing much to do, Jack and Alex just wandered the ship. Eventually, they plopped down in two easy chairs in a small, out-of-the-way reading room. It was an okay spot because there was no one else around.

Alex looked at Jack and said, "So you're an Army brat?"

"Yup. And you're a Navy brat?"

"Yup. So what are Army brats like?"

"We're the smartest, sharpest looking, best behaved children on the planet." Jack spread his arms as if welcoming applause from an audience. Then he cocked his head toward Alex. "What about Navy brats?"

Alex gave him a slow smile. "That's easy. We are the bravest, most honest, hardest working, sincerest kids who ever lived."

Jack pretended to have a new thought. "Oh, and we're the sneakiest, most devious, cleverest children on the planet. We know how to get in and out of any situation." He smirked. "What can you *Navy brats* do?"

"Well, we never get caught at anything, and even if we do, we figure a way out of it."

"That's what I thought." Jack liked this kid.

Alex said, "So where you been?"

Jack ran down the list. "Oh, Monterey, California. You know, Fort Ord. That's where I was born. Then we did a year in Colorado, while my dad was in Korea. My grandparents live in Colorado near the Rocky Mountains. Later we were in Yokohama, Japan, for a few years, then Fort Sill, Oklahoma. This time we moved from Fort Hood, Texas. You know the drill—my ol' man came home one night about a month ago and yelled, 'Saddle up. We're movin' out,' and, of course, we all knew what *that* meant. Next day he left for Germany and my mom went out and got about a million boxes, and we all started packing."

"Oh, yeah, I know that drill."

"So, where *you* been?" asked Jack.

"Naval Base, San Diego. Then Rota, Spain. Then Washington, DC. Then we went to the P.I."

"Where?" asked Jack.

"You know. The Philippine Islands. Subic Bay."

"Oh." Jack was fairly sure Alex could tell he knew nothing about the Philippine Islands, but he didn't want to slow Alex down.

"Next we moved to Great Lakes Naval Training Center, near Chicago. Then, same old routine. My old man comes home a few weeks ago and starts yelling, 'Prepare to ship out, swab jockeys!' So, now we're headed for Germany, just like you."

Jack said, "Tell me about the P.I."

"It's the greatest. We were there three whole years. My best friend was John Jawarski, but everyone just calls him Ski. We did everything together. There's this huge bay right where we lived. In fact, there's ocean surrounding the whole place. See, Subic Bay has got to be the biggest Navy base in the whole world. And they don't just have big ships there, they also have submarines. Ski and I'd ride our bikes down to the docks and sneak around so we could see the subs. Once we even saw the atomic submarine *Seawolf* when she was brand new."

"What's an *atomic* sub?"

"You know, like the atomic bomb."

Jack must have looked confused, because Alex went on, "Ya know, those giant bombs they dropped on Japan to end the war. Man, they're the biggest, most powerful bombs the world's ever seen. One atomic bomb can kill thousands and thousands of people, maybe even a million."

"Gee . . ." For the first time, it dawned on Jack just how destructive an atomic bomb was.

"Now even the Commies have 'em."

"Who're the Commies?"

"I dunno, really. I just know they're the bad guys."

"I don't get it. Why would they make a submarine out of a bomb?"

"It's not a bomb, it just uses atomic power. And don't ask me what that is, 'cause I can't really explain it, except to say it's the latest and greatest. Biggest, fastest, and most powerful."

"And you saw one."

"That was the best. My dad got Ski and me onto a sub, but it wasn't the *Seawolf*. Subs are way bigger than you'd think when you see them up close, but inside, not so much. When you're inside, everything seems real small. This ship's corridors might seem narrow to you, but they're huge compared to the alleyways on a sub. The crew sleep in tiny hammocks stacked on top of each other. Much smaller than the bunks sailors use on this ship. The guy on top has to climb over everyone. And there are no portals, so you can never see where you're going when you're submerged."

"So how can they get anywhere?"

"Charts that map the bottom of the ocean help. But today we saw the sub's best friend."

"Sonar." Jack shuddered. "I don't know, man. Subs are cool and all, but not being able to see where we're going . . ."

"I know," said Alex. "I'd rather be on aircraft carriers, like my dad."

"They must really be something."

"Oh, they are, my man. They have big guns, rockets, missiles, and definitely jets. And you want to talk about big? There are over five thousand sailors and Marines on an aircraft carrier. They make the *Upshur* look like a rowboat."

This was the kind of talk Jack loved. But then he heard himself asking one of the few questions brats never, ever ask. "So, do you think you'll ever see Ski again?"

Alex just sat there, studying him. Jack knew he'd been stupid, stupid, stupid.

Finally, Alex seemed to force himself to say, "Don't know."

Jack was miserable. Here was a great guy who could be a very good friend, and he might have just gone and blown it all up.

Then, for some unknown reason, Alex started talking. "I miss him. At first, when we moved to Chicago, it was really hard. I'll tell you about that move in a minute. Anyway, I think about Ski sometimes even now—in fact the best thing is when I see him in my dreams. Those are my best dreams. I wake up, and it feels like we were back together. Also, it feels okay when I tell stories about him to other kids. It kinda makes me feel like he isn't completely gone."

Jack swallowed to control his insane sense of relief. "So, tell me some Ski stories."

As Alex settled in to tell him more about his old buddy Ski, Jack's brain couldn't help going into analysis mode. *I'd never have asked that question to any of my friends in Texas or Yokohama or Fort Sill. Why did I ask Alex? Why is he answering?*

Jack began sorting out the difference between Alex and the other guys he knew. *He gets the whole brat thing, but so do my other friends. It's more than that. There's just something about Alex . . . That grid-search stuff and everything about subs. I can learn from him. And besides, serious stuff happens when we're together, like the whole whale thing.*

"You okay?" Alex asked.

"Absolutely," Jack said. "Come on, tell me about him."

"Well, a couple of times Ski's dad took us out on Subic Bay in a small motorboat. We went to this really big island where they were moving a mountain."

"They were *what*?" Jack's look said he thought Alex was full of it.

"I'm not kidding. The Seabees were out there with these big bulldozers, and they were scooping away this mountain."

"Seabees?"

"Navy combat engineers. They had tons of dynamite and kept using it to blow the top off the mountain. Afterward, they'd come in with giant bulldozers and push the dirt and rocks and trees over the sides of the mountain. The Seabees just kept chopping that mountain down, one layer at a time."

"But why?"

"Airplanes don't land well on mountain tops," Alex said, grinning. "But if the Navy could remake that island into a huge, flat airbase, they could control the oceans for a thousand miles in all directions. Naturally, everyone said it couldn't be done. But the Seabees said, 'That's a load of crap. Give us the job and that mountain's gone.'"

Jack admired that kind of can-do attitude.

"The Seabees like to say, 'The difficult we do at once. The impossible takes a bit longer.'"

"*That* I have to remember."

Alex said, "The Seabees, with all their equipment, a boatload of dynamite, and hundreds of bulldozers, came in and just started pushing that mountain into the ocean. They also used a lot of the rubble to create this massive runway for the jets. Every so often, we'd go out there in Ski's boat to see the progress. My favorite part was watching them set off the dynamite and blow up part of the mountain."

"Then what happened?" asked Jack.

Alex grimaced. "We moved to Chicago, so I didn't get to see. But later my dad told me it got finished. He called Subic Bay Naval Air Station the biggest land-based aircraft carrier in the world."

Jack sat for a while enjoying that thought. Then he said, "What about fights in the P.I.?"

"Brats are brats, so some were trouble. The local kids were tough because they trained in judo and tae kwon do, but they didn't tend to pick fights. In fact, most of the locals were nice. Our nanny, Maria, took us to play with her cousins. We rode our bikes all over the place, like to the beach. They knew some great places to swim. We'd also go to these big outdoor markets where they had all kinds of odd fruit, strange fish, and amazing shells you never found on the beach."

Alex asked, "Did you have a nanny in Yokohama?"

Jack nodded. "Kazako. I really miss her. She didn't speak a word of English, so we learned to speak to her in Japanese."

"Was it hard to learn Japanese?"

"Dunno. It's not like we took lessons or anything. I was kinda young, and . . . well, she was with us all the time, so pretty soon we figured out what she was saying, and how to say stuff back to her."

"Say something in Japanese."

"*Ko-ni-chi-wa, kyo-wa doe-de-su? Da-ka-ra wa-rei-wa-rei wa nah-ni soo-roo tsu-mo-ri-de-su-ka?*"

"That's 'Hello, how you doing? So what are we gonna do?' I must have said that to her every single day."

Jack and Alex sat there for hours, swapping stories and getting a feel for each other, their lives, and their families. When Alex was talking about the P.I., Jack felt like he'd been there. And when Jack talked about Japan, somehow that became part of Alex's life.

"I really like that part about seeing Ski in your dreams, even if he's not really there. I'm gonna remember that." Jack had picked up a solid-gold nugget worth keeping.

Something made Jack's inner clock go off. He glanced down at his watch: 5:54.

"Rats! I'm late!" Jack shot out of his chair, yelling as he ran, "I'll see you at dinner."

Alex bolted a split second behind him. Obviously, the home-by-six rule applied in the Knox family, too.

They'd had a couple of adventures together that morning and one long conversation that afternoon. By dinner, they were best friends.

4

Jean-Sébastien

Jack entered the cabin at six o'clock on the dot.

"You cut that pretty close, Jack," his mom said, a no-nonsense look on her face. The girls were already getting dressed.

"That's 'cause he was off running around with his new friend, Alexander Knox," sneered Queenie from the bathroom.

"Shut up, Queenie!" Jack yelled back.

"Watch yourself, Jack McMasters." His mom sounded very quiet, very controlled. "One more word out of you, and you'll never see this Alexander Knox again."

Jack was no fool. He clamped his mouth shut and started washing up.

When their mom wasn't looking, Queenie stuck her tongue out at him. Jack's eyes flashed at her and his fists tightened. She was taunting him, trying to get him to come after her. But he knew better than to risk getting banned from playing with Alex.

Queenie always knew when she could push it and just how far. But Jack was doing an excellent job of staying quiet on the outside, even though he was raging on the inside. *She is such a royal pain. Oh, yeah, this chick really knows how to get me going. Why is she messing with me and Alex, anyway?*

He'd just finished getting his clothes changed for dinner when, out of nowhere, Queenie burst into tears. No matter what Mrs. McMasters did or said, Queenie just kept screaming and crying about Janie.

Janie Hunter had been Queenie's best friend back in Texas at Fort Hood. Now that Jack thought about it, he realized Queenie had been upset for days, probably because they were moving again. This must be about having to leave the very best friend she'd ever had. Queenie was smart enough to know there was no hope they'd ever see each other again.

As Jack laced this shoes, he strategized how to stay out of Queenie's way till the storm blew over. But it was strange. All of a sudden he wasn't ticked at her anymore. She only wanted what he had: a new best friend.

It took a bit, but his mom and Queenie finally came out of the bathroom, and they all headed for dinner. On the way, Jack tried to lighten things up by telling his mom about their whale sighting. She just gave him an absent nod. It was clear she was preoccupied with other things.

In the dining room, Ernie came over to seat them. He gave Jack a wink before turning to Mrs. McMasters. "Ma'am, tonight you've been invited to the captain's table."

"How nice," she replied. Then she turned to the kids. "You all know the drill: Best manners. Make me proud of you. Do we understand each other?" They each gave a nod.

As they approached the extra-long head table, the captain, Commander Allen, and the other men stood to greet Mrs. McMasters.

"You must be Mrs. McMasters," said the captain. "How good to meet you, ma'am." He shook her hand and then turned to the kids. "Jack, it's a pleasure to see you and your sisters again."

His mother's eyes flicked over to Jack, clearly surprised. But Rabbit grabbed the conversation, saying, "It's nice to see you, too, Captain. You have a very nice ship. We like it a lot."

The captain beamed at her, as did Mrs. McMasters. But she also shot Rabbit a kind-but-clear look, communicating, "You are a very sweet girl, but that is enough out of you, young lady. You are now to be seen and not heard."

"We had quite a time with the children this morning," said Commander Allen.

Her smile grew wider, but her glance at the kids said, *This had better be good.*

Commander Knox and his family, including Alex, were already at the table and were also introduced. As everyone sat down, the two boys managed to get themselves seated next to each other.

The captain jumped right in. "Mrs. McMasters, we were just talking about what great whale hunters these two boys are. I trust you know about their adventure today."

She didn't miss a beat. "Jack was just starting to tell me about it, but I'd love to hear more."

Everyone at the table began telling their version. Commander Allen started with the kids' visit to the bridge. He explained that he'd asked Alex to join them and how they'd all seen what might be whales on the sonar scope.

The story passed to Jack and Alex, who told how they'd used grid search and eventually spotted a whale's tail and hurried to the rear of the ship for a better look. Jack skipped the part where they'd burst into the kitchen to get to the back deck.

The captain then explained how the boys had spotted not one, but five whales playing off the stern. "That, ma'am, is how I came to meet your children. And thanks to Jack and Alex, a large number of people on the ship—passengers and crew—got to see these fantastic creatures. In all my crossings, this is the first time I've ever seen the right whales. Commander Allen and I wanted to take this opportunity to say thanks."

Once the food came, the officers at the far end of the table began joking about a long-ago operation they'd shared in Italy. They couldn't agree what the objective had been. Jack's brain started grinding on the word *objective*. The more they wrangled, the more he realized he wasn't sure what it meant.

Without thinking, he broke the seen-and-not-heard rule. Spectacularly. He interrupted Commander Knox. "I'm sorry, sir, but I don't quite get it. It seems like every time one of you says that word *objective*, it has a different meaning. What does *objective* really mean?"

When Jack broke the flow of the adult conversation, the whole table went silent. Mrs. McMasters glared at Jack, without even hearing his remark. Jack tensed. That woman had such exceptional mom-radar, as well as unbending rules.

Commander Knox looked at Jack and then at Alex as though he'd forgotten they were even at the table.

Fortunately for Jack, before Commander Knox responded, the captain jumped in. "Well, well, I think Jack might have just hit the nail on the head. You're right, young man. The word *objective* can get pretty confusing. However, without a doubt it is one of the most important, if most misunderstood, words in the military." The captain turned to see his officers nodding.

Mrs. McMasters must have sensed things had settled down, because she went back to her own conversation with Mrs. Knox. The moment she did, Jack relaxed.

The captain continued, "Let me explain. When the military goes to war, in order to be victorious, everyone involved must know what he is supposed to do. This is explained to everyone through a simple Objective Statement. And there must be one, and only one, objective, so that no one gets confused about what to do. The challenge is that, when the bullets start flying and the missiles and bombs start exploding, everything gets very confusing. In the heat of battle, it's hard to remember what you're supposed to be doing."

As the officers murmured their agreement, Commander Allen said, "Captain, I could explain it with a story."

The captain nodded approval.

Commander Allen explained, "D-day was called Operation Overlord, and it was the largest amphibious landing ever attempted in the history of mankind."

"I'm sorry, but what kind of landing?" Once Jack's brain was engaged, he went into learning mode, and his need to interrupt simply couldn't be suppressed.

"An amphibian is a creature that can live both in the sea and on the land. But, in this case, those creatures were the United States military, and the British military, arriving in more than a thousand ships. We were going across the English Channel to attack the Nazis in occupied France. And we were bringing over a million men. It was the most important operation of the war. General Eisenhower was the Overlord commander. So what do you think he came up with as the Objective Statement for Operation Overlord? Remember, it had to be a short statement that all one million men could understand and not forget once the bullets started flying."

Jack and Alex looked at each other, desperate to come up with something.

Alex ventured, "How about 'Cross the Channel, get the men on the beach, and attack the Nazis?'"

"Not bad, Alex. Fortunately, General Eisenhower had a lot more time to think about it than you've had. General Eisenhower eventually got it down to only five words. His was 'Enter the Continent of Europe.'"

Commander Allen let the two boys chew on that for a minute. "Do you get what he meant by 'Enter the Continent of Europe'?"

They both nodded, but still looked a bit confused.

"Okay, let's see if the meaning of 'Enter the Continent of Europe' was clear to everyone involved." He turned to the officers. "Gentlemen, you know Eisenhower must have talked with the president of the United States about this. What do you think it meant to the president?"

Without a moment's hesitation, one of them said, "Get to Germany and totally win the war."

"And to General Patton?"

Another said, "Shoot that son-of-a-B Hitler right in the head." That got a laugh from all of them.

"And to the colonels?"

"Get to Paris and drink champagne." More laughter.

"And to the sergeants?"

"Get off the beach and to the closest village that still has beer."

"And to the lowest private?"

"Just get to the beach without getting shot, and dive into the first fox-hole you find."

When the laughter died down, Allen turned back to them. "You see, boys, an objective can certainly mean many different things to many different people. But let me ask you this: Was Eisenhower's objective a good one? Was it well done?"

"I s'pose so," said Jack, "since we were victorious on D-day."

"I agree. But probably what was most successful about 'Enter the Continent of Europe' was that Eisenhower managed to get all one million men going in the same direction. They might have interpreted how *far* they were going a little differently, but at least they were all headed in the same direction."

Ernie came over with their main course. But before dinner commenced, Commander Allen concluded with, "Boys, I want you to always remember this. In order for an army to win a war, or a battle, or, for that matter, any operation, no matter how small, there must be one simple objective that everyone can understand and follow once the bullets start flying."

He and the other officers returned to swapping stories of Italy so many years before

Jack and Alex were in no hurry for dinner to end.

When it was time for dessert, Chef Porteaux and a bunch of his bakers formed up into a small procession and entered the dining room. Leading the procession, two bakers pushed a rolling cart that held a huge cake with a big whale artfully sculpted in the frosting. On it was written:

Thanks
Whale Hunters
Jack and Alex

The captain rose to his feet and took up a table knife. He lightly clinked the crystal sides of two wine glasses. The bright, tinkling sound hushed the room.

"Ladies and gentlemen, may I have your attention," he said in a commanding voice. "This afternoon, some of you had the rare privilege of seeing right whales off the rear deck of this great ship. If you did get to see them, you know it was a truly magnificent sight. However, you might not know you owe that opportunity to the two young boys beside me. And so, ladies and gentlemen, I would ask that you raise your glasses in a toast to Jack McMasters and Alexander Knox, our great whale hunters!" The captain raised his wine glass to Jack and Alex, and everyone did the same.

"Hear, hear!" they all shouted.

"And now I'll have our excellent Chef Porteaux and his staff share with you the wonderful whale cake they made especially for Jack and Alex."

Cheers and clapping erupted, not just for Jack and Alex, but also for Chef Porteaux, whose food they had come to appreciate.

When dinner ended, Queenie and Rabbit watched the boys hurry through the dining room together. Queenie said to Rabbit, "Those two think they're conquering heroes."

But, truth be known, all Jack wanted to do was make a hasty escape to the evening movie, so he could teach Alex the fine art of sneaking undetected into the sailors' private theater.

As they left the mess facility, Ernie gave them a small salute, whispering, "Bravo Zulu, gentlemen."

As the boys saluted back, Jack turned a questioning eye to Alex, who said, "Navy-speak for *Well Done.*"

The movie turned out to be some lame love story. Fifteen minutes into the show, they'd had enough and bailed. Drifting back to their spot from earlier in the afternoon, they plopped into the easy chairs and began talking about what it might be like living in Germany. After all, that was where the war had been and where so much had happened in their fathers' lives.

"Not a bad story about General Eisenhower and 'Enter the Continent of Europe,'" Alex said. "I love those stories."

"Me, too. I just kinda wish more of 'em had kids."

"Or at least one," Alex smirked.

"Actually, my favorite of all time is about a kid."

"Spill the beans."

Jack said, "You don't have to ask twice. One night a couple of years back, this guy named Col. McHenry was over at our house for dinner. People are always coming over 'cause my mom's a great cook. Anyway, he'd been in World War II just like our dads. After dinner, he told about a French kid who'd helped him during the war.

"It was a spy story, but he called it an intelligence story. Toward the end of the war, when the American and British armies had fought their way across France, the American Army was about to enter Germany for the first time. They were desperate for intelligence on the German defenses. They needed someone to go in and spy on the Germans and determine their strengths and weaknesses. But for the longest time, no one succeeded."

From the depths of his chair, Alex craned his head to look at Jack. "And?"

"One afternoon, Col. McHenry struck up a conversation with an eleven-year-old French kid who was working behind the bar of a café in the village where the Americans were headquartered. The boy was Jean-Sébastien de la Chaussée. He only spoke a little English, and McHenry only knew a little French, but somehow they managed to communicate. The colonel asked him why he was inside working, instead of out playing with his friends. The kid shrugged his shoulders and said he might as well work, because his parents no longer let him play with his best friend, François.

"McHenry asked if he and François had gotten in trouble. But to his surprise, Jean-Sébastien said it was nothing of the kind. He'd made the mistake of telling his parents that the Germans had reoccupied François's village. His parents wouldn't let him go back there. When McHenry learned that François lived only seven kilometers away, McHenry knew this was important intel.

"Jean-Sébastien told McHenry that a couple of days back he'd been on his bike going over there to play soccer. But when he got to François's village, he saw a German soldier posted at a roadblock. He admitted to Col. McHenry that he had been pretty scared. He didn't know if he should keep going or turn back."

Alex said, "This really happened?"

"Word from the bird," said Jack, holding up his hand as if being sworn in. "What would you have done? Would you have bugged out?"

"Dunno. I hope not. But I know most kids would have. In fact, most *adults* would. But let me guess. Jean-Sébastien biked right up to the guard."

"Yup. And he got stopped."

"And . . ."

"The Nazi corporal on guard duty wasn't gonna let him pass, but Jean-Sébastien half told/half pantomimed a sad story about needing to see his friend. Eventually, the guard let him through. Interestingly enough, once past the roadblock, Jean-Sébastien went wherever he wanted. No one paid any attention. To them he was just a kid.

"Jean-Sébastien told McHenry that he made it to François's house, and they played all afternoon. When it came time for him to go home, he chose a trail through the woods to avoid the roadblock. But the woods were crawling with Germans.

"McHenry didn't expect to get much more from Jean-Sébastien, but asked one last question as he left. Did Jean-Sébastien notice which units of the German Army were in the village? To his surprise, the kid told him the 901st Panzergrenadier. McHenry knew *Panzer* meant tanks. On his way out the door, McHenry thanked Jean-Sébastien for giving him something to work with."

"Cool," said Alex. "Wish we could do something like that."

"It gets better."

Grinning, Alex sank further in his chair to enjoy the rest of the story.

"McHenry beelined it for his commander and his unit's intelligence officer. He asked if they knew anything about the 901st Panzergrenadier. The intel officer seemed shocked that McHenry knew that unit and asked where he'd come across it. When McHenry explained that the 901st might be only seven kilometers up the road — let's just say he had their full attention.

"The intelligence guy explained that the 901st Panzergrenadier was an armored reconnaissance regiment that was part of the Panzer Lehr, the most elite Panzer tank group in the entire German Army.

"Jean-Sébastien had definitely come up with some critical intelligence. After talking it over, they figured the French kid might just be able get them more intel. That is, if he was willing to risk his life getting it.

"McHenry went back to the café to discuss it with Jean-Sébastien. He got his dad. Monsieur de la Chaussée threw up his hands in refusal. 'If you're caught spying, the Germans will either kill you or put you on one of those trains to the East, and we'll never see you again. And, God forbid, what if they break through and capture this village again? Then they'll kill or imprison our whole family because you were a spy.'"

"Jean-Sébastien gave that some serious thought. Finally, he pleaded with his father, 'If I don't go, there's even more chance the Germans will capture our village. You, my mother, and my sisters could be killed.'"

Alex asked in a low voice, "He took the job, didn't he?"

"Yes, Jean-Sébastien said he would do the intelligence mission for the US Army. He wanted to help protect his family and his village. His job was to find out anything he could about what was going on behind the German lines.

"Now things really get interesting," Jack said. "Jean-Sébastien took off on his bike for François's village. Again he got stopped at the roadblock. But this time, even though this guard spoke better French, his story about going to see a friend didn't fly. But he was desperate to get past, so he didn't give up. He just stood there, eyeing the guard. Then he put on his most pathetic face and told the guard it wasn't just any old friend, it was a girl. A girl that he, well, liked. The guard looked at Jean-Sébastien and sighed, saying something about the French and love. The guard let him pass."

Alex laughed. "Yes, that boy definitely was French."

Jack nodded. "Once past the roadblock, just like on his previous trip, he was able to go pretty much wherever he wanted. Jean-Sébastien peddled around the village, checking things out. He reconfirmed that the 901st Panzergrenadier was there. On the far side of the village, he saw two Panzer tanks. But when he biked toward them, a German soldier with a submachine gun waved him off. Jean-Sébastien, not being a slow child, decided not to push his luck with the soldier."

"And his deadly weapon," Alex chimed in.

That got a quick grin out of Jack. "From there, Jean-Sébastien went to François's farm, just outside town, and they headed for the woods to play. And, not play. Jean-Sébastien took a major risk and revealed his mission to François, who might have been secretly pro-Nazi. The kid might have turned him in. But Jean-Sébastien needed his help navigating those woods. Turns out, François wasn't in league with the Germans. He knew it was dangerous, but he said yes, he'd help Jean-Sébastien.

"They snuck through the forest to where François thought he'd recently heard German voices. He wasn't certain, because he hadn't stuck around long enough to find out. They were just about blown away when all around them tank engines suddenly roared to life. Both boys hit the dirt. Engines kept roaring as the boys lay face down on the forest floor. Both feared they were about to be taken into custody. But as the minutes crept by, no one came for them. The initial shock wore off, and they realized they hadn't been spotted. They cautiously crawled forward on their stomachs.

"They got close enough to spot four Panzer tanks. Jean-Sébastien was surprised to see a couple of horse-drawn wagons, too. In those wagons there were big, steel barrels from which German soldiers were refilling their tanks with diesel fuel. The boys carefully backed out of there. They made it over to the edge of the woods and almost ran into two more tanks. They hadn't spotted them till the last second, because they were hidden under camouflage netting. The tanks were positioned with a clear view out across the fields and toward the village. While the tanks had a great view, those Panzers would be very hard to spot by anyone advancing on them."

"Jean-Sébastien and his buddy were really pushing their luck," Alex said. Jack could see he was almost unable to stand the suspense.

"Absolutely. If the Germans caught them sneaking around their tanks, they'd be found guilty of spying."

"Not even *we* could have talked our way out of that one," Alex admitted.

"I suppose Jean-Sébastien knew it, too, because at that point, they carefully backed away and didn't stop till they were deep in the forest. From there, they snuck the long way around to the farmhouse. Hiding in one of the barns, they compared everything they'd seen, wondering wildly what it meant. One thing was terrifyingly clear: The Panzer Lehr was lying in wait to ambush the advancing American Army.

"In the early evening, Jean-Sébastien's luck held when he made his way back through the German lines. He had a soccer ball tucked under one arm as he biked past the roadblock, nodding to the guard, and yelling, 'Good evening. We won the game!' The guard smiled back at him, a kid who was the picture of innocence.

"Jean-Sébastien held it together until he was outside the village. Then his hands began to shake so hard he dropped the soccer ball. It rolled to the side of the road and down an embankment—he didn't even consider retrieving it. He forced himself to stay on the bike and cover the seven kilometers back to his own village. By the time he stashed his bike behind the café, all the adrenaline had left his body. He was exhausted, but calm, when he entered the café. His father and McHenry were waiting for him at a small table. His father exhaled.

"The café was empty, so he quickly went over everything he and François had seen. McHenry knew immediately that this was critical intelligence. He thanked him, saying he'd been very daring to take on the mission. As McHenry spoke to the boy, Monsieur de la Chaussée seemed to study his son with relief and a new sense of pride.

"McHenry hurried to headquarters to go over everything he'd learned with his commander and the intelligence officer. It was obvious that the boys had come up with more than they'd realized. They had confirmed that the 901st Panzergrenadier and the Panzer Lehr were there, lying in wait to ambush the Americans. The Americans now knew exactly where the Germans planned to hit them. That meant they could take appropriate countermeasures. If that had been everything Jean-Sébastien had found out, it would have been worth it. But the most important piece of intel actually was about the horse-drawn carts. Think about it for a second, Alex. What do they tell you?"

When Alex didn't venture an opinion, Jack continued. "I didn't get it either. But it told the American intelligence officer that the Germans were running out of fuel! Tanks eat a huge amount of diesel fuel. Being Navy, you might not know this, but a tank uses fifty times more fuel than a car."

"Okay," said Alex. "But why were the Germans using horse-drawn carts to refuel the tanks? Where were their big diesel refueling trucks?"

Jack grinned. "They didn't have enough fuel to run the refueling trucks *and* the tanks at the same time. Jean-Sébastien's intel confirmed that our bombers were successfully destroying the German oil refineries making the diesel fuel. It also meant that whatever battle plans the Americans came up with against the Panzer Lehr, they needed to force the Germans to move their tanks—a lot. The Americans needed to force the Germans to use up their precious diesel fuel."

Jack sank back in his chair. Alex knew the story was over.

"So whatever happened in the tank battle that followed?"

"No clue," said Jack. "That wasn't the point of Col. McHenry's story."

"And a very good story it is," said Alex. "I mean, what kid doesn't want to be Jean-Sébastien biking behind enemy lines?"

"Yup," Jack said. "Jean-Sébastien delivered significant intel about the Nazi Panzer tanks massing on the American Army. That French kid actually did something that helped."

Alex said, "You think we'll ever get the chance to do something like Jean-Sébastien?"

"Dunno. I do think about it sometimes. I mean, our dads did so much stuff during the war. In fact, I'm sure we don't know half of what they've done for this country. I just hope we get our chance sometime."

A long silence followed as the boys thought it over.

"Well, if it's ever going to happen, I suspect Germany's the place where it will," Alex concluded. "It's all conflict and war there." Then, half joking, he challenged Jack, "You think you'll be ready?"

"Absolutely," Jack said, grinning, "and so will you."

"I think you're right," said Alex. "In fact, I think we have a destiny. I think *you* have a destiny. The time will come when you will be a Jean-Sébastien."

Jack tossed in his bunk that night, unable to sleep. So much kept rattling around in his head. Might he really have a destiny? Would he ever get the chance to prove he could do something for his country? Would his chance to make a difference ever really come? And what if it did? He'd told Alex he was ready to be like Jean-Sébastien, but who was he kidding? Alone in his bunk, he couldn't fool himself. He wasn't ready to be Jean-Sébastien . . . at least not yet.

5

White Glove

Why is it that the mornings you desperately want to go out to play with your friends are the mornings your mom insists you aren't going anywhere? It's those mornings you just know she's going to come up with at least ten things you have to do before she'll even think of letting you loose.

That's just the kind of morning Jack woke up to.

The real problem was that his mom was finally feeling okay. She didn't have that greenish look, and she wasn't running for the bathroom. If Mrs. McMasters wasn't seasick, then she was definitely back in charge.

"Okay, everyone, up and dressed," she said, twitching Rabbit's blanket. "We are all going to breakfast together, and afterward we will immediately return to this cabin to give it a thorough cleaning."

Universal groaning broke out.

"Children, this ship reaches Bremerhaven tomorrow, and we want to be totally ready to meet your father. So don't plan on doing anything until we are one-hundred percent packed up, cleaned up, and ready to go. Got it?"

Don't you love it when moms say things like, *Got it?* The question sounds like, *Do you understand?* But every brat knows that's not what it means. The translation in mother-speak is: *You are going to do exactly what I say, and you're not doing anything else until I am completely satisfied that you have done everything I can possibly think of.*

Jack knew from grim experience that it didn't matter to his mom that the ship already had staff that cleaned the cabins and bathrooms. She would still have her kids clean that cabin and the bathroom from top to bottom. Her ground rules never varied. You always leave your quarters scrubbed and clean. And that meant cleaner than when you moved in. She made sure they never violated that rule.

So with this cheerful thought in mind, Jack got ready to go to breakfast. He was waiting with Queenie by the door when he heard splashing in the bathroom. Rabbit was still in the tub playing submarine, showing no hurry to get anywhere. Jack was fed up with her lollygagging and about to clobber her. Fortunately, just when Rabbit had pushed it to that point, Mrs. McMasters came by and yanked her out of the tub.

"Time to go, Sugar. Let's get you dry and your clothes on."

Perhaps breakfast was Chef Porteaux's favorite meal, because it was the ship's specialty. And the ever-hungry Jack did a yeoman's job of ordering it up. Before you knew it, there were eggs, bacon, sausage, fried potatoes, pancakes, waffles, coffee, milk, cocoa, and orange juice on their table. Everyone ate as though it had been a week since their last meal. In Mrs. McMasters's case, that was nearly true.

Alex came by their table and asked if Jack could go play, but Mrs. McMasters made herself perfectly clear that Jack wouldn't budge until he'd finished his chores. Alex said okay, but, as he passed, he leaned over to Jack and mouthed the words, "How long?"

Jack rolled his eyes. "It's the white glove."

"Not the white glove! That'll take forever."

Jack imitated his neck was hanging in a noose. "See ya later, Alex."

"See ya *much* later, Jack."

By the time everyone had finished the breakfast feast, they were more prepared for a nap than a major house cleaning. But naps were not on Mrs. McMasters's agenda. When they got back to the cabin, the first task she gave the kids was to lay out what they would wear on their final day aboard ship, so the rest could be packed. That alone took Queenie almost half an hour.

Then the cleaning began. Unfortunately for the kids, Mrs. McMasters's style of cleaning involved two dreaded objects: an old toothbrush and a white glove. And she never went anywhere without them. So in a game of drawing straws, Queenie lost and ended up with toothbrush detail—just about the worst job any kid could get. It meant you had to clean every corner, crack, and crevice of the bathroom down on your hands and knees with a cup of soapy water. You detail-clean the bathroom in and around the toilet, the tub, the shower, the sink, and even inside any cupboards. Getting toothbrush duty was a world-class horror, and Queenie's expression registered this fact.

The white glove, however, was the sole property of Mrs. McMasters. When the kids announce they're all finished cleaning and they're sure everything's perfect, she puts on that white glove. She goes through the whole house, or in this case, the whole cabin, running a finger of that white glove over anything—along the tops of paintings hanging on the wall, inside the shower, behind the toilet, etc. If she finds even one speck of dust, they start cleaning all over again. It might not be fair. It might not be right. But it is the McMasters way.

So they got down to cleaning. While Jack started in on the bedroom, Queenie began scrubbing behind the toilet. Rabbit's job was to come along with a washcloth and wipe up after Queenie's toothbrush.

The first time Mrs. McMasters came by to check on progress, Rabbit and Queenie were both on their knees in the bathroom. Rabbit looked up at her and said, "Mom, guess what. My friend Ernie saw Santa Claus when he was up by the North Pole."

"That's nice, dear—now keep working."

Rabbit, as the follow-up kid, was also responsible for yelling, "Missed a spot!" if she happened to get any dirt on the white cloth. She took great joy in such announcements, right to the point where Queenie seemed ready to kill her.

"Missed a spot," shouted Rabbit, for about the tenth time.

"Did not!"

"Did so!"

"Show me!" demanded Queenie.

So Rabbit lifted her finger that was wrapped around the cloth to show her the evidence.

"There's no dirt on that!" Queenie's groan was tinged with annoyance and a righteous dose of anger.

"Oh, yeah, there is. Right here is a speck. See?"

"Is not."

"Is so."

And, of course, things just got louder and louder between them.

Queenie shouted, "Mom, she's doing it again! Make her stop it right now, or I'm gonna box her ears!"

Mrs. McMasters marched in. "Knock it off, both of you. Right now!" Almost as an afterthought she glanced at the cloth. "Stop torturing your sister, Rabbit." Then she gave them one of her classic lines. "I don't care how long it takes you to get this place shipshape. It doesn't bother me. I have all day and all night. It's totally up to you. You can cooperate and get it done, or you can make it last all day. You decide."

In the first ninety minutes, they failed the white-glove inspection twice. But before the third try, they re-scrubbed every inch of the cabin. With great ceremony, Mrs. McMasters put on her white glove to move around the cabin testing here and there. Swipe, inspect. Swipe, inspect. The glove showed no dust or dirt, so she murmured, *Um-hum,* and moved on. Then came the bathroom, the scene of both previous failures. Queenie and Rabbit held their breath. After ten swipes, inspects, and *Um-hums,* Mrs. McMasters pronounced the cabin clean. They were leaving the cabin cleaner than when they came aboard ship. The McMasterses, once again, had met their personal standards.

The children's sighs of relief were audible.

"All right, you may go. But be back by six o'clock sharp."

Three children were out of that cabin in less than ten seconds.

And it wouldn't take many more seconds to find trouble.

6

Final Mission

Jack hadn't made it ten feet out the door before crashing into Alex, who sat in the narrow corridor waiting for him to finish.

"Three hours! Man, your mom's tough."

"You should see how things are when my *dad's* around."

Alex jumped up. "Let's go. It's our last day, and we have lots of ground to cover. Wait'll you hear my plan," he said, with a sneaky smile.

"I'm up for it—whatever it is."

Alex narrowed his eyes, giving Jack a long stare. "I think the captain and Commander Allen have a problem. Enemy agents might have taken over the ship's engine room. But Allen and the captain aren't aware of anything, yet."

Jack said, "So our mission is to determine if there's really a threat to the engine room?"

"You got it. We need to get in there and check things out."

"There's no way! It's locked down tight. We've already tried."

"Follow me. I'll show—"

"We'll help," interrupted Rabbit. She and Queenie had come up behind them.

"Don't even think about it," snapped Jack. "This is a mission for just Alex and me."

But Queenie wasn't buying it. With a tone that said, "I'm the oldest in the family, so I'm in charge," she said matter-of-factly, "Jack, you *know* we're coming with you. Either we come, or I tell Mom."

Jack gave her a hard look. He tried to stare her down so she'd leave and take Rabbit with her. But she just stared back, and he knew she had him.

"All right, all right. But you stay behind us, because *we're* leading this mission."

Off they went, the two girls, all smiles, bring up the rear. However, Alex didn't head for the engine room. When Jack questioned this, Alex just said, "Snack bar first. We can't just rush down to the engine room and mount a frontal attack. We need a plan to penetrate it, gather intel, and do it undetected. Besides, it's past noon and I'm starving."

Jack realized the wisdom of this. They all got cheeseburgers and fries. Except Rabbit. She was crazy about grilled-cheese sandwiches. They chose a table at the back of the snack bar, away from anyone who might overhear their council of war.

"So how do we get in?" asked Jack.

Alex said, "The second day at sea I was exploring with a kid named Gus. Low in the ship, we found a passageway that dead ended at a round hatch in the wall—watertight like on a submarine. It had a crank to open it. We decided to play submarine. With work, we got it open.

"It leads into a passageway made of thin sheet metal. It's basically a big air duct. We crawled in and closed the hatch behind us, so no one would know we were in there. The crank works on both sides, like on a sub, so we knew we could reopen it. But once it was closed the space was pitch black. We crawled on our hands and knees, eventually coming to another duct that leads in two different directions. To the right we heard engine-room sounds, like cranking pistons. We crawled in that direction, but after two or three more turns, we got nervous we might get lost in that maze of ductwork. It was too tight to turn around, so we just started backing out. Eventually, we managed to find the hatch and get out. Gus and I planned to get flashlights and other equipment the next day and make it all the way to the machine room."

"And?" asked Jack.

"We never made it. Things kinda went wrong that night," Alex said, explaining that he and Gus had run into Commander Knox, which meant introducing Gus to his father. Commander Knox asked him who his dad was. Gus had said his dad was Master Sergeant Stephens.

"Everything seemed okay until later that night. My dad took me aside for *the talk* . . ."

"We know all about those," said Queenie.

"He informed me I wasn't to play with Gus anymore. For a split second, I thought he'd found out we'd been in those ventilation ducts. But the problem wasn't that. When I asked how come, all he said was, 'It's not a good idea,' with that voice that says the commander has set down the law. The next day, I saw Gus one last time. He had gotten the same message from *his* dad. It was the old rule that officers' kids can't play with sergeants' kids, and they can't play with us."

Queenie said, "Just 'cause sergeants aren't officers. The dumbest rule yet."

Rabbit nodded her head so hard, her brains were close to shaking out. "That's why I can't bring home half the kids in my class."

Jack turned to Alex. "And, as usual, you followed standard operating procedure: Ignore the rule till you get busted."

"But once that happened, we had no choice but to back off and go our own ways."

Queenie said, "Too bad. Lucky both our dads are commissioned officers. Which means we can get on with the mission." She looked from Jack to Alex. "So, what's the game plan?"

Alex laid out the plan.

First, they needed flashlights. He suggested they get those from the emergency evacuation kits they'd been shown at the Abandon Ship Station on the first day aboard.

Second, they needed a big ball of string. They would tie the end of the string to the crank wheel on the inside of the hatch and unwind it as they crawled through the air ducts on their way to the engine room. That way, they wouldn't get lost in the maze of ducts and could find their way back. But Alex didn't have a clue where to get any.

Rabbit was quick to say she'd seen a ginormous ball of string in the galley, near the big ovens, and maybe she could get it from Ernie.

Third, they needed a change of clothes. The insides of the ducts were covered with a layer of dust and dirt that would get all over them as they crawled through. They didn't want to execute a successful mission to the engine room, only to get busted over why they were so filthy.

After going over the plan a few more times, Alex asked, "What d'ya think?"

It was risky, but it would be their last great adventure on the USS *Upshur*.

Queenie spoke for all of them. "Let's do it."

Twenty minutes later, they were back together.

Rabbit presented the string and grinned. "Ernie handed it right over. Didn't have to explain a thing."

"Mom wasn't in the cabin, so I didn't need to explain either," said Queenie. "Got the stuff out of the bags we packed this morning. Oh, and Alex, I also brought you a set of Jack's clothes, so yours don't get dirty, either."

"Wow. Good thinking," said Alex. "Thanks."

She smiled smugly. "Told ya you needed me on this mission."

Jack and Alex gave each other a "yeah, right" look.

Alex said, "We barely managed to score these two flashlights. Jack was acting as lookout. I had just finished raiding the second emergency evacuation kit when he waved me off. Two sailors were bearing down on us. I stuffed both flashlights under my shirt and quickly walked in the other direction." He turned to Jack. "You tell the rest."

Jack grimaced. "They smelled something fishy. I tried to distract them by walking right toward them, but it didn't work. They grabbed me by the collar and wouldn't let go. They kept demanding to know what we'd been up to. To give Alex more time to get away, I went into my dumb-kid act."

Queenie smirked. "Well, that didn't take much acting."

"Piss off, Laura," Jack snapped at her, thinking, *You perpetual pain in my butt.*

"Anyway, Alex, it didn't take those sailors more than a second to see you'd unzipped a kit. They kept grilling me, demanding to know who you were and what you wanted in that kit. But I kept insisting I didn't know a thing about 'that other kid.' They hauled down the kit that was still half open and stood there trying to figure out what you'd stolen. I was so sure we were busted, but, somehow neither noticed the flashlight was gone. They finally let me go."

Alex let out a long exhale. "That was a bit too close for comfort."

Jack just shrugged. "Yeah, but it's over now, so let's keep going."

They decided that since they only had two flashlights, the first person into the tunnel would be Alex, with one of the lights. Then it would be Jack, followed by Rabbit. No one wanted her to be last, fearing she'd somehow get separated. Queenie would have the other light and bring up the rear.

They changed their clothes in the snack-bar bathrooms, and put their original outfits into a paper bag they'd begged off the lady at the snack counter. They knew that in order not to get busted, they had to show up at their cabins in time for dinner wearing the same clothes they'd left in. It's spooky how moms can remember little things, like what you wore that morning. If you've changed, they immediately know something's up.

Following Alex, they made their way into the bowels of the ship. He made a few wrong turns, but eventually managed to find the dead-end corridor with the submarine door in the wall. That round hatch made Alex's story, and the adventure, seem much more real.

Alex tugged on the wheel crank. It didn't budge. "It wasn't this hard the last time."

They tried with Jack pushing up on one side of the wheel while Alex pulled on the other. Even together they couldn't budge it. Everyone gave it a try, but no go.

Without explaining why, Queenie marched off.

Rabbit said, "She's such a quitter. Let me give it a good jump."

Jack and Alex shrugged at each other, and helped Rabbit up onto a lower spoke. She jumped up and down on it, but even that didn't move the wheel an inch.

They were sitting with their backs up against the wall when Queenie swaggered back, a big push broom over her shoulder. "I got this from one of the supply closets."

They watched as she threaded the handle through the wheel. "Jack, get on the right and pull up on the handle with me. Alex, you and Rabbit get on the left side and push down."

They heaved with all their strength. The wheel started turning with a screech.

And their luck held, because the broom handle didn't break. Once they'd turned it a quarter of a crank, they were able to remove the broom. From there, Jack and Alex got it open.

Jack and Alex locked eyes, knowing this was it.

Alex's flashlight revealed a square air duct. He crawled in on his hands and knees. Jack placed the bag of clothes against the right wall of the shaft while Queenie unscrewed the broom from its handle to fit it inside. Then

Jack climbed in. Both boys moved far enough along the shaft to let in Rabbit and Queenie. Once inside, Queenie flipped on her flashlight and tied one end of the string to the inside crank.

As she was closing the door, Jack whispered, "Only give the wheel a small turn, so it's easy to open when we get back."

They crawled along the duct. The flat bottom made things pretty easy, but the thinness of the metal meant moving too fast, or putting their hands or knees down too hard, made the metal reverberate loudly.

"Spread out a little," whispered Jack, "so we don't put so much weight on the same spot." After that, there was a lot less noise from the metal.

A few minutes later, Alex waved his light behind him to signal the others to stop. In a low voice, he said, "Okay, I'm at the first turn. Everyone go to the right."

Soon after they made the turn, they could hear the unmistakable sound of pistons pumping. It had to be the engine room.

Queenie had barely gotten beyond that first corner when Jack called softly back to her, "You still got the string?"

"Yup, still got it," she whispered back.

It was dark in the shaft, but Jack and Rabbit, who had no flashlights, could see Alex's light continually waving around up ahead. They just kept following that light. Even though he couldn't see much, Jack felt the dust and dirt on the floor of the shaft. It was getting thicker. Alex had been right; the further they went, the dirtier it got and the dirtier their clothes must be getting. Jack didn't care. This was the most important and complex mission he'd ever undertaken.

Alex made three more turns. With each one, the engine noise got louder. Then, without warning, he shut off his light and froze in place.

Jack inched close to him. "What's up?"

Alex made a quiet shushing sound. Jack's brat-radar started whirling. He could sense there might be a real problem.

From behind came a loud, "Hey, what's going on, guys?"

Jack's first instinct was to obliterate Rabbit and her big mouth. Instead, he carefully backed up a bit, snapped his head around, and using maximum effort at self-control, he barely breathed, "I don't know, but be totally silent until I find out."

"Okay, big brother," she said, perfectly delighted with herself and the situation.

Jack was crawling forward when Alex backed up to meet him. "Tell Queenie to turn off her light."

Jack squeezed his leg to indicate he'd heard. Then he went back to Rabbit and told her to *whisper* to Queenie to kill her light. Somehow Queenie understood, because before Rabbit could say anything, her light went out. They couldn't even see themselves.

Alex hardly whispered, but they all heard: "Beyond the next curve, a small window-sized return vent looks into a room. Probably high up in a wall. I saw a couple of snipes down there."

"Spies?" demanded Rabbit in her usual Rabbit voice.

Jack wished she could see his death glare.

Alex said, "Be quiet, or go back. Not spies—*snipes*. Navy-speak for *machinist*. Room might be machine shop. They'll see our flashlights. They stay off."

Queenie's answer was hushed but urgent. "Let's—go—back."

"You can go and take Rabbit," Jack suggested, in a rather too-obvious attempt to be rid of her. "Alex and I can go on."

"You come back, too," Queenie insisted.

"Might be bad guys," Alex said, ignoring her. "Can't tell. No uniforms."

"You are so full of it, Alex," hissed Queenie, with alarm in her voice.

But Jack, full of both terror and excitement, ignored her. He and Alex crawled forward. Jack was disappointed when the girls followed. Queenie may have forced him into letting her come with them, but she wasn't going to control what they did on this mission.

When they rounded the next corner, they saw a wide stream of light shine in through the big return air vent. Alex worked his way up to it and cautiously peered down into the room. Then he slipped beyond the opening so Jack could come forward to look. Facing away from the vent stood a guy at a workbench. He had on dark work pants, perhaps Navy-issue. But, on top, he had a grungy undershirt, some kind of black rubber apron covering his front, and dark goggles over his eyes. Those were definitely not standard Navy-issue. The guy was working a large piece of metal on a grinding wheel, sparks flying everywhere.

Eventually, Jack slipped by, and they both moved farther along the vent. Alex stopped and turned toward Jack, stretching his hand, as if to say, "What gives?"

Jack leaned close to Alex's ear. "Sabotage?"

"Hard to tell. They make repair parts there."

"Keep going."

Not long after, they came upon another big return vent. Alex said, "Four guys playing cards."

Jack, leaning against Alex, could hear them joking about the game.

Then another voice came from somewhere so close it seemed directly below the vent. "Wolfgang, you better get back in there and stoke those fires." It didn't sound mean. It was like the guy was messing with him.

"Flake off, Schwartz," said a card player. "I'll get to it soon enough."

"Oh, yeah, soon enough. Just like always," the voice below taunted. "You watch. The chief'll be back in less than half an hour, and he'll tear you a new one if those furnaces are burned way down."

Alex motioned a "Let's go." He inched past the vent.

Before following, Jack stopped at the grate for a look at the room. Four guys played cards around a square table. The grate was so low he could see their dirty undershirts and the black grime on their hands. Only then did he realize what a chance they were taking. Anyone might have looked up and spotted him staring down. But none of them did. Based on what they were wearing, he couldn't tell if they were sailors or not. Jack carefully crawled past the opening and into the dark shaft beyond. Without using any lights, they just kept going deeper into the shaft. As before, Jack noted the girls were following. Even Rabbit was quiet for once.

Once they could no longer hear the card players, Alex said in a low voice, "Ironheads."

"What?" whispered Jack.

"Navy engine-room workers."

"Is Wolfgang messing with the ship, or is he just lazy?"

"Can't tell. Suspicious. Let's keep going."

Alex came to another dead end, but this time the shaft only turned left. As they approached the corner, the engine room sounds grew so loud, they seemed to rattle the air shaft. When Jack followed Alex around the corner, he saw a faint light ahead. The shaft was coming to an end right at another big air return duct. But this time, there wasn't much light coming in. Alex looked through the opening.

The smell of grease reached Jack as he inched up to Alex, who said, "We've arrived. It's the engine room."

Alex pushed against the grate covering the vent. It easily swung open to the left. He peered down, and then stretching his hand through the opening, he gently tapped something just above it. Seeming satisfied, he turned back to Jack. "There's a pipe. Not hot. If it holds my weight, I can swing out on it and drop to a catwalk maybe four feet down. Grip my belt. If the catwalk can't hold me, pull me back in the vent. Got it?"

Jack wasn't sure. After all, he hadn't yet seen the engine room, much less the catwalk. But before he could respond, Alex turned back around and started edging his way through the opening. Jack instinctively grabbed Alex's belt and crawled forward with him.

Reaching way out and over his head, Alex was just able to grab the one-inch pipe. He tugged on it, to test if it would hold his weight. It must have seemed okay, because in one athletic motion he pulled his entire body out of the vent and hung there. Unfortunately, he dragged Jack half out of the vent with him. Jack let go of the belt to keep from sailing headfirst into the engine room. There he was, heart pounding like crazy as he slumped halfway out of the vent, with his friend precariously hanging thirty feet above the engine room from a one-inch pipe. Jack eased himself back into the vent. Breathing hard, he knew he couldn't leave his friend hanging there. He forced himself to reach out and grab Alex by the belt for a second time. He was about to drag him back into the vent when Alex let go, dropping to the catwalk. The motion yanked Jack so hard that there was no holding him back. Jack flew out of the vent, landing on Alex as they both crashed onto the catwalk.

It took a moment for the boys to realize what had happened. Shaken, Jack carefully crawled off Alex. After sitting there for a few seconds, he cautiously stood, holding tightly to the rails. Alex did the same. They held their breath, waiting to see what would happen. But nothing did. There they were, perched on a catwalk thirty feet above the machine room. Still alive.

"Close one," mouthed Jack, heart still racing.

Alex nodded.

Jack looked down on a maze of pipes running everywhere. Steam was hissing and occasionally pouring from them. They had landed on a hanging walkway made of crisscrossed grating. It seemed to run the full length of the engine room, but it was hard to tell through the blasts of steam. Jack couldn't remember a room this big, noisy, or gloomy outside a movie.

Rabbit stuck her head out of the vent. "Hey! Help me down."

Alex moved a little farther along the gangplank, making more room. Jack reached up and pulled her from the vent and onto the catwalk.

"Cool," she said, not bothering to hold on.

Queenie, staring out of the vent, took one look at the situation and said, "Are you guys crazy?"

Jack nodded a mock-sheepish "yes," and motioned for her to join them anyway. "Grab that pipe, pull yourself out, and drop."

"You are *truly* nuts."

He gave her his best "okay, if you're too chicken" shrug. But he knew he had her. She'd never allow herself to come out of this looking less brave than he did.

She reached for the pipe and pulled herself out. But there she got stuck, looking too terrified to just let go and drop.

Jack cut her some slack, gesturing that it was only a two-foot drop to the walk. He ended with a thumbs up sign. When nothing changed, he reached up, grabbed her waist, and helped her drop lightly onto the catwalk. He didn't say anything, and she didn't either. Some things are best left unsaid between siblings.

Alex and Rabbit were already halfway across the room. Catching up, Jack realized just how big the engine room was, and how powerful the pistons. Those monsters banged up and down, turning the giant drive shaft which, in turn, spun the propellers and drove the ship forward. The drive shaft must have been two feet thick. As it revolved, the oil that coated it glistened in the low light. The smell of grease and oil was almost overpowering.

The other day, Jack had thought the Navy officers were just pulling his leg about the ship having 13,500 horsepower. After all, if the most powerful car engines in America were only 500 horsepower, how could a ship's engine generate 13,500 horsepower? But seeing the engine room in operation, with all that noise and all that steam, Jack became a believer.

About halfway across the catwalk, a huge blast of steam erupted out of the gloom. It didn't burn them, but all the same, the hot, wet cloud instantly turned the dust and dirt on their clothes into runny goo. But even covered with slick mud, they kept moving along the catwalk until they'd inched across the entire room and come to a small door in the wall. Alex managed to pull it open. He ducked through and the others followed. The catwalk kept going right across that next room. In the dim light, Jack saw they were at least three stories high inside the boiler room. He could make out six huge, dark contraptions. Next to them was a small mountain of something rough and black.

Jack leaned over the railing, determined to see despite the near darkness. He shouted, "Boilers that make the steam to drive the engine. Coal for fire." The noise from the engine room made it seem like a whisper.

"Engine room, we have a problem!" a massive voice boomed out of nowhere. It sounded like the voice of God. Jack froze in his tracks, not just out of shock, but because he was pretty sure *they* were the problem that "God" was talking about.

The great voice sounded again. "Engine room. This is the bridge. Our systems show boilers four, five, and six are rapidly losing steam. Get on it, engine room, and give me a sitrep immediately!"

Massive relief was written all over their muddy faces. Jack realized it wasn't the voice of God. It was the voice of Commander Allen. And he did not sound happy.

Queenie mouthed the words, "*Sitrep?*"

Before Jack could reply, "*Situation report,*" running footsteps were coming toward them from the engine room. The kids managed to lie down motionless on the catwalk before all the lights came on and five men burst into the boiler room, all yelling at once. Jack recognized the four card players.

"Wolfgang, you idiot! I told you to get the lead out and re-fire the boilers! But no. You had to keep playing cards."

"Shut up, Schwartz. We don't need your mouth now. Just get number five opened up!"

Wolfgang and another guy grabbed big shovels and began filling a giant, iron cart with chunks of coal. Schwartz got the door to boiler number five open. They wheeled the cart over and started shoveling the coal into the boiler. There was a faint, red glow inside the boiler, but even the kids could tell there was not much fire in there.

"Oh, crap, Wolfgang. You better pray that fire don't go out, or the chief's definitely gonna bust you again."

"Just shut up, and get boilers two and three open. One of them should still be running hot. Get some live coals from them, and we'll throw 'em onto the new stuff in five."

The brats hardly dared to breathe. Their only muscles moving were attached to their eyeballs. They watched Schwartz open boiler two. It was like he'd opened the jaws of a dragon who roared flames back at him. Schwartz's sweaty face glowed so red he looked like the devil himself. He barely shut the door without being torched. No one could grab coals out of *that* inferno. Finding the next boiler's fire wasn't so intense, he began shoveling coals into the cart, and from there, into boiler number five.

"Schwartz, use the bellows!"

Schwartz looked right up at the children staring down through the catwalk.

Major alarm bells sounded in Jack's head. *We get to Bremerhaven tomorrow. First thing Dad hears is we got busted in the ship's engine room. I'd rather be Wolfgang, getting crucified for letting the fires die down.*

All of a sudden their biggest adventure didn't seem like such a great idea.

But Schwartz ignored them completely. Instead, he reached up and grabbed a metal chain attached to a wide, flexible hose hanging out of a massive pipe ten feet below the catwalk. The hose attached to some type of accordion that stretched out as he pulled the chain. Schwartz caught the end of the hose and maneuvered it to boiler number five.

Jack lay there in shock. *Why didn't he bust us?*

Schwartz pointed the hose toward the boiler opening. It blew air on the glowing embers so they worked on the new coal. In a matter of seconds, boiler number five began to burn for real.

It took Jack's brain a couple more cycles to realize what had just happened. It wasn't that Schwartz was too busy to bust them. He had never *seen* them. When the ironheads turned on the lights, Jack could see everything because all those big lights were hanging from underneath the catwalk, pointing down on the room. But when Schwartz looked up, he couldn't see past the blinding lights to where they lay. For Schwartz, everything above the lights was in darkness.

Despite his racing heart, Jack knew they had to move. *They won't be busy forever. Time to beat a hasty retreat.*

He signaled Queenie to move back along the catwalk. He tapped on Rabbit's foot and, getting her attention, signaled her to get Alex and move back, too. In this situation, even Rabbit seemed smart enough to stay silent.

Ever so slowly they stood up and crept out through the steam blasts, through the boiler room's upper metal door, and back across the engine room. Because of that miraculous mix of downward lighting and preoccupation, no one must have seen them go.

Once they reached the air vent, Jack put his back up against the wall, bent down, and put his two hands together. First he gave Queenie a boost up into the vent. As she went up, he whispered, "Find the string and follow it."

Boosting Rabbit up to Queenie's waiting hands, he told her to stay close to Queenie on the way back. Finally, he boosted Alex back into the pipe. Before Alex could try to turn around in the pipe to give Jack a hand, Jack vaulted up and grabbed the end of the vent, pulling himself into the pipe—a stunt made easy by all Jack's excess adrenalin.

"You okay?" asked Alex.

"Fine. Just go."

They edged past the vent overlooking the empty card room, past the snipes' machine room, and on into the vent. The further they got, the faster they moved. By the time they got back to the hatch, they'd been moving at a fast crawl.

Queenie, also adrenalin pumped, got the crank on the sub door turned all by herself. She opened it a tiny crack and listened for noise in the hall. Giving them a thumbs-up sign, she flung it open and practically dove back out into the hallway. Next came Rabbit, then Alex. When Jack finally made it out, Queenie immediately slammed the door shut and started cranking.

"Hold up," said Jack. "We need the broom and the clean clothes."

As Queenie dragged the bag out, the messy ball of string rolled onto the floor. Queenie had been trying to roll it up as she went, but it had been hard while trying to crawl.

Obviously, Queenie's nerves were as unraveled as the string, because she grabbed the end still attached to the crank and tugged frantically. But the string was strong and her knots were secure. Alex leaned over to cut the loop with his pocket knife.

Only then was the hatch cranked shut for good. Everyone was ready to bolt. But again Jack held up his hand. "We're not out of the woods yet. Remember our plan. Let's make sure we finish this mission all the way." He held up the bag of clean clothes as a small reminder. They all looked at the bag, and then at each other. They were a mess. They might be out of the air duct, but they could still be busted.

"Okay, first we get to the bathrooms and change. Then give Rabbit all your dirty clothes to put back in the sack. After that, Laura, you get the broom back where it goes, and Alex and I will return the flashlights. Then we'll all meet back at the snack bar to debrief."

They'd almost made it to the bathrooms when a passing officer openly stared and was about to stop them. Without hesitation, they just kept walking. Rabbit grinned at him as she passed by. "We've been on clean-up patrol."

"Looks like it," he said, not sounding convinced. But he didn't call them back.

Rabbit had doled out the clean clothes before the kids hurried into their respective bathrooms.

Jack did a quick wash-up in the bathroom sink. That wash was only one step better than one of Mrs. McMasters's spit baths, when she'd take his dirty face, pull out her handkerchief, spit on it, and scrub. *At least this time there's a sink.* He went into a bathroom stall to change his clothes.

When they all emerged from the bathrooms, Rabbit made a great show of gathering everyone's dirty clothes before they headed for the snack bar. Queenie dashed to return the broom. Jack and Alex went with the flashlights.

Fortunately, it all went without incident. Fifteen minutes later, they were together at the same snack-bar table, drinking Cokes and congratulating each other on pulling off a most excellent adventure.

"I wonder if Wolfgang managed to get those boilers going to Commander Allen's satisfaction," mused Alex.

"Will he get in trouble?" asked Rabbit.

Queenie humphed. "I'm just glad we got out of there before we got caught."

"And I'm just trying to figure out what we forgot," said Jack.

"Forgot?" Alex asked. "What are you talking about?"

"Oh, you know—something you forget can always trip you up."

That made them all start thinking.

"Where is the string?" Jack was urgent.

"In the bag," said Rabbit.

"See what I mean? If Mom found that string, she'd have all kinds of questions. I can hear her now, 'Where did you get this? What did you use it for?'"

"You're right," said Queenie, running a hand through her hair in frustration. "Man oh man, my hair's filthy."

They all touched their hair and cringed.

"We gotta do something about that, too," she said. "And, speaking of dirt, how do we get these clothes cleaned so we don't get sixty-four thousand questions about how they got so dirty?"

While Queenie rerolled the string as best she could, they spent the time talking over other possible gotchas. (Brat sneakiness is a fine art form.)

First, Rabbit brought the string back to Ernie and then met the others at the gym, where they snuck in to take showers.

Their final stop was a dicier mission involving a favor. Once again they found themselves outside the big iron doors of that laundry facility, with a new set of carts lined up outside. Their banging on the door was answered by one of the sailors they'd met the other day. He studied them for half a minute before yelling in mock-horror to the guys inside, "Help! Protect me! The Army is here!"

The laundry crew all burst out laughing.

"What's up, Army?" he said.

Rabbit took the lead on this one. "We were messing around and we accidentally got very, very, *very* dirty. This bag holds the dustiest clothes you've ever seen." She dramatically lifted the big bag over her head, and without the least hesitation, dumped its contents onto the floor. Smiling broadly she declared, "Don't worry. No puke. Just dirt."

That got another laugh from everyone. Then, getting down to the point, she told her growing audience, "But our mothers will never understand. Soooooo . . . we're wondering . . . if you could do us a *really* big favor and wash them?"

The laundry guys looked at each other and cracked up. The first sailor said, "Okay, okay, we'll do it for you, but only 'cause there's no barf involved."

Still laughing, they told the kids to be back for their clean clothes between nineteen and twenty hundred hours that night.

"You're open past bedtime?" asked Rabbit, clearly surprised.

One of the guys explained, "With so many Army pukers aboard, we work twenty-four hours a day."

The brats were so grateful they joined in the laughter. Then promising faithfully to be back, the merry band marched off, satisfied they'd covered their tracks and completed a most excellent mission.

7

War Story

The McMasters kids made it back five minutes before the six p.m. deadline. The moment they entered the cabin, it was obvious something was up. Their mother looked dressed for a ball, and her makeup was already perfect.

"Are we getting all dressed up, too?" asked Rabbit, starting to get excited.

Queenie asked, "Is there a farewell party? Will there be dancing?" Jack watched Queenie in that moment transform from secret agent into dress-up princess.

"Not a party, but a formal dinner dance. And, yes, you girls are to put on your party dresses. Jack, you're to get into your suit and tie. Everything's freshly pressed and hanging in the closet."

This was anything but the standard prepare-for-dinner drill. Mrs. McMasters told them not just to wash up but instead to take showers before putting on their good clothes. The kids knew better than to say they'd showered less than an hour before. They gave each other knowing glances and quickly took a second shower. Their mom helped the girls with their hair and Jack with his tie. Mrs. McMaster finally nodded her approval when they all looked strack—*strack* being military-speak for looking sharp, top to bottom, with not one thing out of place. And, indeed, their clothes did look perfect, every crease straight, no wrinkles to be found. So, off they went to the dinner dance.

When they arrived at the dining room, or, as Jack would say, the *dining facility*, it was clear this was a serious event, with all the ladies in party dresses and ball gowns, and the officers in their formal uniforms: Navy in dress whites; Army, Marine, and Air Force in dress blues. The dining room was set up for a formal dinner, with white tablecloths, crystal glasses, and the best silverware and china. In the middle of each table was a big, fancy centerpiece. A dance floor had been set up, and a jazz band was already playing.

Queenie rolled her eyes at the band and mumbled, "You can bet they won't play 'Wake up, Little Susie," "Great Balls of Fire," or "Peggy Sue.' Those guys look way too square for rock 'n' roll."

Once again Ernie came forward to lead them to their table. This evening they were seated with a couple they didn't know who had two girls and no boys. Queenie and Rabbit seemed happy enough, but not Jack. He kept looking for Alex. He finally spotted him entering the room with his family. Jack wanted to invite him to eat at their table, but his mom said no. And she did it with that "no means *no!*" look.

However, a few minutes later Alex walked up to their table.

"Good evening, Mrs. McMasters. Did you have a nice day?" Alex asked, using his best adult manners.

"Why, yes, I did, Alex. Thank you. And may I say you look very smart tonight?" Alex, too, was in a suit and tie. "How was *your* day?"

"It was just fine, ma'am. Thank you for asking." Then, after a slight pause, he got to the point. "Mrs. McMasters, my father asked me to come by your table to see if Jack might have dinner at our table tonight."

She gave Alex and Jack "the look," clearly communicating, "You guys are really pushing your luck."

Jack's knee started bouncing. In desperation, he tilted his head, as if to say, "Please get me out of here." Both boys stared her down. She finally softened, giving Alex a knowing smile. "Well, Alex, I suppose Jack would rather have dinner at a table with a few less females. Please say good evening to your father and mother for me, and thank them for inviting Jack."

"Yes, ma'am, I will. And thank you."

"Jack McMasters, you remember your manners."

"Yes, ma'am."

With that, the two boys made a speedy exit.

Commander Knox and family were sitting with Commander Allen and some of his officers, as requested by the two commanders, who were close friends. Once Jack sat down, Commander Allen smiled at him and asked if he had finally decided to join the Navy rather than the Army. Jack went eyeball to eyeball with Commander Allen, aware that the other four officers had stopped talking and were sizing him up. Jack took a moment to compose his response. "I haven't come to a final decision, sir, but I am giving it serious consideration." At that, all the men laughed and went back to their own conversations.

After the afternoon's grand adventure, both boys were starved, and ate like it. During dinner they didn't say much. No brat would discuss a secret mission in front of adults. When dessert was finally served, the dancing started up. A young man came to ask Alex's older sister to dance. Commander Knox gave his approval before whisking Mrs. Knox out onto the dance floor. Commander Allen went off to ask Mrs. McMasters to dance. Jack and Alex wouldn't be caught dead on that dance floor. As the officers drifted away to find partners, the boys stayed behind by themselves.

But it didn't take long for Commander Knox and Commander Allen to gravitate back to the table. It was obvious that the ladies were not about to run out of dance partners, since there were far more men on board than women. That gave the commanders a chance to talk. Soon enough, a couple of other officers joined them at the table.

Ernie materialized, offering coffee or drinks. They all seemed happy about that, quickly giving him their orders. Jack and Alex each asked for a Coke. The officers, settling around the table with drinks in hand, began telling stories. Jack and Alex were smart enough to remain silent, hoping the officers would forget they were there.

During a lull in the conversation, Lieutenant Commander Brink, one of the officers who'd been at the captain's table with Jack and Alex the other night, looked over and said, "Young gentlemen, I remembered another story I thought you'd enjoy on the topic of *objective*."

"Absolutely, sir," Jack said promptly.

"Commander Allen was correct about an objective needing to be both short and understandable. It also needs to be *remember-able*. This World War II story proves the value of remember-ability."

Glancing around the table, Jack saw most of the officers looking intrigued. Perhaps this was a story they hadn't heard.

Lt. Commander Brink continued, "To win a war, an army needs more than just fighting men. It needs trucks and tanks and artillery pieces and ammunition, and, and, and. You get the idea. Right?"

Both boys nodded.

"Also, the *longer* a war goes on, the more you need. Because in battle a lot of your gear gets blown up. So your army constantly needs more of everything. To put it simply, the army with the most armaments tends to win. In World War II, the English and Russians were fighting the Germans for years before we joined the war. As the fighting continued, they desperately needed new supplies. So even before we joined the war, we loaded up ship after ship and sent war materials across the Atlantic to help them."

Looking right at the boys, he asked, "So how do you think the Germans felt about us sending their enemies all those weapons?"

"I'll bet they were pis—ah, very unhappy about it," Alex said.

That near slip got him "the eye" from Commander Knox. Fortunately for Alex, Lt. Commander Brink kept right on going.

"You're right, Alex. The Germans were exceptionally unhappy about what we were doing. So, they sent out a bunch of their U-boats. You know what those are?"

"Oh, yes, sir," said Jack. "Nazi submarines." Not being Navy didn't mean he was clueless.

"Right-o, Jack. The Nazis sent out their subs—and not for a friendly chat. The U-boats traveled in what they called Wolf Packs to stop us from resupplying our friends. They started sinking our ships—right to the bottom of the Atlantic. And, as you can imagine, that was a huge loss for the US Merchant Marine."

At this, Jack became confused. "Who is that, sir? Weren't US Navy sailors the ones getting torpedoed?"

"No, our sailors weren't on the cargo ships. There's a difference between Merchant Marine and Navy. Two kinds of people sail ships on the high seas, because there are two kinds of ships. The first are cargo ships. They transport all kinds of goods around the world. Those cargo ships are operated by a country's Merchant Marine. Those mariners aren't fighting men. The second kind of ships are warships: aircraft carriers, destroyers, and troop transport ships like the USS *Upshur*. The war ships are operated by a nation's Navy.

"But don't get me wrong. Even if the US Merchant Marine isn't in business to fight, they were critical to the success of World War II, and to any war effort. Their skills are in transporting huge volumes of cargo across major oceans and getting it there safely.

"The U-boats failed to make our merchant mariners quit, but the mariners did think long and hard about how to evade the subs. They decided their best bet was a more difficult route far north in the Atlantic. Until then, they'd used the same route we're using for this voyage. They started sailing close to the North Pole, where the waters are often rough and treacherously icy.

"If you think the passengers on this ship have been seasick, you can bet your last dollar they'd never want to sail that northern route. The merchant mariners probably didn't like it either, but they knew the U-boat captains wouldn't follow them into icy waters."

Alex blurted, "Did it work?"

"Yes. The U-boats didn't follow, and the number of torpedoed ships dropped dramatically. The English and Russians were once again getting supplies to continue the fight."

"Wow, great story," Jack said, but unable to stop himself, added, "I'm sorry, sir, but did I miss the part about remember-able objectives?"

Lt. Commander Brink's hand whipped up, palm out. "Hold your horses. I'm just getting warmed up. You see, the U-boats quit sinking the merchant ships, but the Germans weren't about to let those ships pass. They, too, were a major fighting force who refused to give up. With the U-boats out of commission, the Germans engaged the Luftwaffe. You boys know what that is?"

Neither boy was sure.

"The Luftwaffe was the German Air Force during World War II. The word actually means air-weapon, and it definitely was. They sent in their long-range bombers to sink our ships. No amount of icy water would stop *them*."

"Did it work?" asked Alex.

"Many times, yes. The Merchant Marine started losing ships again. They needed a new solution, and they came to the US Navy."

Lt. Commander Brink smiled. "That's when I came into this picture. You see, I was stationed at the Pentagon in those days. The Pentagon is that huge, five-sided building in Washington, DC, where the head of the US Navy has his office. Anyway, representatives from the Merchant Marine came to us for answers. We at Naval headquarters gave their problem considerable thought. After all, we wanted safe passage for their crews and cargo as badly as the Merchant Marine did."

There was a pause as Ernie arrived with a platter of German ginger cookies from the buffet table. Commander Allen looked as involved in the story as the kids were. He said, "Boys, we owe the Merchant Marine a great debt. Winston Churchill called their heroic effort to deliver supplies 'The Battle of the Atlantic.' It became the longest, toughest naval battle of all time."

Lt. Commander Brink nodded. "That's right. We lost even more Merchant Marine ships than Navy ships. And even one would have been too many. The Navy offered to put anti-aircraft guns on the ships so that the merchant mariners could defend themselves against the German bombers. It took a bit of doing, but we finally got all those cargo ships outfitted with Navy anti-aircraft guns."

He chose a cookie from Ernie's tray. "And as you gentlemen know, those aren't a bunch of little pea-shooters. They're serious anti-aircraft cannons. We showed the mariners how to use them, and how to record when they shot down an enemy aircraft. Then we sent them on their way. Of course, the Luftwaffe still dogged them, intent to sink them. But this time, the mariners started shooting back. Unfortunately, some months later, the sitrep showed those mariners couldn't hit the broad side of a barn. They hadn't shot down a single German bomber.

"Why? The Merchant Marine isn't a force of fighting men. They hadn't received much training on the anti-aircraft guns—and it showed. They simply couldn't hit anything."

Jack was puzzled. "Why are Navy gunners so much better?"

"Pretty simple: Navy gunners spend years training to hit fast-approaching aircraft. Merchant mariners become expert in safely moving huge cargo. Those skills are too different to transfer from one task to the other."

"Why weren't Navy gunners on the ships, sir?" Alex asked.

Commander Allen smiled. "Well, Alex, that was an issue of politics. We weren't officially in the war yet, so we couldn't use military combatants."

Lt. Commander Brink nodded. "Our hands were tied. Since the mariners couldn't shoot accurately, we decided it was pointless to leave the guns on the ships. Fortunately, the Chief of Naval Operations was also in that meeting, and he'd been quietly considering the whole thing. He finally asked, 'How many ships have been sunk since they started shooting back at the bombers?' And, guess what? When we checked with the Merchant Marine, it turned out no ships had been sunk since the mariners started shooting.

"Seems that the merchant mariners might not be able to hit a barn, but it also looked like the Luftwaffe pilots didn't much like getting shot at. Apparently it messed up the accuracy of their bombing raids.

"So the Merchant Marine kept our anti-aircraft guns, and the mariners kept wrecking the aim of the Luftwaffe pilots. I suppose you can guess the point of my story. In the heat of battle, when the bullets start flying, we often forget what the objective is. In this case, if it hadn't been for the Chief of Naval Operations, we *never* would have remembered. The objective had nothing to do with how many enemy aircraft got shot down, it was about preventing our ships from being sunk. So you see, the objective needs to be remember-able."

He gave them a wink, and they grinned back.

Sometime later, Alex leaned over and said, "So, Jack, can you tell me our Objective Statement for this ocean crossing?"

"Three words: Explore the *Upshur.*"

"Remember-able," said Alex.

Jack leaned back in his chair. "Accomplished."

Jack hated to miss any stories, but he knew he should be the one to pick up their laundry. He was the one with the least supervision. Alex's mom would notice if Alex went missing, and Mrs. McMasters was imagining Jack under Mrs. Knox's protective eye. While his mom was occupied dancing, Jack slipped out with a huge, fancy dinner napkin loaded with German ginger cookies he'd swiped off the dessert buffet. He double-timed it to the laundry facility, thanked the workers with cookies (who enjoyed busting his chops over the greasy napkin to wash), collected the clothes, and hurried to their quarters to stuff them into their bags. Jack slowed his pace on the way back to the dance so he could catch his breath.

When he plopped down in his seat, Alex placed a Coke in front of him. "I promised Ernie you'd be back for this. Would you believe he was the only person who noticed you were gone?"

"Just as it should be." Jack raised his glass.

In bed that night, Jack thought back on Lt. Commander Brink's story. How easy it could be to forget the real objective. Eventually, Jack fell asleep for his last time on the USS *Upshur*, little knowing that the time would come when this war story's lesson would come back to help him— and that, when it did, it would prove crucial to all their lives.

8

Bremerhaven

The next morning, four victorious rascals headed for their usual lookout, knowing that today they'd really see land. The wind was blowing, as always, but for once the sky had turned a beautiful blue, with huge, white clouds, and the sun was out in full force. That sky did wonders, turning the ocean from flat gray to dark blue. Suddenly it seemed like Germany would be a wonderful place.

The wind was freezing as they ran up the port-side deck. The closer they'd gotten to Germany, the more it felt like winter. Rounding a curve, Jack lost his footing when a massive bell clanged directly above him. He thought the sound might split his head open as he slammed onto the deck. When Queenie stumbled over him, she yelled, "Jack, you dipstick. Out of my way."

Alex shot past him. "Come on, Jack. Follow me."

Jack managed to pick himself up and move out. Their private lookout was crowded with people.

"Hey, they're in our spot," yelled Rabbit, as she began squeezing her way to the front.

The others managed to find space along the deck railing not far from the front. Now, after seven days, they saw the city of Bremerhaven.

For some reason Jack glanced over at Alex and Queenie as they stared at the port. Sadness nearly knocked him down again. Why did he care about getting to Germany? How stupid! The moment the USS *Upshur* docked, he'd lose his new best friend. The thought hurt more than the sound of that bell. Sure, he should have realized this from the start. After all, he was a brat. But this was the first time that the impending loss of Alex hit him. They'd been so preoccupied with exploring the ship.

"Okay," said Alex, addressing the group, "it looks like it's gonna be another hour or two before we really get into port. Let's go have breakfast and come back in time to get a decent place."

Jack forced himself to say, "Good plan. Let's do it."

Queenie yelled, "Come on, Rabbit. We're out of here!" She reached a clawlike hand into the crowd, dragging Rabbit along with them.

At breakfast they saw Ernie and started to say goodbye.

"It's not goodbye yet," he said. "The ship won't dock till around fourteen hundred hours. Things slow way down once the ship gets into the harbor. We can say all that at lunch."

As they left the dining room, they ran into Mrs. McMasters. She gave them the same message and told them to meet her for lunch at noon.

By the time they returned topside, the ship was much closer to the port. As the crowd came and went, they edged their way up into better and better spots. About an hour later, they spotted a tugboat headed toward them.

"Hey, remember what Commander Allen said about the pilot coming on board?" Alex said, all excited. "He might be on that tug."

"No doubt," said Queenie. "Let's go."

Rabbit turned, saying, "Are you nuts? We finally got a good spot."

"But it's the *wrong* spot," said Jack. "We want the accommodation ladder, that swinging staircase the pilot uses."

They headed aft, Rabbit naturally in the lead toward the small deck with the ladder. This time she even kind of knew where she was going. Creeping onto the deck, they heard a chief yelling orders. The kids slowed their pace, looking to hide before the chief threw them out. Seeing a lifeboat, they crept up to hide between it and the rail. So far, no tugboat, but they knew this was the right spot to observe, as long as they didn't get caught. They squeezed down tight, staying quiet.

The tug, when it showed up moments later, might have been a pretty good size, but near the USS *Upshur*, it looked like a tiny toy boat. It eased alongside the *Upshur* and drifted right up to the stairway. A couple of seamen from the tugboat held the accommodation ladder while a guy jumped from the tug and mounted the stairs. He was the first German they'd ever seen.

Alex leaned over to Jack and whispered, "You think he was a Nazi during the war?"

"Maybe," Jack said, checking him out carefully.

Almost before they knew it, the pilot was on board and heading for the bridge, Commander Allen, and the captain.

"Wow, without being here to see it, you'd never even know anyone came aboard," muttered Jack.

"Back to the front of the ship!" yelled Rabbit, and she bolted.

As they hurried back, Jack's mood again took a dive. *Things are always an adventure with Alex. How will I ever find another friend like him?*

Back topside, the place was mobbed.

Queenie pointed to a small group of sailors just standing around. "Why do those guys keep looking at their watches? That won't make the ship dock any faster."

"They're probably part of the anchor pool."

"Come again," she said, sounding fed up with the constant Navy-speak.

"They're betting on the exact hour and minute the ship drops anchor or ties up."

"Maybe we could get in on that," Jack said.

"Not likely. It's very hush-hush. They're not supposed to bet on it. But . . ." Alex shrugged. "And they're probably going on liberty. They have on their thirteen-buttons."

Queenie's lip curled in disgust, "Alex, you're such a pain-in-the-butt. Try it again. This time, in English."

Jack gave Alex an exaggerated frown for offending such an oh-so-superior human being. But Alex merely pretended to yawn.

Jack wanted to remember this moment. Life was such fun with Alex.

Perhaps Alex thought he'd tortured her enough, because he explained. "They're going ashore. They probably have a three-day pass. *Liberty* just means time off. Like being liberated. And as for the *thirteen-buttons*, just take a look at their bell-bottoms. There's no zipper in the front—just a big, square flap with thirteen buttons closing up the pants. It's the dress uniform they have to wear when they go ashore."

Rolling her eyes at Alex, and Jack as well, she declared, "Pathetic. Their pants are pathetic and you two are pathetic."

"I'll tell *you* pathetic," said Alex, waiting till Queenie looked away to return Jack's wink. "Pathetic is when one of those sailors has to pee really bad and doesn't get all thirteen of those buttons undone before he starts going all over himself." Jack and Alex cracked up.

Queenie turned in a huff. "Little boys and their obsession with pee-pee talk!"

That got the boys laughing so hard they almost peed their own pants.

Eventually they worked their way up to the rail. They weren't right up front, but they still had a pretty good view. The tugboat was now well out in front, towing the ship, just as Commander Allen had told them it would. After days alone at sea, they were suddenly in a huge harbor surrounded by watercraft of all kinds and sizes.

Alex pointed to a pier anchored out in the harbor. Two ships were tied to it, one on each side. Other ships were lined up, waiting to dock there. "That's where they do the refueling. See the pipes and hoses coming out to the ships from the dock? That's gotta be diesel fuel. That'll be the huge fuel tank on that platform beyond the pier."

Jack knew he should be interested in the discussion. He wasn't. And he could tell Alex's heart wasn't in it either. Alex was just trying to distract them, to keep their minds off what was ahead.

"Wow, that coal loader is choice," said Jack. He would do his part.

"Definitely. The Navy does things on a large scale," Alex said, a hint of pride showing.

The *Upshur* began to slow, waiting for an open berth in order to dock and unload.

The kids decided to head back for lunch.

As they entered the dining room, Ernie gave them his usual grin. "Right this way." He then mouthed, "Hi, Rabbit," and she mouthed back, "Hi, Ernie."

He led them to where Mrs. McMasters was seated with Alex's family. This time it was a bigger table, laid out for twelve people. They were also joined by Commander Allen and some of his officers. Jack and Alex were seated near Commander Knox and Commander Allen. As lunch progressed, Commander Allen turned to the kids and said, "Welcome to Germany. Do you know much about what to expect?"

They shook their heads in silence. Much better than saying, "Nope."

"Alex, your family will be stationed right here in Bremerhaven, by the sea. Jack, you can expect a five-hour train ride south to your father's base in Baden-Württemberg. It's inland, near the mountains."

Commander Allen was just filling the kids in on the score. But for Jack and Alex, his words came as a jolt. They'd been half hoping that "Germany" meant "near each other." This was a death sentence for their friendship.

"You might be surprised to see how well the Germans accept us since only a few years ago we were at war with each other. In fact, World War II was the largest war in the history of mankind. It's considered an epic battle between the forces of good and evil. More than twenty-five million people died in that war." Commander Allen's words were getting Jack's attention off his own troubles.

"Forces of evil. That's the Nazis, right?" asked Jack.

"Correct. The Nazis and the Japanese."

"Are the Nazis still here? Will we see them?"

"That's an interesting question," said the commander. "The answer is yes and no. You see, when we won the war, the Nazi Party was abolished. So technically there are no more Nazis.

However, many of the German adults you will meet *were* Nazis. Most of them won't want to remember that fact, so it would be impolite for you to bring it up."

The boys nodded. This was valuable intel.

"If it does come up in conversation, many grownups will tell you that they weren't Nazis but that other Germans were. That's probably wishful thinking. Many Germans *were* Nazis but no longer want to admit it."

The commander went on, "Some people might want to pretend the war never happened, but you'll see reminders everywhere. Whole towns and cities were destroyed by the bombing runs and fighting. Some have been rebuilt since the war, but you're sure to see blown-up buildings and other scars of war."

Jack had already lived in a country ravaged by war—Japan. But he had been young so his memories were vague.

"How come the Germans don't hold it against us?" asked Alex.

"For the sake of world peace we've had to learn to get along. Today the Germans are our friends. At least, most of them are. I think you will find them quite friendly toward Americans nowadays."

"If they're our friends now, then why do we have all those bases in Germany?" asked Jack.

"We are here to prevent another war," was all Commander Allen said. "If the world has a hotspot, it's Germany." Then he said no more.

Jack had heard that tone before. It meant, "And that's all I'll say." That left him with new questions and no answers. How could the country that caused World War II now be our friend? Why were US troops here to prevent a war? Germany certainly sounded intriguing.

"Here's the most important thing to know: Whatever you do here in Germany, you are not just a bunch of kids running around. Listen to me closely. Always remember you represent the United States Military and, more importantly, the United States of America. That matters. Represent your country well. You will meet many people, and not just Germans, but people from all over Europe. Never forget you symbolize the best of America."

"Yes, sir," they said together.

As a brat, Jack had to say it. But part of him meant it, too, because he knew he represented America. And, because he was very interested in this Germany that Commander Allen had been talking about.

After dessert came the goodbyes. It wasn't hard to shake hands and say goodbye to Commander Allen and his officers, or to Alex's family. But it was hard to say goodbye to Ernie, and definitely tough for Jack to say goodbye to Alex.

Goodbyes are the one thing brats never get good at, but Alex was better than most. He simply said, "I don't know if I'll see you again, but I hope I do."

Jack's tight lips managed a smile. "Me, too. And if not, I hope, at least, I'll see you in my dreams."

And with that, the best friends went their separate ways.

After that, things moved along pretty fast. Back at their cabin, they put on their best clothes to be ready to meet Lt. Col. McMasters and *look sharp, act sharp, be sharp.*

Hearing passengers pass the door, Rabbit was wild to leave, but Mrs. McMasters was firm. "Rabbit, this is one day you will walk quietly by me and *never* drop my hand. Do I make myself understood? I want you to look as neat and clean when we meet your father as you do right this moment."

Rabbit grinned. "But then he won't know it's me."

When they opened the door, their mother's objective made perfect sense. Under no circumstances did she want Rabbit swept off in the river of people walking to the lower deck. But Rabbit surprised them by calmly taking her mother's left hand. (That was the hand farthest away from Ernie's goodbye donut bulging from the pocket of Rabbit's Sunday coat.)

Jack hoped for one more glimpse of Alex on the crowded deck, but all too soon he was walking down the gangplank to Germany, and even greater adventures.

Part II

4th Armored Division

9

Wunderland

Lieutenant Colonel McMasters stood very erect at the end of the pier, watching his family approach. He was tall, with a strong jaw and attractive, hazel eyes that missed nothing. The colonel was good looking, but what stood out most was his military bearing. The man had command presence. When the kids finally spotted him, they started running, Mrs. McMasters not far behind. He kissed his wife, hugged the girls, and shook hands with Jack.

"How was the crossing?" Lt. Col. McMasters said, as they immediately headed for the luggage.

"It was perfectly fine. And the children conducted themselves very well," Mrs. McMasters said.

"Perfectly fine!" exploded Rabbit. "It was for *us*, but Mom puked most of the trip."

That kid was always such a mouth.

"Really?" Lt. Col. McMasters said, with genuine concern.

His wife gave a reassuring smile. "I'm perfectly fine now that we're back on dry land."

"You never did like the ocean, Lorraine," he said to her. "I missed you. And I'm proud of you for making the crossing with the children." Clearly he was as delighted with her as she was with him. Those two had always been tight.

Pausing, he bent down and looked the children in the eye. "And how was *your* crossing?"

Jack couldn't read his look. Was it one of real interest, or were they about to get cross examined? Would this conversation end well or would their father quickly flare up?

Queenie said, "We had a great time, Dad. The ship was fun. It had a movie theater, a game room, and even a snack bar." Leave it to Queenie to try to control where the conversation went so the colonel knew everything had gone well and that there was nothing he needed to concern himself with. She finished with, "So tell us about Germany."

"Do you like it?" asked Jack.

"Am *I* gonna like it, Dad?" Rabbit was bouncing on the balls of her feet, ready to bolt across the entire country.

Lt. Col. McMasters chuckled. "Wow, hold your horses, everyone. You'll see soon enough. And, yes, indeed, I like Germany. And I'm pretty sure you're going to love it, too. Now, guess where we're going first?"

"To our new house?" asked Rabbit.

"No."

"To a hotel?" suggested Mrs. McMasters, flashing him a smile.

"Well, no." He smiled back, almost regretfully. "What's your guess, Jack?"

"No clue. How about a restaurant?"

"Hungry as always, I see. But you're wrong, too," he said with obvious delight. "We have a train to catch, and along the way there'll be a surprise. But don't pester me about it. You'll see when you see."

As they joined the line of passengers wanting luggage, Mrs. McMasters handed her husband the claim checks. He smiled at her efficiency.

Queenie was the first to have eyes on their bags. Sooner than seemed possible, they were in a big Navy van that the colonel had arranged to take them to the station. As it drove off the US Naval base, each kid was hyper aware they were entering a different country. This wasn't like going on vacation. They weren't off for a weekend lark. They were going to live in this foreign place! Jack didn't notice he was squeezing his thighs together as he sat scrunched up. He had already cycled through excitement, to dread, to overwhelming uncertainty, and so far their vehicle was only one block beyond the main gate.

Why he felt the need to absorb everything immediately is anyone's guess—but he did. Jack wanted to digest this new world, understand it, make it part of him. His frustration came from knowing it couldn't be done, at least not quickly.

"Look at how small the German cars are, Jack," said Lt. Col. McMasters.

Three young faces pressed up against the van's windows. The buildings looked strange, too. They were mostly three stories tall and made of beige or light-yellow stucco with gray-tiled roofs. At most windows were flower boxes filled with cold-loving pine boughs. The kids imagined them spilling with spring flowers.

But for Jack something was missing. "Dad, where are all the Nazi flags? In pictures of Germany there are always hundreds of those flags with the swastika."

Lt. Col. McMasters seemed to hesitate. "A lot has changed since the war. Since it ended, the Nazi flag and the swastika have been systematically removed. You won't see many of them anymore. Today the German flag is three strips of black, red, and yellow. "

"Look at how clean all the windows are," observed Mrs. McMasters. Queenie shot Jack a glance that said, *Please don't tell me this whole country is made up of white glove mothers.*

"Look at all the bikes!" Rabbit shouted, as their vehicle swung onto a busier street.

"And not just for kids," said Queenie. "Ladies are biking in dresses. Are those groceries in their front baskets? It's like they don't have cars for shopping."

"And men are in suits with briefcases on the back of their bikes," said Jack. "They must not drive to—"

Their vehicle came to an abrupt halt—clearly not at the train station.

The driver said, "Sorry, sir, but with that truck blocking our way, I can't get through."

Lt. Col. McMasters studied an old, broken-down truck in front of them. Irritated, he snapped at the young driver, "What are you telling me, seaman?"

Not sure how to respond, and worried he was about to get reamed out, the driver lamely blurted out, "Well, sir, I can't get you any closer."

"How far is the station?" McMasters demanded, losing patience.

"Four blocks, sir."

The colonel's head swung around to the kids. "Okay, everyone, let's move out. We're going to walk it."

Each kid picked up his or her personal suitcase and a family suitcase, trying to look like they weren't too heavy to carry. Jack thought about sliding his bags in front of him down the sidewalk, the way he had on the deck of the *Upshur,* but the colonel kept turning around to them, still pointing out the tiny cars, mostly Opals and Volkswagens. Jack knew his father would have caught him. Anyway, the sidewalks were rough cobblestone—no good for sliding. It dawned on Jack that there wasn't an American car in sight. In fact, he noted there weren't many cars of *any* kind. But when a big, shiny, black Mercedes convertible with long swooping fenders and a lot of sparkling chrome glided past, everyone stopped to look, and Jack had a chance to drop his bags and roll his shoulders.

As they slogged their way through the huge, old station made of wrought iron and glass, they could smell diesel fuel and see steam coming off the trains. "Well, at least the windows on the roof of this place are dirty," Jack whispered to Queenie. "I was beginning to think everything in this whole *country* was spotlessly clean."

"Not good," she whispered back. "Mom's gonna get even worse living here and—"

A scratchy voice interrupted over a loudspeaker. The kids stared at each other. The announcement was in no language they'd ever heard. Every word was strange. They definitely weren't in the good old U S of A anymore.

"Are they speaking German?" Queenie's question came out more like a disgruntled grunt than she had intended. But she couldn't help it. Her arms ached, and she was breathing too hard for it to be a normal tone of voice. She immediately checked to see if her father had noticed.

"Of course," said Lt. Col. McMasters, not seeming to have noticed. "You'll learn some of it very quickly."

Queenie shot Jack a look like, *Oh yeah, I'm gonna learn* that *gobbledygook.*

Once on the train, they were met by a conductor, and for the first time the children heard Lt. Col. McMasters speak German. That was yet another shock. It had never occurred to them their father could speak a foreign language.

How'd he learn how to do that? Jack wondered. But after cycling it through his brain a couple of times, he put it together. His dad hadn't magically learned to speak German in just the last few months. His dad had been in Germany during the war. Even so, it startled Jack. Every time he thought he had the ol' man figured out, something like this happened.

His father was, well, a challenge, and often intimidating. But sometimes he was also amazing.

For the briefest moment, Jack wondered if his dad would be proud of him if he learned German.

The immaculately uniformed conductor listened to the colonel very carefully. Giving a slight bow, he led them off to a special private compartment in one of the cars. Their parents began to talk happily, sitting opposite each other on overstuffed bench seats covered in dark velvet. It didn't take long for the train to start rolling. The children made a quick exit to go explore.

From the windows along the corridor they watched as the train pulled out of the huge station. It passed through the inner city of Bremerhaven, and on to the outskirts.

"Wow! Those are bombed-out buildings," Jack said to his sisters in a low voice. Several apartment buildings, and what looked like the remnant of an old church, were now abandoned heaps of rubble.

"That's got to be from the war," whispered Queenie, staring. "It's not the same as seeing it in pictures, is it? I mean, it's right *there*. Think about it—people were living in those apartments."

"Was somebody killed when it blew up?" asked Rabbit.

Every military brat heard plenty about World War II, but suddenly that war was starting to look a lot more real to the McMasters children. As the train rumbled on, one and then another of them would yell, "There's one!" as they spotted more destroyed buildings. They'd never seen anything like this. With each new pile that had once been a house, Queenie and Jack felt more and more uneasy.

Rabbit ran off, but Jack and Queenie couldn't look away.

"What if we'd been living in that house during the war?" Queenie wondered aloud. "I can't imagine what it would be like, going to bed every night not knowing if you and your family were going to get blown up, or shot by soldiers. Whoever lived there, well, they lived in fear of being invaded."

Jack looked at her, thinking about it. War had always seemed like it was somewhere else. "Remember when Commander Allen said Dad was in Germany to prevent another war? Do you think there *will* be a war and we'll be the ones going to bed at night not knowing if our house is gonna get blown up?"

"Dunno." This wasn't the usual self-assured Queenie.

The train picked up speed as they moved into the countryside. Suddenly, there was no more destruction, and everything became beautiful. Even though it was late autumn, there was still a lot of green against a very blue sky. The rich, dark earth of the farm fields were plowed in perfectly straight rows. The train passed through unbelievable forests, with dark green fir trees and sunlight coming through the bare branches of other huge trees. The kids couldn't believe how perfect this part was. Germany was beautiful, even if it showed the ugly scars of war.

The train felt very different from the ship. Where the ship had rocked back and forth in big swells but seemed to hardly move, the train did the opposite. They were no longer moving at twenty-two knots; they were flying across the countryside at almost a hundred miles an hour, often lurching from side to side so violently that the kids had to grab anything solid just to keep from getting thrown down.

Coming back to Jack and Queenie, Rabbit butted in, "I'm tired of all this scenery schmeenery. Let's go explore."

They headed toward the rear of the train, with Rabbit in front. But when she reached the back of the car, she couldn't budge the heavy door leading to the next.

"Out of the way," demanded Jack. Pulling with all his strength, he managed to heave it open—only to be blasted by frigid air and deafening noise. The door hadn't opened directly into the next train car. If they wanted to get there, they would have to cross a short walkway and go through another heavy door. Jack could hear the clattering of the train wheels on the tracks below. The walls of the walkway were like the folds of an accordion with wind whipping through. Jack took a deep breath and moved out, only to find as he crossed that the metal floor shifted from side to side, almost knocking him over. He grabbed for the far door and shoved it open.

"Wow, that was nutso!" exclaimed Queenie, as she followed Rabbit inside.

"Let's do it again!" said Rabbit, delighted.

The first two cars they passed through had private compartments like theirs. The cars beyond had rows and rows of double seats. As they moved through them, the passengers seemed to pay them a little too much attention, which made Jack and Queenie slightly uncomfortable. Some passengers showed just a hint of dislike. Others seemed nice enough, saying, "*Guten Tag.*" The kids had no idea what that meant, so they just nodded politely and kept moving through the car, passing a conductor checking tickets.

Jack looked back. "Some of those Germans didn't seem happy to see us."

"Yeah," said Queenie, "like they definitely don't like us being here."

When they finally came to what they figured was the back of the train, they found a locked door. Unable to get any farther, they positioned themselves about ten feet from the door, looking out the windows. To anyone passing by they appeared innocent enough, but of course they had actually gone into intel mode. After all, no self-respecting brat was going to leave a locked door unexplored.

While they watched the fabulous German countryside pass by, they kept a wary eye on what was happening on board. But eventually the clattering train and the beautiful scenery lulled them into a dream-like state, and they almost missed it when the conductor slipped past them. Fortunately, Queenie glanced up at the last moment and saw the man unlock the door with a giant brass key. She elbowed Jack and nodded over at the guy before he slipped through the door.

"What d'ya think he's doing back there?"

"No clue, but let's hang out here. When he comes back out, let's try and grab the door before it closes." Jack pulled a pen out of his jacket pocket and gave it to Rabbit. "Take this and when the conductor comes back out, jam it in the door so it doesn't close all the way. But be sure to wait till he's past you before making your move."

"How come I gotta be the one?" she asked, suspiciously.

"'Cause you're the youngest. He's less likely to suspect you. We'll distract him for a moment so you can wedge it in the door."

A sly smile came over her face. "I can do that," she said, moving back down the corridor to the door, but turning away as if it didn't exist. Looking perfectly innocent, she stared out a window.

Jack and Queenie moved fifteen feet in the other direction.

Not three minutes later, the locked door opened and the same conductor came out. He seemed in a hurry and walked right by Rabbit, hardly giving her a glance. Once he was past, she made her move. Queenie and Jack turned and looked the conductor right in the eye. They figured that if he was focused on them, he wouldn't turn around to look at Rabbit. It seemed to work, because Rabbit jammed the pen in the doorway and went back to the window. However, the conductor seemed to sense her movement behind him and started to turn around.

Jack grasped for any diversion. He blurted out, "*Guten Tag.*"

The conductor turned back to Jack. "*Guten Tag.*" He pushed by them and was gone.

"Wow. That was close," said Queenie, looking a little shaken. But she smiled when she saw the pen holding the door open by just the tiniest crack.

Rabbit quickly pulled it open, and waved them in with a small bow.

"Nice work, Rabbit," said Jack.

They all entered what turned out to be the baggage car. The luggage was neatly stored on racks. Fortunately, before the door shut all the way, Jack grabbed it, making sure it could be reopened from the inside without a key. He didn't want them to get trapped in the baggage car with no way out.

"Let's find our stuff," said Rabbit, bounding off.

From the dark recesses of the compartment came a bark. Then a bunch of dogs started barking.

Jack and Queenie immediately turned back for the door. Barking dogs were sure to bring the conductor. Time to go!

But leave it to Rabbit to head in the opposite direction. That wild child definitely knew how to strike terror into the hearts of her brother and sister. She went right for the back of the car and dropped down on her knees in front of a big cage filled with dogs. This wasn't just a luggage car; it was also a pet transportation area. Having no choice, the older kids followed the sound to extract her. There was Rabbit, sitting inside the biggest cage with four dogs all over her. That maniac had actually opened the cage and gotten in with the dogs. Rabbit's the type of kid that dogs naturally love. Within seconds they were too busy licking her to bark. Jack and Queenie just stared at her, incredulous.

Queenie whispered very calmly, "Okay, Rabbit, say goodbye to your little friends, and let's get outta here before we get busted."

It took a bit of persuading to get her to come out, but they finally made it back to the door of the baggage car. Slowly pulling it open, they slipped out, unseen.

Making their way forward, they reached their cabin and stopped to check in with their parents.

"Well, well, well, here are my children," Lt. Col. McMasters said with delight. "And what have you little rascals been up to?"

Unfortunately, before the others had a chance to respond, Rabbit rushed in. "Dad, guess what? They have a bunch of really cute dogs in the baggage car!"

Jack and Queenie froze in place, waiting for their father to start asking a hundred and forty-two thousand questions about how they could possibly know what was in the baggage car, and had they trespassed, and what possessed them to think it was okay to do such a thing. But by some miracle of the gods, he just looked at Rabbit and said, "That's nice." Then, looking at Jack, he asked, "Are you hungry?"

"Starved!" Jack said, unable to mask his relief.

"Well, since we still have two hours left of our ride, why don't we get something to eat?"

"Excellent idea," said Mrs. McMasters.

They all saddled up and made their way to the dining car. Their father ordered for them. The kids weren't surprised when their father ordered beer for himself and their mom. But then he gestured toward his kids and asked for "dry Coca-Cola."

The waiter nodded and walked away.

"Dry Cokes? Dad, do they have dry Cokes in Germany? How can they be dry?" Rabbit couldn't ask her questions fast enough. She wasn't the only one wondering what their dad was up to.

"Absolutely, Rabbit. Dry Cokes are very common here. Wait till you taste them—totally unique."

"Dad! What do they taste like?"

"It's impossible to describe. You'll just have to wait and see."

Jack started to imitate a waiter. "Here is your powdered Coke, sir."

A few minutes later, the waiter approached with a silver tray of drinks. There were two big glasses of beer, three bottles of Coca-Cola, and three empty glasses. The Coke bottles looked just like the ones in America.

Rabbit took a swig from her bottle. "Hey," she said, "this isn't dry Coke—it's regular Coca-Cola!"

"Yup, it's exactly the same Coke we have back home," their father said, chuckling. "I actually asked for *drei* Cokes. In German the word *drei* sounds exactly like *dry*, but it means three. I ordered three Cokes, not dry Cokes."

"Good one, Dad," said Jack. Sometimes there were moments with his dad when Jack felt everything was fine. This was one of them.

"Don't worry, kids. Soon enough you'll all speak enough German," reassured their mom.

A few minutes later another surprise arrived. The waiter brought over five big bowls of hot soup with hotdogs in them.

"Now *this* you're going to like," their dad said. "It's lentil bean soup with hotdogs."

Rabbit looked down into the bowl, obviously confused. Then looking up to the waiter, she raised her hands to her mouth pretending to be eating a hotdog, and asked, "Hey, where are the buns?"

The waiter, having no idea what she was saying or wanting, looked at her like she was from Mars.

Their dad told the man that everything was fine.

"Just cut up your hotdog and eat it out of the bowl, dear," said Mrs. McMasters.

For a moment, Jack wasn't sure if he should use a fork or spoon, but once he tasted his soup, there was no question about whether he liked it.

"Hey, Mom, from now on I think you'd better give up the buns and stick with German-style hotdogs," Queenie said with a smile. "This stuff is really good."

Their father smiled back. "Welcome to Germany."

Standing in the dark, looking out the bedroom window, all was confusion and fear. Something had jarred him awake. Then the noise came again. A loud clattering, and then a deep grinding. It was coming from out there. A tank rolled into view, the sounds made by its treads. Were those soldiers coming up alongside it? Who were they? What was happening? It was so dark he could barely make them out. Then came flashes of fire and ear-shattering explosions.

He watched as the machine-gun rounds came ripping through his window and cringed at the sound of exploding glass. Tiny chards of glass flew past him. The tank fired a massive round, and half of the bottom floor of the house exploded. They needed to get out or they'd all be dead—no choice. He screamed as he jumped from the second story window—

"Wake up, Jack. You're having a bad dream," whispered Queenie, shoving him hard enough that his head banged on the window.

"Whaaa . . ." He was hyperventilating.

Mrs. McMasters, hearing him, looked over. "Jack, are you okay?"

"He's fine, Mom. He was just dreaming." Queenie watched her mom turn back to looking out the other window, and then leaning over, she quietly asked Jack, "What were you dreaming about?"

He said nothing. He was totally disoriented. He must have fallen asleep. Where was he? Oh yeah. They were in a staff car. They'd stayed at that castle last night and taken the train that morning to a city called Stuttgart.

"Jack . . ."

His heart was still racing, and he felt clammy as he turned and looked at her. "We were being attacked by invaders. Our house was being blown up. Like the ones we saw on the train yesterday."

"Nazis?"

"Dunno."

"Relax, Jack. It was just a dream."

"Yeah, but it seemed so real. Do you think we might . . ."

"Be quiet, Jack. Don't think about it," she said very softly.

He turned away and stared out the window.

There was snow everywhere. All that white somehow calmed him. About an hour outside of Stuttgart, the German countryside had become hills and even some small mountains. The farther the train went, the deeper the snow got. When they had finally pulled into the station, two staff cars were waiting for them. Jack, forehead pressed against the window of one of those staff cars, thought back over last night.

Their father's surprise had been Schloss Rheinfels, the largest castle on the Rhine River. They had gotten to stay in the castle overnight—something their parents had to explain twice, it was so unexpected. A bed is a bed is a bed—except in a castle. Then it's an adventure. And that night their dreams had been full of adventure.

On the walls of the fortress where it overlooked the Rhine River, they'd found an old catapult. Next to it was a big pile of round boulders, ready for the catapult to fling them down the hill at approaching enemies. They weren't small like baseballs, or even bowling balls. They were enormous, round rocks more than two feet wide. They must have weighed two hundred pounds each. Even their dad couldn't figure out how, in the olden days, they'd managed to get the rocks up into the catapult. But however they did it, one thing was certain: those giant projectiles would flatten anything in their path.

Jack thought about the ancient armor they'd seen displayed in a stone hall of the castle. The antique helmets and armor had been worn by knights. Lt. Col. McMasters had told them an armored knight with a horse covered in armor was the equivalent of a tank today. In fact, a medieval knight riding in full armor was so powerful he could take on a whole bunch of enemy soldiers and win all by himself.

"Since you're a tanker, does that mean you're a modern-day knight, Dad?" Queenie had asked.

Their dad just chuckled.

10

Quarters

Jack leaned over and whispered to Queenie, "Everything's so foreign. I love this."

Queenie nodded. "And like going back in time. Here castles aren't just in library books and fairytales—they actually exist. And the ancient villages and fortresses—they actually exist." Queenie's eyes said it all. She leaned in closer to Jack. "My mind's spinning—in a very good way."

Jack nodded back. "And the whole language thing. I mean, on the train everyone was speaking words we couldn't understand. It's like someone turned the dial on the radio and scrambled the reception and we were getting static."

"Yeah, we could see them speaking and hear them—but it was all gobbledygook."

"And most of them couldn't understand *us* either. It's like we've been dropped down on another planet. We're invisible, looking in on their lives, but they can only sense our presence, our intrusion." He quietly started repeating, "*Guten Tag, Guten Tag, Guten Tag . . .*" He was playing with the words on his tongue. "How'd the Germans ever come up with all those weird sounds?"

"Yeah. And how'd they all manage to learn 'em?"

"Hey. What are you guys laughin' about?" demanded Rabbit, clearly feeling left out.

"Cool it, Rabbit, you're too young," Queenie snapped. "Just slide back into your own little world and leave us alone."

"She's doin' it again, Mom!" Rabbit whined, just a little too quickly. It was less a complaint than a way to get Queenie in trouble.

"Settle down, you three. We'll be there soon." Mrs. McMasters's voice had just that little edge to it that said, *You had better not do anything to upset your father.*

No one said much on the final leg of the ride. They just stared out at the beautiful, white countryside. The car finally pulled up to a guarded gate. Above it, a large sign arched across the road: Cooke Barracks, United States Army, Headquarters 4th Armored Division.

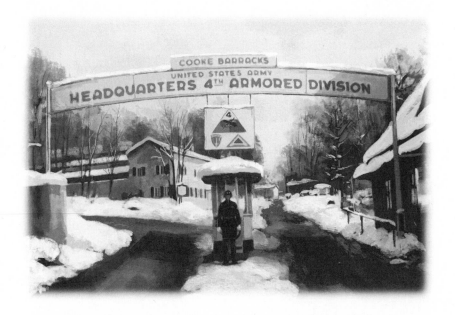

An MP held up his hand, indicating the car needed to stop. *MP* means military police. Saying *MP* is like saying *cop*, but *Army cop*.

Their driver rolled down his window, and the MP peered into the car, his eyes pausing on their dad and the silver oak leaves on his uniform that indicated his rank—lieutenant colonel. The MP snapped to attention and saluted crisply. Lt. Col. McMasters silently saluted back. The guard waved them past the gate house and onto the base.

The staff car slowly moved along the snow-packed street and up a long, gradual climb. Jack had the strangest feeling, as if this were all very important but somehow he wouldn't be able to absorb it. His body was motionless, but his mind was in overdrive. What were these buildings? Where did his dad work? Where were all the tanks? Where was the PX? (The PX is a base's private department store, open only to Army personnel and their families.) Where were the movie theater and bowling alley? His frustration built as the unanswered questions piled ever higher. But his brain wouldn't let up. Where was the school they'd be going to? How hard would the school be? Where would they live? Where would his friends live? Would he *have* friends? Would they be *good* friends? Would he like it here? Would he get along? Where could he build a fort?

Entry into the complete unknown—just a bit overwhelming.

He looked at Queenie, and she looked at him. They each knew all the questions, and they each knew neither of them had the answers. At least, not *yet* they didn't. Rabbit, on the other hand, looked totally unconcerned. She was bouncing up and down.

"Wow!" was all she kept saying.

Fortunately, her attitude proved contagious. Even if they couldn't figure anything else out, Jack and Queenie knew this had to be one of the most beautiful places on earth. White snow covered the hills and fields and forests. It also looked like an exceptional place to explore. So they crammed all those unanswered questions as far back in their minds as possible and just got excited. No matter what else happened, they had each other. And one way or another, they'd make this base into another most excellent adventure.

They pulled up to a large, three-story apartment building and got out. Lt. Col. McMasters pointed to their new quarters. The term *quarters* is the Army's way of saying *your house, your home, your apartment*. Army brats don't have a home, they have quarters.

"This is called The Glass House, and it's where we are going to live. See that second apartment from the end on the third floor? That's ours."

They bumped the suitcases up the stairs of what was now *their* stairwell. With no shortage of excitement, they impatiently waited for Lt. Col. McMasters to get the door open. Entering, they realized it was much bigger than it looked from the outside. In fact, all the rooms were large: large kitchen, large living room, large dining room, three big bedrooms, and a big bathroom. But the biggest thing of all? The toilet.

"You gotta be kiddin'!" yelled Jack "That toilet's big enough for a giant to take a cra—" Jack shut up. He realized he was one swearword away from getting his mouth washed out with soap, and there was a nice new bar within his mother's reach. To Jack's relief, the colonel hadn't seemed to notice.

"It's gigundous!" Queenie exclaimed.

"If I'm not careful, I'll fall right in and get flushed!" exclaimed Rabbit.

Everyone laughed. But Rabbit wasn't exaggerating. They were laughing because it seemed like it could really happen. The Germans had the biggest toilets they'd ever seen.

Queenie turned around. "And look at the size of that tub! I get dibs on the first bath." Queenie loved the idea of an indoor swimming pool, and this tub was almost big enough.

However, when she found out she'd be sharing a room with Rabbit, her look of elation vanished. "Mom! I'm not sleeping with her!" she snapped. "She can sleep in Jack's room."

"Don't start with me, Laura," Mrs. McMasters said, giving her the eye. "You and your little sister are going to share, and that's all there is to it."

When they entered the room, Rabbit scrambled onto the twin bed closest to the window.

"Get off my bed, Rabbit," Queenie snarled.

Rabbit started jumping up and down, obviously enjoying the chance to torture her older sister. Refusing to hear a word that Queenie said, Rabbit shouted, "Look at the beautiful forest out there—it's all ours!"

Queenie could barely control her rage. "I won't tell you again, Rabbit. Move it!"

Pretending not to hear her, Rabbit turned from the window and sprang high into the air to land outstretched on the other bed. Scrunching her back into the mattress, she sighed, "Perfect, just perfect! I'm closer to the bathroom."

Queenie stared out the window. "Rabbit, there are going to be rules."

"Yup," said Rabbit. "If there's thunder, we sleep in the same bed."

Queenie shuddered.

Jack's room was down the hall and looked out in the opposite direction. From his window he saw across the street and into another set of woods. But there was also a big, open area where someone had made a snowman. Beyond that, and way below, Jack could see an airfield for both planes and helicopters. *Not bad*, he thought.

The second time through their quarters, they noticed things they'd missed. They found a big balcony off the living room that looked out over the back forest. Even though it was cold, they all went out to inspect.

Leaning precariously over the rail, Rabbit said, "Wow! We're really high."

Before she managed to fall, Lt. Col. McMasters mechanically grabbed her, hoisting her into the air and pivoting to deposit her far from the railing. "Time to go back in, Rabbit," was all he said.

Next, they discovered a little hallway off the front door. It led to a small bathroom and another bedroom.

"Whose bedroom is this?" asked Queenie, with intent.

"Don't get any big ideas, young lady," her mother warned. "This room is for your nanny."

"Nanny?" said all three kids.

"Well, not right away. But you'll get one at some point. And when we do, she'll stay here." The three knew better than to ask questions that would get no answers, so they moved on.

Then Jack thought of a question that *needed* an answer. "When's our stuff gonna get here?"

Weeks back they'd packed up all their toys, clothes, and furniture to be shipped to Germany.

Mrs. McMasters informed them it would probably be another month before it came over by ship. Basic furniture, pots and pans, and dishes weren't a big deal; the Army had already stocked the apartment with them.

Jack didn't care if his cereal bowl was his own or the Army's. But their toys? That was another matter. A kid's gotta have his stuff.

"Well, at least you have your winter clothes." She was taking stock of the kitchen cupboards. "You get your boots on and go out and play, but right after dinner, it's baths and bed, because bright and early tomorrow you kids are headed to school."

No kid likes being reminded about school. But when it means walking into a new classroom, on your first day, not knowing anyone—that's ugly. And it's much worse when all the other kids have been in that classroom for months.

Saddled with that lovely thought, they bundled up and went out to have a look around the neighborhood. At first there weren't any kids around. Then an OD-green Army school bus rumbled up the street and dumped out a horde of kids. OD means olive drab. Just as everything in the Navy is painted haze gray, everything in the Army is olive drab green.

The McMasterses just stood there watching. A couple of girls about Queenie's age stepped off the bus. One said hi to her. When they found out she'd just moved in, one asked if she wanted to come over. She, of course, immediately disowned Jack and Rabbit and headed off with them. When a bunch of little kids got off, Rabbit walked over and started talking.

Jack watched in amazement as Rabbit suddenly bolted from the group to run around the side of the building. All the other kids followed her. *How does she do that? She doesn't even know where she's going.*

Jack saw no one his age. He started walking without even picking a destination. Soon he was lost in thought, grinding on all the standard questions: Would he like this place? survive school? find friends?

His feet scrunched on the snow. Back at Fort Hood, he would have traded a month's allowance for one Saturday of snow. Now he'd melt it all to be back in Texas with his friends. But they were long gone. Jack's head bowed low, as one foot followed the other, crunching on the hard-packed snow as if his legs belonged to a robot. *Long gone. Long gone.*

Jack began to wonder how Alex Knox was making out. He wished Alex lived here so they could explore this place together. Alex was a friend who believed in him. Together they might have found a way to become like Jean-Sébastien. Could that ever happen here? He worried he'd end up a nobody kid, never making the kind of friends who helped him become a somebody kid.

He wasn't paying much attention to where he was going till he found himself back at The Glass House. That startled him. He'd never turned around, so how had it happened? It took him a moment to figure out that the road formed a circle that took him back to where he'd started. They would be living at the top of this Army base, way at the far end of everything.

Jack wasn't ready to go home, so he headed for the open area across the street from their quarters. The snow out there was a lot deeper, but that didn't stop him. He figured he was headed in the direction of the airfield, and he wanted to check it out. Once across the open area, he came to a clump of trees, the entrance to a small woods. As he made his way in, he could smell the clean forest and feel the cold on his face.

He hadn't gone far when he had to grab a tree limb to save himself from falling. He'd almost walked right off a giant cliff that dropped straight down three or four stories. Heart racing, he slowly, carefully eased back from the edge. He wouldn't make that mistake again. Always keeping a tree between him and the edge, he walked till he found a small opening.

He could see for miles. It was fantastic. Below was a very large building, probably the Army's aircraft hangar, because just beyond that was the airfield. Over to the left were more woods and then fields that seemed to go on forever. To the right were a bunch of buildings and a large section of the military base. Farther to the right, he eventually discovered snow-covered tanks. From his position he could only make out a few, but behind those were hundreds of bumps of snow in regular rows. *Here's where 4th Armored Division parks the tanks.*

He stood there taking it in. Almost unnoticed, his spirits had brightened. He might not have any friends yet, but he certainly knew one thing: He'd found the perfect place to build a fort. His fort. From this vantage point on the cliff he could see the comings and goings of the entire military base. If the tanks ever rolled, he'd know it from here. When Jack finally headed home, he felt just fine. He had plans.

11

New Kid

The next morning they were packed off to the American school on base. Lt. Col. McMasters walked them into the principal's office, where he told the attendant that, starting that day, his children would be attending school. This was not a request; it was a very clear directive from the colonel to the school. A few moments later, Mr. Reynolds, the principal, materialized, and Lt. Col. McMasters introduced himself and his children.

The colonel turned to the kids. "Your new principal, Mr. Reynolds, can handle it from here. I will see you children back at our quarters tonight. You are to take the bus home." With that he turned and left.

Mr. Reynolds told Rabbit to come with him. She jumped up, grinning, all excited to get to her new class. Jack and Queenie remained seated in his office, staring into space, saying nothing. Neither bothered to look at the other. No matter what went down in the next hour, it wasn't something they'd be doing together. They'd be waltzed into a new classroom in the middle of the year—introduced as "the new kid."

The principal came back for Queenie. Now Jack sat alone. *I just want this to be over,* he screamed to himself. *Calm down, Jack. You can do this.* He took a long, slow breath and forced himself to put a positive spin on the situation. *Hey, there's a chance it'll work out okay. Remember that first day back at Fort Sill? Oklahoma was all new and you didn't know a single soul when you walked into school. That time it was in the middle of the year, too. Remember how—*

The door opened, and Reynolds signaled him to follow. Jack prayed he'd be able to just slip in the back of the classroom and find a seat without really being noticed.

But no such luck. The minute he entered the class, everything in the room stopped. Every single kid looked up and stared at him. He stood there in front of everything—and everyone. So much for being stealthy.

The looks on their faces said it all: "Who are you?" Everyone was checking him out, looking for signs of weakness or fear. He stood frozen, trying his best to put on a blank face. His objective was to communicate absolutely nothing. He knew he shouldn't show aggression or disgust toward them. Nor should he show worry or terror. The problem was, Jack had no clue what they were actually reading on his face. His brain kept shifting between overdrive and being numb.

His teacher, Mrs. Campbell, went to talk to Mr. Reynolds for a moment. Then she said, "Everyone, this is Jack McMasters. He's new here. He'll be joining our class. Can you all say, 'Hello, Jack'?"

From the class came the singsong mumbling, "Hello, Jack."

Mrs. Campbell smiled, but by the way the class obeyed instantly, Jack could tell she didn't take crap from anyone. Making matters worse, she asked a girl named Samantha in the first row to move to the back so Jack could sit in the front of the class. Samantha quickly emptied her desk and Jack sat down. He could still feel everyone's eyes on the back of his head. He knew nothing was really gonna get sorted out till morning break.

For the next hour Mrs. Campbell taught English. It had something to do with adverbs and adjectives—stuff Jack hated. When the bell finally rang for morning break, everyone jumped out of their seats. It was like a bolt of electricity had shot through them. They all ran for the gym. There was no going out to the playground because of the snow. Once there, a group of boys gathered around Jack.

"Where are your quarters?" asked a redheaded kid.

"The Glass House," Jack answered.

A couple of them pointed over at a shorter, slightly heavier kid with curly, dark hair. The guy, Charlie, didn't say anything; he just studied Jack.

Another asked, "You any good at dodgeball?"

At that, they all headed off to play. But Jack knew it hadn't been an idle question. And he knew this was not a simple game. No, no, no. This was his first test. You get knocked out early in the game, you're immediately labeled a waste. You last, and just maybe you're okay.

Initially there were lots of kids in the middle, so Jack had no trouble staying away from the ball. Half were quickly eliminated, by which time Jack became a serious target. Everyone wanted to know: Could they get McMasters?

Jack picked up his pace a bit. One sandy-haired kid with ice-blue eyes kept trying to take him out. Jack could tell it was starting to get personal. After another near miss, Jack glanced around, noticing there were only five kids left. One of them was Charlie.

Edging closer to Jack, Charlie whispered, "Watch out for that guy. Ryan Kerrigan's a problem." It was done in a way that indicated he and Charlie were now allied together. For the first time that day, Jack felt a connection. The pressure eased just the tiniest bit.

The game got tougher and tougher, and by then most of their class had gathered to watch. Another kid got taken out. Then Charlie got hit. As he walked off the court, Charlie and Jack made eye contact. Charlie gave him an almost imperceptible nod of approval, but then glanced over at the kid named Kerrigan. "Watch your back," he mouthed. It was done in a way that no one else could see.

"McMasters, you play this game like you're an old lady," taunted Kerrigan. And the trash talk began. "Ya got no moves. Ya got nothin'. You're goin' down."

A few moments later Kerrigan wound up a vicious throw that caught Jack on the ankle. He got back to his feet and, ignoring Kerrigan, left the game. With only two players left, he hadn't done too badly. But he also felt unfinished business with Kerrigan.

Sure enough, the minute Jack was off the dodgeball court, Kerrigan came after him.

"You're a weenie, McMasters," he said in a nasty tone. He walked like someone very sure of himself. Someone looking for trouble. Kerrigan had a small gang of kids following along. "You hear me, McMasters? You're a candy ass. I can take you any day."

Welcome to being the new kid. Still, Jack was shocked when Kerrigan came right up to him and, without another word, shoved him in the chest, knocking him flat to the gym floor. Jack shook it off, and jumped back onto his feet. But, no question about it. He was rattled.

Kerrigan stood there glaring at Jack. He had the look of a mean fighter just waiting to see how Jack would respond. "So what you gonna do about it, candy ass? You gonna cry?"

Jack's head was spinning, and the room tightened in on him. He could sense kids gathering around. He knew they'd be staring at him, not at Kerrigan. None of them wanted to catch Kerrigan's attention, to become his next victim. At the same time, they all wanted to know if Jack would stand up to Kerrigan or back down. Jack could feel it. The betting was going against him. Most kids figured he'd back down, like so many kids before him.

But Jack had seen it all before. He knew that Kerrigan and his gang ran around doing whatever they wanted. They looked for kids to push and pound. Most of the time they didn't have to do anything to get kids to do what they said. They just used intimidation and the threat of violence. Jack could tell that this kid, Kerrigan, was tough—that he could, and would, be more than happy to pound the crap out of him.

His brain was running on overload. It began to shut down. Part of him was screaming to get out of there, while another part stood frozen, repeating, *Why me? Why me? Why me?* That part was having a very hard time dealing with why he was even in this stupid gym, and why this was happening to him. But another tiny part within him knew it was now or never. That part knew he'd be bullied and pushed around by Kerrigan forever if he didn't act.

Jack stood staring at Kerrigan. And then he noticed Charlie standing behind Kerrigan. It confused his brain. Was Charlie actually part of Kerrigan's gang? Had he read things wrong? Nothing had actually been said during the game, but he'd certainly gotten the impression that he and Charlie were together on things. Then Charlie vanished. It took Jack a moment to realize he had dropped down on all fours directly behind Kerrigan. Charlie was looking Jack right in the eyes, silently saying, *Do it now!*

In that briefest of moments, Jack's brain cleared. He understood what Charlie was risking. He'd positioned himself to help Jack take on Kerrigan. Without cycling it through his brain even once, Jack reacted. He crouched his body and then uncoiled, springing directly at Kerrigan in a full body tackle.

Kerrigan didn't react—at least not fast enough. Jack hit him right at chest level. Kerrigan crashed back into Charlie's crouched body, and went flying onto the gym floor. Jack landed right on top of him. The tackle had knocked Kerrigan flat, and now it was Kerrigan who was disoriented—and on the defensive. Jack had his forearm pinning Kerrigan's neck to the ground. But before anything conclusive could happen, two teachers showed up and pulled the boys apart.

With Charlie on his side, and his heart pounding like crazy, Jack was ready to have it out, right then and there. Even if he got his butt kicked. Glaring at Kerrigan, he said in a voice loud enough for kids and teachers to hear, "Who's the candy-ass now?" Jack tried to shrug off the teacher's grip so he could lunge for Kerrigan.

"That's it, young man. Not another thing out of you!" hissed the teacher. "Get to the principal's office!"

As Jack was being led away, he saw Charlie on the sidelines grinning at him. Unable to help himself, Jack grinned back.

Somehow, Kerrigan wasn't in trouble. He was back with his boys, mocking Jack. Even so, Jack was pretty sure their fight hadn't gone the way Kerrigan had anticipated.

∞⦅⦆∞

Jack had left Principal Reynolds's office less than ninety minutes ago, and here he was, back again. He figured Reynolds would be calling his father, and all kinds of bad was about to go down. Initially they stashed him in the outer office, while the teacher who'd dragged him down there filled Reynolds in on the situation. Jack was ushered in. He braced himself, figuring the principal was about to start yelling.

But Reynolds just calmly looked up and said, "Well, Jack, back again already? Have a seat." He studied the boy for a moment, and then continued, "You want to tell me what went down?"

Jack's heart had stopped racing. Just moments ago his brain had been very clear and focused. Responding to the principal should have been easy. But for some strange reason, his mind now seemed to go to mush. He was feeling very removed. Jack knew he was sitting in a chair in front of the principal's desk, but it felt like he was way back in the corner of the room, up high, observing Mr. Reynolds from outside his own body. It felt like he was a hundred feet away. Some small part of his brain knew he was supposed to be answering Mr. Reynolds, but he couldn't figure out how.

Despite Jack's silence, Mr. Reynolds didn't become impatient. In fact, he stayed very calm. "Jack, I know you got into a fight in the gym with Ryan Kerrigan. Just take a moment to gather your thoughts. Then tell me about it."

Jack slowly looked down at his hand. It was there, resting on the arm of the chair. He watched as his fingers stroked the wooden arm rest. But his hand looked ten feet away. He shut his eyes. He just wanted to take a nap, right there in that chair. But from somewhere way in the background he knew he needed to pull himself out of this trance. He needed to deal with the principal. He needed to work this situation so that it didn't get out of control and the colonel got called.

His hand still looked far away. He heard a quiet, remote voice say, "I don't even know Ryan Kerrigan, or whoever that was."

Strange, Jack thought. *That's my voice.*

But that's all he managed to come up with.

"Jack, look at me."

Mechanically, he rotated his head to look over at Mr. Reynolds. It was kind of interesting that Reynolds didn't look all ticked off.

"Jack, I *do* know Ryan Kerrigan. Trust me. He's been down here to see me a number of times. He and his friends can be rough customers."

In a very lazy, still, removed voice, Jack heard himself say, "I really didn't mean to get into a fight. We were just playing dodgeball. After the game it just happened."

"I'm told you were on top of him, calling him names."

"Yes, sir."

"And, I don't suppose you were on top of him because you tripped or accidently fell on him?"

"No, sir."

"I see. Well, how about if you try not to get into any more fights on your first day of school?"

"Yes, sir."

"And, Jack, let me suggest that you also try and stay away from Ryan Kerrigan, for at least the next couple of days." Reynolds studied him for a minute. "I'm going to do my work. When you're ready to do yours, you can go back to your classroom."

Jack was too tired even to nod. But after a while, when he began to feel more like himself, he rose to go.

Reynolds got up, too. He put a hand on the boy's shoulder. Almost in passing, he said, "Jack, I think it's going to be interesting having you in this school."

Jack went back to class.

Except this time when he entered the class, it was different. Oh, everyone still looked up at him, but this time, there were a lot fewer "sizing him up" looks. And, there were certainly no "Who are you?" looks. It was clear they'd all figured out who Jack McMasters was. Some even gave him a slight nod of welcome. A few actually smiled—not *about* Jack, but *for* Jack. Jack's eyes searched for Charlie. He was way in the back of the room. Charlie winked and gave him an encouraging nod.

Maybe his day was finally improving. Maybe. Then he saw Ryan Kerrigan sitting in that front desk at the far end of the room. Kerrigan was glaring at him. Jack couldn't read anything but malice in those cold, blue eyes. Kerrigan wasn't going away any time soon.

Mr. Reynolds may have been finished with him, but Mrs. Campbell wasn't. At lunchtime she announced they could all go, except Jack. She made him eat his sack lunch at his desk. Halfway through lunch, he saw the kids stream past their classroom to go outside, but instead of letting him go to, Mrs. Campbell told him to return to Mr. Reynolds's office.

Now what? I thought Reynolds was finished with me! Would this horrible day never end? Just don't call my dad. Anything but that.

Reynolds looked calm, almost happy to see him.

Bizarre!

"Jack, sit down, and for goodness sakes *relax*. You're not in trouble. I just wanted to talk to you. I've been doing some thinking. You remember when you first got to my office after the fight?"

"Yes?"

"I got the impression your body was shutting down on you. Do you know what I'm talking about? Like your body really wanted to sleep?"

"Yeah, I guess so, sir." Jack was getting progressively more uncomfortable. *How's he know so much about what was going on inside me?*

"Did it start when you got to my office or when Ryan pushed you to fight?"

"It's hard to tell. I'm pretty sure after Kerrigan first shoved me down, when I got back on my feet, my brain just started shutting down."

That same brain was working fine now, saying, *Are you nuts, Jack? Why am I telling Mr. Reynolds all this?* But, there was just something about Reynolds that made Jack drop his defenses. Jack's brat-radar just wasn't going off. Even though Reynolds was an adult, Jack trusted him.

"I thought that might be the case," said Mr. Reynolds. "I think you're going to have to work on that. If you keep shutting down, he's going to keep coming after you."

"I know . . ."

"I wasn't always a principal, Jack. I was in the US Army, in the Korean War, like your dad."

"How'd you know my dad was in Korea?" Jack said, suddenly bewildered. "You just met today."

"The United National Korean Service Medal on his uniform."

Of course. These guys always notice what's on soldiers' uniforms, the patches and stripes, ranks and ribbons that I.D. what they've done and where they've done it.

Reynolds said, "When I was in Korea, I experienced the same shutting down problem you had this morning. A particularly bad problem to have in the middle of a war."

"What did you do?" Jack asked. Part of him was curious, hoping for a miracle cure. The other part couldn't imagine anything that could help. Deep down, Jack worried he really *was* a weenie.

"Well . . . I learned some techniques that helped me to not shut down. They came from a very unusual source. Obviously, we can't work on this your very first day here, but I wanted you to know I think I can help you. If it's a problem, come see me."

"Yes, sir. Can I go back to class now?"

∞⊶⬦⊷∞

Finally the dismissal bell rang, and everyone jumped up to leave. While Jack was getting on his coat, Charlie came up and said, "I'll show you where we catch our bus."

They walked out of the school together and onto the bus. They made their way to the back and sat together.

"It takes a bit, but this bus eventually drops us off right at The Glass House. By the way, my name's Charlie Carron."

"Hey, Charlie. I'm Jack McMasters."

"Yeah, I kinda figured that out." Charlie's dark eyes were full of humor.

Jack exhaled. "I hate the first day at a new school."

"I know what you mean. So, where you been?"

So he told Charlie about California, Colorado, Japan, Oklahoma, and Texas. Reciting all the places he'd lived to Charlie somehow felt good. That *where you been* ritual performed by so many brats all over the world. The way so many brat friendships begin.

"So, where *you* been, Charlie?"

"Oh, lots of places. I was born in Italy. My mom's Italian. She and my dad met during World War II. We were stationed in Torino, but she's from a place called Positano. They say it's a beautiful place right on the ocean, but I've never been there. At least not that I can remember. Then we moved to Fort Bragg, you know, in North Carolina. We spent two years there. Then moved to the P.I. You know what that is?"

"Yeah, I guess. The Philippine Islands, right?"

"Right," said Charlie, surprised. "A lot of people don't seem to know that."

"I met a kid on the ship coming over. He'd been stationed in the P.I. at Subic Bay. His name was Alex Knox. You know him?"

"Nope, but we weren't at Subic. We were in Manila."

"No big surprise. He's Navy, not Army."

"I don't know many Navy brats. Anyway, afterward we went to Kentucky for a couple of years, and then here. I've been here about three months."

"You like it?"

"Oh, yeah! You wanna come over?"

"Sure. Just let me check in with my mom so she doesn't flip her lid. You know, first day of school and all."

"Deal. I'll come with you."

The bus dropped them in front of The Glass House. Jack did the world's fastest introduction of Charlie Carron, and they were off to Charlie's place. His quarters were on the first floor of the other stairwell, on the far end of the building.

When Jack met Mrs. Carron, he couldn't help but like her. She was a short, dark-haired, heavyset woman who asked about a thousand questions, mostly about his family.

"Mom, you writin' a book?" groaned Charlie, rolling his eyes at Jack. "She's famous for asking questions no one else would ever dare ask."

Jack didn't care; he actually enjoyed talking to her. But when she asked if he was hungry, well then he *really* liked her. Jack told Mrs. Carron he was just about on death's doorstep from lack of food. Grinning at his starving-kid act, she said she might be able to find them something.

"That's great, Mom," Charlie said, as he dragged Jack off to his room.

A little while later, Mrs. Carron came in, carrying two bowls of steaming-hot pasta, with some kind of meat sauce. "Here, try this mostaccioli with Bolognese sauce."

Jack had no clue what she'd just said, but one bite made him think he'd found heaven. The noodles looked like miniature pipes. The sauce was nothing short of spectacular. Jack began thinking it was best to come to Charlie's place every day after school. At the McMasters house, if you asked, "Can I have a snack?" you usually got a response like, "Don't eat too much or you'll spoil your dinner." Jack's mom was all about the dinner. Charlie's mom was all about serious food any time at all.

"Want to see something smokin' cool?"

"Sure," mumbled Jack around a mouthful of noodles.

Charlie went digging in the back of his closet while Jack turned back to his pasta.

Eventually, Charlie emerged with a large shell casing. To Jack, it looked like a bullet without a tip. It was the larger brass part that once held the gunpowder. But at eighteen inches long with a two-inch-wide opening, it was fifty times larger than any regular bullet. It probably weighed eight pounds.

"Wow," Jack whispered. "Where'd ya get this?"

"Found it in the woods. I actually tripped over it."

"What?"

"See, I was out in the woods behind here. It's amazing back there. Anyway, I'm runnin' full speed, catch my toe on something, and go flying. Next thing, I'm face-down on the forest floor. I sat there trying to get my head to stop spinning. Ya know how it does that sometimes when ya go flyin'?"

Jack just nodded, and Charlie kept talking.

"Anyway, there were leaves everywhere so I couldn't really see what I'd tripped over. I assumed it was a tree root. But when I looked back, I wasn't that close to any trees. So I started feeling around in the leaves. Eventually I felt something hard sticking out of the ground. When I brushed the leaves away, there was the shell. Well . . . I didn't actually know what it was, or how big it was, till I dug it out. It took me a while, 'cause it was buried in there tight."

"How'd you get it out?"

"I marked the spot so I could find it again. You'll see, the woods are huge. It's pretty easy to get lost. At least, until you learn your way around. Don't worry. I'll teach you all the tricks. Anyway, I went home and snuck one of my dad's hunting knives and dug it up. Man, I was amazed how big it turned out to be.

"Yeah," Jack said, holding the shell, loving it. "Did it still have gunpowder in it when you found it?"

"Not a drop left. I think this one had been fired."

"Where do you think it's from?"

"It's definitely a Nazi shell. You know about the Nazis, right?"

Jack looked at Charlie, considering the question. "Yeah. I mean I know they were our enemy and we defeated them. My dad fought over here during the war. But how can you be sure it's a Nazi shell?"

"One day I had it with me, over at this other kid's quarters. His dad came in and caught us playing with it. When he asked to see it, I thought we might be in big trouble. But his dad stayed cool, just studying the shell. He asked where I'd found it, so I told him I got it from another kid who said he found it somewhere around here. I figured it was best not to tell him too much. Anyway, his dad said it was most likely a Nazi anti-aircraft shell. He told us that during World War II there were *Soldaten der Flak-abteilung* here. They were an anti-aircraft unit."

"So right here where we're living, there were Nazi soldiers during the war?" The question was hardly out of Jack's mouth when he began to cringe inside. *This guy's gonna think I'm an idiot. Of course there were Nazis here during the war.*

Charlie didn't seem to notice. "Yup." He disappeared back in his closet and came out with an old photo that said, "Nazis. 1937."

"That's just before the war," said Charlie.

Jack studied the picture of the Nazi troops marching their famous goose step. The shell and photo made the Nazis somehow come to life. They were no longer just stories.

Jack said, "This *Flakabteilung* shell might have shot at an American plane."

"The Americans or the British. Hard to believe."

"Interesting word, *Flakabteilung*," Jack said. "It sounds like the word *Flak jackets*. They protect from shell fragments. That makes more sense now."

"If you like Nazi stuff, I have to show you something else. It's in the woods."

That got Jack's attention. Before tearing out of the apartment, Jack scraped the last bits of sauce out of his pasta bowl and placed it in the sink.

"Mrs. Carron, this was the best pasta I've ever had," he said and meant it. "If I'd had any better, believe me I would have remembered."

Her big, dark eyes lit up. But just as the boys made it to the door, she yelled, "Charlie Carron, you get back here. Right now!"

"Did you boys forget something?" She looked from him to the floor.

"Oh, yeah," Charlie said with a sheepish grin.

"Oh, yeah," she said mocking him, but with humor.

Jack and Charlie pulled their big black rubber galoshes over their shoes and clipped them up. Jack might be on the other side of the Atlantic, but galoshes seemed to be standard issue for Army brats everywhere.

There was quite a bit of snow, but not so deep that it prevented them from moving through the woods. The land gently dropped away, and soon Jack could no longer see The Glass House, or any other buildings. The only sounds were their footsteps crunching snow. Jack looked up at the huge trees, with their limbs dark against the white, late-afternoon sky. All the leaves were long gone. The whole scene was black-and-white and shadowed.

Sensing motion in all that stillness, Jack paused as two black squirrels came out of nowhere. They sprang along the treetops, leaping from limb to limb in a game of chase. He studied them, thinking how excellent it would be to fly across those treetops like the squirrels. Then they were gone.

The two boys moved deeper into the woods.

Finally, Charlie stopped, saying, "What do you see?"

Jack took his time, doing grid search. *Man, if it's obvious, Charlie will think I'm a complete flake.*

Jack finally gave up. "I don't see anything."

"That's just the point. You're not supposed to notice anything. But see that slight mound in the snow down there?"

"Yeah. It just looks like the ground's a little higher there."

"You're right. But, my-man-Jack, that's no ordinary rise in the forest floor—it's a Nazi pillbox. Come on!"

As Jack came around the mound, he could just make out the opening to a concrete bunker. Both boys crawled down inside the frozen structure.

There was a cement platform just below the opening, with metal rings anchored into the concrete walls. "This must be where the machine gunner set up," suggested Jack. "And the spotter positioned here, right next to him."

"I figure it was a listening post," said Charlie. "They probably had a field phone, so they could report in on enemy activity."

Jack agreed. "It has a perfect view of the woods."

"Even better, it's in a great place to defend the airfield if an attack came in this direction."

Jack and Charlie hung out for a while, pretending they were Nazi soldiers waiting for the Americans to attack. Jack was great at pretending, but it felt strange to know that Nazi soldiers had actually manned this bunker. Perhaps they had fought and died right here.

Wow, Jack thought—*real shells, real bunkers. World War II was real!* He'd always known that, but somehow being here made it come to life.

"Charlie, do you think there are still Nazis around here?"

"Probably lots of the Germans around here were Nazis during the war," said Charlie.

"Yeah, I know that. But what I mean is, are there *still* Nazis around?"

"Dunno," said Charlie. "I suppose it's possible."

It was starting to get dark, so they headed back. On the way, Charlie pointed out a couple of noteworthy landmarks. He was beginning to teach Jack how to navigate the woods.

Back at The Glass House they each headed toward his own stairwell.

"See you at the bus stop in the morning, Jack."

"See ya."

Jack made his way to his own quarters. He had made a real enemy that day, but he had also made a good friend. Not a bad first day.

12

Flugplatz Spies

The next morning a mob of kids were out in front of The Glass House waiting for the bus. *Day two,* Jack said to himself, hoping he'd survive this one, too. He spotted Charlie waving from the crowd. Yesterday he had no one, today he had Charlie.

When the bus rolled up, he and Charlie plopped down in a seat together like they'd been friends since birth.

"Hi, Charlie," said a blond girl seated across the aisle. She sort of had a Queenie look. Not the "I'm obviously superior" part, but certainly the natural-confidence, good-posture, socks-pulled-up part. Jack immediately thought, *Yup, probably likes school, gets good grades, obeys the rules—at least most of them. Always has friends.* She seemed the type who didn't exactly skate through life, but definitely made it work for her.

"This is my friend Sam Sands," Charlie said. "Her real name's Samantha, but everyone calls her Sam."

"Hi, I'm—"

"Jack McMasters. I know," she said.

"How do you know that?"

"You kidding? After yesterday's recess, we all know who *you* are. I'm in your class, too, in case you didn't notice."

"I guess yesterday was a blur. Nice to meet you, Sam."

"You better watch out, Jack, 'cause Ryan Kerrigan is a complete psycho. And he has lots of kids under his grip."

Jack nodded that he understood. But inside, he felt his stomach tense. He didn't need this crap. Suddenly, being a nobody seemed very attractive. Not the target of a psycho. He felt lightheaded.

Get me off this bus. Get me out of this new school.

Based on yesterday, the other kids might think he could handle himself against Ryan Kerrigan, but Jack knew that was a load of crap. Next time, he would panic and show he was the weenie Kerrigan had said he was. Yesterday he'd gotten lucky. He'd fought back and won, but only because Charlie had helped. If the teachers hadn't broken things up when they did, he wouldn't be looking so good right now. He knew Kerrigan could, and probably would, beat the crap out of him. Next time everyone would find out who he really was.

"Best thing to do is to stick together," said Charlie. "Alone, he'll kick either of our asses; together, maybe he'll leave us alone. Anyway, one way or the other, we'd better try and avoid him."

Jack nodded. He was really glad Charlie was around.

By whatever miracle of the gods, that day actually went okay. And it was Friday.

At least it went okay till they were headed for the bus home. That's when Kerrigan made a point of ramming Jack into Charlie.

Over his shoulder Kerrigan yelled, "Don't worry, McMasters. I haven't forgotten about you. We're still gonna go the rounds, you and me. And as for you, Charlie Carron, yours is coming, too. You don't *really* think I'm gonna forget you helped Panty-waist McMasters yesterday, do ya?"

Before either had a chance to react, Kerrigan was gone.

"Just ignore him," said Sam, when she caught up with them. "What are you two gonna do when you get home?"

Almost without thinking, Jack said, "We're going down to explore the airport."

"Yeah," Charlie said, as if they'd been planning it all afternoon.

"By *airport*, you mean *der Flugplatz*, right?" Sam asked, wanting to make sure she knew where they were headed.

"Yeah, yeah, Sam, the *Flugplatz*," Charlie said.

"Okay, maybe I'll see you down there."

∞✕∞

They went to Charlie's to get refueled. Mrs. Carron fed them cut-up apples and different kinds of lunch meat. Good stuff. Not as good as her pasta, but still better than what Jack would have gotten from his mom.

"We need to explore the airport," said Jack. "We gotta figure out how everything works down there. What did Sam call that place?"

"*Flugplatz*. It's what the Germans call it. Not sure what it means, except that in German class I did learn that *Platz* means *place*."

Jack thought about that for a minute. If *Platz* meant *place*, then that left *Flug*. He figured that must mean fly. So translated, *Flugplatz* meant *fly-place*. He liked that.

They headed through the open field across from The Glass House and into the small woods beyond. Jack led Charlie to the lookout spot he'd found the other night. But despite the amazing view beyond the cliff, they didn't get too close to the edge; it was a sheer, three-story drop.

Jack said, "Perfect spot for us to build a fort. Don't ya think?"

Charlie nodded. "Great lookout. Very secluded. But I don't see any obvious way to do it. The trees are too big to climb, so a tree fort is out."

Jack smirked. "That'll be our engineering challenge for next spring when the snow melts." He studied the airfield below.

They made their way along the horseshoe-shaped cliff till they came to where it wasn't quite so high and the drop-off was less steep. Charlie watched tensely as Jack stretched out on his stomach into the snow, edging his legs over the side of the cliff.

"You sure about that, Jack? There's a path that goes around through the woods."

Jack was nowhere *near* sure, but he said, "Show me another time. I want to try this." He pushed off over the cliff, first sliding on his stomach, then tumbling head over heels, and finally sliding to the bottom on his butt. Seeing that Jack had survived, Charlie reluctantly followed. Like Jack's descent, his was a bit out of control.

"That was okay, I guess," Charlie said, out of breath and surprised to be in one piece.

Jack gave him a grin.

Then they turned their backs on that impossibly high cliff. They had no idea how they'd get back up the incline, but for the moment they didn't care.

They cautiously waded through snow-crusted brush to make their way toward the big airplane hangar, only to hear Sam Sands yell, "We'll see you guys down on the side of the airfield."

How could anyone know their whereabouts?

"She musta spotted us from up on the cliff," said Charlie. "You *said* it was a great lookout spot."

"She'd better pipe down or she'll blow our cover."

Jack and Charlie made their way to the back of the structure to begin exploring.

The hangar was huge. It had no doors on the back side, but windows covered the entire upper arch, reaching all the way to the roof, too high for anyone to see through.

Learning nothing, they rounded the corner and found a couple of very dirty windows closer to the ground. The boys were just tall enough to peek inside. Because the lights were on, they could make out several helicopters. Two Army guys in overalls were moving around one.

Charlie barely whispered, "Don't move a muscle or they'll spot us."

"I know. Let's stay put. Looks like routine maintenance." Jack and Charlie were in spy mode, motionless, unobserved.

They nearly jumped out of their skins when something tapped them on the shoulder. They whipped around to see Sam and another girl.

Shaken, the boys slowly backed away from the window.

Clearly delighted to have scared the snot out of the boys, Sam said, "We took the trail that goes through the woods."

"Oh, you took the long way," Charlie said, grinning at Jack. Then he introduced him to the other girl, whose name was Jayla Jones. She was thin and wiry, with dark-brown skin and jet black hair.

Jack brought both girls up to speed on their recon mission.

"A what?" asked Jayla, a bit bemused.

"Recon," said Jack. "You know, a *reconnaissance mission*. A mission designed to gain intelligence. And not get caught."

Jayla, not exactly a slow child, immediately nodded. In fact, it didn't take Jack long to realize she was extremely bright. This was disconcerting, since she gave Sam a skeptical glance that said, *You sure about this guy?*

But Jayla and Sam followed the boys around to the front of the hangar. There they found two huge doors that could be rolled up to let aircraft in or out. Both doors were closed, but the *Flugplatz* obviously was open for business, because the snow had been cleared off the tarmac, as well as from one runway.

Not far from the building was a huge earth mover, with enormous tires and a large blade. Clearly this was the Army's version of a snow plow. It was parked and unattended. Beyond the runway was an air-traffic-control tower. On top they could see a curved panel spinning round and round.

Sam asked, "What's that thing up there?"

"Everyone, back up very slowly," Jack said. "Right now!" They heard the alarm in his voice and watched as he retraced his steps. They promptly obeyed.

"Why'd we need to do that?" asked Jayla once they were safely behind the building.

"That was a radar tracking station," Jack said, as if the situation were obvious.

"Soooo?" Jayla didn't find that any kind of answer.

"It's their eyes in the skies. With it they can see approaching aircraft, and track their direction and speed."

"How do you know all that?" challenged Sam.

"I saw one like it on the ship coming over." He told them about Commander Knox and the USS *Upshur*'s tracking systems and how there was probably a round screen up in that tower with a light green line of light going around it, showing bleeping dots of light if any aircraft were approaching. "They can probably see at least ten miles from the base."

"So why'd we have to get outta there?" demanded Sam. 'We're not approaching aircraft."

"Because the tower was manned," said Jayla. "The radar was spinning. Someone might have spotted us out in front of the building."

"Exactly," Jack said, surprised at how fast she'd caught on. *Who are you, Jayla Jones?*

Jayla further impressed him by guessing his thoughts. She gave him a little wink.

They eased around to the back of the hangar and over to the other side. There, again, they found a set of dirty windows. But this time the windows were a little too high. So Jack leaned back against the wall and put his hands together to give Charlie a leg up. Stretching, Charlie got a momentary peek, before ducking and jumping back to the ground.

"Two guys were sitting at a small table drinking coffee," he whispered, "but they just got up and I think they're headed this way. Let's go!"

Faster than saying Jack Robinson, the four got behind the building. Charlie peeked around the corner. "Two GIs coming right for us."

Sure they were about to be busted, with nowhere to run and nowhere to hide, the four brats pressed up against the wall.

But the two men stopped before they rounded the corner of the building.

"Let me bum a smoke," came a voice not three feet from where they stood. They could hear a match being struck.

"I heard a good one the other day," came another voice. "Ya know how no one really knows if Hitler died at the end of the war, 'cause his body was never found?"

"Yeah."

"Well, supposedly, a bunch of the old Nazis found out he's still alive and living in South America. So they go over there to convince him to come back so Germany can take over the world."

"And?"

"And Hitler says he'll do it. But under one condition."

"Which is?"

"Hitler says, 'This time, no more Mr. Nice Guy.'"

Both soldiers began laughing. Then, to the brats' relief, the men slowly headed back into the building.

"That was too close!" whispered Sam.

"Way too close," said Jayla. "Let's get up that hill and into the woods before we really *do* get busted."

Once safely among the trees, they crouched in the frozen undergrowth. They were now hard to spot, but the leafless trees afforded them a decent view. Out beyond the hangar they could see a huge, round cylinder lying on its side and raised up on iron legs. A big hose dangled from it like an elephant's trunk.

"That's got to be the aircraft fueling station," said Charlie.

Jack's mind was racing. Relieved they hadn't gotten busted, and at the same time excited by what they'd figured out, Jack couldn't just turn it all off. He saw a white, two-story, u-shaped building beyond the aircraft hangar. Most of its windows glowed yellow. He knew people were working in there, because lots of cars were parked outside. Besides, an American flag hung from a giant pole in front of the building. He pointed to the building. "What's that place?"

"That's Headquarters 4th Armored Division," said Sam.

"So all the brass are in there?"

"Yup, commander of 4th Armored is a two-star general."

Almost to himself, Jack said, "So when the tanks roll, that's where the order comes from."

"That's the place," came back Jayla's voice in a whisper.

Finally Jack whispered, "I think we have the lay of the land. Let's get outta here."

Jack checked his watch. He knew the drill. The people inside wouldn't leave until "Retreat" was blown and the Stars and Stripes were lowered at seventeen hundred hours, sharp.

Slowly, four cold bodies strained to get back on their feet. They gingerly followed Sam as she headed for her secret path. But she hadn't gone far when she suddenly stopped, dropping to one knee. In that same movement she raised her right arm, forming her hand into a fist. This, as most Army brats know, is the infantry signal to stop, get low, remain silent; the person on point has spotted enemy activity.

They each soundlessly took a knee, remained motionless, and kept a wary eye out for activity ahead.

Sam lowered her arm, and turned to make eye contact. Without saying a word, she brought the fist up to her face and extended her index and middle finger toward her eyes. Then she lifted just one finger upward and pointed it off to a ridge above them. These were Infantry signals communicating that she had spotted one enemy up and to their left.

They each nodded understanding.

Pointing at Jack and Charlie, she made a little walking motion with two fingers. They were to work their way up and around in order to get a better look. She signaled for Jayla to stay put.

Jack wasn't sure if this was a game or a real problem. Opting to take it seriously, he and Charlie remained low and inched soundlessly backwards. Then, slowly, they made their way around and up the hill. But then, Jack felt a wave of apprehension; in the woods just below them stood a man. He had on a short, dark coat and a dark hat. The brim covered most of his face, so Jack couldn't really see what the guy looked like. But one thing was certain: he wasn't just a hiker in the woods. First, he was too well dressed. Second, he stood perfectly still, not moving a muscle. All his concentration was on the airfield and the headquarters building. Clearly, the brats weren't the only ones watching the comings and goings down there.

Jack glanced at Charlie. For once the playfulness had left his friend's eyes. They showed fear. While down at the hangar, the boys might have been concerned about getting busted for being someplace they shouldn't be. But this? This was different. This guy radiated danger. There was something truly scary about him. Ever so slowly, ever so quietly, Jack and Charlie retreated. Working their way back to within twenty feet of the girls, Jack signaled them. Pointing two fingers to his eyes, he then held one finger up and nodded yes. Next, he used two fingers in a walking motion to communicate that they should back away, circle around, and come up the hill.

When they met up, Jack put a finger to his lips. He signaled for them to continue crawling up the steep embankment. It took ten painful minutes to reach the path. Getting to their feet, they double-timed it out of there. The tension didn't ease until they'd made it to the clearing in front of The Glass House.

"What was *that* all about?" asked Jayla, obviously rattled.

"I don't know, but, well, look, you know those two GIs down at the hangar? They might have been joking about Hitler coming back to power, but that guy on the hill was no joke," said Jack. His eyes darted back to where they'd just come from, as if he expected the guy to appear at any moment. "Let's go to my place. We have to figure this out."

Inside the front door, everyone peeled off their snowsuits. They made a kid-sized pile on the boot tray, but at least they had somewhere to melt. Jack was glad they'd been so careful when his mom came into the hallway. He introduced Sam and Jayla.

"What have you four been up to?" she asked.

Jack limited his response to "Hiking in the woods." Then, to deflect further questions, he said, "Mom, can we have cocoa?"

He wasn't all that hopeful she'd agree, because she was right in the middle of making dinner, but it was worth a shot. It surprised him when she smiled and actually said okay. As she poured the milk into a pan, they disappeared to Jack's room.

Once the door closed, Sam immediately started in with, "Who do you think he was?"

"And what was he doing there?" wondered Charlie.

Jack agreed. "Something doesn't feel right about this."

So many questions. They sat on his bed collecting their thoughts. Ever so slowly, Jack said, "*We* know what *we* were doing there. We were *spying* on the place. But what was *that guy* doing there? Was he spying on the place, too?" He exhaled. "Let's see what we can figure out about him. Like, for instance, he was definitely a man, not a woman. Right?"

"No question about that," said Sam. "I only saw him for a moment, but he was definitely a man."

"Also, I didn't get the impression he was US Army," said Charlie. "We didn't stick around long once we spotted him, but I'm pretty certain he wasn't in uniform. And I mean, come on. How many Army guys go around dressed in civilian clothes when they're on base? Am I right?"

"You're right," said Sam. "So probably not Army. Let's see. What was he wearing? I remember a dark coat."

"And he had on a brimmed hat, kinda like Dick Tracy's. I remember because the brim kept me from seeing his face," said Jack.

"Yeah," said Sam. "Now that you mention his hat, things are starting to come back to me. Like his hat was kinda dark, but not black. In fact, I think it was dark green, and the fabric of that hat was different from the kind my dad wears. It was more like a fuzzy felt or something."

"Wow, Sam! You are so on the stick. Leave it to you to register the fashion stuff." Jayla said it good naturedly.

"You're also right about the dark coat," Jack said. "But it was pretty short."

"So?" Charlie said.

"Well, most men don't wear short coats. They all have long ones that cover their suits. Right?" suggested Jayla.

"Yeah. Now that you mention it, I guess that's right," said Charlie. "But what does that tell us?"

"It means he wasn't American!" said Jack. "He was dressed more like a German than an American. He was German, or from some other foreign country."

"Probably German, and not military," recapped Jayla.

No one said anything for a few moments. Then slowly, Jack said, almost to himself, "No, I don't think that's right. I actually think he *was* military—just not US military. Okay, maybe he was dressed like a German civilian, but he didn't *act* like a civilian. Remember how he stood. Did you see how straight he was? how little he moved? how completely silent he was? That takes discipline. To me he seemed military. But *whose* military?"

"Okay, if he's German military, or someone else's military," said Charlie, "what's he doing on a US military installation? Someone all alone, watching the airfield *and* the Headquarters Building of 4th Armored Division? Doesn't add up."

"Minimum, he's a shady character. Worst case, I say he's a spy," said Jayla.

Jack's mom entered the room. She was carrying cups of cocoa on a tray. The marshmallows floating on top were just beginning to melt.

There was a chorus of sincere thank-yous. Mrs. McMasters seemed pleased.

Sam kept her feelings in check until Mrs. McMasters left, but then she said, "This could be *so* serious. Should we tell anyone?"

A look passed between Jack and Charlie. Then Charlie answered for both of them, "No point in telling anyone now. The guy's probably long gone. But we better keep an eye out for him."

Before they left, he had a name, The Watcher, and they committed to look for him wherever they went.

They made plans to meet at Charlie's the next day and go to the Saturday movie.

"Be there at eleven thirty sharp, Jack," said Sam. "We don't want to be late."

"When we're late we don't get good seats," said Jayla.

Charlie grimaced. "And we won't get to sit together. The place packs out every week."

"Copy that," said Jack.

∞⎯⫱⎯∞

Later that night, the man in the woods was still bothering Jack. He just knew something wasn't right about that guy. So when his dad was saying good night, Jack told him they'd seen a German man over by the cliff.

Lt. Col. McMasters could tell Jack was worried about it, so he made an effort to reassure him. "I wouldn't worry about it, Jack. Germans love to go for walks in the woods."

"But why would a German guy be walking in the woods of a United States Army base? I mean, how'd he even get *on* the base?"

"Your imagination's running wild, Jack. The guy's probably a German civilian who works for us. He was probably just out for an evening stroll." Before Jack could say any more, his dad said good night and left his room.

Jack lay in his bed, thinking that Charlie had been right: There was no point in saying anything to adults about the guy. Without more evidence, no one was going to take a bunch of kids seriously.

∞⎯⫱⎯∞

Fear came. . . . Fear kept coming. . . . *He* kept coming—the man in the dark-green felt hat and short, dark coat. Everywhere Jack went, The Watcher was there. Jack struggled to make him go away.

Jack forced his eyes open. The room was dark. But his eyelids were so heavy. His covers were twisted as he rolled back over, desperately hoping the nightmare would not return.

. . . There he was in that green hat, sitting in a room, talking to Hitler. . . . He followed Jack into the PX. He sat behind Jack in the movie theater. He joined the dodgeball circle, faking throws to see Jack jump away. He wove his way through the rows of tanks. *Please. Let me sleep. Please, just let me sleep.* But The Watcher on the cliff wouldn't go away. . . .

13

Cowboys Against the Indians

Saturday was allowance day in the McMasters household. This week, getting it was essential. Jack had been singing the blues all week about not having a thin dime to his name. Without allowance, there'd be no Saturday movie. And there'd be no allowance if their Saturday chores weren't completed to Mrs. McMasters's satisfaction. Unfortunately, the lady is no pushover. Making matters worse, she never gave her kids a list of the chores before they started. Instead, she just kept coming up with an endless set of things for them to do. Thus, there was no guarantee the McMasters kids would finish in time. But Jack wasn't the only seriously motivated troop. Queenie and Rabbit had also made plans to go to the Saturday movie with their new friends.

"Rabbit, you vacuum the living room," said Mrs. McMasters. "Laura, you and Jack get at those dirty dishes from last night." Then she headed out the door of their quarters and down the stairwell to the basement to put in a load of laundry.

"Oh, great!" said Queenie. "This'll take forever." They had accidently—on purpose—forgotten to do the Friday-night dishes the instant their parents had gone off to a cocktail party. "You wash, Jack."

"Not a chance. But I'll flip you for it."

Desperate to get a move on, she agreed.

Jack won the toss.

Queenie got washing; he got rinsing and drying.

Everything went fine until it came time to wash the coffee pot. The contraption was composed of two big, round parts. The bottom was the pot, where the coffee ends up. The top was a big, stainless-steel bubble where the coffee was brewed. Coming out of that top was a spout shaped like a long cone.

Queenie, still ticked off at losing the coin toss, filled the bubble with water from her sink and washed it. Normally she'd have swished the coffeepot and dumped the dirty water back into the sink before passing it to Jack to rinse. But instead, she held a finger over the tiny end of the spout, lifted it high, and released her finger. A giant stream of dirty dish water shot out like a water cannon. That would have been fine if she'd aimed into *her* sink. But she shot the sludge into Jack's clean rinse water.

Now he'd have to drain his sink and completely refill it. Time for payback. Laughing, he reached into his sink and flung water right on *her*.

Shirt all wet, she screamed, "Oh! Now you're gonna get it." But she was shrieking and laughing at the same time.

That's when The Great Dishwashing War erupted. She quickly dipped the coffee bubble back in her dirty wash water. But this time, when she took her finger off the small end of the spout, it was aimed right at Jack. Brown water gushed toward his chest.

Jack tried to evade the stream, but Queenie chased him around the kitchen, spraying him and just about everything else.

The coffee bubble ran out.

Jack doubled back to the sink and grabbed a glass. He scooped up rinse water and threw it at Queenie.

Half the water hit her, and the other half flew all over the cupboards and counter. Jack was about to launch another glassful when in walked Mrs. McMasters.

"Mom! He started it!"

She took one look at the mess and said, "Hmm, the Saturday movie is looking more and more doubtful. Now you two can not only finish the dishes but also scrub the cabinets, counters, and floor. Then report to me for your next assignment."

She left the kitchen. Before either of them could even react, they heard her from the next room.

"Rabbit, start all over again with the vacuuming. This time do it *right.*"

Mrs. McMasters wasn't taking any prisoners today.

"Your fault, Jack."

"No, yours."

"You threw water on me first."

"You sabotaged my rinse water."

But they both knew it was time to call a truce and get back to work. If they wanted to make the movie, they needed to get it in gear.

"You deal with the cupboards and counters; I'll get the floor," Queenie said. And they were off to the races.

Mrs. McMasters kept them working on one chore after another for the next three and a half hours. And without a single break. Dishes, bathrooms, bedrooms, blah, blah, blah. The closer it got to eleven thirty, the faster they moved.

Finally, at 11:25, she called it quits.

"You can go," she said, "but make sure you three stick together at the movies."

Three greedy hands shot out to collect allowance.

The minute Jack walked into Charlie's place, Sam said, "Okay, let's get outta here."

"Jack," Charlie said, shaking his head, "you forget the old Army saying, 'If you're on time, you're late.' Always better to be a little early, especially for the Saturday movie."

It wasn't hard for him to read their impatience. They had probably been questioning whether he was even going to show.

Great way to make new friends, Jack, he tortured himself. *Oh, yeah. Be the one who's late and keeps everyone waiting. At this rate they'll probably dump me by next Saturday.* Then, making matters worse, he was forced to explain they couldn't actually leave without his sisters.

Fortunately, when they came out of the building, Queenie and two of her new girlfriends were already waiting on them. Queenie introduced Jack's crew to her new friends, Camila and Liz.

But Rabbit? No Rabbit!

Just at the point Jack was ready to ditch her, she and two other little kids ambled around the corner as if they had all the time in the world.

Queenie assumed her totally superior, oldest-child, "I'm in charge" persona. She growled, "Move it, Rabbit, or we're leaving without you and your l-i-t-t-l-e friends." Like Jack, she was feeling embarrassed for making her new friends wait.

Double timing it all the way down the main road that cut through the base, they actually got there just before the show started. Late or not, Jack, Charlie, and the others naturally had to load up on candy and popcorn first. Charlie didn't say it, but Jack was certain they were too late to find seats together.

Fortunately, the GI in charge of things that day must have forgotten his watch, because he opened the main doors to the theater a little behind schedule. So, pushing and shoving their way through the enormous crowd of kids, they managed to be some of the first inside. Charlie and Jack had already decided the objective was to sit in the front row. But they obviously weren't the only ones with that idea. By the time they got there, the whole first row was full. Still, they managed to get seats together in the third row.

The lights dimmed partway, and the whole theater went quiet. A picture of the American flag came on the screen, and they all stood, placed their right hands over their hearts, and sang the "Star-Spangled Banner." The lights went out completely and the preview of next week's movie began, looking so promising that Jack decided to declare a truce with Queenie during all of next Saturday's chores. Then there was the cartoon. And, to no one's great joy, Bugs Bunny was followed by the newsreel. Jack and Charlie ignored most of the news from around the world . . . except the piece about a big military parade in Russia. They definitely paid attention to that part because it showed tanks rolling down a wide street.

Charlie leaned over to Jack and whispered, "Now *those* could do some major damage. I've never seen any like 'em. Have you?"

"Nope. Sure different from our dads' tanks."

Jack thought, confused, *The officers on the* Upshur *said Russia was our friend during World War II. This newsreel guy says the Russians are our enemy.*

Jack forced his mind off that puzzle and onto the serial, an outer-space adventure about a guy named Flash Gordon. Jack loved the title, "Flaming Torture," but since this one was the sixth installment, Charlie had to fill him in on the story as it went along. Flash had been taken prisoner on Mars. Today's episode abruptly ended with Flash in the Static Room strapped to a Sparking Machine about to burn Flash to death. By the time the screen said, "See 'Shattering Doom,' Chapter 7, of the Flash Gordon

Serial to be shown at this theater next week," every kid in the theater couldn't wait for next Saturday.

And last but not least—the real movie. It was about cowboys and Indians. Jack loved cowboy movies. Sounded like they all did.

The Glass House kids piled out of the theater's side doors: Queenie with Camila and Liz, Rabbit with her friends, Jack with his crew. Everyone was talking about the movie as they headed home, and nobody was paying much attention to what was going on around them. A block from the theater, Ryan Kerrigan and a few of his gang were standing on a street corner. Kerrigan was facing away from them, giving some kind of instructions to a guy named Tony Keach, whom Kerrigan treated like a sidekick. But as if Kerrigan had eyes in the back of his head, he glanced around, focusing on them.

Jack felt his face go hot and his stomach tense. There was going to be trouble. There was no time to avoid it.

Some of the others had also spotted Kerrigan. It was as if someone had just pulled a pin on a grenade.

Kerrigan said, "Boys, it looks like we need to hold up on that mission for a moment."

"But . . ." said Tony.

"Relax, this won't take long. I just need a quick time-out to kick McMasters's ass." To Jack, he shouted, "Yeah, Jack, I'm talkin' about you. Time to find out who the real candy-ass is!"

Even though it was cold outside, Jack started to sweat. Everything closed in on him. His brain started firing questions. *Why can't Ryan Kerrigan just fall off the cliff by the airfield? Why can't this guy's dad just get transferred somewhere else, preferably on the other side of the world?*

Jack hated this! He knew he needed to clear his head and *focus*. But the questions were coming at him so fast he couldn't. *Why am I such a target? Why does Ryan want to obliterate me? Why did he hate me from the start?*

"Yeah, that's what I figured, McMasters," Kerrigan sneered. "You're a complete panty waist!"

"Hey, tough guy, you want Jack, you get all of us!" The voice came from behind Jack.

Queenie. Even without turning, Jack knew she had her "kill look" on.

"Yeah, you, tough guy. You want to take on all of us?" Jack knew she was staring Kerrigan down and that everyone knew Jack's friends outnumbered Kerrigan's gang two to one.

It was Kerrigan who finally blinked.

"Yeah, that's what I thought." Queenie's eyes never left Kerrigan. "Come on, guys. Let's go."

And to Jack's amazement, Kerrigan didn't do anything about it.

Once past them, he did hear Kerrigan taunt, "Don't worry, Jack. Your ass whuppin' is still coming. You just wait. One of these days your sister and her girlfriends won't be around to protect you."

But everyone knew that Ryan Kerrigan had just backed down. No one said anything until they finally turned the corner at the main gate and headed up the long hill to The Glass House.

"Who was that jerk?" Queenie asked. "Why does he hate you, Jack?"

Before Jack had a chance to answer, Charlie said, "He's in our class. He's the guy who pushes everyone around. Jack was just today's target. Next time it'll probably be me."

"Well, piss on him!" said Queenie, breaking into a big smile. "Were we great or what!"

They all started laughing about how Kerrigan and his gang had backed down. Jack knew he should be feeling like crap, but for some strange reason he suddenly felt great. Queenie could be a real pain-in-the-butt; however, right now she was okay in his book. For some unexplainable reason, this band of Glass House kids had come together. It was one of those deciding moments. Jack knew that they'd be together from then on.

As they neared The Glass House, Rabbit and her friends cut and ran . . . to who knows where. Queenie eased over to Jack and said in a low voice, "I know you don't want to, Jack, but one of these days you're gonna have to deal with Kerrigan."

"I know," Jack said, reluctantly.

But before their discussion got much further, Camila interrupted, "So what are we gonna do?"

"I don't know about you guys, but I think we're gonna play Cowboys and Indians," said Charlie. "Remember in the movie how they circled the wagons and the Indians attacked? Let's do that."

"So, who's gonna to be the Indians and who's gonna be the cowboys?" asked Queenie.

"If you want, we'll be the Indians," said Jack.

Camila nodded.

"I got it," said Charlie. "Since we don't have any wagons, you cowboys set up in the Nazi pillbox and make that your fort. We'll go hide out in the woods and attack."

"Perfect. Laura, we'll show you where," said Camila.

"As for weapons, what do you guys have?" asked Charlie. "I have two six-guns the cowboys can use."

"We have a rifle I can get," said Jayla.

Camila called over her shoulder, "I think my little brother has a bow and arrows. I'll get 'em."

"Everybody back in fifteen," Charlie yelled after them.

Jack looked at him. "And let me guess: If you're on time, you're late."

"You're catching on," his new friend said with a grin.

They scattered to get weapons, but were soon back together, dividing them up. Charlie and his Indians got the rifle and the bow with three rubber-tipped arrows. Queenie and the cowboys, actually cowgirls, got the two six-guns. They hiked to the Nazi pillbox. The cowgirls started setting up their fort. Charlie and the Indians headed deeper into the woods to prepare.

Once out of sight, all the Indians started talking at the same time about the best way to attack. Jayla whipped out a tube of red lipstick.

Jack raised an eyebrow. "What's that for?"

"War paint."

Opening the lipstick tube, she put a bright-red slash across his forehead. Everyone grinned. Then she applied red lightning bolts down each of his cheeks, declaring, "These are the war symbols of our tribe."

Everyone nodded.

She applied the same slashes of red to Sam and Charlie. Sam then drew the marks on Jayla.

By then most of the tube was gone. Almost to herself, Jayla said, "Oh well. I don't suppose my mom is gonna be too happy about this, but on with the battle plan."

"Okay. What do we have for intel?" asked Jack, as if he were a major general commanding a huge army. They went over the location of the pillbox and how the cowgirls would probably position themselves. Finally, they went over the routes they could take.

"Good. Very solid intel." Jack was morphing into full commander role. "But how are we gonna handle the security and surprise?"

Jayla cracked up. "Security and surprise?" Her giggles grew louder as she looked from warrior to warrior wearing winter coat, snow pants, hat, gloves, boots, and . . . lipstick.

Sam and Charlie started cracking up, too.

But Jack wouldn't shift out of commander mode. "Yes, security and surprise. *Security* is how we're going to sneak up on them without getting busted. *Surprise* is how we're going to catch them unawares so we can shock the snot out of 'em. That's how we get them: before they get us."

He sounded cool, but their laughter, even more than Kerrigan's taunts, shook his confidence. Was he making a fool of himself? Would any of them follow him?

Fortunately for Jack, their laughter quickly died away, and everyone started sharing ideas for their battle plan. They figured all the cowboys would stay inside their fort, protected from attack, with clear visibility of what was in front of them. So, instead of mounting a frontal attack, the Indians decided to approach the bunker, unseen, from the rear. The plan was to make their way up and over the bunker, lean over the top, surprise the cowgirls, and shoot them all.

"Okay, so we're all clear about the objective, right?" questioned Jack. Jack couldn't help himself; he'd jumped right back into being General Jack.

Sam cracked up again. "Man, where do you come up with all this stuff? *Intel, security, surprise,* and now *objective.*"

"Don't ya get it? We need to fight for the same thing. Our objective for this battle is 'Overrun the bunker and kill or capture all the cowgirls.' Are we each clear on that?"

With enthusiasm, and a broad smirk, Charlie yelled, "Overrun the bunker and kill or capture all the cowgirls—*hooah!*"

"God bless you," said Jayla, as if Charlie had just sneezed.

"Come on, Jayla, you gotta know *Hooah!* It's the best of all tanker cries. Like '*Geronimo!*'"

"For tankers, yes," said Jayla. "But I seriously doubt Indians ever yelled '*Hooah!*' before a battle."

Unfortunately, for all their talk of objective, security, and surprise, they hadn't planned for the unexpected. But they certainly got it. As they climbed onto the pillbox from behind, Queenie came sneaking up the side steps and out on top—*Bam, Bam, Bam!* She unloaded on them. Whether she had come up by luck or had planned to, they didn't know. But either way, she spotted the Indian attack and started shooting her pistol at them. The noise alerted the other cowgirls.

Charlie, reacting quickly, shot an arrow at Queenie. Of course, the suction-cupped arrow barely left the bow.

Jack, aiming a stick at her, yelled, "Bang! Bang! Bang! I got ya."

"No, you didn't! You're long dead!" she yelled back, "I got Charlie, and I got you, too!"

Sam and Jayla left Charlie and Jack to deal with Queenie. They sprinted over the roof of the pillbox and leaned over the front edge to shoot Liz and Camila. The two cowgirls were ready with guns raised.

Everyone was screaming, "I got you!" and "Did not! I got you first!"

They were all arguing, all laughing. It had been a great battle because both sides had surprised the crap out of the other.

They sprawled on top of the bunker and talked about having another battle, but they never quite got around to it. Everyone figured nothing would be as good as that first one. Then just as they were getting ready to head back to The Glass House, Queenie spotted movement in the woods. She quietly asked, "Who are those older kids?"

Jayla, caught up in the conversation, finally glanced up—and froze. "It's Kerrigan's gang!" she whispered. "Maybe they haven't spotted us yet. Quick everyone, get back into the pillbox. Do it now, before there's trouble. And don't make any sudden moves that attract attention."

"What d'ya mean by trouble?" demanded Queenie, not being quiet at all. "Aren't those the same creeps who gave Jack a hard time?"

"Shhhh!" said Camila. "We'll explain later. For now, just move out before something bad happens."

Queenie trusted her friend and decided not to make a fuss. She followed the others who were quietly slipping back into the pillbox.

"Scrunch down on the floor below the opening in case they happen to look in," Charlie hissed.

"Why are we avoiding those toads?" asked Queenie, getting impatient.

But Jayla, looking alarmed, put a finger to her lips.

Sam whispered to Queenie, "Let's just sit quiet and see if they pass by."

Jack wondered wildly if hiding would do much good. Kerrigan had probably spotted them. Jack had seen Kerrigan take a knee and pass back hand signals.

The brats remained frozen in place for the next ten minutes.

Dampness from the concrete wall penetrated Jack's winter coat. Remaining motionless was getting harder and harder. The cold was robbing him of what little patience he had.

Finally, Jayla lifted her head a few inches above the opening of the pillbox. Then, turning to the others, she mouthed the words, "I think they're gone." She motioned for everyone to stay put as she checked behind the bunker.

It seemed to take forever before she returned. But in a low voice she said, "I think they went right by us. Anyway, they're gone."

"Okay," said Queenie, exasperated, "you want to tell us what *that* was all about?"

"That," said Jayla, "wasn't just Kerrigan and his gang. They were with some of the Sevens."

"Who are the Sevens?" asked Jack. "Why are you afraid of them?"

"If you think Ryan is bad, you ain't seen nothin' yet," Charlie said. "They're a badass bunch of older kids. They call themselves the Sevens because there were seven of them when the gang formed. Some originals were transferred, but no matter. Today there are more than seven, and they think they own these woods. They've beat up lots of kids they've found out here."

"That sounds like a load of crap," Queenie said.

"But it's not," said Charlie. "A couple months ago they beat a kid so bad they put him in the hospital. And the younger kids they recruit—they're the worst. They'll pound you into the ground over nothing—just to prove themselves to the older kids. We don't let them stop us from playing in these woods, but we definitely try not to cross paths with them."

Jack said, "But why would they let Kerrigan hang out with them? He's our age."

"Close as I can figure," said Jayla, "they'd only include him in things that are risky or bad."

Sam nodded. "He thinks he's cool, because he gets to hang with the Sevens. He doesn't want to see they're just using him."

"If Kerrigan and his gang do their dirty work," said Jayla, "it's Kerrigan who takes the rap, not the Sevens."

Jack sighed. "Nothing's ever simple, is it?"

"Probably not. But, hey, no big deal. Shake it off. We ducked 'em . . . at least for today," said Charlie.

On the way back to The Glass House, the mood lightened. Laughter broke out as they told and re-told The Battle of Fort Pillbox.

Jayla said, "I guess *surprise* works both ways. We planned to surprise the cowboys, and we did. But they definitely surprised us, too. Next time, we better work a little harder on the *security* part of our battle plan, so we don't get caught with our guard down."

Jack grinned at her. "Wow, you get it."

She rewarded his smile with a smirk. "I'm not an idiot, Jack. I *do* catch on."

She does, Jack thought to himself, liking her. *And she's right. We need to work on our security. Not just for war games—to avoid serious problems with Kerrigan and the Sevens.*

The Indians all went to Charlie's place to wash off their war paint. And they certainly made a valiant attempt. But no amount of soap and water faded the lipstick. At first, it was funny—at least until it dawned on them they might be wearing red lipstick for the next week. Then mild panic set in.

Charlie, in desperation, got his mom. Easygoing as always, she just chuckled. But she wasn't much help.

The vinegar she brought smelled awful and did nothing.

Sam said, "What are we gonna do about this? My dad'll lose it if I don't get this stuff off."

"So will mine," said Jack. "In fact, I don't even want to think about what he might do."

Charlie stayed calm. "Whose mom knows more about makeup than mine?"

There was silence for a bit, until Jayla finally coughed up that her mom was really good at makeup. She hated to ask her mom for help, and they didn't blame her. Mrs. Jones thought her lipstick was tucked in her makeup bag—not on them.

"Jayla, there's just no choice. We need her help. If we stay like this, we're all in big trouble." Sam pleaded.

Reluctantly, Jayla trudged up Charlie's stairwell to her quarters on the third floor, with the rest of the Indians in tow.

Jack had never even met Mrs. Jones—definitely an awkward situation. This time, his special talent for meeting parents deserted him. The first thing that slowed him down was what a fox Mrs. Jones was. No one—kid or adult—ever failed to notice that Mrs. Jones was beautiful. She was a statuesque Negro woman. Jack was sure she was, or at least had been, a fashion model.

The second thing that messed him up was her "Who do you think you are, young man?" look. Which was immediately followed up with a glare that seemed to say, "Just what kind of trouble have you gotten into?"

Jack knew he'd better come up with something fast. After a quick breath, he put on one of his charming smiles and extended his hand. "It's nice to meet you, Mrs. Jones. My name is Jack McMasters. My father is Lt. Col. McMasters. We just moved into one of the third-floor apartments on the other side of this building."

She seemed to soften just a hair, giving him her hand to shake. He took his next shot. "I'm sorry to be introducing myself when I'm all painted up like this. But you see, we all got very excited by the Saturday movie. It was a cowboy and Indian movie. Afterwards, we decided to have a cowboy and Indian war." He paused to get a read on how he was doing.

"And let me guess," she said, with just the hint of a smile. "The four of you *weren't* on the side of the cowboys?"

"Exactly right, ma'am," he said. "But before I head home, I thought it might be a good idea to . . . to give up being an Indian and turn back into Jack McMasters. Unfortunately, we are having a rather hard time getting our war paint off. We tried soap and water at Charlie's quarters, but that didn't work too well."

"And, pray tell, what form of Indian paint are you sporting, young Jack?"

"Well, a rare, and precious variety, called . . . lipstick."

"What!" she exclaimed. And then, she *did* crack up.

"Yes, ma'am."

For the longest time, she got all serious, studying poor Jack. None of them could tell if she was just torturing him or truly stumped. "Are you sure you really want it off? It's a great color."

Doing his best to keep a straight face, Jack said, "Yes, ma'am, I definitely want it off."

"I guess I see the dilemma. You girls by no means look great, but you boys will definitely look funny at school with lipstick all over your faces. You might have a tough time explaining it." Another pause.

"Now, let me see . . . getting lipstick off a child's face. Surely there must be a way. That is, without a doctor performing surgery. I doubt we'll have to burn it off. Do you—"

"Mom! Stop torturing us. This is serious! Just tell us the answer," Jayla pleaded.

Mrs. Jones flashed them a radiant smile. "My beautiful band of Indians, the magic answer is nothing other than . . . baby oil."

"Baby oil?" they all shouted in disbelief.

"Yes, indeed. Come right this way, you wild warriors." She gestured toward the bathroom.

"You first, my fine little brave. It's time to turn you back into Jack McMasters." After spreading baby oil on Jack's face, she rummaged through her washcloths for a red one. By then the oil was doing its magic. With just a bit of elbow grease on her part, Mrs. Jones wiped the lipstick off his face.

Glancing in the mirror, he smiled at her reflection.

"Welcome back, Jack McMasters," she said.

"Really, Mrs. Jones. You're a life saver."

"Okay, Jayla, you now know how it's done. Do the others." With that, Jayla's mom left them to solve the war paint problem on their own.

When she was gone, Jack said, "Your mom's a genius."

"Told you. She's great at all things makeup," Jayla said, smiling.

"Was she a fashion model?" Jack asked.

Jayla stopped smiling. "Are you messing with me? Of course not," she said coldly.

"What?" he asked, confused. "Did I say something wrong?"

Her expression softened. "You really don't know?"

He shook his head.

"Me, neither," said Charlie.

"There are no Negro fashion models," Jayla said.

"What do you mean?" Jack asked.

"Think about it. Have you ever seen a colored fashion model in *Vogue* magazine or for that matter *any* big magazine? No, you haven't. That's because no magazine will show colored people and white people together in the same magazine."

"Hey, you're right," said Sam. "Why didn't I ever notice that?"

"So there are no colored fashion models?" asked Jack.

"I've only seen them in *Ebony*, but that's a magazine for colored people," said Jayla. "Look, things are different for brats. Our whole lives, we've gone to school with white kids, colored kids, Korean kids, Japanese kids, and who-knows-what-kinda kids."

"Sure," said Jack.

"The rest of America goes to school with white kids or Negro kids, but not both. When you went to church off base back in America, were there any Negro people in your church?"

Jack's brow wrinkled. "I guess not."

"If we weren't part of the US Army, I'd be in some all-colored school right now."

They were silent till Charlie blurted out, "Hey, what time is it?"

Jack looked at his dad's old Elgin watch. "Fifteen minutes till six. I gotta split."

＞＜○○╼╉┝╾○＜

On his way out, he said thanks again to Mrs. Jones.

"Say hi to your mom for me, Jack, and tell her it was nice to meet her."

"You know my mom?"

"Absolutely. She and your dad were over here for our cocktail party last night. In fact, I have a feeling your mom and I are going to be good friends."

That gave Jack a rather nice feeling. He was starting to like Cooke Barracks.

14

Sunday Ritual

When Jack went to bed that night, he never imagined he'd spend the next day in an ancient civilization. But that's exactly what happened. The Sunday ritual started the same as usual: Lt. Col. McMasters prepared to take the children to church while Mrs. McMasters stayed home to create the great banquet she called Sunday breakfast.

They loaded into their dad's big, blue '55 Buick Roadmaster, which the colonel had had the Army ship overseas the moment he got orders for Germany. But instead of going to church on base, the colonel had decided they'd go to the cathedral in the center of Göppingen. As they walked across the square of the ancient city, Jack saw no other Americans. No English was being spoken. And as they entered the four-hundred-year-old cathedral, it felt like they were walking into the Middle Ages.

The church felt like a tomb, cold and dark, with its only light from candles flickering on the stone walls. Once inside, Jack's eyes lifted from the well-worn stone slabs of the floor, traveling way, way up to the vaulted ceiling. It must have been four or five stories high. Halfway up the side walls, he could make out recessed walkways visible through stone archways.

Wonder where those archways lead, he said to himself. *Wish I could get up there to explore.*

As they moved farther inside, music erupted from out of nowhere, really amazing and really loud. Turning, Jack spotted a huge organ up high in the rear of the church. Rapid notes shot out of its giant pipes, raising the hairs on the back of his neck. *Maybe Bach or Beethoven. Doesn't sound much like heaven,* thought Jack. *In fact, it sounds more like God is really ticked off this morning.*

As they walked up the center aisle to find seats, the organist suddenly stopped; the only sounds were their Sunday shoes striking the stone floor.

Jack winced. *Now everyone in this whole place can hear us coming in late.*

Fortunately, most people ignored them, remaining eyes-front as a priest in long, green-and-silver robes walked toward the altar.

Finally, halfway up the aisle, the McMasterses managed to find a place. Before entering the pew, each kid knelt on one knee, making the sign of the cross. They hadn't been seated long when the priest began shouting something. Everyone got on their knees, so they did, too.

Is that German or Latin? Jack wondered. Catching a few familiar words, he knew it must be Latin. Then for the Gospel reading and the sermon, the priest switched to German. *He sounds as irritated as I am about being here this early. That's not preaching, it's yelling and screaming,* Jack thought. *No wonder no one's looking at us. They're too afraid if they look away he'll storm off the platform to smack the snot out of them.*

Even with eyes-front, Jack took it all in. It was mysterious, reverent, ancient. He liked it. Especially when the priest, surrounded by his altar boys, started swinging an ornate, golden ball that had white smoke pouring out. It smelled amazing. There was something about the cold air, the smell of incense, the sound of the organ music, and the Latin chants that made this dark, candlelit tomb seem magical. It put Jack into a kind of trance.

While he knelt, he imagined the stone cutters working year after year to build the place. He envisioned a man in medieval robes kneeling in this same spot hundreds of years before. The man would have been listening to a priest chant the same Latin phrases.

Jack's eyelids grew heavy and his legs tired of kneeling. Without a conscious effort he could no longer maintain the straight-up kneeling position he was supposed to. His butt leaned back against the bench. His body slouched. Jack nodded off.

Queenie jabbed an elbow into his ribs.

His eyes sprang open. When he turned to scowl at her, she nodded toward their father.

The colonel was giving Jack the "kill look."

That was all the adrenalin Jack needed. Fully alert, his back went ramrod straight.

But as the service droned on, the same drugged feeling came back. The longer he listened to the organ music and Latin chants, and smelled the thick incense, the sleepier he got.

He started yawning. The first were little yawns that he could stifle. But it wasn't long before his head rocked back, his eyes closed, and his mouth opened wider than seemed humanly possible. He made a deep groaning sound, gulping in a massive amount of air. The yawns kept coming, one after another. He just couldn't help himself. Jack was in a trance, hit by a spell—

Whack! Another elbow to the ribs from Queenie.

Another "kill look" from the colonel.

Snapping back into focus, Jack knew he'd better wake up—and fast. *What's wrong with me? I keep shutting down. I do it when Kerrigan comes at me. I even do it in church.*

He made a valiant effort to remain awake, but within ten minutes he was nodding off again. Mercifully, at that moment the service ended. In a near catatonic state, Jack shuffled behind Queenie out of the cathedral. But that catatonic state didn't last long.

They were only a few steps outside the cathedral when Jack was yanked back into reality. His dad placed a vice grip on his shoulder and whipped Jack's body around to face him. Jack looked up into the glaring eyes of one seriously pissed-off military officer. Never releasing Jack's shoulder, the colonel growled in a whisper, "Jack McMasters, don't you *ever* embarrass me like that again. You sorry excuse for a human being. You are one extremely poor representative of the United States of America. Every self-respecting German in that place saw your slothful, bored, lazy demeanor. You had better learn to get more sleep before church on Sunday mornings. Do it, or you and I are definitely going the rounds. Do I make myself clear, young man?"

"Yes, sir," was all Jack said. After all, there was nothing more to be said—if he knew what was good for him.

The colonel didn't say another word, but his angry scowl kept on talking. *You keep yawning like that in church, or slouching back instead of kneeling upright, and I'm going to punch your lights out.*

Jack had violated the McMasters motto: "Look sharp, act sharp, be sharp."

With their brother in trouble, the girls knew enough to keep a low profile. Everyone marched back to the car in silence. That is, until they were
almost there and Queenie called, "Shotgun!"

For once Jack was just fine with her having dibs on the front seat. He
slipped into the back seat, scrunching down to stay as far away from his
father as possible. Somehow he needed to make it through this, make it
till the old man cooled off. *How long is it gonna take this time? How bad
is it gonna get?*

What can I do to make it stop?

He hated being in the car when his dad was ticked off. It was too
easy for the colonel to focus those hard, gray, laser-beam eyes on him. In
laser-beam mode, those eyes could always find yet another thing wrong
with him.

An alarm went off in Jack's head. He screamed to himself, *You idiot!
What are you doing scrunching down?* He straightened himself up before
the colonel could catch him and again start yelling that he was a worthless,
slouching slacker. For the first time all morning, Jack sincerely prayed.
God, just let me get through this car ride, so I can get away from him.

"Look at those German people leaving the church. Look how nicely they're
dressed." In the front seat, Lt. Col. McMasters was talking to Queenie.

He seems to have calmed down. Has the anger gone? Jack pretended
he wasn't listening, but his radar was on high alert. *Dad really likes the
Germans. He likes being stationed in Germany. Please, God, let him focus
on the Germans and not on me.*

"I think we'll stop at one of the bakeries and get a nice loaf of hard-
crust bread."

Jack could feel the tension in the car lessen. Whenever the colonel's
tension eased, the whole family's tension eased. Staring out the car window, he tried to think of ways he could stay awake in church. Maybe he
should keep a safety pin in his pocket and stab himself if he started to nod
off. But he didn't really think a pinprick would have helped today. Was his
dad right about getting more sleep? No, he'd slept great last night, but his
whole system still shut down in church.

Crap, I'd better figure somethin' out or I'm gonna get killed. His mind turned away from an image of the colonel looming over him with his belt and brought up the face of Mr. Reynolds instead. That conversation they'd had. Jack decided he'd better go find out what the principal knew about shutting down. Better yet, what he knew about *not* shutting down.

He would have kept grinding on it, but Rabbit was next to him behind the colonel, and she chose that moment to mimic his yawns during church. Jack flashed her a "cut it out" look, but that just seemed to encourage her. At first, hers were just silent, mocking yawns, but with each one she got a little louder. Any moment the colonel would notice.

Jack swatted her leg. "Stop it," he hissed, "or you're gonna get it."

"I will if you play with me one whole hour this afternoon."

"Nope," he mouthed.

She spread her arms, preparing to let loose the loudest yawn yet.

Jack caved. "All right. One hour. Now knock it off."

She gently patted his knee. "I love when we play together, big brother."

Trying to ignore her, Jack glanced out the window at the German people his dad had been talking about. A group of men were walking along the sidewalk. One of them was wearing a rather short, dark coat and a dark-green hat with its brim pulled down. Jack wasn't paying all that much attention, but the sight jogged his brain. Something about those men. . . . He kept staring. Then it hit him: that guy in the wood by the cliff had the same coat and hat. Could this be The Watcher? No sooner had he put it all together than the guy was gone. Jack whipped around to stare out the back window, but his dad had gone around a corner. Nothing.

Five minutes later, they pulled up to a bakery and the girls got out with the colonel. Wanting to distance himself from his dad, Jack stayed in the car. He scanned the near-empty street. *Why haven't I thought about The Watcher since that night? Guess I didn't figure we'd actually find him. Now he pops up out of nowhere.* Jack nervously rubbed his hands on his pants.

Up at the corner, two men crossed the street. Both had on short coats and dark-green felt hats with brims. Clearly neither was the guy he'd just seen.

Jack sat very still, trying to remember other details about the guy in the woods. Jack saw his sisters and father coming out of the bakery, just as a man and woman were walking in. To Jack's absolute astonishment, *that* guy had on the same coat and hat, too. *Come on! How many of these guys can there be?*

When they got in the car, Jack said, "Dad, look in the bakery. Do you see that man with the short dark coat and the green hat like Dick Tracy's?"

"I see him, Jack. What about him?"

"Have you ever seen anyone wearing a green hat like that?"

"Those hats? Sure. You see them all over Germany. Why do you ask?"

"Oh, nothing. I've just never seen a hat like that before."

"Now that you're in Germany, you'll see plenty."

That's that, thought Jack. *We thought we could identify him by his clothes. That won't be happening. So much for trying to be like Jean-Sébastien.*

One good thing about Jack was he never stayed down for long. A most excellent breakfast restored his spirits. Mrs. McMasters had really outdone herself on their first Sunday in Germany. She had made them bacon, sausage, and fried potatoes, and promised to fry or scramble eggs, whichever way they wanted.

Not for the first time, Jack thought to himself, *Other moms could try to make this breakfast, but it would never taste as good.*

For his mom, breakfast was a major art form. It was entertainment. Her scrambled eggs seemed so simple, but they were pure genius. First, she never made them till the very last moment. Second, she pulled out her old cast-iron frying pan and lit a huge flame under it. She let the pan get so hot you'd think it would melt. (Jack figured there must be magic in that old frying pan, and that was why she packed it in her own suitcase for the trip to Germany, rather than entrusting it to the movers.) Third, she put bacon grease in the pan.

"Now," she'd say, "don't *ever* let *anyone* give you any grief that bacon grease is bad for you! Bad, my eye! Bacon grease is the secret ingredient to the perfect egg." She'd let the bacon grease get so hot it began to smoke. Then, with great flare, she'd say, "Is your plate ready? Don't blink twice or they'll already be done."

In one big swish, she'd pour in the eggs, stirring them like crazy from the moment they hit that pan to the second they were done. It actually *did* take less than two blinks of an eye.

Her real genius in cooking was insisting on only the best ingredients. But it didn't hurt that she had exceptional cooking technique, combined with a killer sense of timing.

The eggs delivered, she didn't miss a beat. Next came coffee for the parents and cocoa, with marshmallows, for the kids. The feast began! But, like all great performers, she saved the best for last. What none of them knew was that she'd made something else—something amazing.

A moment later she glided back into the dining room with a huge smile and a platter of her world-class popovers.

Everyone went crazy, especially Lt. Col. McMasters. They were his absolute favorite. Her popovers were a light and airy pastry that the colonel would load up with butter and jam. Scrumptious. Sunday breakfast at the McMasterses' was a sight to behold.

While they were feasting, Mrs. McMasters said, "Jack, your friend Charlie Carron came by just before you got home. He wants to know if you want to go sledding."

"Absolutely," was all Jack said.

"I want to go!" said Rabbit. "Jack, you promised."

"Me, too," said Queenie, piling on.

Their dad winked at their mom, saying, "I guess we know what the children are up to this afternoon."

In the smoothest and nicest way, Lt. Col. McMasters had just given Jack good news and bad. He'd said Jack could go sledding. But only if he took the girls along.

Jack didn't want them tagging after, but if his sisters had to be part of the package, so be it.

Charlie came back just as breakfast was concluding. Jack said he could go on two conditions: if he could bring Queenie and Rabbit, and if Charlie could wait till the dishes were done. Because, of course, the kids had to wash all the dishes before they could leave; cooking and serving such a feast generated plenty of dirty pots and pans and plates. Charlie said he'd wait.

As soon as Mrs. McMasters pronounced things spick-and-span, the kids bundled up in their winter gear and headed for Charlie's. Those dishes had been done in record time. Sledding is important.

When they got to Charlie's, Sam was there, too. As always, she was anxious to get going.

"What about sleds?" asked Jack. "We don't have sleds yet."

"No problem. We got you covered," said Sam. "I have two. Charlie has one. And Jayla loaned us two."

Charlie described in detail where they were going as they dragged their sleds from The Glass House, all the way across the base, out the main gate, down a big hill, and back up another long hill. There were at least fifty other kids already sledding.

It was indeed a great sledding hill. Perfect for racing. All five of them lined up next to each other and took off together. Jack's face cut through the icy air, his heart racing. He loved it. As he traveled down, the hill got steeper and steeper. Scraping sounds came off the blades as they cut over the hard-packed snow, and he flew faster and faster. Only at the bottom did it smooth out enough to slow him to a halt.

He was still lying on his sled when Rabbit glided up alongside him.

She vaulted off her sled, grabbed the tow rope, and started sprinting back up the hill, yelling, "Let's do it again!" Rabbit was Rabbit.

He followed her up the hill.

At first they rode down on their stomachs. Later Charlie suggested they try sitting. That was tougher. But once Jack got the hang of it, Charlie decided to see if he and Jack could both go down seated on the same sled. They wrecked the first couple of times, but finally succeeded. Back at the top of the hill, they got back on the sled.

"Outta here, Carron. This is our spot!"

Startled, Charlie looked up at a giant head covered in a ski mask that made it look like a big, brown basketball. The guy stood grinding a fist into the palm of his hand. "Get to the far side of the hill where you belong. Or else!" Behind him, Kerrigan, Tony Keach, and a whole bunch of their gang nodded slowly.

No choice. Charlie got up and they all followed.

Rabbit planted herself in front of the bully. "Hey! This is *our* spot, Basketball Head, and we're not—"

Queenie grabbed her, covering her mouth to cut her off. "We're moving along," she said, dragging the struggling Rabbit.

Once over on the far side, Rabbit started mouthing off. "Hey, why should we listen to Basketball Head?"

Queenie had loosened her headlock on Rabbit, but now retightened it and calmly explained that they had been hopelessly outnumbered. None of them liked it, but under the circumstances, they might as well try out this side of the hill.

Other than being pushed around by Basketball Head, it was a great afternoon on the sledding hill. While they were trudging along the long road to The Glass House, Jack asked, "How come Jayla didn't come with us? Doesn't she like sledding?"

"Oh, she loves sledding, but her parents wouldn't let her come today."

"Is she in trouble?"

"Not too bad. Mainly it's because she has family stuff—a trip to some castle. But she won't be going to the Saturday movie anytime soon. Mrs. Jones finally put two and two together about where we got the Indian war paint. She said Jayla has to buy her a new lipstick, which'll take all the money she gets from her next two allowances."

"Hmm. Guess it could have been worse. Her parents certainly aren't shy about giving her grief."

"Yeah, they hold her to a crazy high standard," said Sam.

"What do you mean?" asked Jack, figuring he had it just as bad.

Sam asked, "Would your parents, or mine, give us a hard time if we got a B on a test? Never, right? Well, remember our reading test last week?"

"Please. I'm trying to forget about tests," Jack groaned. "I only *wish* I'd gotten a B. I haven't caught up with you all in the book, so I had no clue about half the questions."

"Well, Jayla got just one question wrong. Unfortunately that gave her a B on the test."

"So?"

"So Jayla's parents go ballistic if she gets anything but straight A's. Her mom stormed around yelling, 'Lt. Col. Jones's daughter does *not* get B's!' Then she marched up to Mrs. Campbell after school and demanded an A. Jayla said she'd given the right answer but our book had the facts wrong. She then produced not one, but two different library books proving her point. Would you believe it? Mrs. Campbell actually seemed pleased by the whole thing and gave her the A."

"Jayla reads library books?" Jack asked, incredulous. "Even when they haven't been assigned?"

"McMasters, sometimes you are so blind. Haven't you noticed Jayla carrying a ton of books everywhere? Her parents make her read two or three extra library books a week."

"Wow," Jack said. "Good thing Jayla's the smartest kid I've ever met, or she'd never survive her parents."

Trudging along, Jack was grinding on Jayla's situation. It didn't feel right. "Sam, I've been thinking about it, and we all used that lipstick. Jayla shouldn't have to take the whole rap. Shouldn't we each pay our share of the new one?"

Surprised by his suggestion, Sam studied him for a moment. "Good idea, Jack. I'll let her know."

Queenie and Rabbit were moving fast, desperate to get home. Rabbit had been complaining that if they didn't get there soon she was going to wet her pants. Jack let them run ahead. He dropped back to be with Sam and Charlie. That gave him a chance to fill them in on his morning in Göppingen and the man in the exact same coat and hat as The Watcher.

"I mean, I really thought it was our guy. He was just four feet from my car window—it scared the snot out of me."

"And?" Charlie demanded, getting excited.

"And I kid you not. I kept seeing more and more Germans in short, dark coats and green hats. I began to think Göppingen was a town full of spies. Then it dawned on me, short coats and green hats don't mean *anything*, except that a lot of German men like 'em."

"Guess I never noticed that," said Charlie.

Sam frowned in thought. "Well, I suppose I have, but I never put two and two together till now."

It got them debating whether The Watcher really had been spying. They still had no idea why, but in their gut they knew he was a spy.

By the time they reached The Glass House, they were cold, wet, and worn out. Jack's sisters were long gone, so they went to Charlie's to warm up . . . and try to convince Mrs. Carron they needed cocoa.

When they got inside, Charlie went with the direct approach, yelling at the top of his lungs, "Mom! We're home! We're starving! Can we have cocoa?"

Mrs. Carron's heart melted at the sight of three frozen snow children. "How was it?"

As she helped them peel off their snow gear, they all talked at once to answer her question. They were still giving details as she arranged the marshmallows on their hot chocolate. Chuckling over their sledding stories, she piled warm cookies on a plate.

Life was good at Charlie's.

15

Grafenwöhr

Three nights later, in the middle of the night, Jack's father vanished. So did most of the other fathers. Jack didn't find out about it until breakfast the next morning when he asked, "Where's Dad?"

"He's on maneuvers," his mom said airily. "All the tanks rolled out of here at zero four hundred this morning."

"Four o'clock in the morning?" Queenie said, concerned. "They must have been up most of the night. Is something bad happening?"

"Your father got a phone call about one o'clock this morning. The whole base went on Full Alert. He just grabbed his gear and left."

"When will dad get home?" Rabbit asked in the middle of a big yawn. She was still half asleep and not really paying much attention.

Their mother shrugged. "I don't know. It could be days or weeks."

"Mom, you're not telling us. Has something bad happened? I mean, Dad's not going back to war, is he?"

Queenie—always with the questions, thought Jack, but he wanted to know, too.

"Now don't be worrying about all that, children. Your dad will be just fine. He'll get home when he gets home. Eat up, and get ready for school. The bus will be here soon."

Jack knew his mom was done talking, and that she probably didn't know that much herself. All the same, he studied her face for signs of tension. It was a complete mask. Jack wasn't really all that worried. He and Queenie had been through this plenty of times. As for Rabbit, she was so young she didn't know to care.

Then Jack started thinking, *Most of the other times, we were stationed in the States, not overseas. In the States, it was always just training. They'd go off for a few days with all their tanks and equipment to practice war exercises. Even though Dad took those mock battles very seriously, there was no danger. It was no big deal. But would they do mock battles in Germany? Was this the real thing?*

∞✟∞

When Jack got to the bus stop, all the talk was about the tanks rolling in the middle of the night. Jack and Charlie sat together, trying to hear what the older kids were saying.

"Hey, if the entire 4th Armored Division rolled outta here in the middle of the night—that's some serious *Scheiße*," said a good-looking kid with a dark crewcut. "It could be the Nazis are coming back to throw us out. I figure they're trying to take over the world again. We probably gotta go shut 'em down."

"You really think the Nazis might be coming back?" asked a girl sitting across the aisle. She seemed more interested in him than in what was going on.

"Obviously," he said, ignoring her and speaking to anyone else willing to listen. "They tried in World War I, and they tried again in World War II. What makes you think they'll quit now?" He turned to the girl. "Why do you think we're in Germany? We're here to stop the Nazis from coming back to power."

"Shut up, big mouth," hissed another a kid sitting in front of him. "Next, you'll be broadcasting our plans to the entire bus."

"I'm not talking about finding the Nazi's *stuff*," the kid hissed back. "I'm talking about finding *Nazis*."

"Shut your face, dink, or you're out."

Charlie and Jack looked at each other, not sure what to make of all that. But they certainly knew better than to let the older boys know they'd overheard. Turning away, they focused on two high-school kids sitting behind them.

"Yeah, and I'll tell you something else. My ol' man's the S-3. He runs Plans . . . so one of his jobs is to draw up a lot of plans for what 4th Armored should do if war comes. Anyway, I remember one time last summer after they'd been out on maneuvers. I asked if 4th Armored ever went on maneuvers in the winter. He said, 'Not if we can help it.' He said that it's a real pain to move out in the snow. So, I ask you this: Why did they mobilize last night?"

In the seat across from them were two high-school kids. So far they hadn't said anything. But one leaned over to his friend and in a low voice said, "And they carried live rounds."

"How do you know that?" asked his friend.

"You know what my dad does."

"Head armorer."

"Last night I heard him barking orders into the phone to get more staff on the shift. He said they needed to equip every tank with live, armor-piercing rounds as well as simulation rounds."

"Why the extra staff?"

"The short notice, I guess. The shells are about a hundred pounds each so it's not a one-man job. It took some hustling, but they rolled out on time, armed to the teeth."

"Know where they were headed?" asked a kid behind him.

"Dunno, but they normally go to Grafenwöhr."

"Yeah, up in tank land," said another kid. "During World War II, Graf's the place where Rommel trained his Panzerkorps before going up against General Patton in North Africa."

"Rommel was Hitler's best tank commander," a kid piped up. "Graf's up there on the East German border right near Czechoslovakia. Land of the Commies."

"Oh, yeah! One-on-one with the Commies!" shouted someone in the back of the bus.

Charlie raised an eyebrow in Jack's direction.

Jack leaned over to Charlie. "You know who the Commies are?"

"Not really," he whispered back. "All I hear is they're the bad guys."

When they got off the bus, Charlie said, "I don't get half that stuff about the Nazis coming back or about the Commies. You?"

"Me, neither," said Jack. "But it seems like something serious might be going down."

They were both lost in their own thoughts as they wandered into class.

∞⊶⊷∞

Mrs. Campbell began the day by writing a math problem on the blackboard. She called on child after child to try solving it. Kerrigan was the third one to get twisted up and fail. He didn't seem the least concerned.

Then she called on Jack.

Jack tried to ignore Kerrigan's dagger eyes on him. He knew Kerrigan wanted him to fail. But, unlike reading, math came naturally to Jack. He'd seen the solution while the second kid tried to do it, so he calmly solved the problem and sat back down. On the way back to his seat, Mrs. Campbell gave him a knowing nod. *She knows I can do math.*

Unfortunately, the next thing she announced was reading discussion groups. Jack hated reading, but he hated reading discussion groups even more. He'd asked Jayla for the lowdown on how they worked in their class. He'd heard there were about six kids in each group, and Mrs. Campbell worked with one group at a time. She'd go from group to group, checking their comprehension by having each kid read part of the passage *out loud*. No group was called the best or the worst; they were named for colors. But everyone had ears so they knew the red group was best and the purple group was worse. Jack got started off in that group.

The red group sat by the window. Both Sam and Jayla were in that one. Jack's heart sank when he saw Kerrigan strutting over. Kerrigan shot him a look that said, "Oh yeah, baby. You may be a math whiz, but watch this." When he finally got called on, Kerrigan sounded like a great actor reading his lines. He never messed up.

Mrs. Campbell came to the purple group next, and to Jack's horror, she asked him to read first. At that moment, he'd have chosen to *fight* Ryan Kerrigan over reading where he could hear.

My brain's gonna scramble. All the words will jump around on the page and nothing I do will keep them still. How am I supposed to read with the letters dancing?

Jack had tried to explain to his friends back in Texas about his reading problem. He'd even brought it up with a teacher once. But none of them got it. In fact, they had looked at him like he'd lost his marbles. "Printed words are stamped on the page. They don't move around, Jack." That was all anyone ever told him. So he quit talking about it. However, the more pressure he was under (including finding out he was in the worst reading discussion group), the more the words danced. For Jack, reading in front of other kids was like shouting, "Look everyone! Look how stupid I am!"

His brain was in turmoil. *My new friends think I'm halfway smart. This will kill that idea faster than a ray gun.*

The door cracked open. Everyone watched a student aide cross the room to hand Mrs. Campbell a folded note. She carefully read it, and then nodded to Jack. "Mr. Reynolds wants to see you."

Jack was stunned, completely forgetting he'd tried to see Mr. Reynolds that morning and the secretary had said she'd let the principal know.

Jack followed the aide gratefully. *Wow, Mr. Reynolds just saved me from reading discussion group!*

"Glad you decided to come and see me, Jack," Reynolds said, lifting his head out of his paperwork. "Can I assume this is about your shutting down?"

"Yes, sir," Jack said, suddenly very unsure of himself.

They sat at a small table.

"As I told you, I used to have a problem with shutting down, too." Reynolds's tone was confidential. "It was during the Korean War. No one really wanted to hear about it or help me. That is, until one day when I happened to meet a Buddhist monk. You see, Jack, that old monk somehow realized what was happening to me. You know, the shutting down thing."

How did Mr. Reynolds do that? Just a few, short words, just mentioning an old Buddhist monk, and all Jack's defenses dropped. Now he *wanted* to be in this room.

"That old monk called it 'mindfulness' or 'remaining in the present.' He told me people shut down for many different reasons. Certainly, it can happen when you're confronted with violence or danger . . . such as when Ryan Kerrigan attacked you. The monk believed he could help me redirect my brain away from its normal reaction to stressful situations—away from thoughts like, *Why me? What did I do to deserve this? I just want to go to sleep.* He said I could even learn to *appreciate* the moment. This may sound confusing, Jack, but he showed me how to stay awake and remain in the moment, instead of shutting down. That way I could deal with what was happening around me. You get what I'm saying?'

"Yeah, I *guess* I get it. But how do you do it?"

"Do you know in advance when you're about to shut down?"

"I try to fight it, but it doesn't help."

"The monk had me focus on my senses. Things like touch, sound, scent, and sight. Let's run through them."

Jack nodded.

"Great. We'll start with touch. You concentrate on the things that you can feel physically at the moment you start to shut down. What does the ground feel like beneath your feet? Can you feel a breeze against your face? Are your clothes rough or smooth? Be aware of what everything *feels like*. It works even better if you do it with your eyes closed. Of course, that's not practical if you're standing before Ryan, but if you're shutting down someplace where you're not directly confronted, try it with your eyes closed."

Like in church, Jack thought.

"Now take scent. Can you smell anything right as you're shutting down? Does the gym smell sweaty? Does Ryan have bad breath when he's up in your face?"

That made Jack laugh.

"Then there's hearing. When you're about to shut down, try to listen, *really* listen, to the things around you. Can you hear a ball being bounced? birds singing? a car going by? Maybe Ryan's new Converse

All Stars are squeaking as he bounces on his feet getting ready to punch you. This one also works better if your eyes are closed, and sometimes that's possible."

Jack nodded, but there was hesitation in the nod.

Mr. Reynolds didn't let it stop him. "Now think of sight. Let your eyes rest on an item near you and really look at it. Does the ball being bounced have dirt on it? Is there something written on the ball?"

"You sure?" Jack challenged, unable to control himself. "I mean, won't this slow my reaction time even more? It just sounds a little crazy."

"I know it does, Jack. But it's designed to help you focus, to stay in the present, to remain fully conscious of what is going on around you. If you practice, you just might find it helps. It did for me."

"Okay, but . . . isn't there anything else I can do when Kerrigan comes at me?"

Mr. Reynolds smiled. "This one will sound even crazier. You could try having an imaginary friend with you."

"You're kidding, right?"

"Actually, I'm not. Think about it more like having an imaginary *protector*. Say, Superman, or Batman, or your guardian angel. However, if you choose the angel, I'd suggest choosing one of those warrior angels with a big sword and shield. The idea is to have someone tough with you."

Jack tried not to roll his eyes. "And this imaginary protector is gonna punch Ryan Kerrigan's lights out for me?"

"No, of course not. They don't fight your battles *for* you, but somehow just having them there can make *you* be tougher."

Jack liked this idea a little better.

"Another thing you might want to do: Put a rubber band around your wrist. Then when you're in trouble or shutting down, give your wrist a good snap with the rubber band."

"But why?"

"When you give yourself a twang with the rubber band, it'll signal you to start exercising your senses and for your imaginary protector to show up. Jack, nobody's going to wonder why you wear a rubber band on your wrist, and they won't have any clue that you're signaling yourself to fight the shutdown. And it just might help."

"Yeah, okay," Jack said reluctantly. He'd been hoping for something else.

"I know it sounds a bit crazy, but give it a go, Jack. It helped me."

"Yes, sir. Thank you." He got to his feet to leave.

"One last thing, Jack. This one's not so much about shutting down, but it might help with Ryan. Try and look as if you're not easy to bully. Give him a look that says, 'Don't you dare mess with me.' Stand tall and look tough, even if you don't feel tough. Got it, Jack? Now, show me your tough look."

Jack stood a little straighter and locked eyes with Mr. Reynolds. He tried to put on his dad's "kill look."

Reynolds chuckled. "Okay, Jack, maybe you'd better practice your tough-guy look in the mirror a few times before you try it out on Ryan."

That made Jack smile, even if it embarrassed him. Somehow it broke the tension that had built up in the room.

Mr. Reynolds pointed an index finger at Jack and cocked his thumb back, as if he were pointing a gun at him. Then he loaded a wide, blue rubber band into the imaginary gun and shot it at Jack. "Try this one on for size. Maybe it'll do the trick."

The rubber band hit Jack in the chest and bounced off. Jack picked it up and put it on his wrist. As he turned to go, he gave it a snap. "Thank you, Mr. Reynolds."

The principal said, "I shared all this because I thought you could understand, and I think you do. But remember, Jack, it only works if you practice before you need it."

❁

"What'd Reynolds want?" Charlie asked, as they headed for recess.

"Not much. He was just goin' over the Kerrigan fight again. He said Ryan probably won't back off, and I better learn how to look tough."

"Look tough? I think you're gonna need a little more than that."

"So do I," Jack said ruefully.

"Did he say anything about the base going on full alert last night?"

"Not a thing."

"Shoot. I thought he might have said something."

The dodgeball game wasn't getting many takers. The older kids were off, talking among themselves, mostly about the tanks rolling. Jack and Charlie wandered toward them.

"I'm not really surprised they took live rounds," Charlie mused. "I mean, think about it. Simulation rounds are for practice battles. Nothing actually blows up. "

"So why would they carry live rounds unless it's a real battle?"

"For range practice—shooting practice for the tanks. You need range practice to improve accuracy. Mock battles help with maneuvering. For the battles, they divide into two teams. My dad calls it force on force, or BLUEFOR and OPFOR."

"What?"

"*BLUEFOR* means Blue Forces, or the friendly forces. *OPFOR* means Opposition Forces, or the enemy forces. Good guys and bad guys. Get it?"

"Okay," Jack said. He had stopped trying to hear the older kids. Charlie had his full attention. Jack's dad talked to him about global history, but nothing about this stuff.

"Anyway, that's when they use the simulation rounds. It's like fighting a real battle, but nothing really gets blown up. The second thing they go for are range scores. That's shooting practice. They use live ammunition and actually blow stuff up. Of course, they aren't shooting at each other. That'd be crazy."

"Yeah," Jack said, grinning.

"Instead, they shoot at old, broken-down tanks or trucks. Stuff the Army doesn't care about anymore. It's really sweet 'cause if they get a direct hit, it blows an actual hole in it. On some tank ranges, they even build reinforced concrete bunkers to shoot at, like the Nazi pillbox in our woods."

Charlie was in his element. His eyes sparkled as he got his friend up to speed on how their dads prepared for war. "When the tankers are out there during shooting practice, there are guys with binoculars watching every shot. They mark down if you get a hit or a miss. That's why they call it *range scores*. Each tank crew gets a score on how well they shoot. I mean, think about it. You can't really tell if a tank crew is good at hitting something unless they use live ammunition."

"So you're saying they might have headed out last night with live ammo not to stop something bad, but for target practice?"

"Bingo. You just broke the code."

"So this could be fun and games, not a major battle."

"Well, *we* might call it fun and games, but that's *definitely* not how my dad looks at it. To him it's serious stuff. The tank crews go through tank tables, which are qualification exercises covering everything a tank unit has to know and do well. And the conditions are tough, even at night and near live fire."

"Okay, *not* fun and games."

"And they'd better be good at hitting stuff. The tanks have to move from one place to another, shooting from different positions. While they're moving, someone radios in with their next target. The tank crew is scored on whether they hit the target and how long it takes them to take their shot. If it takes too long to get the shot off, they lose points, even if they hit the target. Flunking says you're not combat ready. And that is the definition of a big problem."

Jack laughed ruefully. "And I thought nothing could be worse than reading discussion groups."

Charlie laughed, too.

"Charlie, how do you know all this?"

"When we lived in Kentucky, we were at Fort Knox, with 3rd Armored Division. My dad was an instructor at the tanker school. He also designed and set up the new tank range at Knox. He spent a lot of nights and week-ends out in our garage building a model of the proposed range. It was really keen. It kinda looked like the layout for a train set on a giant piece of plywood, except without the trains and tracks. It had hills and trails and little, tiny trees. The targets were tiny tanks, trucks, and bunkers."

Charlie paused as the school's janitor asked to go past them. He had a thick German accent. The spikey-haired guy was wiping down the gym walls with a damp rag, but at the pace of a slug.

"Why's he doing that while the gym is being used?" whispered Jack.

"Dunno," shrugged Charlie, preoccupied with his story. "One of the neatest things my dad did was set some of the model tanks and trucks on fire and get the plastic burning. Then he'd dunk 'em in water so they only half melted. They looked like they'd been hit by tank rounds. Anyway, I used to hang out with him while he worked on the model, and he told me lots of stuff about how the range worked."

"Nice." Jack wanted that with *his* dad.

They headed toward the water fountain to get a drink before the bell rang. Jack saw the janitor again. Charlie's eyes followed Jack's. "That man is sooo strange," said Charlie. "What's he doing in here anyway?"

Jack nodded. "He's like that girl in the bus who kept leaning across the aisle to catch whatever that one boy said. But why would a janitor be so interested in what kids are saying?"

For the next several days, not much intel was forthcoming about what the tankers of 4th Armored Division were up to. There was a rumor they were up in Grafenwöhr, but Charlie and Jack had no verification. When they asked their moms, they got the standard answer: "Oh, honey, I have no idea. You don't need to worry about that. Your dad will be back soon enough."

Translation of adult-speak: "It's none of your business."

Finally, one afternoon about a week later, Jack and his gang picked up a rumor that the 4th was on their way back to Cooke Barracks. The brats headed for the cliff overlooking the *Flugplatz*. For once, this rumor proved correct. They could just make out a long convoy of tanks, lights on, rolling toward the right side of the airfield, headed for the tank lot.

Jack had brought his binoculars. Actually, they were his dad's, but he had recently taken near-permanent possession of them. Through the powerful lenses, he could see that the tanks hadn't stuck to roads and highways. They had snow, mud, and tree branches all over them. They'd obviously been out who knows where, tearing up the German countryside.

Everything was left to Jack's and Charlie's imaginations. No one ever sat them down and said, "Here's where we went. Here's what we did. Here's the outcome." Parents, especially Army ones, just don't cough up that kind of info. But the tighter the information flow, the more Jack and Charlie wanted to know. They wouldn't let it go.

"So how are we going to figure out what they were up to?" Jack asked.

"What *won't* work is asking them questions like, 'Where'd you go?' They'd just say something lame like, 'Oh, up the road a bit.' And if we ask, 'What'd you do?' they'd probably just say, 'We were working.' All we're gonna get are standard non-answers." Obviously, Charlie had given it some thought.

They kept struggling with it, but couldn't come up with a way to find out.

The day after Jack's dad got home was a Sunday. Lt. Col. McMasters had to work that whole weekend. The 4th's absolute priority was getting the tanks, trucks, equipment, and men back into a state of readiness so they could roll again at a moment's notice. But Lt. Col. McMasters did manage to get his kids to church before returning to duty.

Everything went fine until Jack yawned. At that first yawn, Queenie dug him in the ribs and the colonel glared in his direction. That panicked him. *I can't shut down now. I can't get in trouble just when Dad gets back in town. It'll spoil everything.* He chomped down on the inside of his cheeks to keep his jaws from opening in another yawn. That seemed to help. But then they had to kneel. His legs started to weaken and his mind to drift. He caught his head just as it fell to one side, sleep almost overtaking him.

He screamed inside his head. *Snap out of it, Jack! You're gonna ruin everything.*

Desperate, he knew he had to do something. *What had Mr. Reynolds said? Why'd I take that stupid blue rubber band off and throw it in my desk? Dumb, dumb, dumb!*

He pretended it was on his wrist and gave it a pretend snap. But he knew it was a useless gesture. He could hear Mr. Reynolds's words: *'That only works if you practice before you need it.'* And, of course, he'd never practiced. Not even once.

Jack tried coming up with an imaginary protector, but that proved worthless. He didn't need somebody tough to help him fight. He just needed to stay awake. When he imagined Superman, the Man of Steel was smacking him upside the head for letting his eyes drift shut.

Mr. Reynolds had said that I should *close my eyes. Why?* Jack remembered. *To use my senses.*

Jack squeezed his eyes. *Think, Jack. What can you smell?*

Heat.

Heat wasn't exactly a smell, but that's what came to mind. It was very hot in the Army chapel.

Concentrate, Jack!

He tried to detect the smell of incense. Nothing. Not in this church. He just wasn't any good at this.

What was that?

He'd heard a click.

Ah, the heater must have kicked on. Great, just what we need—more heat. Concentrate.

He felt a slight breeze on his face. Hot air from the chapel's heating system. Maybe he *could* do this.

The next thing he knew, they were walking up to communion, and shortly after that mass ended. He'd made it. He wasn't convinced the techniques had worked, but then again, he hadn't shut down.

∞⛓∞

Later in the week, Jack's mom went on a tear. She started working the entire household mercilessly, having them shine and double shine everything. Seems that on Friday night his parents were having one of their cocktail parties.

When Jack found out that Charlie, Sam, and Jayla's parents were on the invitation list, he asked to invite a friend and his mom agreed. He invited Charlie, because this was their best opportunity to get the intel. He and Charlie devised a plan for how to extract it. They wouldn't ask any questions about where 4th Armored had been. Instead, they'd ask something totally different: a question that made it sound like they already knew.

They figured 4th Armored had been up to Grafenwöhr. Since everyone and everything came back in one piece, it must have been an exercise and not a real battle. Since they needed the live ammunition, they must have used it for range scores. All that decided, they came up with an irresistible question Charlie could ask his dad at the party.

Mrs. McMasters had, of course, laid down the law about how things would operate. Queenie, Rabbit, Jack, and Charlie were given clear instructions: The kids would greet the guests when they arrived. They would be on their very best behavior. Once the party got going, they would disappear into their bedrooms and not run around the apartment during the party.

All four children solemnly agreed to these rules, knowing that occasionally they could sneak into the party to snitch food, provided they ate it back in the bedrooms.

By Friday evening, everything at the McMasterses' quarters was set and elegant. Jazz music was playing in the background on their new Grundig hi-fi turntable. The dining-room table was lit with candles, and some of Mrs. McMasters's best appetizers were already on it. Lt. Col. McMasters had a bar set up off to one side of the living room. Bartending was his main job. The kids, including Charlie, were dressed up, shined up, combed up, and strack. Now that all the preparations were complete, it was starting to get fun. Jack and Charlie greeted the arriving guests, taking their coats to lay on Mrs. McMasters's bed.

Mrs. McMasters was about to introduce Jack and Charlie to Lt. Col. and Mrs. Jones, when Mrs. Jones gave them a big smile and said, "Good evening, Jack. And, good evening to you as well, Charlie. Don't you two young men look sharp."

"It looks like you already know my son," Mrs. McMasters said, seeming a bit surprised.

"Oh, absolutely! You must realize that Jack knows how to make a first impression," she said, giving him a quick wink.

"I certainly hope that that first impression was good," his mother said, giving him "the eye."

"Oh, definitely. In fact, it was quite memorable." Mrs. Jones quickly added, "Jayla brought Samantha, Jack, Charlie home on Saturday."

His mom smiled. "Isn't that nice. Jack had them all over here for hot cocoa another day after playing outdoors. The Sandses should be along any moment. Jack, Charlie, why don't you take Colonel and Mrs. Jones's coats?"

As Mrs. Jones shrugged off her coat, Mrs. McMasters's face lit up. "Shannel Jones, that is a fabulous dress. You put us all to shame."

"Why, thank you, Lorraine. That's high praise, coming from the best-dressed woman in Göppingen."

Jack looked around at that. Every lady in the room was dressed up very fancy, but these two ladies *did* look the best.

Friday-night cocktail parties were dress-up affairs, but since this was the first social event since the tankers returned from maneuvers, everyone seemed especially motivated to come all decked out and ready for a good time.

Heading down the hall with the coats, Charlie said, "Jayla's mom definitely was messing with you, Jack."

"She certainly was," he said. "I thought she was gonna spill the beans about the lipstick."

After finishing coat duty, they hung out in Jack's room, letting the party get going. Jack wanted to time things so they didn't miss out on the big roast beef his mother had made. He was desperate to sink his teeth into that rare roast. They also wanted their dads to be in relaxed, happy moods when Charlie sprang the question.

When their growling stomachs could be patient no longer, the boys made their move. The plan was simple: Get their food (their excuse for being out there), casually pass by Charlie's dad, and spring the question.

"Excellent," exclaimed Charlie, growing wide-eyed at the feast. "But where are the real plates?"

Being a cocktail party, there was no formal, sit-down dinner. Instead all the food was served in small portions, designed to be eaten with fingers or tiny forks. Guests just walked around with tiny plates of food they ate standing up, or sitting on chairs or the couch. They would come back to the table and add to their plates as many times as they wanted.

Well, that system didn't suit Jack and Charlie. Eating off those tiny plates would have required too many return trips, and Mrs. McMasters would never put up with that. She'd throw them out after their second trip to the table. Jack went into the kitchen and got them regular dinner plates.

That luscious roast beef had little buns next to it. Most people were making tiny roast-beef sandwiches.

The boys passed on the sandwich idea and piled massive mounds of beef on their plates. Jack's mouth was watering by the time he had added ham, shrimp with cocktail sauce, some cheeses, apple slices, and grapes. They passed on the smoked oysters, the stuffed dates, and a bunch of other adult-looking food.

Plates loaded, they scanned the party for Charlie's dad. He was sitting with some other men near where Jack's dad was tending bar. It didn't look like they'd gotten food yet—only drinks. The boys eased over, and Lt. Col. McMasters immediately spotted them and their mountain of food. "Whoa! You boys get enough to eat?"

"Holy cow, Charlie, did you leave any roast for us?" Lt. Col. Carron asked, flashing a quick smile at the other men. Fortunately, the boys could tell they were kidding around with them.

"Oh, don't worry, sir. That roast beef is really big," Charlie said, with the well-practiced look of an innocent angel. Then, before they were told to get lost, he sprang the question on his dad. "So, was the tank range at Grafenwöhr tougher than the one you built at Fort Knox?"

Before any of the men had time to wonder how two young kids knew enough to ask such a question, one grinned at Charlie and said, "Oh, the one your dad built at Knox was a lot tougher. I know. I got scored there twice, and I did a lot better up at Graf."

All the men laughed at that, and another said, "Yeah, but that's just because you like shooting in the cold and snow."

"And you, Harry, never did like gunning up in the winter."

"You got that right!"

They all laughed again.

The men were no longer paying much attention to the boys. They were back to smokin' and jokin' with each other. Jack and Charlie would have gladly hung out there longer, trying to learn more, but Jack's dad started shaking the ice cubes in his own drink. The tinkling sound of the cubes was a clear signal to Jack. His dad was getting impatient. He'd been okay with the boys stopping by, but clearly it was time for them to hit the dusty trail.

"Let's am-scray," said Jack.

Charlie looked at him, confused.

"That's pig Latin for *scram.*"

Once back in Jack's bedroom they grinned, victorious.

Charlie slammed his palm down on the edge of Jack's desk. "We did it!"

"Indeed, we did. We broke the code on that one. It *was* Grafenwöhr. The live rounds were for winter range exercises," Jack said triumphantly.

While most adults considered it an exceptional cocktail party, Jack and Charlie thought of it as a roaring success.

16

Ingrid

Jack's eyes were closed in concentration. It was one of those slightly warmer January days. He could actually feel the sun's warmth on his face. He breathed in the faint smell of the forest floor, dampened by the melting snow. And maybe he was picking up on the scent of pine—or was he making that part up because he knew there were some evergreen trees out there?

I'm wasting my time, Jack thought. *This is never gonna work.*

He was alone on the balcony of his quarters, practicing his self-imposed drills. He thought of them as his anti-shutdown drills; touch, scent, hearing, sight. Once again his doubts broke his concentration. *Why am I doing this? Even if it somehow manages to keep me awake in church—so what? It's not like I'm going to shut my eyes and try to smell pine needles the next time Kerrigan is standing there ready to kick my—*

"Jack!"

He whirled around and saw his mother rapping her knuckle on the large, glass panel, signaling him to come back in.

Had she been calling him?

As he walked into the warm living room, she said, "There's someone I want you to meet."

Queenie was shaking hands with a rather thin young lady. She was a head taller than Queenie and had short, dark, spiky hair.

"Jack, this is Ingrid, your new nanny," Mrs. McMasters announced.

Nanny—she's a nanny? Definitely not what Jack had expected. An older woman, sure, but . . .

Mrs. McMasters inconspicuously reached down and took hold of Jack's arm, digging her long, red nails into his bicep just hard enough to get his undivided attention. "Manners," she said, ever so sweetly.

He'd been staring a bit too long. "How do you do? I'm Jack McMasters." He shrugged off his mom's claws to extend his hand.

"Ah, yah, Jack. Guten Tag," she said, shaking his hand with a firm grip.

Those eyes! Jack locked on them. They were huge. They were *purple*.

Rabbit burst through the front door. Dropping a toy-filled knapsack and her coat, she became an airplane, arms outstretched, lips making the engine noise. The plane barely screeched to a halt before colliding with Ingrid. Rabbit demanded, "Who are you?"

"Manners," Mrs. McMasters said again, trying her best to sound pleasant.

"Also das ist sicher Kirsten. Oder soll ich dich Rabbit nennen?" Ingrid said, delighted with Rabbit.

The fact that Rabbit didn't understand a word Ingrid said made no difference. Rabbit grabbed Ingrid's arm and tugged. "You wanna see my room?"

Ingrid's big, purple eyes danced with delight as she allowed herself to be dragged away from the others and down the hall. Mrs. McMasters followed after them, deciding to let things take their course.

Queenie spun around to glare at Jack. "Did you know anything about this?"

"Not a thing," Jack said, wondering why Queenie was getting so hostile.

"I don't think she even speaks English," Queenie whispered before storming off down the hall to supervise Rabbit's tour of their bedroom.

By the time Jack arrived, Rabbit was conducting an English lesson.

Pointing, she said, "Closet."

"Schrank," said Ingrid.

"Toys," she said, pointing to a pile of yesterday's playthings.

"Kinderspielzeug," replied Ingrid.

Rabbit jumped onto her bed, pointing at the same time.

"Okay, Kirsten. That's enough language lessons for now," said Mrs. McMasters, semi-amused by her antics. "You'll have plenty of time to play with your new nanny later."

"Nanny! Ya mean she gets to *stay*?" Rabbit bounced up and down on the bed, thrilled to have found a new best friend.

"Come along, dear," her mom sweetly insisted.

They all made their way back to the living room. Mrs. McMasters began a litany of roles and responsibilities, including how the children were to interact with their nanny. Queenie could tell that Ingrid was pretending to pay attention to what was being said, but not understanding a word of it. She shot a "didn't I tell ya" look at Jack.

Jack just stood there, taking it all in. He'd liked Ingrid from the start, but she puzzled him. He could see she'd picked up on Queenie's attitude.

When his mom finished listing all the new rules, Ingrid reached into her small, yellow purse for a wrapped package. As she started to unwrap it, Rabbit bounced up and down on the couch next to her and said, "Here, I'll help you."

Rabbit grabbed the package and tore it in two. What looked like light yellow, green, pink, and blue pieces of chalk tumbled into Ingrid's cupped hands.

"*Saure Stücke*," Ingrid said. She held them out to Queenie first. Jack could tell his sister was about to refuse, but Mrs. McMasters gave Queenie the look, and she reluctantly accepted one.

Rabbit grabbed one next, but then wasn't sure what to do with it. She looked up at Ingrid and shrugged her shoulders.

Ingrid pretended to eat one.

That was all the information Rabbit needed. She immediately popped an end of the light-blue stick in her mouth. Jack reached for another of the three-inch-long candies. It was the perfect blend of sweet and sour.

"Oh, *Saure Stücke* means sour sticks!" Rabbit shrieked with delight. She had no idea what *Saure Stücke* really meant. She'd just chosen something that rhymed in English. But from that moment, *sour stick* became the McMasterses' name for their favorite German candy.

As Jack savored his light-pink sour stick, he glanced at Queenie. She might not be happy with these new arrangements, but she was enjoying her third piece of Ingrid's gift.

Later that afternoon, Queenie condescended to play a rare game of checkers with Jack. The conversation soon got around to Ingrid.

Queenie scoffed, "Mom told me she's only seventeen! I told her how ridiculous that was, and that she needed to find someone older."

"Older? Please! I like that she's young. And she seems nice. Did you see her eyes?"

"Yeah. They're beautiful. So what?" Queenie wasn't giving an inch.

"That's not it. When she was having fun with Rabbit, her eyes almost danced. But they turned into cold, purple stones once or twice. I think when she'd realized I'd noticed, she immediately turned the bright eyes back on. There's something about her, nothing bad, but something I can't put my finger on. Like she's hiding something. I gotta figure her out."

"Forget about figuring her out. She can try and buy us off with all the German candy she wants, but I'm not learning German just to talk to *her*."

That was a battle Queenie would lose.

From the very first day, Ingrid only spoke to them in German, and she insisted they use that language, too. When they replied to her in English, she pretended not to hear. They knew she understood *some* English; she spoke to their mom in very bad English as well as German. But that never happened with the kids.

As the days passed, Queenie's hatred grew. She did everything she could to resist Ingrid's requirement that they speak to her in German. And she complained to her mother.

"Mom, this is totally ridiculous! It's just not normal. All my friends with nannies have ones that speak English. Why do we have one who only talks to us in German? I know she can speak at least a little English. I hear her talking to you. Why can't she do that with us?"

"Our family is our family; we are not your friends' families. We do things our way, they do things their way. So you'd better learn to speak to her in German." And that's all Mrs. McMasters ever replied.

Queenie held out, not speaking or listening to Ingrid, for about a week. Then, reluctantly, Queenie gave in.

Early communications involved Queenie talking a blue streak of German and then trying to show what she was saying with motions.

"*Zeit zum Mittagessen,*" Ingrid said one day.

When the kids only gave her blank stares, she put her hand up to her mouth and pretended she was eating.

"*Essen, essen, essen, verstanden?*" she said, as she put their lunch on the table.

"Eat," Rabbit yelled out, delighted with herself.

It didn't exactly take a genius to figure out that *essen* meant *eat*. Ingrid had gotten pretty good at making a guessing game out of what she was saying. And it usually resulted in a lot of foolishness and laughter.

"*Mittagessen,*" she said again. Then she started making this big karate-chopping motion with her hand.

At first they had no idea why she was doing it. Then they figured out that her karate chopping meant to cut the word into pieces. That's because the Germans are always jamming two or three words together into a single, long word. So she took *Mittagessen* and karate chopped it in half so it became mittag/essen.

She again said, "*Essen.*" They knew that meant *eat*. Then she took the word *Mittag* and started pointing to her watch. She adjusted the big hand and the little hand to the 12 position. Everyone started guessing.

"*Twelve o'clock,*" Jack yelled. Ingrid kept shaking her head. Wrong!

"*Noon,*" yelled Rabbit. Wrong again.

"*Noon/eat, noon/eat, noon/eat,*" Queenie repeated, trying to figure it out.

Finally Jack got it. "*Noon/eat* means *lunch*!"

Before they finished eating that day, they'nd figured out that *Zeit zum Mittagessen* meant *Time to eat lunch*. After winning that guessing game, they were so happy they went around all afternoon saying, *Zeit zum Mittagessen*. And none of them ever forgot what those words meant or how to say them.

No matter what the conversation was about, Ingrid kept using the word *verstanden*. She would say, "*Essen, essen, essen, verstanden?*" It only took the kids about a week of hearing "*blah . . . blah . . . blah, verstanden,*" "*blah . . . blah . . . blah, verstanden,*" "*blah . . . blah . . . blah, verstanden,*" for them to finally figure out that *verstanden* meant something like, "*So, you understand?*" or "*Did you get it?*"

Little by little, the kids picked up a lot of German. Little by little, Queenie started to like Ingrid.

The McMasters household fell into a new rhythm. On school days, Mrs. McMasters got the kids up, gave them their breakfast, and (like any good drill sergeant) got them out the door in time to catch the school bus.

Ingrid didn't have to get up and start work till ten o'clock on school days. While the kids were at school, she picked up the place, made the beds, and then most days made her way to the basement to do the laundry. Next to the coal-fired boiler that heated the whole building, there was a room that contained a bunch of washing machines, and outside of it there were clothespins hanging from clotheslines strung the entire length of the basement hallway. Whenever the kids played in the basement, they'd run in and out of the clean laundry drying on the lines. Once Ingrid started doing the family's laundry, Mrs. McMasters never set foot in The Glass House basement again.

Jack knew that doing the laundry was a bit of a social thing for Ingrid. There were usually other nannies or maids down there doing laundry, too. They all sat around chatting as the machines worked on the dirty clothes.

If no one else was around, Ingrid would talk to the old German man who lived in the basement. His job in the winter was to keep the furnace fires going. Jack liked to watch him, too. Seeing him shovel in big chunks of black coal reminded Jack of the boiler room on the USS *Upshur*. Jack tried to ask Ingrid what the man would do once the furnace was turned off in the spring. She pantomimed planting and weeding, making it look like a lot of work.

Ingrid always had the laundry done by the time the children got home from school. She got them a snack and took care of anything they needed. As far as dinners were concerned, Mrs. McMasters never gave up control. Occasionally she let Ingrid help, but she remained the master chef. No one was ever allowed to interfere with her fine art of cooking. And, of course, cleanup remained the kids' responsibility.

"Why can't Ingrid do the dishes?" demanded Queenie one night.

"Because I say so," came Mrs. McMasters's response, in a tone suggesting one's life might be in danger for asking such an impertinent question. No McMasters child ever brought up the topic again.

On the nights Queenie and Rabbit did dishes, Jack got an earlier start on his nightly shoe-polishing job. When Jack and Queenie did the dishes, Ingrid got Rabbit her bath and into her pajamas. After the dishes were put away and Jack had finished the shoes, Ingrid made sure the other two got their baths and were ready for bed.

The final act of most nights belonged to their father. The kids would gather on the couch in their PJs, and he would read them a story. Lt. Col. McMasters was a very, very good reader of very, very long stories. Since coming to Germany, they had gotten most of the way through *Oliver Twist*. Everyone liked to listen to the stories, even Mrs. McMasters. Naturally she was *much* too busy to sit on the couch and listen with the others. There was always some critical chore in the living room, dining room, or kitchen that needed her attention. But they all knew she was listening. They knew it because every once in a while, in the middle of a really good part, their father would lower his voice to a dramatic whisper, and from another room would come, "Hey, speak up! I can't hear!"

Every time, they all roared with laughter.

17

Call from the School

It was mid-February when Kevin Duncan was escorted into their class. Jack studied the look on his face. Except for the no-nonsense flattop crew-cut and blond hair, this must have been the way he looked coming in that first day. Kevin was doing his best to show nothing, but once he'd been at his desk for a while, Jack had a chance to read his eyes. Jack knew right away the kid's brain was fully engaged . . . and that the boy was no fool.

Kevin had just moved in to one of the houses on The Circle up from The Glass House. He'd be riding the same bus as Jack and Charlie. His family had just come in from Fort Knox, and it didn't take a rocket scientist to figure out his dad was also a tanker.

There wasn't much snow on the playground, so the teachers let the students go outside for morning break. Jack got there late because he'd made a pit stop at the bathroom. Coming out of the door, he spotted Charlie on the far side of the playground and headed that way. Kerrigan and his guys materialized out of nowhere. There was a nasty sneer on Kerrigan's face.

Jack tensed. Things started to close in. His system was flooded with panic. *Think fast, Jack.*

But he couldn't help himself. He began shutting down. His brain was stuck on a single thought: *Why me? Why me? Why does he hate my guts?*

"McMasters, you're such a candy-ass! I'm just gonna have to pound ya." Kerrigan's eyes were filling with an eerie delight at the idea of cleaning Jack's clock.

Somewhere, way in the back of his mind, Jack knew he needed to resist shutting down. A distant voice urged, *Do something, Jack!* But pinpricks of light started flashing in his eyes. He'd been holding his breath. It took all his effort just to suck in a small breath. *Clear your head, Jack!*

Somehow Mr. Reynolds's advice came back to him. He stood taller and did his best to look tough. He snapped the blue rubber band against his wrist. Then he half spit out the words, "Kerrigan, you're—a—complete—nutter!"

Kerrigan's face turned angry red. He gathered his strength and took a swing. Fortunately, he hesitated just long enough for Jack to get his fists up and partially duck the punch. It hit Jack on the shoulder, causing no real damage. Jack punched back, but being off balance, he didn't connect with any real force either.

Having no idea what possessed him, Jack screamed, "You're a total nutter, Kerrigan!"

Unfortunately, his brain then retreated into the ozone. Instead of concentrating on Kerrigan, he was wondering, *Where'd I come up with the word* nutter? *I'm not even sure what it means.*

Kerrigan's fist hit him in the eye, launching him off his feet. As his head smacked the ground, his brain began to short-circuit, but out of instinct, he rolled into a ball to protect himself. Good thing, too, because Kerrigan started kicking him. Pain shot through Jack's back as the second blow connected for real. He had to get out of there—now.

Forcing his eyes open, he rolled away, trying to get back on his feet. Just as his vision cleared, he witnessed the strangest scene. Kevin Duncan was racing toward him from across the playground and flew through the air, crashing straight into Ryan Kerrigan.

Jack staggered to his feet.

Duncan and Kerrigan were sprawled on the ground. But, lighting quick, Duncan jumped back on his feet and calmly said, "Get up, scumbag!" He didn't kick Kerrigan while he was down. He just stood there and waited till Kerrigan got back up.

One of Kerrigan's gang was about to sucker-punch Kevin from behind, but by then Charlie was there. He punched the guy in the ribs, knocking the wind out of him. Arriving late to the action, Sam and Jayla were now shoving another one of Kerrigan's guys. Kerrigan, by now crazed, came at

Kevin. But cool as a cucumber, Kevin just punched his lights out—*boom, boom, boom*. Kerrigan went down.

To Jack, the fight seemed to last forever; it really was over in a flash. But even the shortest fight is long enough for a swarm of kids and teachers to gather.

This time it wasn't just Jack who got hauled off to the principal. It was all of them.

Shaking his head, Mr. Reynolds said, "I don't have room for half of Mrs. Campbell's class in my office." He quickly ushered Jack and his crew, along with Kevin, into a separate room. Kerrigan and his gang were told to remain in his office.

Jack's eye was developing a most excellent shiner. But for some reason he felt great. Looking right at Kevin, he said, "Whoa, thanks, man! Sorry to get you in trouble your first day."

"My pleasure." Kevin raised his shoulders in an innocent shrug. "It was bound to happen, one way or another."

"You're outta control," Charlie said, grinning at Kevin.

"You certainly are," said Jayla, delighted with the whole thing.

In fact, they all were.

"Best fight this year," said Sam, looking right at Kevin. "You took Ryan Kerrigan *out*! That's big."

"It is?" he asked.

All talking at once, they filled him in on Kerrigan and his gang. He listened, all the while rubbing his hand over his flattop, a thoughtful look on his face.

"Well, I guess now they know who *we* are, too," he said, with a little smile. And it was obvious they were all going to be serious friends.

Mr. Reynolds came in and, as usual, kept his cool. "Mr. Duncan, it looks like you've met Jack McMasters and the others."

"Yes, sir," he replied, very respectful and standing a bit straighter.

"It only took Jack about ninety minutes to end up back in my office on his first day. You, Mr. Duncan, seem to have tied his record." But Reynolds had a twinkle in his eye.

"Yes, sir."

"I understand the original fight was between Jack and Ryan. How'd you managed to get involved?"

The other kids stayed quiet. They all knew that with adults, the less said the better, especially when you're in trouble. But they looked at Kevin, who finally said, "Well, sir, I just kinda figured it seemed wrong to kick a guy when he's on the ground."

Reynolds kept his eyes locked on Kevin, but Kevin didn't offer up anything else. Finally Reynolds said, "Seems like you live by that rule. The way I hear it, *you* didn't kick Ryan Kerrigan when he was down. Seems like you waited till he was back on his feet before you dealt with him."

Kevin looked Mr. Reynolds in the eye but didn't respond.

Reynolds turned to Jack. "This time I can't just let it go. The fighting has to stop, Jack. I've told Ryan the same thing. All your parents have been called to come and pick you up. Just sit tight until they get here."

He reached for the door but turned back. Looking directly at Kevin, he said, "Well, at least you know how to choose the right friends." Then he was gone.

Even with him gone, the room remained quiet.

Until Jayla seemed to come to life. She shuddered. "Arghhh! My ol' man is really gonna lose it. I can hear it now, 'Fighting! Have—you—lost—your—mind, young lady! You're in so much trouble.'" Warming to her own imitation of her father, she continued in the same gruff voice, "'Shannel! You'd better start getting something through this renegade child's thick head about how to act like a lady, instead of a hoodlum!'" She started laughing.

That got them all laughing.

"And what about *my* mom?" smirked Sam. "I get to hear, 'Samantha Sands, I raised you better than this! Wait till your father gets home!'"

For a long time the nervous laughter didn't stop.

"Thank goodness it's only Tuesday. I need to get paroled before the Saturday movie," said Jayla. "Like *that* will happen." This time she pretended to be her mother. "'The next movie you'll see, young lady, will be in college.'"

That cracked them up again.

Theirs was a comradeship forged in battle. Ryan Kerrigan had once more inflicted damage. Jack's eye wasn't looking any too good. And it wasn't as if they no longer feared him, but this time Ryan Kerrigan had also walked away worse for wear. That part was new.

The first parent Mr. Reynolds walked in with was Col. Duncan. The room went silent as a stone. Every kid stood tall, though their faces had the thousand-yard stare of a shell-shocked soldier.

The man was in his Class A uniform, with *Duncan* written on his nametag, a rack of ribbons on the other side of his chest, and shiny screaming eagles on his shoulders. This was one pissed-off full colonel. He didn't say a word. Nor did he look at Kevin. Instead he stared directly at each kid in the room, one at a time. He glared with an "I'll eat you alive" look. As intimidating as he was, not one kid broke eye contact. They knew better. The minute he finished silently grilling the last kid, who happened to be Jack, he turned on his heels and headed out of the room. Over his shoulder, he said in a quiet-but-deadly voice, "Let's go, Kevin." The entire time Col. Duncan was in the room, he never once looked at his son.

Then they were gone.

"Whoa, Kevin's dad is really intense!" said Jayla. "My dad is beyond tough, but that guy is hardcore."

"Man, I hope Kevin's okay. Col. Duncan looked like he might kill him," Jack said, with genuine concern.

But before anyone else said anything, the door swung open and in walked Lt. Col. Jones. The only kid he even looked at was Jayla. All he said was, "Let's go." And the two of them were out of there.

"Boy, oh, boy. I couldn't read a thing on his face," said Sam. "I have no clue if she's in trouble or not."

"*You* heard her earlier," said Jack. "She's in big trouble. Lt. Col. Jones is the highest ranking Negro officer I've ever met. I overheard my dad say he's amazing, and that one day he'll be a general. So I know she gets held to a ridiculously high standard. "

"I think he expects a lot from her 'cause he's been through a lot," said Charlie. "Like when he was at West Point."

"He graduated from West Point?" Jack said, stunned.

"Sure did," said Charlie. "He's one of the first colored men to do it. But the way I hear it, he had to deal with four years of the silent treatment.

Except for official communications, no one ever spoke to him because he's a Negro. I guess after he tolerated all that, nothing he puts on Jayla seems tough to him."

About twenty minutes later, Sam's and Charlie's mothers picked them up. Jack was left there to sweat it out all by himself. No question about it: *He* was in big trouble. If the school calls your dad, and he has to leave work because of something his kid did, that kid should watch out! Jack knew it didn't matter whether it was his fault or not. It didn't matter if he had stuck up for himself or not. If your actions bring negative attention to the colonel, you're in deep trouble. Right, wrong, or indifferent, you are going to get it. The rules are clear: You never, *never* make a military officer look bad. You do, and it can affect that officer's career. As he sat alone, Jack could feel his body fill with dread.

Lt. Col. McMasters came barging through the door with Mr. Reynolds in tow. He wasn't even *trying* to mask his anger. Jack could see he was fired up. He glared down at Jack's swollen eye and said in a very surly voice, "Well, it looks like I don't have to kick your ass, since it's *obvious* someone's already done it for me." Without another word, he grabbed Jack by the ear and yanked him out the door. He didn't let go of that ear till he forcibly tossed Jack into the car.

Jack sat, petrified, waiting for his dad to come around and get in, wishing he was anywhere but in that car. Slamming the door shut, the colonel yanked the car in gear and pealed out of the school parking lot. Gravel kicked up. Tires squealed. He hadn't gone two blocks before he started screaming at Jack, "Have you lost your mind! I don't need your stupidity! And I certainly don't need this crap. You—are—a—complete—idiot! If I *ever* have to come to that school again, you'll by God pay the price. Do you understand me, young man?"

"Yes, sir," Jack replied just above a whisper.

"What did you say!" screamed his father, as the car roared toward The Glass House.

But before he even had a chance to reply, his father lost it, smacking Jack hard across the face with the back of his hand. Blood erupted from his nose.

"I said, what—did—you—say!" his father screamed again.

"Don't make me ask you one more time, you—sorry—excuse—for—a—human—being. Or you'll get it again."

Jack desperately gasped for breath, finally managing to blurt out, "Sir, it won't happen again, sir."

"You're damn right it won't!" screamed the colonel. He brought the car to a screeching halt in front of their building. "Now get your sorry ass upstairs, and clean yourself up. And don't come out of your room till I tell you to. Do—you—understand—me?"

"Yes, sir." Jack got out of the car and headed into the building. He was hoping against hope his father would stay in the car and head back to work. But a second after he entered the building Jack heard his dad's car door slam.

He mounted the stairs as fast as he could, but his father's footsteps were coming rapidly. He had almost made it to the third-floor landing. *WACK!* The colonel slapped him a hard one upside the back of his head. Jack went down hard. Jack forced himself to climb, desperately trying to get away. Just before he got to their door, his father latched onto the back of his neck with a vice grip. Leaning down to his ear, he said in a low voice, "And I better not hear any crying out of you, or I'm going to come in there and give you something to cry about! Do—you—understand—me?"

"Yes, s—sir."

Jack headed straight for the bathroom and worked to get his nose to stop bleeding, all while trying to wash up. Nothing would stop the blood flow. He grabbed a huge wad of toilet paper and held it to the eruption. His brain was mush. The only thing he focused on was not getting more blood on his clothes than he already had.

He grabbed the extra roll of toilet paper off a shelf, went to his room, closed the door, and cautiously lay down on the bed. Tilting his head back, he tossed the blood-soaked toilet paper in the waste bin by his bed, and pressed a fresh wad to his nose. He forced himself to remain motionless, hoping that would help stop the flow.

Jack could hear the colonel ranting and raving out in the living room. He sensed him pacing up and down like a caged tiger. His mom was the only one home at this time of day. Jack knew she was getting an earful. Every time it went quiet out there, Jack drifted off, only to be jolted back to reality when the colonel resumed yelling. Jack's whole system would rush back on high alert. Was his father coming to his room to give him more? Was his father going to lose it with his mom because of what he'd done? Were the girls going to get it, too, when they came home, for no reason at all? Jack lay there, dreading whatever was coming. If his father would just go back to work, then he could shut down and drift away.

The apartment door slammed. He knew someone had gone out. Had his mom finally had enough and walked out on the colonel? Had the colonel finally gone back to work? He forced himself off the bed and toward the window. He was careful not to get too close. He knew the colonel had the kind of radar that would sense Jack's presence at the window. If his dad glanced up and saw Jack staring down at him, he'd probably come storming back in and kick his ass all over again. Jack was in no position to risk anything, but he couldn't stand not knowing if it was his dad or his mom leaving. Placing a chair well back from the window and praying he wouldn't be seen from below, Jack slowly stood on the chair and looked out. The car was pulling away. Lt. Col. McMasters was in the driver's seat.

Once the car was down the street, Jack got down and put the chair away. As he eased back onto his bed, he realized his nose had stopped bleeding. He knew eventually his mom would come in, but for now he was just too spent even to think. Jack's eyes wouldn't stay open. Jack shut down.

Sometime later he heard her come in. But, he kept his eyes closed, not moving, pretending he was asleep. After a few moments, she left. The second time she came to check on him, he opened his eyes and looked at her.

"Sit up and let me have a look at you."

She examined his eye and his nose, and then left. A few minutes later she returned with a dish towel full of ice cubes. "Here. Put this on your eye."

He did as she asked, not saying a word. He simply lay back down, putting the ice pack over his eye and nose.

She walked out.

A while later, she came back and took the ice pack away, saying, "I have a bath ready for you. Go in and take it now." She didn't show anger, nor did she show sympathy. She didn't show anything at all.

He took his bath, put on a clean pair of jeans and a white T-shirt, and went back to his room. He was there quite a while before she returned.

She sat on his bed and studied him. Finally she asked, "Do you understand why your dad is mad at you?"

"Because I got into a fight?"

"No, it's not the fight. It's because you got in trouble with the principal, and because the school called him."

"But it wasn't my fault—"

Her eyes flashed, and she gave him a "don't even *think* that" look. "Jack, who started it doesn't matter. What matters is that you made your father look bad. You kids simply can't afford to make your father look bad. Do you understand that? Do you understand why?"

Jack looked her in the eye but didn't respond.

She said, "If his boss, Langford, or if the commanding general ever get the idea that your father can't even control his own children, they will question whether they can trust him to command a bunch of men in battle. If you or your sisters do anything to make your father look bad, he might never make full colonel. Do you understand?"

"Yes, ma'am."

"Don't you just 'Yes, ma'am' me, Jack McMasters," she said with real irritation. "Either you actually understand what I'm talking about or you don't. But this is far too important for you *not* to understand. So which is it?"

"I understand, Mom. I really do. It won't happen again. I promise."

"It had better not!"

She got up to go. But she turned back to him, and said, "If your father talks to you tonight, or if he asks you any questions, you keep your answers short. You look him right in the eye. You tell the truth. And for goodness' sake, don't ever say it wasn't your fault. Got it?"

"Yes, ma'am."

She left.

He heard the girls get home from school but he knew they wouldn't be by to see him. Word passes fast in a brat school, and nothing passes faster than news of a fight and kids being sent home. Before they ever walked in the door of their quarters, the girls knew Jack was in trouble. And in the McMasterses' household, when one kid was in trouble, all kids were subject to trouble. Even Rabbit knew to keep a low profile. Queenie and

Rabbit got in, and they got out—fast. Jack knew they wouldn't be back till dinner. He also knew they wouldn't risk getting home late.

Jack's adult-radar went off at five-thirty. His dad had returned. This time there was no yelling and screaming. Actually, things remained a bit too quiet. He figured his parents were in a private powwow.

He had no idea what that would mean. But this lying around, not knowing, drove him crazy.

Later he heard them eating dinner. Again, no one had come to get him.

Sometime after seven-thirty, his door opened and Queenie came in. She gave him a "you're such a dork" look, followed by one that said, "God, I'm glad I'm not you." But out loud, all she said was, "Dad wants to see you. He's in the living room."

Jack got his shoes and socks on. Earlier, he'd made sure that the shoes were properly shined. The last thing he could afford was a confrontation over un-shined shoes. He put on a clean shirt, carefully tucking it in. At the last second, he even remembered to put on a belt. He made a quick stop at the bathroom to make sure his hair was combed. Yup. Both his eye and nose were swollen. Then he made the long death march into the living room.

His father looked at him as he came in. He could feel the colonel inspecting him as he walked across the room.

There was a long silence. Jack stood there not moving a muscle. He made sure he stood erect.

"Who was the fight with?"

"Ryan Kerrigan."

"Tell me what happened."

"He came up to me on the playground during morning break. He called me a bunch of names and slugged me."

"What did you say to him beforehand?"

"Nothing."

"You're telling me this was totally unprovoked?"

"Well, the guy definitely doesn't like me."

"Why?"

"I don't know. He started yelling at me the first day of school. I got into a fight with him then."

"Well, it certainly looks like he kicked your ass today."

"Ryan Kerrigan kicks everyone's ass."

"Shake it off, Jack, and get your licks in when you can."

For the next five minutes the colonel gave him the third degree about who had been involved. Jack explained about Kerrigan's gang and about those involved on his side. The colonel asked a lot of questions about Kevin Duncan.

"Do you know why I'm upset with you?"

"Yes, sir."

"I don't want to *ever* get another call from that school—or from anyone else—about your behavior. Do I make myself clear, Jack?"

"Yes, sir."

He thought he was about to be excused, but instead his father told him to take a seat on the couch. That made him even more nervous.

"Earlier today I said you were stupid. Jack, you're not stupid. But you certainly need to get a lot smarter. And you need to do it fast. Here's what I'm thinking. This Kerrigan kid is going to keep coming after you. Am I right?"

"Yes, sir."

"Face it, Jack, sooner or later you're going to have to figure out how to cool his jets, or he'll never stop coming after you. Am I right?"

"Yes, sir."

"Okay, ground rule number one: No matter what he does, what he says, or if he attacks, you never fight him on school grounds. You tell him you'll meet him somewhere after school where there are no adults around. Got it?"

"Yes, sir."

"Second, you always show. And you show early if you commit to a meet. If he doesn't show, he's the coward, but don't *you* ever be the coward. Got me?"

"Yes, sir."

"You get your ass kicked—that's your problem. But I better never get a call about it. Got it?"

"Yes, sir."

"Last thing. Not to be repeated. Col. Duncan is new here, and I don't know him. But I hear he's one tough son-of-a-B. So if his kid is a friend of yours, and he's anything like his old man, you better keep him close to you. "

"Yes, sir."

"You don't leave your room, except to go to school, for the next two days."

"Yes, sir."

"Dismissed."

"Yes, sir."

Jack lay down on his bed studying the cracks in the ceiling. His brain was fried. He just wanted this day to end. He was still staring at the same stupid cracks fifteen minutes later when his mom came in with a scrambled-egg sandwich and a glass of milk. She didn't say anything; she just put it down on his nightstand and walked out.

Jack didn't really care about the food. He only ate half the sandwich before giving up. Lying back down, he resumed his study of the ceiling. How long he'd been at it, he didn't know, but Kevin Duncan suddenly popped into his head. He wondered how Kevin was making out. His stomach started tightening. Thinking about Kevin made him feel worse. In his gut he knew Kevin was taking some serious heat. And he knew it was his fault. His father's words kept swimming around in his head, *One tough son-of-a-B*. A new wave of guilt washed over him. He'd gotten Kevin into hot water. And Jayla. And maybe Charlie and Sam. *Why me? Why does Ryan Kerrigan hate me so much? Kerrigan is my problem, not theirs. I'm the one who's a panty waist. If I weren't such a weenie, they wouldn't have gotten involved—I am one sorry excuse for a human being.*

18

Guilty Before Proven Innocent

Kevin's cheek looked really bad. Jack didn't see it till he was halfway down the aisle of the school bus. The left side of Kevin's face was swollen and dark. For the briefest moment Jack thought it was from the fight with Kerrigan. Then he realized how Kevin got it, and guilt flooded him.

He was about to say he was sorry, but realized it would just make things worse. Kevin couldn't control Col. Duncan any more than he could control his own dad. So, instead, he opted for humor that he didn't feel.

"Nice cheek," said Jack, by way of greeting. "You run into a door last night?"

Kevin touched the side of his cheek, and winced. "Yeah—same door you ran into with that nose."

Jack couldn't help smiling. "Yup, I gotta learn to watch out for that door." He plopped down next to Kevin. Charlie jumped into the seat across the aisle. Jayla and Sam sat down just in front of them and leaned over the back of their seat.

"Sooooo . . . ?" asked Sam, scanning everyone in turn.

Jayla offered up, "I can't play for the next three days. The only time I'm allowed out is to go to school. My dad was really ticked off. In the car I got the total silent treatment. He never said one word to me the whole way back to our quarters. He just drove along, grinding his teeth. You know you're in major trouble when his jaw starts movin' back and forth that way. He dumped me off at home, leaving my mom to deal with it. He told her he thought I'd been recruited by a bunch of hooligans, blah, blah, blah, and that she'd better sort me out."

"So what'd your mom do?"

"She was really put off by the whole thing. She gave me the third degree for about an hour. When I finally told her what happened, she looked at me like I'd lost my mind and lectured me about how young ladies never, ever, ever get into a physical altercation. You like that one? *Physical altercation.* That's my mother's way of saying fistfight. She went through this whole drill about how I am never to embarrass my father with any of my behavior, and how my actions reflect on my father's character. She got so worked up that she stormed out of our quarters, marched into the muddy woods, got a pine switch, and tested it on me."

Sam said, "Good thing she didn't permanently ground you from playing with us. Sounds like you'll be paroled by the time the Saturday movie rolls around."

"Which is perfect timing. What about you guys?"

It turned out that because Sam and Charlie had been picked up by their mothers, they got off light. Charlie just got lectured, and Sam's mom was downright sympathetic. She was sure it was all just a little misunderstanding.

Sam said, "On the way home, before I could even explain about the fight, she said, 'Well, whatever happened, I trust that you did the right thing.'"

"Yup," said Sam, "that all took about half a second, and then my baby brother started to cry. He was in the back seat of the car just waking up from his nap. My mom smiled at me and said, 'Well, as long as you're here, honey, will you crawl over the seat and feed Mikey his bottle? You're just so good with him."

In fact, both of Sam's parents were certain that their ever-so-sweet, ever-so-good, ever-so-perfect daughter couldn't possibly have done anything wrong.

"Trade ya parents!" Jayla scoffed. Half of her was in disbelief, and the other half was just plain jealous.

"What about you, Kevin?" asked Charlie.

Kevin held up his hand as if to pause the conversation. All his concentration was on a huge wad of Bazooka bubblegum in his mouth. It seemed to pain him, but never the less, he worked that big, pink wad around, trying to get it into just the right position to start a bubble.

They all watched as the pink ball grew to the size of a baseball. Time to suck it back in before it popped. But no. Kevin kept blowing, way beyond the natural point of explosion. The bubble got to be the size of a softball, its ultra-thin skin starting to wobble. Only then, just when they were sure it would explode all over his black-and-blue face, he sucked it back in.

"Not a bad one," he said. "Now what was it you were asking, Charlie?"

"I was asking what happened. How did Full Colonel Duncan react to your first day of school?"

"Oh, that. Trust me, the colonel was one ticked-off commander. You know the drill. He gets a call from the school, and it immediately becomes my problem. It doesn't matter if I'm innocent or guilty! It doesn't matter what went down. If he gets a call, I'm guilty. 'Innocent before proven guilty' is definitely not in my father's vocabulary!

"I never quite know how this kinda thing is gonna go down, but in this case, he wasn't angry about the fight. In fact, he said it wasn't even a surprise I got in a fight on my first day. I started to think I might even get away with it. But, no. He found me guilty on two counts."

Imitating his father, he recited, "'First, you had the fight on school property. When you get into a fight, young man—and you will!—you take it offsite. You got that? Second, it wasn't even *your* fight, it was someone else's. You don't stick your nose in someone else's fight!' Blah, blah, blah . . .'"

"So what happened with your cheek?" asked Jack.

"Well, let's just say he felt poorly about my choices."

Jack couldn't help it. He burst out laughing. It made him feel better, but only for the briefest moment. "I'm sorry I got you guys involved in my problem. I should be able to deal with Kerrigan myself."

"That's a load of crap!" burst out Charlie. "That guy's a complete mental case. There isn't one kid in our whole class that can take Kerrigan by himself." Then a grin crossed his face. "Well, maybe there is *now*."

They all looked at Kevin.

"How'd you learn to fight like that?" asked Jayla.

"I don't know. I guess it didn't hurt that my ol' man made me take some boxing lessons back at Fort Knox."

"Wow!" Jack was incredulous.

"Yeah, for about the last year. It's actually kinda fun. The guy who taught me was this really small guy. They called him a featherweight. He worked with me a lot. If we go to the gym sometime, I'll show you. So, what happened to you, Jack?"

"What you'd expect," Jack answered. "The colonel exploded in the car. Actually it's kinda amazing we made it back to The Glass House without getting in a wreck. He was driving like a bat out of hell, and screaming at me the whole time. His eyes were on me more than the road. I was immediately sent to my room. Then he stormed around the place yelling and screaming at my mom. Sometime later he went back to work. That's when my mom ripped me up for embarrassing my father and possibly ruining his career. You're right, Kevin. No matter what goes down, no matter who starts it, or who did what, if the ol' man gets a call—I'm guilty! Basically, neither of my parents give a crap about what happens, as long as it doesn't come back to bite them.

"Then last night, my dad called me in for *the talk*—"

"No! No! Not *the talk!*" Jayla said in mock horror, and they all laughed.

"Yes, brace yourselves, brats. It was indeed the dreaded *talk*," said Jack. "My dad grilled me about what happened, and who was involved. His conclusions were very simple." Jack rattled them off like a rapid-fire machine gun:

"Ryan Kerrigan won't stop coming after me.

"Never fight on school grounds again.

"The school better never call him again or I'm dead meat.

"Pick some place other than school for the fight.

"But don't get caught fighting anywhere else.

"But don't ever back down from a fight.

"And if I get my ass kicked, it's my problem.

"Dismissed!

"Oh, yeah, and he restricted me to quarters for the next two days. I am not allowed to leave my room except to go to school."

"And that fine-looking face?" asked Charlie.

"Black eye courtesy of Ryan Kerrigan. Nose courtesy of the colonel," smirked Jack. "To quote our new friend, Kevin, let's just say the colonel 'felt poorly about my choices.'"

They were all laughing as the bus pulled up to school. But as they got off, Jack's smile faded, and he thought, *We weathered this one, but I need to do better at keeping these guys safe.*

∞⧓∞

In the playground after lunch, Jack, Charlie, and Kevin gravitated to the back fence to hold a short war council. They came up with the Ryan Kerrigan Solution. First, they'd stick together—alone, they made easy targets. Being together might slow Kerrigan down. However, they concluded, no matter what they did, sooner or later he would pick another fight at school. So they decided when that happened, they'd agree to fight him—just not at school. They decided the best place would be out behind the post gym. It was a location any kid could get to, but one that was far from school. Also it was a spot where no one was likely to bust them for fighting.

Kevin added, "And remember, if he doesn't show up, it makes *him* look like the weenie."

Kevin scraped up some snow, formed a snowball, and threw it onto the roof of the school. He said, "I hate math, and I just know Mrs. Campbell's gonna make us do that next."

Jack said, I'm okay at math. I'll help you."

"Even that might not be enough. Is math your best subject?"

"Yeah, that and German."

"Ugh! Do we have to take German?"

"Yup. Twice a week," said Charlie.

"And you *like* it?"

"Yeah, I guess," said Jack. "I want to learn it so I can understand what the German people are saying. Sometimes my dad takes us to Göppingen on Sunday for church, and I have no idea what the priest is talking about. But I like to try and figure it out."

"Not me, man. I hate languages almost as much as math."

"What's your best subject?' asked Charlie.

"History and maybe geography," said Kevin. "What about you?"

"Me?" said Charlie, "Definitely not science. Last week's test almost killed me."

Jack shook himself to forget the memory. "You had company there, Charlie. I bet we *all* failed."

"Glad I missed it," said Kevin. "So what subject *do* you like?"

Charlie thought a moment. "Lunch."

Kevin winked at Jack, nodding toward Charlie. "I knew I liked this guy."

The bell rang and they had to head back in. By the time they got to the school door, everyone else was off the playground. Mrs. Campbell was a stickler for getting back to class on time, so Jack picked up the pace. Unfortunately, halfway down the hallway some kid had barfed. The sight and smell made Charlie so sick, he thought he might lose it, too. He bent over as the other two scooted down the hall. It was only a second, but when Charlie straightened up, the janitor was blocking his way with a slimy puke mop. It seemed to Charlie like Mr. Electric Shock Hair actually took pleasure in not letting him get past. Charlie had to go the long way around. He was still in the hall when the late bell rang.

Mrs. Campbell glared at him. "Charlie, yesterday you never even made it back to class after fighting at morning break. That should have put you on your best behavior today. You owe me 'I will not be late from lunch' one hundred times. Have it on my desk first thing tomorrow morning."

Charlie looked ticked as he headed for his seat. But before he reached it, there came a sharp sound of metal banging metal.

Clang! Clang! Clang!
Clang! Clang! Clang! Clang!

Every kid in the room, even Kevin, knew that sound. Every kid in every military school around the world knew it.

Air-raid drill.

Kevin ducked into a cross-legged position under his desk, but all the other kids headed for the door. Jack leaned down and said "We don't do the duck and cover here. There's an old Nazi bomb shelter in the basement. Follow me."

Their class formed an orderly line and made their way, along with the rest of the school, through the hall, down two flights of stairs, through a large iron door, and into a cavernous, concrete room. Mrs. Campbell's class stayed together as one very silent unit. The minute they were up against a far wall and seated on the floor, she did a head count to make sure everyone was accounted for.

Kevin leaned into Jack and whispered, "At Fort Knox we just got under our desks. There was no bomb shelter. And we kept our eyes shut tight so we wouldn't get blinded from the bright flash of the nuclear bomb."

Jack nodded. "We don't have to shut our eyes here, 'cause with no windows, there's no giant flash."

From Kevin's other side, Charlie cocked his head toward where the janitor stood in front of a closed door. "Man, I hate that creepy guy." He told them how the janitor made him late for class.

"There's definitely something off about him," Jack said.

"It was like he was pushing the puke mop at me. I thought I was gonna lose my lunch."

Kevin studied the man. "Looks like he's guarding that door. What's behind it?"

"We don't know," said Charlie. "Someone told us it's a storage room."

Jack added, "But we're not sure. We're only down here for air-raid drills. It looks suspicious. Why would a storeroom door be solid iron and and have no door handle?"

Mrs. Campbell, looking seriously irritated, hissed, "You three stop talking this instant!"

They immediately piped down. But a few minutes later, when her head was turned the other way, Kevin said under his breath, "Is she always such a dragon lady?"

"Mostly she's nice, and, as teachers go, we all like her," Jack said very quietly. "But air-raid drills get her upset."

Mrs. Campbell, jumping up, headed right toward them.

Jack was sure they were in big trouble. But she passed them by and started yelling at Kerrigan for something he'd done. Today was not the day to push their luck. This time they stayed silent.

Once back in class, Mrs. Campbell began handing back their science tests.

As they looked at their scores, a collective groan came from the class.

"You *should* be ashamed of yourselves," she said, glaring at them. "You not only failed to learn the new material, you even missed the extra-credit questions about Sputnik! I mean, come on! Four months after the Russians launch the first satellite into outer space, you can't even remember enough to answer some simple questions?"

Jayla raised her hand. "Last week's newsreel said President Eisenhower was completely taken by surprise when the Russians won the race to launch the first man-made moon. It said our scientists are way behind the Russian scientists."

Mrs. Campbell's expression turned even sourer. "Well, maybe that's because our scientists are as bad at science as you children are. That's probably why we've been forced to use old Nazi scientists on the project instead of American scientists."

"So the Russians really *are* ahead of us?" Jayla asked, obviously concerned.

Mrs. Campbell began pacing back and forth in front of the blackboard, snapping a ruler into the palm of her hand. "Absolutely, they are! Two years ago America said we would launch a satellite by 1957 or 1958. But did we? We most certainly did not! Two years ago the Russians predicted they would conquer space long before any US man-made moon appeared. And did they? Yes, they did!"

"Who cares?" Kerrigan blurted out defensively. "What good is a hunk of metal in outer space when all it does is go *beep, beep, beep*?"

"That's enough out of you, Ryan Kerrigan. One more smart remark and you go to the principal for a second day in a row."

When Kerrigan glared back, his swollen black eye made him wince.

"Well, we will catch up. Won't we?" Jayla said, concerned.

Mrs. Campbell snapped at her. "I find that highly unlikely. And especially if your generation has anything to do with it. Compared to Russian children, American children are lazy and incompetent. Instead of being willing to put real effort into math and science homework, all American children want to do is sit around playing board games. Counting out play money in Monopoly won't get you anywhere. But Russian kids? They have the resourcefulness and determination to overcome any obstacle or barrier, no matter what it takes. American children couldn't plan their way out of a paper bag."

Jayla went speechless, her endless supply of questions dried up. But not Mrs. Campbell. She was just getting warmed up.

"Russian children aren't over-privileged—the way you are. And they aren't spoiled. After the war, many of them were left as orphans. All on their own, those kids had to walk halfway across Eastern Russia to hunt up whichever relatives they had left. You kids couldn't even make it to that mountain on your own." She pointed out the window in the direction of the Hohenstaufen, ten miles away.

Mrs. Campbell stayed a dragon the rest of the day. At the final bell, the boys escaped as fast as they could; even solitary confinement at home was better than any more time with her.

Jack turned to Charlie. "Don't sweat having to write those hundred lines; I'll help you on the bus."

"Does she always give so much math homework?" moaned Kevin. "I *knew* when she yelled about Russian kids doing better at science and math that we'd spend the rest of the day on math, and I was right. But did she have to pile on the homework? I don't have a clue what she was even talking about. Why does anyone need fractions anyway? Jack, you help *me* with the math homework and *I'll* help Charlie with the lines."

Charlie wrote the sentence on multiple pieces of notebook paper. Sam and Kevin each took a couple and made a contest out of who could make their handwriting look most like Charlie's.

Jack glanced up from Kevin's math. Jayla's contorted face glared at him.

"What?" he demanded.

"We have a lot more important things to do than writing 'I will not be late from lunch'! We *are* going to get from here to the Hohenstaufen. And we're going to do it all by ourselves. I don't care how many obstacles we have to face, or barriers we have to get over."

"What are you talking about?"

"I'm talking about Mrs. Campbell and her superhuman Russian children. *We* are going to prove we are just as good as Russian kids. Do you hear me, Jack McMasters?"

"Yeah. I hear you." But, truth be known, he couldn't make out if she was serious or just mad at their teacher. "Do you realize how far away that mountain is?"

He knew that was the wrong thing to say when she flipped around in her seat to stare out the dirty bus window.

Kevin wordlessly communicated to Jack, "What's she so worked up about?" Aloud he said, "Mrs. Campbell was right about one thing. I love Monopoly. I wouldn't even let the packers get their mitts on it; I brought it with *me*. Come over Saturday afternoon and play Monopoly in her honor."

Jack nodded.

"Can't say I'm any good at it," Charlie said, "but I'm in."

So began the longest Monopoly marathon in the history of Cooke Barracks. After lunch on Saturday, Jack called for Charlie at his quarters and they hoofed it up from The Glass House and around The Circle

to the third duplex. Beside one of the doors was a stenciled sign: Col. Duncan.

A girl about Queenie's age answered the doorbell. She yelled up the stairs, "Kevin, your little friends are here."

Kevin came bounding down the stairs, shaking his head in frustration. "Guys, this is my sister, Karen. And as you can tell, she makes my life a constant delight."

Jack said, "Oh, Kevin, you won't know delightful till you meet my sister Queenie."

"Queenie? Your sister's name is actually *Queenie*?" demanded Karen.

"Well, no. But it's a long story. Her real name is Laura, but we call her *Queenie*."

"Surely you don't mean Laura McMasters. I know her. You're her *little brother*?"

"That would be me." Jack gave her one of his world-beater smiles.

Karen just walked away.

After she was out of earshot, Charlie said, "By the way, Kevin, don't ever call her *Queenie* to her face. You'll get a knuckle sandwich."

Kevin assured, "I am a pro at dealing with a superior older sister." He flashed his own dazzling smile.

He led them into the living room, which was surprisingly dark. All the drapes were pulled, and not one light was on. Jack assumed they were passing through an empty room, but out of the gloom came a low, gravelly voice. "Hello, boys. It's nice to meet you."

Jack all but jumped. He hadn't noticed anyone as they came through the room. In fact, he could barely see the lady now. She was seated in an old, overstuffed chair in a far corner. She seemed slightly heavyset and strangely removed. Remaining perfectly still, she was like a female Buddha sitting in the dark.

"Could you get me my medicine and refresh my drink?" the gravel voice said.

"Sure, Mom. Come on, guys."

They followed him through the dining room and into the kitchen. "I'll help her and then get us our stuff."

Jack noticed Kevin smelled the glass before refilling it with ice water. Jack thought, *Probably deciding if it needs to be washed.*

Kevin was back in a flash. He got them each a Coke. Then said, "Okay, boys, let's go to my room."

As they walked up the stairs, Jack thought, *When your father's a full colonel, you must get quarters with an upstairs and a downstairs.*

Kevin had the game set up on the floor over in a corner and they got right down to playing. It seemed only minutes before they had to head home for dinner—right in the middle of a game.

"I vacuum my own room, so this will never be disturbed."

Thus began their winter series of Monopoly games. Within weeks, Charlie and Jack rivaled Kevin as Monopoly masters.

∞⊱✦⊰∞

Jack did his best to practice Mr. Reynolds's exercises, but he knew it would take more than staying engaged to deal with Ryan Kerrigan. It would mean learning how to defend himself. So he reminded Kevin of his promise to show them how to box.

Kevin was more than willing, if they could find a place. The post gym was the most likely location, so one afternoon, Jack, Sam, Jayla, Charlie, and Kevin just showed up there. They had no idea if kids were allowed, and that was definitely *not* the kind of question they would ask an adult—especially their parents. The certain "parent answer" would be, "Even if you *are* allowed, we don't want you hanging around a bunch of GIs." So, of course, no one asked.

When they reached the front desk, they again figured that if you ask, you get told no. That first day they just marched right in and started using the stuff.

The gym had all kinds of fun equipment to play on: a rope climb, parallel bars, weights, and the horse for gymnastics. But for them, the main attraction was a boxing ring that had gloves and everything they might need. Kevin invited them into the ring to show them how to box.

It didn't take long for the guy in charge to tell them to get lost.

That didn't stop them from coming back another day. And that afternoon a private named Finnegan was on duty. Jayla tried a new approach. She walked right up to him and said, "Is it okay if we use the boxing ring? My friend Kevin is a boxer, and he wants to show us how to do it."

"Which one is Kevin?" Finnegan asked.

"I am."

Finnegan said, "So, Kevin, where'd you box?"

"Fort Knox, sir."

Private Finnegan just nodded. "Okay, kids, I don't care. Go knock yourselves out." Then he added with a smile, "But don't *really* knock yourselves out."

Without the slightest hesitation, they started putting on the gloves. That turned into a laugh. They soon realized they couldn't tie up their own gloves. And once on, there was no way to tie up someone else's gloves. Sam was the last person with untied gloves. She asked Private Finnegan for help, and asked which days he worked at the gym.

Tuesdays and Thursdays.

They started showing up on those afternoons.

At first, Finnegan just kept an eye on what Kevin was showing them. But about their third session, Finnegan realized they were getting serious about boxing. He started showing them a couple of things, and acting as the referee. He explained about holding your guard up, how to move your feet, and how to punch, not just with your arm, but with your whole body. He also showed them how to train with the big punching bag and the speed bag.

The speed bag looked easy when Kevin or Finnegan did it, but when Jack tried, it took him a while to get the hang of it. Finnegan also made them jump rope. That, too, was a riot. Right from the start both girls could do it, but it took Jack and Charlie quite a while to figure out how to jump rope without looking like a dip stick.

In the beginning, everyone but Kevin was terrible at boxing—and sore after every session. Their bodies hurt, not just from the punches, but also from the workouts—punching the bags, jumping rope, scrambling up the climbing rope, and everything else to improve their strength, stamina, and agility. But they steadily improved. The one who surprised everyone was Jayla. From the start, she was fast on her feet and had a good eye for what her opponent was going to do. The two things that helped her most were long arms and being fearless. Jayla became Kevin's regular sparring partner. *Sparring* was a Finnegan term, which basically meant having a boxing match with an opponent. They all took turns sparring.

Boxing wasn't the only way they improved. At first, none of them could reach the top of the rope climb. But as with boxing, over time, they got better at it and could touch the ceiling.

∞⊰✕⊱∞

One night Kevin and Jack were having a sleepover at Charlie's. The Monopoly board was sleeping over, too.

"McMasters, you stink," Kevin said, laughing. "That's the third game in a row you've won."

"Can't there be *something* I'm better at?" complained Charlie.

Jack wouldn't take that sob story for a minute. "Don't give me that. You certainly have the best comic book collection of any of us, not to mention you read better than we do."

Charlie only shrugged. "Yeah, you might hate reading, but somehow you still know more war stories than both of us together."

"You don't have to read to know a ton of stories," Jack said simply. "You just have to be good at listening and remembering what you hear. When your mom is as great a cook as mine is, the officers come to *you*, and so do the stories."

Kevin said, "Okay, then, Mister Great Listener, tell us one."

"Make it a war story," said Charlie, "from one of those foreign officers in love with your mom's cooking."

Jack had told them some of his best tales came from military men from places like Japan, England, Iran, Pakistan, France, and Indonesia. How they made it halfway around the world to find Mrs. McMasters's dinner table was something he couldn't begin to explain.

Jack said, "Well, one night a few years back, this tall, very dignified gentleman came to our house for dinner. His name was Col. Jean-Jacques Boutrigue. He was a French Infantry officer, and boy was he strack. He showed up at our quarters in a perfectly pressed khaki uniform, a broad, brown leather belt around the jacket, and plenty of ribbons on his chest. He had on a round, flat-topped, dark-blue hat with plenty of gold braiding around it, and a small bill in front. He was a French colonel. When I was introduced, he shook hands with me and then handed me that hat, but with such a serious look I felt like he was making it my personal mission to keep it safe. I carefully put it on a small table just inside our front door.

"But while the adults went off to have a cocktail before dinner, I snuck back and tried on his hat. As I looked at myself in the mirror just above that table, I wondered what it would be like to be a French Infantry officer. I loved that hat, even though it was way too big.

"After dinner and coffee, my father brought out the decanter of cognac and two crystal brandy snifters. He poured cognacs for himself and the colonel. The colonel had a large, thin beak of a nose, and he used it to take a deep smell of the cognac. He closed his eyes and smiled with delight. He and my dad started talking. For some reason, he told this story about why he admired our General George Washington.

"Early on, during the American Revolutionary War, the British had occupied Boston. General Washington and his Continental Army had them surrounded. Old Washington was in a perfect position to attack. But he had one major problem: He was desperately short on gunpowder. In fact, his men only had enough gunpowder for several shots each.

"But, boys, General Washington was the only one who actually knew how short on gunpowder the Continental Army was. His men did not know, and his officers didn't either. If they had known, they'd have realized that instead of the American Army being in a position to attack the British, it was really the British Army who could have wiped *them* out.

"Whenever gunpowder came up, Washington told his officers and men that he had plenty stored away in a secret place. But in fact, there was no such gunpowder. Washington knew he had to keep it a secret until he could get more. And he needed more before the British got wind of his problem.

"Washington made a number of attempts to get more gunpowder. Once he sent ships down to the Caribbean to get it. But the British had created a blockade and the ships couldn't get through."

"And nobody figured it out?" demanded Charlie, getting impatient.

"Charlie, General Washington was really good at bluffing. In fact, he had to keep up his bluff for almost six months.

"Fortunately for Washington, one of his generals, Benedict Arnold, along with Ethan Allen and his Green Mountain Boys, won the Battle of Ticonderoga, and they took over Fort Ticonderoga up in New York."

Kevin spoke up. "But Benedict Arnold was the traitor who tried to give West Point to the British."

Jack nodded. "This was before he switched sides. Fort Ticonderoga had lots of British cannons and gunpowder. Then, in one of the greatest feats of the Revolutionary War, Benedict Arnold was able to drag those big cannons and all those barrels of gunpowder hundreds of miles from Ticonderoga to Boston.

"Once Washington had the guns and gunpowder, he threw the British out of Boston."

"Great story," said Kevin.

"Yeah, but that wasn't Col. Boutrigue's point. He looked me in the eye and said, 'Consider for a moment what might have happened if Washington had *not* been able to keep his secret. What if his troops found out, lost confidence, and deserted? What if the British had found out nothing could stop them? You, Jack McMasters, might be British today.'"

"From this story, my friends, we learn the importance of certain skills."

Charlie said, "Bluffing."

Kevin agreed. "Knowing what to tell and what to hold back."

"Yes." Jack nodded.

"Wonder if we're ever gonna have to keep something like that secret," Kevin mused aloud. "You know, like about gunpowder?"

Little did Jack know he would soon hear just such a secret.

19

Cut and Run

Spring meant exploring the woods without boots or heavy coats, as well as hitting the post gym every Tuesday and Thursday. Private Flannigan seemed to like being their coach and referee. But for Jack, boxing didn't seem to get easier. His brain shut down whenever someone attacked him. He didn't tell anyone, but some nights he'd lie awake, wondering, *What's wrong with me? Why am I such a complete weenie?* Jayla was so cool-headed when she boxed, which made him feel worse.

Finnegan made them wear face guards when they sparred. One day Charlie got in a lucky punch, hitting Jack full in the face. The punch turned out to be lucky for Jack, too. When the face guard did its job, Jack's mind stopped shutting down as a punch came at him, freeing him to watch his opponent. He began to protect himself in the ring, and to get in a half-decent punch himself.

For Jack's birthday, Charlie and Kevin slept over, and his father presented him with a Fleischmann train set. Things were going fine that spring.

Then came Little League signups.

Jack, Kevin, and Charlie were on the Cooke Barrack's Cougars. Two afternoons a week, they would go to Little League practice. In a while, they'd have a game once a week. Some would be home games, others away games. For the away games, they would ride in an Army bus to play a team on another base. Every boy Jack knew was crazy about baseball. Jack assumed he'd like it, too. That assumption was about to strike out.

As he got suited up for the first practice, Jack studied himself in the mirror. He liked how he looked in his Cougars uniform. He started getting pumped about being part of the team. But things took a serious dip an hour into that first practice. As they each tried throwing, Jack soon realized he could *throw* the ball but it rarely got over the plate. He'd never be a pitcher. Besides, that position was quickly reserved for Kevin, who demonstrated decent ball control and even a bit of a fastball.

Charlie Carron got selected for third base. It seemed there was little he couldn't catch. Jack, on the other hand, didn't catch much better than he threw. That put him out of the running for any infield position—not second base (which went to Kerrigan), not shortstop, not anything.

In less than no time, Jack became an outcast. By the second practice, no one but Charlie and Kevin would even make eye contact with him. If anyone else looked at him at all, that guy's eyes seemed to say, *What kind of dorf can't catch a ball?*

Jack just couldn't get that hand/eye coordination thing going. His glove and the ball were not on good terms. The other boys seemed to catch instinctively. Jack had zero instinct in the catching department. Kevin and Charlie tried to help, but he was pretty much a lost cause.

By the third practice, even his best friends had started to avoid him on the field. *Why am I such a stupid klutz? I hate this! Quit looking at Kevin! Quit looking at Charlie! Make like a nobody, Jack, or they're gonna dump you.*

Jack had been relegated to the outfield, where he endured both mind-numbing boredom and constant dread that he would miss a fly ball?

Jack hated Little League.

One evening after baseball practice, Jack was scrunched down on the couch in the living room, flipping through the latest *Life* magazine. He liked how it had the best pictures and the least words.

Rabbit and Queenie were both in their room, and his parents were on the balcony having a drink. They probably had no idea he was there. Through the open door, he heard them mention his name. Jack's brat-radar flipped on.

"You don't need to tell me Laura is doing great in school, but what did Jack's teacher have to say about his reading?" asked Lt. Col. McMasters.

"Still very little progress," he heard his mother say.

"Lorraine, what are we going to do about that kid?"

Jack was surprised, not by his father's words, but by his tone. Instead of sounding frustrated or angry, he sounded concerned.

"Relax, John. Jack is smarter than people think. In fact, his teacher thinks he's doing fine in math and science. "

Jack thought, *She's just trying to smooth it over so he doesn't get bent out of shape about how I'm doing.*

"And as for German, she thinks he's nothing short of amazing," said his mom.

"The German is Ingrid's doing," said his dad. "I just worry about his ability to read. He's got the kind of mind that needs to be fed."

Whatever that *means,* Jack thought.

Their conversation moved on to other things.

Nothing to worry about. Relieved, Jack went back to an article in the magazine showing space pilots and the kind of suits they might wear.

A few minutes later, his brat-radar tripped back on, not from hearing his name but by the rising level of tension in his mother' voice.

"Relax, Lorraine, that new lieutenant's wife is an alarmist."

"Don't tell *me* to relax. You heard what she said." His mom's voice was getting more and more demanding. "Stop ducking the issue, John. I have a right to know. Is this base likely to be attacked or not?"

"She was overreacting." Jack heard growing frustration in his dad's voice. "There's no threat of attack right now."

"Maybe not now, but it is possible. Correct?"

"I've told you before. There's no way to know for sure." Jack heard him adopt a more calming tone. "It is possible, yes. But I don't think it's likely. Our defenses are solid, and for them the cost would be too high."

"She said that if the base were attacked, it would be overrun from the northeast."

"Probably, but that's all been taken into consideration. Look, honey, you really don't need to worry about this. If it ever does actually happen, there will be plenty of warning. Plenty of time to get you and the kids out."

Jack, whose instincts were usually pretty good, decided it was time to slip away. Better to not be caught eavesdropping when they came back inside.

Charlie and Kevin were stretched out on Jack's bedroom floor, tinkering with his new train set. Everything *seemed* to be great, but Jack still couldn't shake the fear they might dump him for being such an embarrassment in the outfield. He couldn't help looking for telltale signs. *Is everything still okay? Are they just hanging out with me because I'm the only one with a train set and none of the other kids will know?*

"The Germans certainly know how to make a train," said Charlie. "The only problem is, you have more track than bedroom. You could use it all if we made a loop run under your bed and out the other side."

Jack nodded, so Charlie said, "Hand me one of those switches, Kevin."

Kevin passed it over. "I overheard my dad talking about the Nazis last night. What he said struck me as strange, and at the same time kinda scary. A few weeks back he was off doing something with the German Army. What, I have no idea. Anyway, he went out drinking with a bunch of German officers who were former Luftwaffe officers. I mean, word from the bird, these guys had been Nazi Air Force officers. My dad said something to them about the Germans having such a good Air Force during the war. An old colonel, who was a little drunk, said something like, 'Give us another Luftwaffe, and we'll conquer the world!' His German buddies quickly hustled him out." Kevin looked at his friends. "Is that eerie, or what?"

Charlie gave an involuntary shiver. "You're right. Definitely scary."

"Do you think the Germans are really planning to try and take over the world again?" asked Kevin.

"I don't know," said Jack, thinking it over. "It's possible. Otherwise, why would the younger officers try to shut him up?"

"I dunno," replied Kevin. "Maybe the guy was just drunk and shooting his mouth off."

Jack shook his head. "No, something's definitely going on. I heard something, too." He relayed his parent's conversation on the balcony.

"So you're saying if they come back and attack us, it will be from the northeast?" asked Charlie.

"Dad said, 'Probably,' right before he told my mom it wasn't all that likely."

Charlie's knee started bouncing up and down. "Maybe he just said that to calm her down. And what about all the other stuff we've heard?"

"What stuff?" demanded Kevin.

Jack related what the older kids said to each other the morning the tanks rolled. Then he told Kevin about the joke they'd overheard at the airport about Hitler coming back to power.

"When we were on the ship coming over," Jack added, "one of the naval officers told us the American military was in Germany to prevent another war. So maybe we're here 'cause the Nazi's *are* coming back."

When Charlie told him about The Watcher, Kevin was barely breathing.

Kevin studied his friends and finally took a deep breath. "We need to find that spy. We need to figure out what's going on with the Nazis."

"Yeah," said Jack. "It feels like there's an enemy empire out there getting ready to crush us. Unfortunately we're totally in the dark about who they are."

"*Dark* is the right word," Charlie said, grimly. "Boys, we're up against a Dark Empire. Time to figure out who they are and where they are.

Jack was by himself in his room. Recently he'd been spending a lot of time in there working on his train set. And not just because he liked it. Something about the work helped him think over stuff. Things he'd normally avoid. The work somehow freed his mind to think about Little League, Kerrigan, the Sevens, the Nazis, his shutting down, and even Ingrid.

Unlike the other things, he puzzled over Ingrid because he *liked* her. The more she became part of their lives, the more intel came his way. For example, he'd made a note that she never got any phone calls. And one time when a letter from his grandma arrived, he realized that Ingrid never got any mail from *her* family. In fact, she got no mail at all. He logged that in the back of his mind as somehow worrisome. Was she really all alone in the world? Why?

Little League and Kerrigan were the most urgent, and they took up most of his brainpower.

He put a railroad car back on the track but, for the third time, its wheels weren't lining up correctly. Jack wasn't concentrating on the task. Instead, he was imagining himself on the Little League bus, isolated and miserable. Even though Charlie and Kevin told him not to sweat it, he still worried he'd lose his best friends over being a klutz at sports.

He blamed his eyes. He hated his eyes. But there was nothing he could do about not having 3D vision. Seeing in 2D was what made it hard to catch. Should he say something to his parents? Forget it. They knew about the problem. His dad would just say to suck it up and move on. Should he tell the coach or the other players? That was never gonna happen! He was already pathetic enough without piling on lame excuses.

So much for processing time—Jack was still in a box.

A week later, Lt. Col. McMasters came home with a giant train board tied to the top of the Roadmaster. It was so large, it took his dad and a huge guy to get it up the three flights of stairs to their quarters and into Jack's room. What most stunned Jack was the landscape painted on the board. There were big brush strokes of different shades of green and brown showing fields and forests, dark charcoal for the roads, blue and purple splashes making up a stream that flowed across the board into a lake.

"Jack, this is Corporal Harding," his dad said. "He works for me now, but before he joined the Army, Harding was a professional artist."

"Your dad told some of his men you got a train set for your birthday," said Harding. "So, as a favor to the colonel, the men got together and made you this train board and the sawhorses to hold it up."

"Wow." It was all Jack could think to say.

Corporal Harding smiled. "Jack, that was all fine and good, but I gotta tell you, once we got it built, the board looked a bit naked. So I decided to whip out my brushes and paints, and see if I could dress it up a little. I hope the landscape I came up with works well for you."

"Thanks," Jack said, simply amazed. "You're a really great artist. It's perfect. I'm gonna call it *Wunderland*."

Corporal Harding's smile got even broader. "I'm glad you like it. And that's a swell name. How'd you come up with it so fast?"

"I guess 'cause my sisters and I like Germany so much that we call it *Wunderland*. That's the German word for Wonderland. And this board looks just like Germany."

The corporal knelt on one knee to look Jack in the eye. "I really am glad you like it. I painted this board for you, and for your father, because we Army guys stick together. We help each other out. For me, the Army *is* my family, and family sticks together. Sound good, Jack?"

"Yes, sir."

"Oh, you don't have to call me *sir*. I *work* for a living." His eye twinkled as he looked up at the colonel, who seemed to be smirking at an inside joke.

Jack didn't know what the joke was, but he loved his train, and he sure was glad to get the board.

During school the next day, Jack and Charlie had a minor run-in with Kerrigan. They'd been out on the playground and watched as Kerrigan held the attention of a group of kids. Some were older.

"How's he do that?" Jack wondered aloud.

"What?" Charlie asked.

"Well, the guy's a psycho, right? He's definitely not what anyone would call a *nice* guy."

"So?"

"So why are they listening? Especially those older kids."

"Dunno. Let's wander over there and see what they're up to."

As they approached, one of the older kids said, "How much?"

Kerrigan quickly stuffed what looked like a Nazi helmet into his backpack. Then he whipped around and glared at Jack and Charlie. "Get lost, McMasters. I'd spell it out, but I'm not sure you could sound out the letters."

It took everything Jack had in him to turn away.

Jack and Charlie were almost out of earshot when they heard Kerrigan say to the guys around him, "So, you interested in it?"

Jack and Charlie kept walking. "He's selling Nazi stuff," whispered Charlie. "Wonder where he got it."

"Dunno," Jack said.

That evening Jack finished the dishes in record time. He wanted more train time to grind on Kerrigan.

How's he getting kids to follow him? He's intimidating. He's mean. He's violent.

He plugged more track together. *Kerrigan's also smart and good at controlling his gang. He's helped them believe they're somebody.*

Jack thought back on the scene of Kerrigan coming toward them when they'd been playing Cowboys and Indians at the pillbox. Kerrigan hadn't just been with kids his age. There had been older kids. He remembered them moving through the forest like a well-disciplined military unit. Kerrigan had been out in front, walking point, leading the squad. He'd just taken a knee and had been passing back hand signals. Kerrigan had real leadership skills.

Everyone, even the older kids, obeyed his commands without hesitation. How's that possible?

He rummaged through the box for some curved track to route around the pond painted on the train board. *And why do the Sevens let Kerrigan hang out with them? He's two grades younger than they are. Maybe Kerrigan had something they wanted—like that Nazi helmet.*

As he snapped two pieces together, something clicked in his brain. *Kerrigan and the Sevens aren't hunting for the Nazis. They're hunting for Nazi stuff to keep or sell. They don't want us in the woods in case we find something before they do. . . . Bingo!*

By their fifth Little League practice, Jack realized playing outfield had two advantages: few balls reached him, and he had a prayer of catching the ones that did.

He was so far out, it took longer for the ball to arrive. That gave him enough time to adjust his position two or three times as he figured out where and when it would land. One afternoon, Jack actually caught a long bomb, and Kevin gave him an amazed thumbs-up.

After that, Charlie and Kevin started helping Jack catch long balls. They'd practice most afternoons in front of The Glass House. Jack never got great at catching, but his friends did help him improve his game and calm his fears that they would ditch him. Even so, he still wished Little League would just go away.

One afternoon Jack was in the outfield, bored and unfocused. Just when he realized the whole team was yelling at him, a long ball whizzed low over his head. He'd been so lost in a daydream he hadn't even known the ball was hit, much less in his direction. But he was wide awake for the groans of all his teammates.

Jack had had enough.

He barely held on until the inning ended. He headed for the dugout with the others, but, instead of entering, walked right past and didn't stop until he was all the way back to The Glass House. He just wanted his old life back, his life before baseball.

He didn't see Kevin or Charlie until the bus ride to school the next morning.

Jack decided on a preemptive strike. "I'm done with baseball. I hate standing there waiting to make an idiot of myself."

"But you were getting better," said Kevin. "I told the coach you started to feel sick and went home. Thought that would keep him off your back."

"Thanks." Jack didn't know what else to say.

For the next two days, when Kevin and Charlie went off to Little League, he stayed home, alone, working on his train set. He accomplished almost nothing.

He had assumed that after practice Charlie and Kevin would come by to play. But they must have gotten preoccupied with other stuff on the way home, because they never showed. Not the first day, and not the second day. Jack dreaded the third.

But Kevin and Charlie did come by after practice that afternoon.

Out of the blue, Kevin said, "We all want to be warriors, right?

Jack sensed a trap. "Yeah. So?"

"Well, don't you know about the Spartans?"

"I know they were great warriors in ancient Greece."

"Great?" Kevin said with delight. "They were way better than *great*. The Spartans were one of the most feared military forces of all time. A Spartan was the M-48 tank of his day, and all he had was a spear, a sword, a shield, and some body armor. One Spartan was worth several men in any other army. That's 'cause Spartans started military training when they were babies. By our age, their life was focused on two things: war tactics and sports. Spartans believed sports were critical to becoming a real warrior."

Jack rolled his eyes. "Spartans didn't play baseball." Then, hesitating, he finally added, "Besides, what's the coach gonna say if I just show up again?"

"We've got that covered," said Charlie.

Kevin grinned. "We've been telling him you're home sick. Didn't you wonder why he hadn't called your parents?"

I was too busy wondering why you *hadn't called.*

"So forget the coach. Think about the Spartans," said Kevin.

Jack shrugged. "I'll be there tomorrow."

Little League practice was just as painful as ever, but a load was off his shoulders, and working on his train set had become fun again. He hurried home to work on the board. Except he couldn't get anywhere near it. Some days, Rabbit and Ingrid had a parade of stuffed animals marching down the hallway to the bedrooms. Every other day, Queenie, Camila Alvarez, Liz Harrison, and a bunch of other girls were hanging around the bathroom so Ingrid could show them how to do their hair in different styles. Lately, it seemed like all Queenie and her girlfriends wanted to do was hang out with Ingrid.

While Jack had a very low tolerance for this girly, girly stuff, he was still okay with Ingrid. Mainly because she sometimes did things just with him. In fact, one afternoon shortly after he'd gotten his train set, she had taken him along with her to Göppingen. That's when she'd introduced him to the hobby store where his father had bought his Fleishmann train. It instantly became his favorite place in Göppingen. He bought a dining car that afternoon, but it took him almost an hour to make up his mind; he wanted just about everything in the store.

He especially liked a model of a rock quarry but thought it wouldn't fit with Wunderland.

Ingrid said, "But it would! Last Sunday, I was out with a guy, and we took a ride up to the Hohenstaufen. At the bottom of the mountain we found a rock quarry like this model."

"You go on . . . what's the word in German for when a guy asks you to go out?"

"*Auf ein Date gehen?* Is that what you are asking?"

Weird, Jack thought. *We say 'going on a date' and they use the same word in German. I guess that's one German word I won't forget.* Then, unable to contain himself, he said to her, "Yes, that's it. So, do you go on dates?"

"Don't you think I'm pretty enough?" she said, flirting with him.

Jack went red. He had no response in either German or English.

On his second trip to the hobby store, Jack fell in love with an old mill with a water wheel. It came as a kit to assemble with model glue. The problem was he didn't have enough money to buy it. He finally settled on a small farmhouse, which was half the price.

Jack loved his train set, but he worked on it mostly when he needed time alone. Jack's train set had become his private sanctuary, his place to think.

He spent the next several days carefully building that farmhouse, while his brain was preoccupied with Kerrigan. As he attached a piece of the model, he examined another piece of intel he had on the guy.

Unfortunately, unlike the model that came with all required parts and specific assembly instructions, it was clear to Jack that he didn't have all the pieces when it came to Kerrigan. Nor did he have a clear idea of what Kerrigan was up to. That worried him.

He mentally turned over the pieces he *did* have. *I know he and his gang are out in the woods trying to find caches of Nazi stuff from the war. And I can guess they keep some and sell the rest to make money. I get all that . . .*

Jack balanced a tiny, green rectangle on the tip of his finger. With his other hand, he dipped a toothpick into a drop of glue he'd squeezed on some newspaper. Then, ever so carefully, he dabbed the glue onto the green window shutter and placed it beside a window.

But why has Kerrigan hooked up with the Sevens? Why let himself be used to do their dirty work? That doesn't make sense. He's too smart to let himself be used by those guys. What's in it for him?

Jack studied the farmhouse assembly instructions and then broke off the next piece he needed.

Maybe Kerrigan thinks it's the best way to search for Nazi stuff in what they consider "their woods." If he couldn't lick 'em, he'd join 'em.

An hour later, Jack glued the last piece onto the farmhouse.

Ryan Kerrigan, if I know anything about you, you think you're smarter than the Sevens, even if they're older. You plan to stay one step ahead of them and to find things first. You're not being used, you're using them. And they don't even know it. You might be a psycho, Ryan Kerrigan, but you're a clever one.

Jack put the completed farmhouse on the board. It looked great. But it also highlighted how empty the rest of the board was. Clearly he needed a lot more buildings, trees, people, animals. . . . Lots more than he could ever buy with his weekly allowance.

Starting that moment, Jack became a hustler. He left his room to see if his mom had any paying chores. She set him up polishing the silver. As he rubbed her silver teapot, he made a mental list of other adults who might need help.

From then on, he asked every adult he met, "Do you have any jobs you need to have done? I'm desperate for money." He got all kinds of reactions. Mostly *no*. But he did occasionally pick up an odd job. Among other things, he became pretty good as a carwash guy. He took every job, and every spare nickel went into his train set.

On the way to their first game, everyone on the bus was laughing and yelling and having a great, old time. Everyone except Jack. He wanted to be anywhere except on that bus. He was envisioning all the other kids playing with the skill of Major League baseball players. They would be flawless. Only *he* would be the idiot who couldn't play ball.

However, once the game started, it didn't exactly go as he'd antici-pated. Being in an actual game was a lot different from practice. Kids were making all kinds of errors. Balls were being dropped, under thrown, and over thrown. Few kids even got a hit when they came up to bat. In fact, most of them froze up, not even swinging at the ball. And the pitchers weren't much better. They walked a lot more kids than they struck out. The coach was trying to stay positive, but every kid knew he wanted to pull his hair out.

Fortunately for Jack, by the bottom of the fifth, only one kid had actually managed to hit a ball out in his direction, and even Jack's grand-mother could have scooped up that one. It was a slow-rolling grounder.

As for batting, early in the second inning, Jack struck out. He was sure the coach was going to cuss at him, but instead he said, "Keep at it, Jack. You'll get it."

The coach might have been okay with it, but when Jack walked back to the dugout, everyone was avoiding eye contact, and he heard someone whisper, "McMasters stinks."

Jack came back up to bat in the bottom of the sixth. They were losing three to one. He was so nervous he struck out again. This time he figured even the coach would be pissed at him.

"Crap, McMasters. You're pathetic," yelled Kerrigan. "You can't hit the broad side of a barn."

That's when the coach had had enough. He stormed over, not to Jack, but to Kerrigan. He bellowed, "Look at me! All of you look at me, right now! Shut up, and listen up!"

For a moment there was dead silence.

"At least that guy," and he pointed right at Jack, "has what it takes to swing at the ball. You're never going to get a hit if you don't swing. You want to know pathetic? I'll tell you pathetic. Pathetic is not having the nerve to swing at the ball!"

After that, no one said another word about Jack. But when he went to the plate in the bottom of the eighth, things were different. Oh, the score was still three to two, with their team down by one. That hadn't changed, but Jack had changed. For some strange reason, he was now calm. That annoying voice in his head had suddenly gone quiet. No more, *You're gonna mess this up, Jack. You're gonna miss, Jack. You're a loser.*

Even, amazingly, his heart rate slowed. Then it happened. He had the bat cranked back, ready to swing. He was watching the pitcher wind up the throw. Somehow the guy seemed to go into slow motion. Jack watched the ball leave the pitcher's hand, floating toward him. Jack felt he had all the time in the world to figure out when the ball would get to him, and where it would pass him. This was a math problem, not a vision problem! Math, he could solve. He calmly plotted it all in his head and then swung with everything he had. The bat actually connected. As the hit jarred Jack's hands, his brain said, *Run!*

Jack ran.

His solid grounder got him to first base. Everyone but Kerrigan cheered.

Kevin was up next and hit such a long ball, he brought Jack home from first, and himself home, too. The Cooke Barracks Braves actually ended up winning the game, four to three. By hitting his way to first base, Jack had made one of the key runs.

The bus ride home was a lot more fun than the ride to the game.

Bouncing along in the seat, Jack grinned at Kevin, remembering how his friend had persuaded him to come back. "Tell me more about those Spartans."

Kevin paused to blow one of his giant, pink bubbles. "They were some of the greatest warriors of all time, and pros at tactics. Their heavily armed foot soldiers, the hoplites, had an unstoppable fighting formation."

Charlie's eyes widened. "Where is all this military smarts coming from?"

Kevin ran a hand across his flattop, obviously thinking. "I talked to my dad about the Sevens . . . without actually mentioning them. I asked him a 'what if' question. I just said, 'What if a group of us kids were being attacked by a larger group of kids who were stronger? How could we defend ourselves and beat the bigger force?'"

"And?" said Charlie.

"He loves military history and told me how the Spartans were often outnumbered, and if they had tried to fight their enemy one-on-one they would have been crushed. So they would form a special fighting formation called a phalanx.

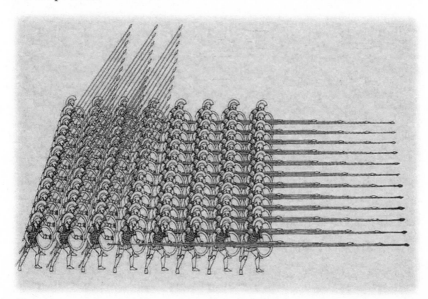

To this day, it still means a formation of infantry carrying overlapping shields and long spears. The foot soldiers formed themselves into a square, say ten men in a row and ten rows deep. Instead of relying on their individual strength, they became a single fighting unit, a single stronger force made up of one hundred men.

They fought as one. In order for an enemy to beat them, they had to break through this tight formation—something that was very hard to do. And if enemies ever did break through, the center of the square would drop back to let them in. Then the square would close up, surrounding the intruder. They would reverse themselves and all attack the intruders at once, overwhelming them."

"Now if only there were a hundred of us, we could form a phalanx to deal with the Sevens," said Charlie, sounding glib.

But Jack got all excited. "Wow! Imagine a whole army of Charlies, Kevins, Jaylas, and Sams. How most excellent would *that* be?"

Kevin burst out laughing. "And just one Jack to lead the army."

"That's our Jack," Charlie said, grinning.

Jack laughed, too, glad to be back with his friends.

20

The Cost of Freedom

"Die, you little sucker!"

"Fry, you pinko Commie."

Jack and his crew had pretty much given up playing Monopoly now that it was nice out. Like all the other kids in the neighborhood, they spent most of their free time running around outside. That afternoon, a whole bunch of kids were lying in groups of twos and threes on Kevin's driveway, magnifying glasses pointed to burn holes in leaves and bits of paper. Even though the magnifiers were the cheap plastic kind, when held just right for a minute or two, a spot on the leaf would start to smoke and then burn right through. The kids had decided during science that day that the magnifying glasses would make excellent laser weapons to destroy America's enemies, so they took the whole box home overnight for a little extra homework.

Smoke curled up on one of the dry leaves Kevin had found in the forest behind his quarters. He'd burned the biggest hole yet. He glanced up at Charlie, whose left eye was bloodshot and ringed in shades of yellow and purple. "That eye looks like it got hit by an enemy laser, not Kerrigan's fist."

"I'd pick the laser beam," Charlie said, wincing when he tried to grin. "It's a much better story to tell. If I admit that Ryan cleaned my clock, one of his snitches would pass it on, and he'd just come after me again."

Charlie was his latest victim.

Jack frowned. *We gotta do something about that guy,* he thought for about the hundredth time.

"Die, Commies, die!" shouted Karen Duncan. She was there on the driveway with Queenie and Liz.

Jack lay there, smelling the smoke of the burning leaves. His mind shifted from the age-old topic of Kerrigan back to the topic at hand. *Strange,* he thought. *Commies. Why don't my parents even mention them?* He said out loud, "Who are the Commies?"

"Oh, you know," said Charlie, "they're the enemy."

"Oh, yeah! Destroying the Commies!" said Kevin, his leaf smoking in a new spot.

Almost by accident, Jack found out who the Commies really were. After that, the word wasn't nearly as much fun to say.

The bigger surprise was who clued him in.

For the first time, Ingrid had decided to take both Queenie and Jack to Göppingen. Queenie protested that she didn't want someone else tagging along. Jack said the same thing. But there was no budging Ingrid on the idea. She'd taken Rabbit the week before. Now she was taking them. So they both went.

And that made all the difference.

They went first to the open-air market, where farmers had set up large folding tables to display everything they'd grown or raised. In between, there were a shoe-repair guy; a woman selling toys; and other vendors with clothes, kitchen stuff, and strange odds-and-ends. As they walked through the market, Ingrid made them tell her the names of everything.

"*Käse,*" Queenie said, pointing to a table full of cheeses.

"*Schwarzbrot,*" Jack said, eyeing a pile of brown loaves in a baker's display.

But Ingrid wagged a finger at him. Incorrect. Then she made him get into a full conversation in German with the baker and have the man explain the names of each and every kind of bread and pastry. Jack should have said, "*Pumpernickel,*" which in English is . . . *pumpernickel.*

They passed some of the farmers' trucks all lined up next to each other, and Ingrid said '*Lastwagen,*' which they figured meant *trucks.* The market finally ended at the big church they'd gone to on Sundays with their dad.

Ingrid pointed to it and made Jack tell her all about attending that *Kirche* on Sundays.

Jack was reminded of the early days, when Ingrid would point to something and say the word once. Then she'd made him repeat it ten times. The locals had gaped at them like they were flakes. That never bothered Ingrid. She'd march him right back through the market, re-pointing at the various things she'd told him. She just stood there waiting until he came up with the German word. Ingrid's idea of a pop quiz. If he missed even one, she'd bring him back to where they'd entered and make him start all over again.

That seemed hard at the time. But it was nothing like being expected to have full conversations with the merchants. Ingrid never, never let up on their German lessons. But at least she kept them from getting boring.

They made their way to a small *Gästehaus* for lunch, and one of Ingrid's girlfriends joined them. It was the first time they'd met Lena.

Lunch was amazing, because Lena insisted on ordering them *Schnitzel mit Pommes frittes und Salat*. Both Jack and Queenie were glad to practice *those* words, so they could order it any time they had the chance. *Schnitzel* was breaded veal, better than the best chicken nuggets, but twenty times bigger and three times thinner. The *Pomme frites* were the most excellent french fries. And, of course, *salat* was salad.

It was during lunch that Queenie, trying to speak German, asked Ingrid, "*Wo wohnen Sie?* (Where do you live?)"

That cracked Ingrid up. "*Dummkopf, Ich lebe mit dir.* (Dumb head, I live with you!)"

In frustration, Queenie turned to Jack. "I'm trying to ask her where she's from. You know, as in where she grew up."

"*Ach so,*" Lena said. Turning to Ingrid, she spoke in rapid German. The two of them went back and forth for a bit. Then, Lena surprised them by speaking English. "Ingrid grew up in Dresden. It is a beautiful city in East Germany."

"Did she like it?" asked Queenie.

Ingrid and Lena said a few more things, again in German, and started laughing.

"Ingrid says she liked it when she was a little kid. But when she became a teenager, she hated it. She told me Dresden was called *Tal der Ahnungslosen*, which means *The Valley of the Clueless*."

That got a laugh from everyone. Everyone, except Jack.

"I don't get it," he said.

"It's because they weren't able to get any Western movies and TV, or any West German newspapers and magazines," Lena said, as if that explained everything.

"Still don't get it," insisted Jack. "And another thing, I also don't get the part about *East* Germany and *West* Germany. I hear people talking about that, but are they really that different from each other?"

A strange expression came over Lena's face. Jack wasn't sure why, but he was pretty sure he'd just said something very wrong.

Lena's voice got quiet and even stern. "Jack, you know exactly what I mean. East and West. Communist and Free!"

This time it was Jack and Queenie's turn to stare. "That's another thing," Jack said, more cautiously. "People say *Commies*, or *Communists* all the time, but we don't know who they are. We know they're supposed to be the bad guys, but . . ."

Lena started to look at them as if *they* were in The Valley of the Clueless, too.

Ingrid's eyes darted between Jack and Queenie and Lena. She and Lena went off into their own hushed conversation, too quiet and too quick for Jack to understand. There was no more laughing and joking. Queenie tried to interrupt a couple of times, but Lena just held up her hand, signaling to let them finish. Toward the end, their conversation seemed heated, and Ingrid looked annoyed. She made little chopping motions, as if to cut off further discussion.

Lena leaned toward them. "Ingrid says we can't tell you." Her quiet voice was very sad. Jack just stared at the wet ring his Coke bottle had made on the table.

It was a long time before Queenie said in a voice as soft and sad as Lena's, "Please tell Ingrid we are very sorry if we said something wrong. We want her please to forgive us. It's just that no one will explain things to us. They think we're too young." Unable to look Ingrid in the eye, she stared down at her tightly interlaced fingers.

Eventually Lena leaned over and whispered to Ingrid. Suddenly, Ingrid lifted her hand for silence. Her bottom lip quivered, and tears rolled down her cheeks.

Queenie felt so bad that she, too, began to cry. "I love you, Ingrid, and I am sorry you hurt. You don't have to tell us anything."

And then, for the first time ever, Ingrid spoke real English. "But I wish to. I wish to tell you so very badly."

Both kids were stunned. Had Ingrid really just spoken to them in English?

"I remember my first day at The Glass House, Jack. From the start you've tried to figure me out," Ingrid said.

"Me? What?" *I've been found out.*

"Oh, it wasn't what you said. I saw you trying to read my eyes. You try to figure everything and everybody out."

"But . . ."

"It's not bad, Jack. It's who you are. So now you'll know." She sighed. "My mother and father live in Dresden with my two brothers and older sister. I love them very much. I miss them terribly. I'll *never* see any of them again."

"How come? Won't they let you?" asked Queenie. "*We* want you, Ingrid."

"That's not the reason. It's not their fault. It's the way things are. There are two Germanys. At the end of World War II, Germany was split into East and West. The West is where we are now. West Germany was helped by the Americans, and it's *free.* You have no idea what free really means. You can't, because you've grown up free. I grew up in the East, and it was *not* free. The Russians took over East Germany after the war.

"They, the East Germans and the Russians, are Communists, and the Communists rule everything there. Jack asked what Commie meant. Commie means Communists. And the Communists don't just control East Germany and Russia, they control all of Eastern Europe, as well as China. That's half the world. Queenie, Jack, look at me. I couldn't be more serious. The Communists are your enemy. They want to destroy you."

Her quiet words drowned out the talk and laughter beyond their table. The kids stared at Ingrid and Lena. This was the truth.

Jack imagined the wall-sized map hanging in his classroom. *Half the world is my enemy?*

"The adults don't want to tell you about the Communists because you're just kids. You're right, Laura. They think you're too young, and they don't want to scare you. I'm worried, too, that I shouldn't tell you."

For a moment they thought she might not continue. Finally, and very slowly, she said, "I know who I was at your age. I know you're old enough to know—and need to know so you can be prepared. But if I tell you, it must be our secret. You can't tell any adults that I've told you these things or I'll get in a lot of trouble. I could even lose my job and have to leave your family."

Ingrid would have to leave us? Is knowing worth putting Ingrid at risk? Jack looked at Queenie. They both stared into Ingrid's purple eyes and nodded that they understood and would never tell.

She nodded back. "The Communists hate America. They want to destroy it. Which means they need to destroy the American Army. Their objective is to take over all of West Germany, and then the rest of Europe, and then the world. The only thing that stands in the way of the Communists conquering the world is the Americans and their friends.

"There are over three thousand Russian tanks up on the East German border ready to attack the West. The Communists have far more tanks than the Americans. That frightens me."

Since their first train ride through Germany, Jack had sensed an unknown enemy but had mostly tried to ignore that fear. A moment ago, the *Gästehaus* had seemed so safe. Now Jack glanced from table to table, wondering if anyone was listening in. He felt the threat level increasing.

"Why would they care about our family?" Queenie asked.

"Your dad and 4th Armored Division is what is holding the Communist Empire's tanks back from attacking."

Once again, Jack saw himself with Kevin and Charlie looking out over the tank lot at Cooke Barracks. They weren't just impressive machines. The fate of half the world might be resting on those tanks. Jack shivered. "They can't do it alone!"

"You're right. And they're not alone. For instance, remember telling me about your friend Alex, from the ship coming over to Germany? Well, his father is helping to prevent an attack from the Communist Empire's ships."

Jack placed his hands in his lap so he could snap the blue rubber band without being noticed. He wasn't shutting down, but he thought it might just give his brain an extra shot of clarity. "Ingrid, what about the Nazis? Where do they fit in?"

Ingrid gave him an indulgent look. "You're always seeing Nazi ghosts. The Nazis were yesterday's great threat to freedom. Today's threat aren't ghosts but very real Communists."

Jack struggled to make sense out of this. *Our allies are now the enemy. American troops had stayed after the war to help rebuild Germany, but the Nazis weren't why we never left. We're here to keep our old allies, the Russians, as well as the other Communists, from attacking West Germany and the rest of the world.*

More things made sense. *Grafenwöhr's up on the East German border. Our dads aren't going up to Grafenwöhr just to train. If a war starts, it's gonna start there.*

His throat tightened. Jack remembered the day at the castle when Queenie called their dad a modern-day knight. *She was right. The free world depends on him, and the other knights, to protect it. But this is no fairytale, and there could easily be no happily-ever-after.*

Jack heard his sister ask, "What was the war like? What were the Communists like when you were growing up?"

"I was pretty young during World War II, so I don't remember much. My family was mostly on my uncle's farm near Wernigerode. I loved that farm. But near the end of the war, we returned to Dresden. It had been very badly bombed. My most vivid memories are of how the Russian soldiers overran the city, killing people and stealing anything they could get their hands on.

"They didn't only steal little things like watches, jewelry, and silver. Once I saw them drive trucks up to a big factory and steal everything inside. The owner just stood there, watching. He told my mom they were taking all his equipment to send back to Russia."

"The war suddenly ended, but the Russians didn't go home. They stayed, and not to help."

"Lots of my friends no longer had dads. They'd been killed in the war. And lots of the other dads didn't come back for months or years, until they were eventually released from prisoner-of-war camps in Russia. Somehow we still had fun. After all, we were kids. We even played games pretending to be Russian soldiers. My favorite game was *Gib Mir Deine Uhr*, which means *Give Me Your Watch*. We thought it was funny when a soldier raised up his shirtsleeve and had five or six watches on his arm."

Jack was taking in everything about the Russian soldiers. But, as always, he had many other questions about her childhood. "Did you build a lot of forts?"

"Oh, yes," she said, smiling at those memories. "We loved to make forts. There certainly was plenty to build with." She described the massive piles of brick, stone, and wood everywhere—rubble from the war. Mainly from the devastating bombing raids.

Queenie abruptly held up her hand for silence. "Enough with the war," she declared. "I have been sitting here listening to you, and, well, until today I thought you only knew a couple words of English. But you could have grown up in America, your English is so great. How is that possible?"

Ingrid's eyes grew worried. Quietly, she said, "That I speak your language so well, and how I learned it must be our secret. That means you can't *ever* tell. If your parents find out, they too will want to know how I learned, and that I can *never* tell them. But if you'll keep my secret, I'll tell you."

Jack had no idea where this was going, but he knew that, more than ever, he believed in Ingrid, and trusted her. "I can keep your secrets."

"So can I," Queenie said.

Ingrid exhaled. "When I was young I was selected to learn English. Kind of like you, Jack, I've always had an easy time learning languages.

"What about me?" demanded Queenie.

"You? Well, you'd do a lot better, Laura, if you didn't always strive for perfection."

Naturally, Queenie couldn't let that pass. "How can striving for perfection *ever* be bad?"

"Jack never cares if his German is perfect; he just plows forward, desperate to communicate. By making more mistakes, he gets more practice and helpful corrections. I know it might sound strange, but his willingness to fail helps him learn faster."

Queenie just rolled her eyes. "Oh, Jack is *definitely* willing to fail."

Seeing that Queenie was ready to fight this one out, Jack cut in. "Can we just get back to the story?"

Ingrid continued, "It began when I was little. I loved my teachers, and I knew they loved me. One of my teachers recommended me for a special program to learn English. It was so exclusive, I wasn't even allowed to tell my friends that I was learning extra English. My teachers, and even my mother and father, were very clear on this point. I was never to tell anyone about my language classes. I told my friends I had extra chores all those afternoons I couldn't play. They thought I had the strictest parents in the world. But I knew different.

"The longer I took the classes, the more fun they became. I was taught to read and write in English. To help me learn, the school distributed American books and magazines, which I loved. My teachers told me to read the words but not believe them. They said they were all propaganda. But the more I read, the more I came to believe the things I read and *not* my teachers. As I read, I fell in love with America.

"Anyway, I loved my lessons. We even saw movies! No one else could watch Hollywood movies, but *we* could. To my amazement and delight, they started showing us American movies in the auditorium of our language school. After watching these movies, they'd have us practice speaking with an American accent and lots of American slang. I was so good at it! At language school, I loved to show off the American me. I could be from Boston, or I could be from the South." Ingrid switched effortlessly between a Boston accent and a Southern drawl.

"I noticed that I was the youngest person watching those movies, and my teachers told me it was because I was such a promising student. They made me feel important."

"But you couldn't tell your friends?" Queenie sounded incredulous.

"That was one of the hardest things. How do you *not* talk about some great movie you've just seen?"

Raising an eyebrow at Jack and Queenie, she said, "I know you two, and you'd have blabbed. But you've never lived with constant fear that if you told your friends, and they got caught, you'd cause something bad to happen. In East Germany there is no freedom.

"But, except for not being able to tell anyone, you had a good life, right?" Queenie said.

"At first, yes. But as I got older, things began to change.

I realized my parents and other adults were nervous around people they didn't know. And they often lied about things. Everyone seemed afraid of one woman in our apartment building. At first I didn't understand why. I just knew my parents said to stay away from her. Then one time my mom told me to be ready to lie to her. A couple stayed in our apartment for a few days. They were old friends of my parents. My mom made me promise if that woman asked who they were, I should say they were my uncle and aunt, which of course wasn't true. Sure enough, the next day that woman cornered me in the hallway and asked who was staying with us. But I was prepared and did as my mom had asked. I didn't like it, but I did it. As time went by, I realized more and more adults were lying about where they'd been or who they'd been with."

Queenie seemed to notice her Coke for the first time. She took a sip. "My mom threatens us within an inch of our lives if we tell a lie. Your mom, well, she was *making* you lie!"

"Precisely. My life was so dif-ferent from yours. Especially once I found out about the Stasi. They are the East German secret police. They're hardcore Communists who spy on everyone. When I was twelve, my dad finally explained that the Stasi were everywhere, listening to everyone's conversations. He said I needed to be very careful what I said, or I could be arrested and sent to prison—and my whole family, too. The scariest part was the Stasi don't need a reason to arrest you. They can send you to jail without a trial. At first I thought my dad was just trying to scare me into behaving. But later I learned the truth.

He was trying to protect me. I learned to fear the Stasi.

"He told me that that snooping woman worked for the Stasi. She told the Stasi everything that went on in our building. Later I heard that the Stasi had a watchdog in every apartment building in East Germany. My dad hadn't been exaggerating. There really *were* spies everywhere. Some-times the Stasi drill tiny holes into the walls of apartments and hotel rooms to film people with special movie cameras. They're always watching what people do and say. Every school, university, and hospital has Stasi spies and informants in it. They can be bus drivers, trolley conductors, jani-tors, doctors, nurses, and teachers. The Stasi recruit them because they're around lots of people and can overhear what's being said. The Stasi are much worse than the Gestapo, and the Gestapo were terrifying."

Jack had seen plenty of Gestapo in movies. They were the ruthless Nazi Secret Police, with their long, black leather coats. *How could* anyone *be worse than* they *were?*

Ingrid's eyes darted over to the bartender, and then around the room, as if she were scanning for problems. "Then, when I was fifteen, things suddenly went very bad for me. My language school said I would have the honor of spending that summer holiday at camp. For the first time in my life, I told them to forget it! You know how it is. I wanted to stay home with my girlfriends and enjoy the summer *our* way.

"The next day I was called down to the office. A malicious-looking guy glared down at me, saying, 'You are a very spoiled girl, and we are finished with all that.' How could he say that about me? I was a model student!

"The way he looked at me, I knew he was thinking, *It would give me great pleasure to torture you.* His mocking smirk dared me to challenge him. I was smart enough not to say a thing, but I think he wanted me to react with anger or tears. When it didn't happen, his impatience seemed to grow, and he got down to business, with, 'You have two choices, young lady: you go to this camp during the summer and do absolutely everything they tell you without one word of complaint, or there will be no more books, no more magazines, and definitely no more movies. What do you choose?'

"It was clear. This was not a choice.

"Unfortunately, I hesitated just a moment too long. Before I could give him the answer he wanted, I found he could look even more evil. He said, 'Either you go to the camp and perform perfectly, or your brother Klaus will not be attending the University of Dresden, or any other University, for that matter. But, of course, it is your choice.'

"Needless to say, I went to camp. To my surprise, it had nothing to do with language studies. It was military training. They put us in uniforms and taught us how to march in formation, recognize all the military ranks, act military, and obey orders. They made us do all kinds of exercises and physical-fitness stuff. We had to run up and down hills while carrying a fully loaded backpack and a rifle. I hated that part.

"And we never got enough sleep. They woke us at five every morning and worked us till late at night. Only then did we drop, exhausted, into bed. By day we learned military tactics and underwent weapons training. We all but lived on the rifle range."

"You can shoot?" asked Jack, excitement in his eyes.

"Absolutely. And you'll never believe what else. Toward the end of camp, small groups of us got specialized training. First, it involved shooting pistols. We spent hours becoming decent shots."

"They're harder than rifles, right?" Jack said.

Ingrid nodded. "I was the best shot in my squad." She said hastily, "Actually it wasn't all that cool. Mostly just repetitive, boring, and exhausting. But I never complained, not once, that whole summer. I didn't want to make problems for Klaus. Then one day I realized that no one else complained, either. I asked a guy why. He said, as if it were obvious, 'The Stasi won't want us if we question or complain.' I was stunned. *Willingly become Stasi? Certainly not!*

"Oh, don't get me wrong, some time back I'd guessed that the guy who forced me to attend camp was Stasi. But until that moment, it had never dawned on me we were being trained to become Stasi. In fact, I'd spent most of that summer believing I'd been sent to the wrong camp by accident. I hadn't said anything in case it looked like a complaint. I was just sticking it out. But that guy's answer shattered that illusion. I knew that somebody, somewhere, had chosen me to be Stasi. I couldn't sleep that night.

"Even without that conversation, I would have started getting suspicious. Soon after, they began teaching us personal fighting skills, espionage techniques, and surveillance methods."

Jack's eyes widened. "Whoa. What was *that* like? What kinda things did they teach you?"

For a moment, Ingrid's purple eyes sparkled back. "Jack, you'd have loved it! We learned things like using invisible ink and secret codes, detecting people tailing us, making dead letter drops."

Jack gave her a quizzical look.

"It's where you hide a message or a key or something in a public place for someone to pick up later. You might hide it under a rock or behind a loose brick in a wall—that's called the dead drop. The person you're leaving it for knows all about the drop and where to look for it."

"Nifty," said Queenie.

"But," continued Ingrid, "you also signal that the drop was made, so the person doesn't arouse suspicion by checking needlessly. We learned to chalk an X or a plus sign as a signal. But you make that chalk mark somewhere far from the dead drop, in a spot they would easily see it."

"Great idea," Jack said.

"And, Jack, we did micro-photography, too. We used these itty-bitty cameras to photograph documents."

"Charlie would love that." Jack was in spy heaven.

"There was a whole course on how to observe a suspect without being seen. We learned how to hang out on a street corner reading a newspaper or a bus schedule until the suspect came by, but without being obvious. We'd go out in teams and follow someone, giving each other signals for things like *back off* or *switch places*."

"What signals?" Jack asked.

"Simple stuff like removing your sunglasses, or switching your newspaper from one hand to the other, or blowing your nose with your handkerchief. Always something ordinary. But for us, the communication was clear. Disguises were also important. When you're following someone, or being followed, and you figure you've been spotted, you try to fade away by changing your appearance."

Queenie said, "How?"

"We'd carry a briefcase, knapsack, big camera bag—that sort of thing. In it we'd have a change of clothes, a hat, and maybe glasses. There would be a wig with hair of another color, and for men a realistic-looking moustache. Also shoes or boots with thick soles or lifts inside to make you much taller. You'd be surprised how different a person can look after changing height or hair."

Jack couldn't believe his nanny knew all this neat stuff. "Are there other ways to tell if someone is spying on you?"

"Here's one—say you have something hidden in your briefcase but you have to leave it alone and you're worried someone will search through it. How would you know if the briefcase had been tampered with?"

"Fingerprints?" he asked.

"Too complicated, and takes too long. Try this sometime." She reached for her purse and placed it on the table. Then she yanked a single hair from her head, and wet it with her tongue. She stuck it next to the latch of the purse. "If you come back and the hair is still stuck on the latch, then no one has opened it. But if the hair is gone, it means someone has opened it. Watch this." She snapped open her purse, and then reclosed it. Sure enough, the hair was nowhere to be seen.

Jack's glance to Queenie telegraphed, *We've gotta remember this one.*

"Our instructors also taught us how to conduct investigations and recruit informants. They wanted us to convince wives to spy on their husbands, and children to spy on their parents."

Ingrid's expression was suddenly serious. "It mostly involved the *dark* art of persuasion: bribery, blackmail, and threats. At first, all this spy stuff was fun and games, kind of like pretend. When I understood they actually expected us to *do* that kind of thing, I could hardly wait for camp to end. Back at school, with my friends, I tried to put it all behind me."

"It was only after I turned sixteen that I realized the Stasi had been involved from the very start. The teacher who saw my talent had been Stasi. The teachers at the English school were, too. They hadn't been trying to nurture my love for languages. They did it to make me an operative—whether I wanted to or not. And not just as an informant like that creepy woman in my building. I was pretty sure they planned to send me to Western Europe or America as a spy. At that point, I realized all the people in my language classes were, or would be, Stasi agents. We would end up working for Hauptverwaltung Aufklärung, what we call the HVA. It's the Stasi Main Directorate for Foreign Intelligence. That's like America's CIA. I became desperate to get out of East Germany. That's when I began to plan." Ingrid went quiet.

Queenie was staring at Ingrid, almost unable to comprehend what she had been through. But finally she asked, "Your life was so twisted up with the Stasi. How could you possibly get away from them?"

"It seemed impossible," said Ingrid grimly. "First, no one in East Germany is allowed to travel without written permission. If we wanted to visit my grandmother who lived a hundred kilometers away, my family couldn't just do it. We had to go to the police station and tell them exactly *why* we wanted to visit her and get their official permission.

"Second, even if you could figure out a way to travel, the Communists have their Iron Curtain. It's a wall along the border that stretches over a thousand miles. Some parts are concrete, some are barbed wire. There are also guard towers all along it, and guards with machine guns and attack dogs. Their job is to stop anyone trying to get over the wall."

Jack piped up, "If it's so bad in there, why would people want to get into East Germany?"

Ingrid laughed at that. "Most of their work is to keep East Germans from getting *out*. Anyone caught trying to escape is sent to prison. But they also want to keep outsiders from telling East Germans what the rest of the world is really like. The Stasi have shut East Germany off from the outside world. The only information comes from the East German Communist government and the Russians. Citizens aren't allowed to get news from West Germany or France or England and certainly not from the United States. If you are caught with any American newspapers, magazines, or books, you can be arrested and jailed.

"The Stasi arrested a literature professor because he had an American book. His wife and children never saw him again. He just vanished. I've heard about people the Stasi killed with a single shot to the head or with a guillotine. Maybe those rumors aren't true, but I know people who vanished—never to be seen or heard from again. I don't know if they were killed or imprisoned or shipped off to Russia. I *do* know I hate the Stasi. In East Germany, I worried all the time that someone might report me for saying something I didn't even know was wrong."

Queenie and Jack glanced at each other, glad they weren't hearing this alone.

"So how'd you get *here*?" Queenie asked quietly.

Lena said, "Perhaps you need to tell them."

Ingrid took a deep breath. "Laura, can you imagine always being afraid? I wanted my life to be the way yours is. I love to hear you laugh with your girlfriends and say whatever pops into your head—no matter how crazy or silly or funny. I wanted that, and to go anywhere and read anything without worrying I'd be reported." Her eyes brimmed with tears.

Lena said, "We need more beer." She waved at the waiter. "*Zwei Bier, und zwei Coca-Cola, bitte.*"

They were quiet till the waiter brought their drinks. Lena lifted her glass and said, "*Prost.*"

They all clinked glasses and drank. Queenie, trying to lighten the mood a little, said to Jack, "At least these Cokes aren't too dry." She told about their father's practical joke.

Laughing about it and a taking few sips of beer seemed to calm Ingrid. "I dearly love your sister, Rabbit, but she would never survive in East Germany. Can you imagine it? She is so trusting of adults and has no ability to control what she says. It would be a disaster."

Queenie's eyes grew wide. "I don't even want to think about it."

Ingrid went silent, fading back into her memories. "For a long time, I desperately wanted my life to change, but it took much longer to realize my desire had a name. It was called *freedom*. Once the word entered my head, I couldn't get it out. I decided I had to do it."

"It?" ask Queenie, confused.

Ingrid nodded. "It. I would leave my family and all my friends, get over the Iron Curtain, and find my way to West Germany and then America. No matter what it took, I would make my way to freedom."

"Over the Iron Curtain? That's how you got to us?" Jack was stunned.

"Yes."

The word said so much.

21

Iron Curtain

"How'd you do it?" Jack didn't think he could listen any harder.

"It took me a long time. The two hardest parts were being patient and not telling anyone. I knew I couldn't tell my parents, brothers, or sister—that would put them at risk. They might even try to stop me."

"They thought life was better in East Germany?" asked Queenie.

"No, but getting caught trying to escape would mean prison or being shot on the spot. I simply couldn't put them through that worry or risk. So for the next year I planned and told no one.

"My biggest problem would be getting to the border. It was hundreds of miles from Dresden. Remember, the police must approve all travel. I thought of idea after idea, but none seemed safe.

"I needed a miracle. Then my aunt and uncle in Wernigerode sent us an invitation to my cousin Franz's wedding. That invitation was my ticket to freedom; Wernigerode is very close to the Iron Curtain. However, my parents decided we wouldn't go, because it was too far and cost too much. Oh, they had a bunch of stupid excuses. I was furious—panicked. My parents probably thought I was just upset because when we lived there during the war, Franz and I were best friends. But there was no way I could let this opportunity pass me by. I started bugging my parents to let me go by myself. I said that at least *one* of us should go. I could represent the family. And I kept at them till they finally gave in.

"My father took me to the police station, presenting the wedding invitation as proof that Franz was family. The desk sergeant, never responding to us, pressed an electronic button wired to his desk. An unsmiling officer came and took us to a small, windowless examination room. My father's eyes widened just enough for me to see this was not good. He calmly explained that we couldn't *all* go, but that he wanted me to represent our family at the wedding. The officer shifted his cold eyes to me. I felt like he could see right into my heart and read my true plans. I forced myself to stare back, to show nothing. Finally he turned on his heel and walked away.

"We were escorted back to the desk sergeant, who kept us standing there, waiting, until his phone finally rang. He answered respectfully but hardly said another word. His eyes never left me. I was sure he was hearing that guards would be in to arrest me. I could tell my father was uneasy, too. But when the sergeant put down the phone, he picked up an iron-handled rubber stamp, slammed it on an ink pad, and then onto some paperwork, saying, 'Fill this out.' An hour later, I walked out with my travel permit.

"I took a train to Wernigerode, and my aunt and uncle greeted me like a long-lost daughter. I hadn't seen them since I was a little girl. I'm sad now how little I enjoyed that visit. I was so preoccupied with my escape plans—or lack of an escape plan. I had no idea where the stupid border was! And there was no one I could trust. For all I knew, Franz was a Stasi agent. I felt such pressure; my travel permit lasted only five days. I spent the first two trying to pick up information about the border without ever asking. With all the wedding stuff going on, the border wasn't exactly a major topic of discussion.

"So what *did* you do?" asked Jack.

"On the third day, I got a break. Franz received a message that his best friend couldn't come to the wedding. His idiot boss had scheduled him to work the next three nights and wouldn't change the schedule.

"Truthfully, Jack, I didn't care that the guy wasn't coming. Frankly, I wasn't even paying much attention to the conversation. Oh, I tried not to let it show, but you have to understand, I was obsessed with escaping.

"Trying to be sympathetic, I asked what his friend did. I just about fainted when Franz said that Manfred was a guard on the border. In a flash, my whole attitude changed, but I had to stay casual. I asked, 'How far away is he?' Franz said, 'Just up the road maybe seven minutes' drive.' I couldn't believe I was so close to the border!

"Franz said, 'I wanted Manfred to meet you.'

"It took all my acting ability to stay casual. 'Well, he isn't that far. Couldn't we just go by to say hi?'

"Before I knew it, we were in an old farm truck heading for the border. You can believe I paid attention to every turn and the surrounding landscape. We hadn't gone more than five kilometers when we came to a low, concrete building next to a tall, barbed-wire fence. *Could that be it?* I wondered.

"Franz said he'd bring Manfred to the truck. Cute girls weren't welcome in the guard building.

"Acid pooled in my stomach as I waited for Franz to come back with Manfred. He was very good looking. Which made it more believable when I turned on the charm. Manfred and I talked and laughed for about twenty minutes, and then he had to get back to work. But in that short time, I learned a great deal."

Queenie's eyes lit up. "Spill the beans. How'd you get him to talk?"

"You should have seen me." Ingrid batted her lashes. "Franz had gone back into the guard house to talk to the other guard, so I had a chance to get Manfred talking. I started by asking if that barbed-wire fence could possibly be the famous Iron Curtain. I acted dumb, saying I thought it would be solid iron. Grinning like a fool, Manfred assured me, 'Barbed wire is plenty strong for this stretch. Around here, no one tries to get in or out.' I wanted to melt in relief, but I just kept acting cute and dumb. Make a note of that, Laura. Boys love cute and dumb."

Jack groaned. "Can we just get back to the story?"

The girls giggled at him.

Ingrid said, "Sorry, Jack. I asked him what he did. Laura, men love it when you ask them about themselves."

Jack knew she was trying to torture him as well as teach Queenie about men.

"Manfred told me he walked his German shepherd, Adelfried, along the fence to guard it. So, of course, I told him how much I loved dogs. Well, that got him talking about Adelfried, who was lazy, lazy, lazy. That's when I got him. I told him that if I had to walk that fence for eight hours a day, I'd be a lazy dog, too. He burst out laughing. He said, 'Since nothing ever happens here, we only go out for about ten minutes each hour, and Adelfried doesn't even want to walk that much.' I, of course, laughed with him and said I wished he could come to the wedding. He asked me to visit before I went home, and I said I hoped I could.

"On our way back to the farm, I made my final plan. I would escape as soon as possible after the wedding.

"The wedding was the next day, but before it ever began, I was prepared. I had brought a good pair of hiking boots with me, but not the right clothes. They would have looked suspicious. I managed to find some old farm clothes that fit close enough. On one of my walks around the farm, I'd seen a rusty pair of wire cutters. I got those, too, hoping they were sharp enough to cut barbed wire.

"I went to the wedding and danced till the end. But as soon as we got back to the farm, I told everyone I was exhausted and went off to bed. It was about eleven or twelve, but I knew I couldn't allow myself to sleep. I sat in a corner for two hours, until every sound died away and I was sure everyone was asleep. Only then did I dress in the old clothes and my boots. With the cutters stuffed deep in my pocket, I headed out.

"Every time the floorboards squeaked, I was sure someone would hear. But I think all that beer and wine at the wedding made everyone sleep soundly. I headed up the road with no suitcase, no extra clothes, no money, nothing but the wire cutters. I kept rehearsing my best excuse if I got caught: I was sneaking off to see Manfred. I would get in trouble, but not *big* trouble.

"There was a bit of a moon, but clouds, too, which made me feel safer. It was eerily quiet. Then I heard a car behind me. I whipped around to see lights coming straight for me. I was sure it was the Stasi, that someone had guessed and ratted me out. I managed to jump off the road and into a field. I lay face down, wishing the plants were tall enough to cover me. I expected to hear screeching brakes as they stopped the car to grab me. But it went right by."

Ingrid's speech had gotten slower and slower. Her sentences dragged out, devoid of emotion, as if the words were coming from far away—almost another world. Jack watched her purple eyes—dull. This time she made no effort to hide that cold, distant stare. She was no longer there in the *Gästehaus* with them. She was back reliving the whole thing.

"Even now I can smell plowed earth and sugar beets when I think of that night. I forced myself to lie still for a long time, straining to hear the car return. If they had spotted me, they would be doubling back. Eventually I got up. It was over an hour before I saw the lights of the guard hut maybe two hundred meters away. It was around three in the morning, or a little after.

"I wasn't going any closer in case the dog could hear or smell me. Instead, I went back about a hundred meters and then walked into the woods for about five minutes, before heading back in the direction I hoped would be the fence. It was dark in those woods, but my eyes adjusted. Then, the clouds briefly parted and I saw the fence. I was on a little hill only seventy meters from the Iron Curtain."

Jack saw Ingrid's hands press against the table as she forced herself to tell more.

"Thorns from some bush poked through the legs of my pants, but that was the least of my worries. I felt so jumpy I had to force myself not to run down toward the fence."

"Why didn't you?" asked Queenie in a soft voice.

"I feared the guard dogs. If I went down there, they might pick up my scent. I knew I had to wait until I'd seen the border guards pass by for their ten-minute stroll. Then I'd have an hour to make my attempt.

"Believe it or not, I began to fall asleep. I know it sounds crazy, but at this most important moment of my life, my fear became too much, and my body seemed to wind down. Despite my panic, I had to keep waking myself up.

Jack nodded, understanding too well: her "winding down" was his "shutting down."

"So many nights, I have a nightmare that I wake up in those woods to find a guard prodding me with his rifle."

Queenie shivered. "That's awful."

Ingrid only shrugged. "Spotting the guards turned out to be easy. They were smoking cigarettes! Even with the moon behind the clouds again, I could see the two tiny, red glows heading away from the guard building. And I could hear their voices, though not the words. I realized if I could hear them, they could hear me. I was so scared I might make a sound that I even stopped breathing, until I realized I was holding my breath. I forced myself to exhale. Falling asleep was no longer a problem, my heart was pounding so hard, I worried they'd actually hear it. Manfred had said they only went out for ten minutes, but to me, it seemed an hour before they finally passed by again. I learned over and over again that night that when terror grips you, time slows dramatically.

"Finally, I started toward the fence, expecting every moment to be caught. My hands were shaking when I reached for the barbed wire. I thought, *I'm actually touching the Iron Curtain.* My mind went wild with questions. *Was I too clever with Manfred? Had he seen through my flirting? Does he expect me to make a break for it?*

"I was so angry with my brain that I yelled inside my head, *Shut up. Just shut up! I need to think.*

"I didn't want to cut through the fence unless I had to. That would leave proof someone had escaped. My disappearance would point to me. I hoped to scramble over the fence and be gone without a trace. So I climbed onto the wires. But I'd only made it up about three feet before the wires started shaking like crazy. They were too loose to climb. I lost my balance, falling forward against them. The moment that happened, the wires acted like a spring, catapulting me backwards. Completely off balance, I let go and went flying. But I never hit the ground. Somehow I was left hanging from the fence. I realized the sharp barbs were hooking my clothes and struggling made it worse. I hadn't thought I could feel more afraid, but this was worse than all the rest. I was sure searchlights would come on to find me hanging there. Then a horn would blast, and guards with machine guns would run up to rip me from the fence. My brain screamed, *What in God's name was I thinking? I'm out of my mind!*

"But nothing happened. Eventually the wires calmed, and my body didn't bob so much. My hands stopped trembling enough that I could begin unhooking my clothes, one barb at a time. When I was down to the last few barbs, my clothes ripped free, and my body smacked the ground. I was pretty jarred, desperately trying to catch my breath, but I fought down my panic long enough to pull out the old pair of cutters and attack the bottom wire. It wouldn't cut! I just wasn't strong enough. My heart began beating so hard I thought I would burst a blood vessel. But for some strange reason my hands filled with superhuman strength. Squeezing the cutters with all my might, I snapped the wire. I didn't dare pause for even a second. I moved on, cutting the next two. Then my hands cramped so badly, the cutters fell to the ground. But I'd done enough.

"I was terrified I would get snagged on the barbed wire again, and this time not be able to get unhooked, so I lay on my back and began wiggling through, face up. That way I could keep an eye on those vicious hooks. I had intended to use my hands to keep them away from me. But my hands were useless once I had to keep them pressed against my sides—that was the only way I could fit through the opening. Inching my way forward, it was amazing my face didn't get sliced up. One hook was only a millimeter or two away. I finally managed to slip through the fence.

"I staggered to my feet and ran toward the West. I probably hadn't made it more than half a kilometer before I tripped and went flying to the ground, flipping head over heels, somehow landing face up. I had nothing left. Everything spun around, and I passed out."

Ingrid stared at her beer glass, as if she once again had nothing left.

Jack shifted his head from side to side, trying to loosen his shoulders. Glancing around the *Gästehaus*, he thought of another café, where Col. McHenry had talked to Jean-Sébastien. *What is it about these European kids? They're so brave. How would I react? If my time ever comes, will I hold it together the way they do?*

Ingrid stirred, coming back to them.

"I'm sure hours passed before I woke. My two conscious thoughts were daylight and pain. My entire body ached. Slowly, things began to come back to me. I was pretty sure I was in West Germany.

"I managed to sit up. I was in a big, open field. Struggling to my feet, I put one wobbly foot in front of the other. But I had no idea which way to go. If it was the morning, then west would be away from the sun. If I'd slept into the afternoon, west would be *toward* the sun. I gambled it was still early and I headed away from the sun. When I came to a road, I could no longer get my body to budge. I lay on my side by the road for hours. Not a cart or car or person passed by.

"Gradually, a new fear replaced my fears from the night before: What if the road and fields were deserted because West Germany was all a myth? What if no one had actually lived there since the war?"

Her lips twitched into a brief smile. "Guys, what I hadn't put together was that it was Sunday morning. No one was out and about.

"Eventually, a man drove up the road. I managed to sit up and his car slowed down. He leaned out his window and asked if I was okay. I didn't know what to say. My life was based on *not* trusting people. But when he asked a second time, I blurted out, 'Please, sir, am I in West Germany?'

"He stared at me, and then a welcome spread across his face. 'Have you come over the wall?'

"I just nodded yes.

"'Well, come on. I'll give you a hand,' he said.

"He helped me into his car. Then all my alarm bells went off. I thought, *Is he taking me back to East Germany and the Stasi? I'll be jailed or shot!*

"But none of my terrible worries came true. He was a local farmer. He took me home to his wife and children, and they fed me hot food and put me to bed. When I finally woke up, I found myself in a pretty room, with sunshine pouring through a big window. I thought, *Real people do exist in the West!*

"I regained my strength quickly. Even my hands healed after a few days. From there I was introduced to the local police, who, instead of being cruel or scary, actually helped me get through the political-asylum process, which basically meant I was allowed to stay in West Germany and start a new life.

"I was allowed to go anywhere, say anything, and read anything. It was all pretty strange, and pretty wonderful."

Ingrid was done, but Queenie wasn't. She asked, "What about your family? Don't they think you're in prison or dead?"

"Good question. I left my parents a letter at my uncle's farm, and I have to assume they received it. Unfortunately, since I had to cut the fence, my escape was certainly detected. I just hope my uncle's family and my parents were believed that they had no part in my escape."

Jack and Queenie could tell Lena was glad it was all out in the open. She hailed the waiter to bring them some Black Forest cake, and coffee for Ingrid and herself. The conversation became much more lighthearted. But not for Jack.

Finally, Ingrid noticed this, and studying Jack for a moment, said, "You are very quiet. I think you must have another question, so go on and ask it. After all, it seems that today is the day to get all the questions out of the way."

"I'm afraid to ask," Jack said. "But there might not be another time."

"Go on, Jack," she said. "Besides I'm pretty sure I know your question: Were my parents Nazis during the war?"

Jack sheepishly mumbled, "Well, were they?"

Finally she said, very matter-of-factly, "Yes, they were. My parents were teachers. You couldn't even be a plumber, let alone teach school, unless you supported the Nazis. Many Germans will tell you they weren't Nazis, but the truth is that more Germans were Nazis than will admit it now. I'm not saying they all believed in Adolf Hitler or everything the

Nazis stood for. Many didn't. But if you wanted to survive, to feed your family, to stay out of jail, you couldn't oppose the Nazi Party.

"Look, kids, for you this will be very hard to understand. It's hard for you, because you are Americans. For you, freedom is as common as air. You don't say every minute of every day, 'There's plenty of air.' You just breathe. In the same way, you were raised to believe that people are free to make their own choices. That would mean a German person could simply chose to be a Nazi, or choose to be a Communist, but just as easily could choose *not* to. This was not how it was for us Germans. My brother Klaus is a Communist. You know I hate the Communists, but I don't hate Klaus for being one. I know he didn't become one because he believes in what they say or stand for. He did it because he desperately wants to become a doctor, and only Communists can go to the University of Dresden. He could have said no, but then he would never become a doctor.

"I crawled through that barbed-wire fence so I'd never have to make a choice like that. But the price for my freedom is never seeing my family again. It's a price I pay every single day."

"Ingrid," Queenie whispered, "you're amazing."

Jack knew the conversation was over. Ingrid confirmed it when she said with pleading eyes, "Remember, children, we must *never* speak of these things again."

Jack and Queenie nodded.

As a way to lighten the mood, Ingrid added, "And remember, I hardly speak any English, so don't even think about saying anything to me, unless it's in German. *Verstanden?*"

"*Oh, wir verstanden!*" Jack's head bobbed up and down in his insistence. Then, just to prove his point, he added in his best German, "*Lena, wenn das Mittagessen immer so ist, dann sollten wir wieder mit Ihnen gehen.*" Roughly translated, that means, "Wow, Lena, we gotta do lunch again. Especially if it's always like this."

Jack could see pride in Ingrid's smile. He sensed she was thinking, *Jack, you're finally getting it.*

22

Enemy Empire

In the nights that followed, Jack kept having tortured dreams about the Stasi. Dreams that didn't make a lot of sense. Sometimes he was spied on. Sometimes the Stasi overheard him telling one of Ingrid's secrets. He knew better! Why had he talked? Often, he was running and running and running. He would jolt himself awake, his mind as jumbled as his sheets and blanket. He'd have to reassure himself that he hadn't told Ingrid's secret.

On Friday, Charlie asked him to sleep over. Jack said no, afraid he would wake up thrashing around and sweating. He spent the night with Charlie anyway—in his dreams.

Tanks were crashing through barbed-wire fences. They were coming to get them. He was searching everywhere for Charlie. Had to find him. Had to!

Jack's heart was racing when he snapped awake. It was still dark out, but Jack was afraid to go back to sleep.

When the sun came up, Jack quietly got out of bed and pulled on a pair of jeans and a white T-shirt. But he didn't leave his bedroom. Instead, he sat down at his train board and started working on the old mill with the water wheel, the model he'd wanted to buy the first time he went to the train store. He'd finally bought it when he'd gone to Göppingen with Ingrid and Queenie. He squeezed just the tiniest drop of glue ever so gently out of the tube and onto a tiny piece. He was mastering the art form. It required extreme concentration but, as usual, it freed his mind to think, to figure out what was bothering him.

Normally, he'd be brooding over plans to get Jayla to the mountain. But since Ingrid's confession, her new intel was all he could think about. As he positioned the piece, it finally came to him. Once he got it, it seemed pretty obvious. He needed to clue his friends in on who the Commies really were—and why their families were *really* in Germany. His friends needed to understand that the Dark Empire they'd talked about wasn't the Nazis, but the Communist Empire. But he knew he needed to be careful. He needed to do it in a way that did not reveal any of Ingrid's secrets. He built for an hour. In that time, he worked it all out.

Jack was at the table eating breakfast with Queenie. His day was improving; there were Frosted Flakes.

"What are you guys up to today?" she asked.

"I think we're gonna go hang out at the cliff to keep tabs on the activity down on the *Flugplatz.*"

Queenie's eyes brightened. "What's up there?"

"Sam heard that a big Sikorsky chopper is coming in this morning to hoist a giant generator and fly it out for repairs."

"Okay," Queenie said. "We'll see you down there."

"Wow, you can see everything from up here," said Sam.

"Yeah," said Jayla. "No wonder The Watcher used it for his lookout last winter."

"Who?" said Kevin's sister, always gathering intel about what happened before they were on base.

Jayla hesitated, "Long story." She turned to Kevin, "Sorry, I wasn't thinking."

He shrugged. "She won't let you stop now."

Jayla turned back to Karen. "Last winter we thought we saw some guy spying on the *Flugplatz.* Possibly a Nazi spy."

Jack decided now was the time. "Not a Nazi. The Nazis are ancient history, but he *could* be a Communist spy."

While everyone else looked confused; Charlie started chanting, "Commies, Commies, Commies . . ."

Camila talked over him. "What do you mean, Jack?"

Queenie shot Jack a warning look, but he shook his head, saying, "They need to know."

"Know what?" Camila edged closer.

"Wait one minute, Jack! You and I need to talk. Right now!" Queenie grabbed his shirt and tugged him away from the staring group.

Queenie's whisper was quiet but explosive. "What exactly do you plan to *tell* them?"

"It's not what I tell them. It's what *we* tell them."

It took all Jack's persuasive skills to win her over, but as the others took turns trying to inch within hearing range, only for Queenie to shoo them away, she and Jack worked it out. They would explain about the Communists, East Germany, Russia, the Stasi, and the Iron Curtain. They would even say the intel came from Ingrid, but they wouldn't mention a single word about Ingrid's life, training, or language skills.

Once out of their huddle, Queenie took charge. "Okay, gather 'round. We need to talk." She sat down in a clearing where they could see anyone approach. The others promptly followed.

Jack knew it was best to let Queenie take the lead, so he made a show of giving her his full attention.

She began, "You cannot tell *anyone* what Jack and I are about to tell you—do we understand each other?"

Every head nodded.

"We figure your parents don't want you to know *any* of this. And we're pretty sure our parents don't, either. It's the usual they're-kids-and-don't-need-to-know routine. But Jack and I found out something you *do* need to know. This is some heavy stuff, and it's pretty scary, so if you want to leave now, no one will blame you."

Queenie and Jack looked around the wide-eyed group. Not one kid budged.

"Anyone know what a Commie *really* is?" Jack asked and then waited for an answer.

When no one spoke up, he asked, "What about why we're all here in Germany?"

"To contain the Nazis," said Sam, with certainty.

"No, Sam, that's old intel," said Queenie. "The Nazis aren't the enemy anymore. The Commies are."

"*Commies* is a word for *Communists*," said Jack.

He and Queenie laid it all out for them. Jack, being Jack, was tempted to finish with the story of Jean-Sébastien, challenging everyone to be on the lookout for intel, but his friends looked too stunned to handle any more that day. Jean-Sébastien would have to wait.

Finally, Kevin spoke up. "You're telling us that the Communists control half the world? You're saying that Charlie's Dark Empire actually exists and they *are* out to destroy us? You really think our dads and the whole 4th Armored Division are here to stop them from invading West Germany on their way to taking over the rest of the world? Is that your intel?"

"That's about the size of it," said Jack very soberly.

"Damn!" was all Kevin said.

"And the East Germans and Russians have three times as many tanks as we have."

"That's what we've heard," Queenie said.

"Damn!" said Charlie. Then very quietly, with worry written all over his face, he added, "No wonder our dads need range practice up at Grafenwöhr. They have to be three times better than the Commies or we'll get overrun."

"I guess that's why my mom keeps suitcases packed and ready to go," said Liz.

"What?" Queenie asked. Now it was her turn to look confused.

"I never put it together till now," Liz answered. "Mom keeps a suitcase for each of us packed with stuff that we'd need if we left for a few days. I caught her adding sweaters when the weather got cold. When I asked why we didn't unpack them so we could *use* the stuff, she just said, 'This way, we can just get up and go on a quick vacation.' It was all a lie. Those suitcases are ready in case tanks come rolling through that Iron Curtain and we can't stop 'em. My mom knows the threat is real, and she's prepared to evacuate."

"Holy crap!" Camila said. "I saw suitcases in our back closet, too. I'm opening them up when I get home. This really *is* scary."

Jayla said, "So you figure The Watcher is working for them?"

Jack's face was grim. "I think we detected a Communist spy."

When they got back to their quarters that evening, Jack and Queenie investigated. Sure enough, they found four fully packed suitcases in the back closet.

Queenie went to her mother. "I like my green skirt. Why is it sitting in a suitcase?"

Mrs. McMasters seemed really annoyed. "Why did you even open that suitcase?"

"It was heavy," Queenie said innocently.

"I call that snooping. It could have been filled with your birthday presents."

Queenie waited for more.

"I have suitcases for each of us all packed and ready in case we want to take a quick, little trip. If you want that green skirt, swap it for one you don't care so much about."

Later, when they were alone, Queenie rolled her eyes at Jack, saying, "Right! I'll tell you what she means by a quick, little trip. She means getting out of here in the nick of time, just before the Communist Empire overruns us with its tanks! Why does she always treat us like we're too young to be told anything?"

"I got an idea," Jack said.

Queenie raised an eyebrow. "Yeah?"

Checking that their mom was busy in the kitchen, Jack walked to the back closet. Queenie followed.

"I figure Mom and Dad rarely mess with these suitcases."

"So?"

"So if they ever *do* mess with them, it would mean something serious is up."

"Maybe."

"More like probably," said Jack. "Give me a hair."

"What?"

He yanked his own hair. "Mine is too short to use."

Queenie quickly plucked out a hair and handed it over.

Jack licked it and placed it next to the right latch of Queenie's pink suitcase.

"Our early warning system," he said. "We'll check it at least once a week."

Jack had no problem remembering to check. From that day on, it was hard to get the Communist threat out of his mind.

23

Facing the Challenge

Unfortunately, other things didn't change. Jack was great at reading people, but he couldn't seem to figure out what would set Kerrigan off. It was as if Kerrigan had a bully's handbook, and he randomly chose the look, gesture, or comment to threaten or embarrass Jack on any given day. Things came to a head on the playground after lunch one day. Kerrigan and his gang charged right at Jack as he walked onto the playground.

"This time it's your turn, punk!" Kerrigan shoved Jack in the chest, knocking him to the ground.

A crowd quickly gathered. Jack had learned his lesson about getting kicked if you stay down, so he leapt to his feet before Kerrigan could make another move.

"Not here, Jack!" Sam screamed from yards away.

Jack hated this. He just hated it! *Why me?*

His brain began wandering into the land of wishful thinking. *If I had a magic wand, I could make Kerrigan disappear. . . .*

Kerrigan shoved him again, snarling, "You hear me, punk? You're going down!"

Jack almost lost his footing. By zoning out, he was backing down. He nearly took a swing at Kerrigan, but his brain cleared long enough to warn him, *Sam's right—not here.*

He couldn't risk getting thrown out of school again. He needed to control the situation. *Mr. Reynolds said to think up a helper. Oh, yeah! Batman!*

He imagined Batman standing beside him. Jack straightened his shoulders, looked right at Kerrigan, and did his best to strip all fear from his voice. Half-turning to the crowd, he said, "Okay, Kerrigan, you want a piece of me? You got it. We meet behind the post gym after school, and you get your shot. But you don't show, and you're the one who's a panty waist."

Kerrigan studied Jack for a minute. Then he chuckled and said so everyone could hear, "Don't flip your lid, McMasters. Me and my boys will be there. You're the one who needs to worry, 'cause I'm definitely gonna enjoy taking you down." With that, he walked off.

Sam came over. "Good job. That was the way to handle it."

But Jack wasn't feeling like he'd handled anything. He dragged himself back to class and spent the rest of school with his eyes glued to Mrs. Campbell, pretending to pay attention so she'd leave him alone. He couldn't nudge his brain onto anything but *after* school.

Word of a fight spreads fast. By the time he and his crew walked behind the gym, half the school was there. He noticed even Queenie and Rabbit and their friends had shown up. Just one more thing he didn't need. Kevin was trying to coach him about handling Kerrigan, but not much was getting through.

An electric ripple went through the onlookers. Kerrigan and his boys paraded in, grinning and very pleased with themselves. The crowd quickly spread out, forming a circle. Kerrigan pranced into the center, his fists held high, as if already the champ.

"Okay, punk," Kerrigan taunted, a mean glint in his eye. "Let's do this thing."

Jack didn't say a word. He looked calm as he stood there, snapping his blue rubber band, but inside he was still trying to jog his brain into action. Jack raised his fists in boxing stance, somehow remembering to keep his elbows tight to his sides. Both boys started circling. Something about Jack's controlled stance made Kerrigan seem to hesitate, possibly reassessing him.

On the inside, Jack felt more like a zombie than a boxer. As they circled, he glimpsed his sisters, Kerrigan's gang, and his friends. Their unspoken expectations were like a cloud of gnats flying in front of his face, fogging his vision.

Kerrigan seemed to sense it, because he smiled as he came at Jack with a fast right jab and then a hard left hook to the head. But even though

Jack's brain wasn't cooperating, those hours in the gym had sharpened his reflexes. He automatically dropped one knee and dodged most of the punch, only getting a glancing blow.

Again, out of habit, Jack countered quickly, jabbing with his left, going for a power shot with the right. But in his foggy state, he didn't expect Kerrigan's backward dodge, so Jack's hit seemed more like a push than a punch.

"That all you got, weenie boy?" mocked Kerrigan.

Both boys backed away, regrouping.

Jack knew he was just going through the motions. *Stop shutting down! Get it together!*

Kerrigan covered the ground between them to deliver a series of punches—one of which Jack failed to block. He got clocked in the left eye. Staggering backward, his head was rattled. He started seeing stars. But for some strange reason, that punch shook the fog from Jack's brain. Filled with rage and energy, he no longer gave a crap if he got pounded by Kerrigan.

Kerrigan was dancing around, telling the crowd how great he was. And while his head was turned, Jack charged, tackling him to the ground. The move took Kerrigan by surprise, and before he could recover, Jack ended up on top, pounding at least one solid punch into Kerrigan's face.

With the tide now turned, Basketball Head, one of the leaders of the Sevens, moved in to drag Jack off Kerrigan. But Jayla, about half the kid's size, pushed him away before he could grab Jack. B-Ball Head made the serious mistake of swinging at Jayla. She exploded with the fastest series of punches any kid in that crowd had ever seen. The big guy went down—hard.

"All right! That's enough!" came a shout from the back door of the gym. It was Private Finnegan, striding over to the circle, with Rabbit marching behind. With more command presence than he'd ever shown before, Finnegan pulled Jack, still swinging like crazy, off Kerrigan and dumped him on the ground. When Kerrigan tried to come at Jack, Finnegan merely shoved him back.

"It's not over, McMasters," snarled Kerrigan, as he and his boys helped B-Ball Head to his feet and guided him out of there.

Finnegan watched Kerrigan reach the road before his glance rested on Jack's swelling eye. "Have a nice rest of your day." He gave Jack an unreadable look and headed back to the gym.

The crowd went wild, boosting Jayla up on their shoulders to parade her back to the street. She was the obvious star of this fistfight. Word was about to spread across the base: Smart brats who want to live won't mess with cute, little Jayla Jones.

Queenie gave Jack a thumbs-up as she left with her gang, wanting to escape Rabbit, the one-girl mob scene shouting, "Did you see him? That's my favorite brother!"

"Not too bad, Jack," said Kevin. "Maybe Kerrigan will back off, at least for a while."

"Let's hope so. I like our boxing matches, but I really hate these Kerrigan fights. I'm just glad Rabbit ratted to the one guy who wouldn't come down on us."

Kevin smiled at him. "You did all right, Jack. You didn't back down. And by the end, you almost had him."

Charlie threw an arm over his shoulder. "You fought like a Spartan."

"I guess I did." Jack was relieved and a bit surprised.

"Will your dad give you crap about that black eye?" asked Kevin.

"Probably not." Jack was strangely at peace with himself. "I mean, I didn't get thrown out of school, and he didn't get called because of it, so he probably won't care."

Kevin said, "My guess is you're right."

Jack was just glad it was over, at least for now.

24

The Ravine

Any afternoon they didn't have Little League, Jack and his crew spent exploring Cooke Barracks, especially the woods behind The Glass House. Since no one was stopping them, they kept penetrating deeper and deeper.

Used to the plains of Oklahoma and Texas, Jack thought this was the most beautiful place he'd ever known. If Jack had pictured the perfect forest, it would have looked like this.

Rays of sunshine shot through the new, green foliage, creating a thousand combinations of dark shadows and explosions of light. The forest floor, instead of being full of brush and briers, thickets and brambles, was a lush carpet of soft leaves that hardly made a sound as Jack's crew moved through the trees. The land contoured up and down, with very few large stretches of flat land. Over the last month, they'd realized The Glass House and The Circle occupied the high ground of the base.

From there, the deeper they moved into the forest, the more they descended into some kind of valley.

Tree climbing became a key skill. There were so many trees begging to be climbed. And they proved a great place to hide.

One Saturday morning in April, they chose to maximize their exploring time by bringing picnic lunches with them to the movie. The moment the screen flashed, "The End," they bolted out the side doors, headed for a part of the forest not far from the theater. They'd picked up rumors that a path near the theater led through the woods and eventually connected to another behind The Glass House.

It took a bit to locate the path, but once on it, they moved along quickly, covering all new ground. Initially, they were powered by candy and popcorn from the movies, so they didn't bother to stop for lunch. But once back on familiar ground in the woods behind The Glass House, they found a fairly secluded spot for their picnic.

Jack glanced down at his watch, calculating. "Well, that was certainly no shortcut. In fact, it took us an hour and a half to get back here, and it only takes us twenty minutes by the road."

"Nice trail, but too many twists and turns," said Sam.

The boys were juggling the balled-up wax papers left from all the sandwiches when Jayla abruptly signaled for quiet. They immediately went silent, the wads of paper forgotten where they dropped.

She whispered, "Someone's coming. Hide!"

Fearing the Sevens, they vanished up nearby trees. Their theory was simple: This was their woods. All others were intruders, but, when possible, they would avoid confrontation.

Jack chose the oldest and tallest tree around. From above, he watched as Rabbit and her best friends, Joni Portwine and Mark Sanchez, came wandering through the trees. The little kids never even looked up.

"Hey, what's this?" Rabbit said, scooping up the wax-paper balls. "Somebody's been littering."

"Who'd do that?" Mark wondered.

"Dunno," Joni said, "but it's kinda strange. Don't ya think? No Germans would ever litter in the woods."

"And brats know better than to litter," Mark said.

Rabbit shrugged, cocking her head to one side as if to say, *Who knows?*

Jack made a mental note to ensure they never again left anything on the forest floor that could get them busted, especially by intruders more dangerous than Rabbit.

As Rabbit and her friends moved on, he lost interest in her, but not in climbing. The higher he got, the more things opened up and seemed, somehow, more important than anything below. Looking down from his perch, he could see the tops of the nearby trees and the crows nesting in them. Or were they ravens? Hanging from the branches, he watched the large black birds take off, soar through the brilliant blue sky, and eventually return to the trees.

He spotted the Hohenstaufen in the distance. From here it looked so much closer than ten miles away. That mountain had become a royal pain in the butt. He'd stopped hoping Jayla would give up on her march to the mountain. She was even more determined they make it their primary objective. Yet, from this exhilarating height, the path seemed clear. *I guess I have to figure out how to make it happen.*

His mind flashed back to the Sunday afternoon his family drove up to the castle ruins that topped the mountain. The countryside below had looked like a prince's kingdom. Jack felt that way again. *This really is Wunderland.*

"Jack! Coast clear! Jack!" Jayla was calling him.

Reluctantly, he yelled, "Up here."

Giving up his fabulous view, he started back down.

By three o'clock, they were deeper in the woods than ever before, sprawled on the damp forest floor and lost in their own thoughts as they stared up into the interconnected limbs of the trees. The longer they lay there, hardly talking or moving, the more the world above came alive. The air was still around them, but up in the canopy all the branches were waving in the breeze. Suddenly, appearing out of nowhere, two black squirrels chased each other across the treetops at breakneck speed, jumping from tree to tree along the crazily swaying branches.

Jack stared. *How? They're just one step from a spectacular fall. They're flying without wings. Why can't I be a black squirrel living that magic—*

"And just what do you little creeps think you're doing in our woods?"

Jack sat bolt upright, but Jayla was first on her feet.

A whole pack of Sevens started forming a circle around them.

Jack scrambled up, scanning for a way out. But the Sevens were closing ranks.

Right in Charlie's face, one hissed, "I asked you a question, punk! You know better than to be in—"

"What're you talkin' about? It's not your woods. It's *our* woods," shouted Rabbit, coming out of nowhere to stand right behind the guy hissing at Charlie. "And if you don't leave us alone, my big brother, Jack, is gonna pound ya."

Jack knew they were outnumbered and out-gunned, but when the Sevens all turned to look at Rabbit, it broke the situation their way.

"Run for it!" he shouted to his crew. Rabbit shook her head, hands on hips, legs planted on the ground.

"Not this time," Jack hissed, yanking her away as the Seven lunged for her.

"Okay. Later." Rabbit smiled as if it were a promise.

To Jack's relief, once she knew they were running, she was in front of the pack.

Given the adrenalin pumping through their bodies, they might have outrun the bigger kids. But suddenly there was nowhere to go. Jack pulled Rabbit back just as she sprinted to the edge of a ravine as steep as the cliff by The Glass House.

The panting Sevens caught up in seconds.

One taunted, "And which of you is Big Brother Jack—the one who's gonna kick our ass?"

That got a nasty laugh from some of his friends.

Jack tried to swallow. *How could Rabbit be so stupid?*

His brain kept saying, *Trapped, trapped, trapped, trapped.* He forced through a new thought: *Do not shut down! What can I smell? What can I hear? Oh, please—you're joking, right?*

He could tell the guy was scanning their faces, looking for one like the little girl's.

Jack forced himself to stand taller and step forward. "I'm Jack. And that was my crazy little sister. She didn't know what she was saying. Just let us go, and we'll get out of here."

"Jack, Jack, Jack, too late for that," the boy scoffed, wiping his snotty nose with the back of his hand.

"Yuck! What's your name? Snot-Nose?" squealed Rabbit.

Every eye was on the snot glistening along the guy's knuckles. He winced at his own snotty hand before carefully closing it into a fist. He lunged at Jack's jaw with a lightning-fast uppercut. Jack dropped one knee and shifted just enough to keep the damage minimal. But two other Sevens grabbed his arms and held him in place for Snot-Nose to stomach-punch the wind out of him.

Before Jack could catch his breath, they threw him over the edge of the ravine.

He went crashing down, head over heels, finally slamming into a tree. He couldn't move. His lungs locked up. Starving for air, he forced his jaw open wide. Just when lights started to dance before his eyes and he knew he was going to pass out, a trickle of air burned its way down to his lungs. His only thought was pain.

The others had no time to come to his aid. Nor did they fare much better. Mayhem had broken out, with all of them being attacked at the same time. Four big kids started swinging, and both Kevin and Charlie went down. Sam and Jayla were hanging over the edge of the ravine, trying desperately to get away from the chaos. But B-Ball Head stomped on their hands, breaking their grips. They, too, went crashing into the ravine. Rabbit, Joni, and Mark somehow got away during all the confusion.

"Don't let us catch you in our woods again!" shouted Snot-Nose, as they walked off.

Jack was so banged up, it took Kevin pulling and Charlie pushing to get him up the side of the ravine. After that, the two girls managed to scramble up, smashed fingers and all, with further help from Charlie and Kevin.

They sat in a circle trying to recover before the hike home.

"I can't believe Rabbit. I'm gonna kill her," Jack fumed.

Jayla shrugged. "I know she's a mouth-and-a-half, Jack. But it wasn't really her fault. We were in for it, with or without her mouth."

"She's right," said Sam. "Actually, Rabbit was trying to stop the whole thing. Maybe she was a little half-cocked in her approach . . ."

Jayla cracked up at that. "And has a little too much confidence in her Big Brother Jack. But her heart was in the right place, even if her head wasn't."

Grudgingly, Jack added, "Yeah, I guess it wasn't her fault—but what a mouth on that kid."

Charlie laughed. "What does she weigh? Fifty pounds? Yet there she was, standing up to the Sevens."

That got a fresh chuckle.

Jack turned to the girls. "How are your hands? B-Ball stomped them, didn't he? Unlike Rabbit, *he* weighs a ton."

Jayla shrugged. "We'll live. Better a B-Ball stomping than getting slimy boogers punched on you by Snot-Nose."

The others laughed, but Kevin seemed lost in thought. Then he carefully unwrapped a piece of Bazooka Bubble Gum and placed it in his mouth. He slowly chewed, his absent look changing to cold determination. "We won't be giving up these woods. Piss on those guys. This is *our* place."

"No, we're not!" Jayla said.

"We aren't," Jack conceded, "but *they* aren't either. Think about it. Why are they so determined to keep us out of these woods? The reason came to me the other day. It's possible they're searching for Nazi war stuff. In fact, I figure Kerrigan is using the Sevens as much as they're using him so he can find stuff from the war."

"Actually, that makes sense," said Charlie, rubbing his sore ribs. "Remember when Kerrigan was trying to sell those older kids a Nazi helmet? They're probably worried we'll find stuff before they do."

Jayla nodded. "If they don't want us finding stuff, too bad. We're still not leaving."

Charlie's face turned grim. "Well, if we want to survive out here, we'd better improve our security and stop getting surprised. There are more of them than us, and they're bigger and stronger."

Sam nodded. Sure, we've been boxing, but they know some moves, too, and I doubt we could beat them in a fair fight—much less an unfair fight. We've got to outsmart them."

"Or at least outrun them," said Jack. "In fact, we *were* outrunning them until we hit that giant ravine. If we don't find a way over or around it, they'll trap us every time."

"Easier said than done," said Charlie.

Sam stretched. "Right now, let's hit the gym to get cleaned up. If our moms find out we got pounded by a bunch of older kids, *they* will be the ones who put the kibosh on our playing in these woods."

"Good point," said Jayla. "Mum's the word."

25

The Map and the Mountain

Charlie, Jack, and Kevin were bombing around on their bikes when they found themselves down by the ammunition dump. Burly GIs were passing huge tank rounds from an olive-drab storage locker to an iron dolly hooked to a small tractor.

"Just look at the size of those babies," Kevin said around a wad of gum that seemed almost as big. "They're like giant crayons lined up in the box."

The pointy shells did indeed look like enormous crayons whose tips had never touched paper.

Jack eyed the live rounds. "But a lot more deadly. Finnegan said that if a missile hit this ammo dump, it would level all of Göppingen."

Kevin cringed when two shells clanked together. "Forget an enemy missile. I'm more worried about an accident." He blew a giant bubble and popped it. *Boom!*

Charlie winced. "I bet each one weighs at least a hundred pounds. Hope these are full of paint."

"What are you talking about? They might *look* like crayons," said Kevin, "but they're full of gunpowder."

"Nope. I know of three different kinds of shells," said Jack. "Standard, armor-piercing rounds for a tank battle; phosphorous rounds that blow stuff up and create major fires; but also the ones Charlie's talking about—paint rounds for making pretty pictures."

"You guys . . ." Clearly, Kevin wasn't buying this.

Charlie cut in. "Paint rounds are for target practice. When the Army doesn't want to actually blow up a target, they fill the shells with paint. Dad calls it 'painting pretty pictures.'"

Kevin nearly swallowed his gum. "Now *that* would be fun. Let's watch 'em unload these down at the tank lot."

Jumping on their bikes, they headed that way. But when they were almost there, Jack yelled, "Hold up, guys."

Jack whipped his bike around and headed for the open door of a gigantic maintenance shed they'd just passed. He was studying a huge map before Kevin and Charlie were even off their bikes. The map showed every detail of Cooke Barracks, as well as the surrounding German countryside.

"What do you little brats think you're doing?"

Startled, they turned to see a young, snooty-looking lieutenant who didn't appear to be a big fan of kids hanging around his maintenance shed.

Jack definitely wanted to study that map, so retreat wasn't an option. He decided the guy might not like brats but that he could work the guy. Looking him right in the eye, he said, "Good morning, lieutenant. My name is Jack McMasters, and my father is Lt. Col. McMasters. My friends and I were just going by on our bikes when we noticed this map. We're trying to figure out where we are on the map right now."

Jack saw the annoyed look disappear the moment he mentioned his father was Lt. Col. McMasters. *What a weenie.*

The lieutenant poked a finger at the map. "We're here." Then he walked his fingers to the PX and the movie theater.

By then Jack had also located The Glass House and The Circle up where Kevin lived. "What are these squiggly lines on the map?"

"Those are contour lines," the lieutenant said. "They indicate changes in elevation. The ground either goes up or down ten feet between each line. See over here? You can tell it's flat because you don't see any lines." The lieutenant was pointing to the big open area in front of The Glass House. "But when you come to a hill, you get a bunch of lines much closer together." He pointed to the hill leading down to the rifle range. "And look over here where a bunch of lines are squished right next to each other. That's a cliff."

Jack said, "So, the closer the lines, the steeper the terrain?"

The lieutenant nodded. "Correct. Okay, boys, enjoy yourselves. I have *important* things to do."

Jack was careful to thank him, and the other boys chimed in. The officer went back inside.

At first they studied everything of interest within the base's perimeter fence. But soon they were focused on the German countryside beyond their forest.

Jack pointed to the far northeast sector of the base. "Remember how my dad said this is the most probable location of an enemy attack? Well, it just so happens that if we could somehow figure out how to get over the barbed-wire fence at that exact spot, we might be able to get Jayla to the mountain."

Kevin started snapping his gum in frustration. "We've been over this before. There's no way to get to that mountain and back again in a single day."

Jack said, "If we didn't have to go out the main gate and all the way around the post, it would save a great deal of time."

Charlie's gaze tracked Jack's finger as it swept from the northeast end of base, all the way over to the Hohenstaufen. His eyes went wide. "That's a little nutty, even by our standards. How would we even *get* to that northeast sector, much less over the perimeter fence?"

"No clue," Jack said. "Those must be Mrs. Campbell's 'serious barriers and obstacles.' So that makes it our job to get over them, around them, or through them." Jack stared at Charlie and Kevin each in turn. "Doesn't it?"

Kevin was chewing slower by now. "Maybe."

Jack could feel him coming round. "Jayla is hell-bent on proving we're tougher than those Russian kids."

Kevin's eyes never left the map. "We're tougher. Probably smarter."

Jack and Kevin looked at Charlie. He shrugged. "Okay. If you two are going for it, I'm in."

Jack tapped the top of the Hohenstaufen. "We'll call it Mission Mountaintop."

The other boys cracked up at yet another Jack-ism, but he didn't even notice. His eyes never left the map.

26

Wet Shoes

"Saddle up, boys. We have a mission," Jack announced as he entered Charlie's bedroom on Saturday morning.

Kevin was already there, thumbing through one of Charlie's comics. "So it's the Hohenstaufen and Mission Mountaintop, is it?"

Jack smiled. "Ah! Now wouldn't it be nice to get on with *that*. Unfortunately that doesn't have a prayer till we complete Operation Ravine Crossing."

Charlie caught Kevin's eye. "If he's given it one of his wild-ass names, there's no backing out."

"But why do we need to deal with avoiding the Sevens right now?" asked Kevin. "Forget the ravine. It's not our mission."

Charlie moved closer to Kevin, as if siding with him. "Yeah, let's blow this pop stand and conquer the mountain."

But Jack just shook his head. "Didn't you see those tight contour lines on the map yesterday? They run across our entire woods. We either figure out how to cross the ravine or we never get to the Hohenstaufen."

A mile or so into the woods, they reached the deep ravine where the Sevens had trapped them. Scrambling down the steep slope of loose dirt, they were surprised to see a wide creek running through the ravine. The current was fast, and the water looked much too deep to wade across, at least without getting seriously wet.

Kevin was looking up and down the creek. "It's too deep to cross here, but maybe it gets shallower."

They picked a direction and hiked for more than an hour without finding a better spot to cross.

"Jack's right. It goes on forever," complained Charlie.

Kevin pointed to a spot where rocks rose above the surface in a straight line. "Could we jump from rock to rock? They're not that far apart."

Charlie stepped back. "You show us how it's done."

The first few rocks were close enough that Kevin simply stepped from rock to rock before reaching a long rock in the center. But after that the rocks were not so close or tall. Even so, Kevin managed to reach the other bank without slipping. Coming back he knew what to expect. He managed the widely spaced rocks with a series of running steps, then jumped onto the center rock with arms outstretched in victory. But it was slick from the splashing creek, and Kevin's feet started sliding. He whirled his arms round and round in a vain attempt to maintain his balance, but his windmill motions didn't keep him from going in. No Saturday-morning movie was funnier, and Jack and Charlie were pounding the ground, laughing.

Somehow Kevin managed to stand as he hit the water, so he was only soaked from the knees down. He waded back to Jack and Charlie, laughing. "Something tells me we need to find a different way across the creek."

Kevin walked into his house and started across the living room, heading for the laundry area off the kitchen. *I gotta get these things washed before anyone finds out.*

He'd almost made it to the laundry when the Buddha stirred from her trance. "Kevin, honey, I believe you might have left wet footprints on the carpet."

"Nothing to worry about, Mom. I'll take care of it." He tried to sound reassuring.

"Is there something on your shoes?" Her gravelly voice was rising in volume.

Kevin's radar switched on. He knew that escalating tone. *Gotta get this stuff off! Should never have worn my shoes into the house!* He took his shoes and socks off and tried to wipe his shoes with his soggy socks. He stuffed his socks into the pocket of his pants.

"Come over here. Let me see those shoes," she commanded. "Is that mud I see?"

He knew she was going off the wall again. *Why? Why now? God, please let my mother just slip back into herself.*

"Kevin Duncan, you've gotten mud all over my living room!" she screamed. "Give me those shoes immediately."

He handed her the shoes, sensing the moment that she felt how wet they were.

She pushed them in his face, shouting, "You've ruined these shoes and tracked mud all over this house. In fact, you've *destroyed* these shoes!"

I'm sorry, God. Please help her. Calm her down.

He watched helplessly as she wrestled with her demons. He could almost hear the struggle in her mind: *If I just stay in my chair I won't cause anything bad to happen. I have got to stay in my chair!*

Then, with more energy than Kevin thought possible, his mom pushed out of her chair and charged into the kitchen, screaming, "Why have you *done* this to me?"

By the time he reached her, she had water filling the sink. Wrestling the cap off the dish soap, she poured in almost half the bottle. Then she started dunking his shoes in the slippery water and grabbed a metal Brillo pad to scrape their soft leather sides. She ripped the shoes with amazing force, all but peeling them apart.

She growled, "You think we have money to spend on new shoes? No! We! Do! Not!"

Kevin was desperate. "Mom, I'll take care of it. Just go back and sit down."

"Sit down? No! No! No! I'm forced to deal with your mess."

Kevin watched as she lifted the shredded shoes out of the sink. He'd seen that look on her face before. He knew the split second when she realized she had made everything much worse.

The next second it would be *his* fault again. There would be no stopping her.

She plunged the shoes back into the sink, muddy water splashing up onto the clean dishes in the drying rack. She picked up the entire drying rack, tipping the dishes on top of the shoes in the sink. Some broke. With her hands dripping slimy water, she stormed over to the dirty-clothes hamper. She began dropping clothes onto the wet floor.

What's she doing? But then he knew.

He pleaded desperately, "Mom, please. Just let me help."

From deep in the hamper, she yanked out a bottle of bourbon. Hands shaking, she half-filled a water glass.

"No, Mom. Please don't start drinking."

"You!" she said, an ugly snarl on her face. "You *made* me this way."

In three quick swallows, she drained the glass.

Karen came running downstairs. She entered the kitchen just as Mrs. Duncan was pouring another glass.

"Oh, Mom, please don't drink," she pleaded.

Mrs. Duncan turned unsteadily, sloshing half her drink on Karen. "Look what you made me do! Get out of here!"

Karen looked down at the yellow-orange stain on her blouse.

Kevin handed her a towel. "Karen, fix it later. Please go back upstairs." Kevin kept his voice quiet, emotionless. "I caused it. Just go back up before Dad gets home. This time it'll just be on me."

The next day, Kevin showed up with a red, swollen nose. Jack's eyes grew wide for just a moment. "Let me guess. Your dad thought you made bad choices yesterday when you got your clothes wet."

"Let's just say my mom was kinda ticked off about it. And when she gets upset, the colonel gets upset. And when you're the son who caused this tragedy, the colonel concludes you're an ass-wipe. But you know *that* drill."

"Yes, I do."

But not the whole drill, thought Kevin. *And you're lucky you don't. With you, when it's over, it's over. With me, it will never be over.*

He forced a smile. "Besides, the important question is, How are we gonna get across that ravine? If we don't, the Sevens could trap us again. And even more important, we won't find our shortcut to the mountain."

"Right you are!"

Kevin was glad Jack had let him change the subject. Long ago, Kevin had promised himself he'd never tell anyone about his mom's drinking. It was just something he couldn't reveal. So once again he resisted his need to talk about it—even to Jack.

27

Black Squirrel Jack

Kevin's dip in the creek didn't keep the kids from continuing the search for a crossing that day, and many days after that. Having to watch out for the Sevens made their progress slow, but they only stopped when they hit the perimeter fence running around the base.

Jack plopped down on the ground a few feet away, staring at the end of their world. "Even if we could get some metal snips, we aren't going to cut it. That would compromise the safety of the base."

"Roger that," said Charlie. "The only other way is up and over, but that barbed-wire overhang makes scaling it impossible."

Kevin smirked. "The engineers who designed this fence must have been brats once upon a time."

Jack walked over to the fence, yearning to walk through it. Grabbing on, he shook it a few times, and then he leaned his back against the fence and pretended to bounce off. "We go back the way we came and recon in the other direction."

Two days later, they found a stretch where the ravine wasn't very steep, so the creek was wide and shallow, exposing dozens of stepping stones.

"Hey, Kev," said Charlie, "here's a place even I could cross without any of your famous ballet moves."

The boys raced each other back and forth from side to side, until Charlie happened to look at his watch. "Crap. It's already five o'clock."

Jack groaned. "An hour to get home! We'll have to double-time it the whole way."

Kevin was scrambling to put on his shoes and socks. "It's great here, but too far away to be an escape route or to explore beyond the ravine. We need something closer."

Jack said, "You're right. The run home is gonna kill us."

From then on, they hung out near the place the Sevens had smashed them. But now they designated a lookout at all times.

One afternoon, Charlie was on sentry duty when he spotted some Sevens heading their way. He gave their "take cover" whistle.

He and Kevin disappeared up trees. But Jack couldn't. He was near plenty of trees, but none with branches low enough to reach. He darted one way, then the other, frantic that he was running out of time. He could even hear the Sevens joking with each other.

His brain drowned out the Sevens. *Which way? Which way? Find something or you're gonna get caught. There's one, just below the ledge of the ravine. Why didn't I notice it before? Go! Go! Go!*

The tree was partly uprooted, as if a hurricane had screamed through and yanked it half out of the ground. But somehow the tree had managed to keep growing out over the ravine at a steep angle. Adrenalin and fear pumped through Jack's body as he ran onto the trunk and got onto all fours, scrambling like a monkey. The farther he climbed, the deeper the ravine dropped off, and the higher he was over the creek. But Jack knew better than to slow down till he reached a spot where the leaves covered him. Once there, he froze.

His brain was quiet now, and so were the Sevens. Had they moved on? Without a visual, he couldn't chance moving a muscle.

An all-clear whistle eventually came from somewhere down below. Only then did the tension leave his body. Jack began to tremble. *Another close call.*

"Jack, where *are* you?" came a shout from the ground.

"Up here," he yelled, pushing limbs away to see where the others were. He was surprised to find that right next to him was another tree growing from the opposite side of the ravine. He climbed up to where the two trees crossed. Jack needed a better look. It was hard to size things up because some of the limbs from each tree actually intertwined. He pulled out his KA-BAR knife and hacked off some thin branches blocking his view.

Charlie stood on the rim of the ravine, watching small limbs fall into the creek and float away. "What are you trying to do? Cut that stupid tree down while you're *in* it?"

Jack ignored him. He could see no limbs that were sturdy enough to get across on, so he eyeballed the gap between the tree trunks, and it didn't seem that bad. The two trunks were about five feet apart. If he could get onto the other tree, he could climb down to the far side of the ravine. He would jump five feet without thinking twice—if he were just a couple of feet off the ground. But at four stories above the creek bed, he hesitated a whole second. He said, "Charlie, look at this."

Charlie shouted, "Don't you *dare*! You'll kill yourself!"

Jack waved, as if not hearing him. He pressed a foot against a branch so he could get a decent push off. Crouching, he uncoiled and leapt into open air. Fortunately for him, he came crashing down onto the trunk of the connecting tree. His legs instinctively wrapped the trunk, while his hands grabbed the closest limbs to keep from rolling upside down. As his heart slowed down, he thought, *Amazing! I didn't even get scraped up.*

Jack wasn't as fast as the little black squirrels and he couldn't exactly fly through the air the way they did, but he had managed to cross from treetop to treetop the way they do. Descending that tree, he made it to the other side of the ravine. And he'd done it all with dry feet.

He made the treetop crossing three more times before coaxing Charlie and Kevin to try it. They managed the climb to the crossover point, but once they saw the four-story drop to the rocky creek bed, Charlie and Kevin scrambled back down the tree even faster than they'd come up. Jack followed them, shaking his head in exaggerated disappointment.

Kevin spoke first. "Not a chance I'd *ever* attempt that jump. It must be forty feet down."

Jack grinned. "You wouldn't be jumping *down*. You'd be jumping *across*."

Kevin opened his mouth, as if to argue further, but scowled instead. "You're completely insane, Black Squirrel Jack!"

"I'll say," said Charlie. "You're Black Squirrel Jack with a nut-sized brain. A brain too small to take in the laws of gravity."

For the next two days, they called him Black Squirrel Jack. Once Jayla and Sam found out why, they refused to call him anything but crazy.

28

Property Disposal

Jack dragged Charlie and Kevin over to the edge of the playground after lunch one day. "I have a little project and, Charlie, you're my man."

"What's up?" Charlie felt suspicious. Whenever Jack had that look, it usually meant work.

Jack stuck two fat sticks into the ground, pointing them toward each other. "Pretend these are the trees down by the ravine. At one point, they're only five feet apart." He held a piece of bark in between them. "What if we built a bridge from one tree to the other? Then everyone could use Black Squirrel Crossing."

Charlie's mind easily replaced the bit of bark with a wooden bridge. But one thing puzzled him. "How am *I* your man?"

Jack smiled. "We need to hunt up building stuff—probably six-foot boards. When we were stationed stateside, there was always scrap lumber free for the taking. Lots of houses were being built and the carpenters left piles of junk boards till the dump truck came around. I haven't seen any here, but if there are some, you're the guy to find 'em."

Kevin nodded slowly. "If you could find a Nazi shell casing, you can find us something for a bridge."

Charlie took a mental tour of the base—behind the PX, the gym, the airfield, The Glass House. He couldn't see a scrap of lumber. But at the same time, when he thought about the ravine, he definitely could see a plank bridge between those two trees, so he gamely said, "I'll try."

For the rest of the week, Charlie scrounged Cooke Barracks high and low. Riding in the school bus, or in a car, he scanned for possible scrap locations. As he'd feared, there wasn't a stick of lumber to be found. The Germans were so well organized, and so neat, there were no castoffs of any kind, anywhere.

However, Charlie didn't give up. When he was poking around behind the PX, looking for wooden pallets, the guy on trash duty took pity on him. "Lost cause, son. They're always reused. Scarce as hen's teeth."

The very next day, Charlie got a break. Walking toward his reading discussion group,

he picked up on just one word: *go-cart*. Go-carts needed wood.

Charlie plunked down in his usual spot, by Ben Kramer, the boy who had said it. "You made a go-cart? Where'd you find wood? I've been looking for some all week."

Ben grinned. "So did we. There's no wood around anywhere—at least, that we could find. We used scrap tin. My old man helped us."

"The Sargent Major got you the tin?"

"He helped us fine-tune the plans. I got the tin from my best source."

"Yeah?" Charlie almost pleaded.

Ben studied him for a bit, as if deciding if he could share this key piece of intel.

Then he leaned toward Charlie. "I got the tin from Ol' Henry. He runs a place called Property

Disposal—a place you're gonna love. It's where the Army stashes old stuff it doesn't need anymore. Things like old furniture, scrap metal, and beat-up army equipment."

Ben began flipping through his textbook for the story they were reading, all the while quietly explaining how to find Property Control.

Charlie said, "Thanks. School's out next week. Maybe we could build stuff together. Too bad we live on opposite ends of the base."

Ben gave him a crooked smile. "We'd do great. But I can just picture the Sargent Major finding out my new friend was some colonel's kid. He'd blow a gasket."

Mrs. Campbell started glaring at them; Charlie cocked a head in her direction. "That reaction times ten billion."

They joined the book discussion.

The very first day of summer vacation, Charlie made his way down to the Cooke Barracks Property Disposal. He dug around for a bit, but nothing. He was starting to get discouraged. That is, until he met Ol' Henry.

"Our Boy Scouts troop wants to earn a merit badge this summer by making a small bridge, but we can't find any wooden planks." Charlie's desperation was true, even if the story wasn't.

"That's on account of you're lookin' at the problem all wrong. See, yer in the great land of 4th Armored Division. You need to consider this here project more like a tanker would."

"How's that?"

"Lookie here, you need to be thinking *metal* rather than wood."

"Metal?"

"Yes siree, Bob!"

Ol' Henry took Charlie outside to an area way in the back. He showed him a five-foot-high stack of corrugated-steel sheets. Each was about eight

feet long and two feet wide, with regularly spaced holes. They were obviously well used, a bit bent up, and rusty.

Ol' Henry flipped one off the top of the stack and it clattered to the ground.

"This here is a metal skid. Combat engineers put 'em on top of mud so trucks and tanks and such can drive across the mud without getting stuck. See how it's kinda beat up? That's why the tankers don't want this one no more. But it's still plenty good for a small bridge, don't ya think?"

Charlie nodded, trying to look interested but not *so* interested the price would go up. "How much?"

"Well, lemme see," Ol' Henry said, rubbing a gnarled hand across his chin as if giving the matter serious consideration. "Since it's for the Scouts and all, I guess I could let her go for fifty cents. That sound about right to you?"

"More than fair. Thanks, Henry. I'll be back for it tomorrow."

Kevin dropped the handle of the Radio-Flyer and rubbed his tingling hands together. "This better be good, Charlie. I've *had* it with pulling this stupid wagon."

"You didn't say it was an hour away," grumbled Jack.

Charlie was unapologetic. "Don't be such party poopers. You'll see. This place is outtasight."

In a few minutes, they walked into Property Disposal.

Charlie called across the warehouse, "How you doing, Henry?"

"Just swell, Charlie. How *you* doin'? You come back for the skid?"

"Could be. We'll just go check it out."

The three boys studied the big hunk of iron out on the back lot.

"I see what you mean, Charlie," Jack said. "It just might work."

Kevin hadn't spoken yet, obviously focused on the skid. And as usual, when he was thinking something over, his hand glided over his flattop. At the moment, his hair was unusually short, because he'd been to the barber the day before. Kevin had to get a haircut every single week, no matter what. Col. Duncan's orders. That's when he would go by the PX to stock up on Bazooka Bubble Gum. If Jack was famous for spending half his allowance on his train set, the same people knew Kevin spent half of his on bubble gum. He pulled one end of his current wad into a long rope and then wiggled it back into his mouth. "It's certainly strong enough to hold us for an air crossing. And it's wide enough to be safe. We could pound big nails into the tree trunks and branches, and then bend them through the holes in the metal to secure it."

"That is, if we had big enough nails," observed Charlie. He leaned down to try and pick the thing up. "Whoa, this baby is really heavy! How are we gonna get it up there?"

"Ahhhhh, that's no problem," Kevin said, grinning. "We'll just strap it to the back of the greatest tree climber on the planet, Black Squirrel Jack, and he'll run it up."

Even using both hands, Jack could barely lift one end of the skid. "I don't think so!"

"Well, we gotta find a way," said Charlie.

Kevin thought some more. "With enough rope we could hoist it up."

That meant they needed rope as well as ginormous nails. They trooped back inside to see Ol' Henry, hoping he'd have a suggestion or two.

Ol' Henry had no nails, but he did have huge wood screws, which they settled on. When it came to rope or chain, he had none. However, after much consideration, he dragged out some flat, OD-green cord. "This here's parachute cord."

When the boys said it couldn't handle the weight, Ol' Henry just scoffed. "Now, boys, lookie here. The 101st Airborne Division used this to tie *jeeps* to three parachutes and drop 'em out of C-47 aircraft on D-day. If it worked for jeeps, it should hold that little slab a iron."

"How'd 4th Armored end up with parachute cord from the 101st?" asked Jack.

"Call it a present. For rescuing their ass."

Charlie was fingering the cord, but at that he looked up. "How?"

"You don't know that story?" Ol' Henry sounded incredulous. He waved them to a table little better than the metal skid. "It was World War II. General George Patton and his 3rd Army had hightailed it across Europe to crush the Nazis. Back then, 4th Armored Division was part of Patton's 3rd Army.

"The 4th was called Patton's Vanguard. Everybody knowed they was Patton's best. It was the last winter of the war, and 3rd Army was almost to Germany. Then them Germans mounted a major winter offensive at Bastogne. Became known as the Battle of the Bulge. German Panzer Divisions had the 101st Airborne Division surrounded. Those Panzers kept pounding 'em. The 101st was barely hanging on when Patton commanded 4th Armored to rescue 'em.

"The 4th had just come out of a major battle, and they was exhausted. But General Patton didn't give them one bit of down time. He made 'em race across Belgium, through the snow and freezing cold. They covered a hundred and fifty miles in just nineteen hours. No sleep and no rest. And believe it or not, boys, they went right into battle against them Panzers. They did the impossible. They rescued the 101st."

"Wow," said Charlie. "I never heard that story."

"Haven't you seen that little patch on your fathers' uniforms? The one right under their 4th Armored Division Patch? It says, 'BREAK-THROUGH.' They got that 'cause they're the ones who did the big

breakthrough, coming outta one battle, doing an impossible advance through the snow, and right away breaking through the *Panzers* to rescue the 101st. Made them famous, even if the 101st ain't ever admitted they needed help."

Jack thought about the time their dads had gone off to Grafenwöhr for winter combat exercises and range qualifying. It now made a lot more sense.

Then he realized Ol' Henry was still talking.

"Yup, that's when Ol' Bazooka Charlie was flyin' Two Star General Wood, 4th Armored commander, in a little Piper Cub airplane. 'P' Wood, he liked to command from the front, and Bazooka Charlie flew him in to recon every big battle. We have that Piper Cub parked down on the airfield right now, 'cause General O'Hara acts just like 'P' Wood, runnin' around in that ol' Piper Cub. And good thing he does."

"Why?" Kevin asked.

"On account of when war breaks out again this is the place it's gonna happen. And we're gonna need commanders like General O'Hara."

"What?" Jack demanded, hardly believing what he'd just heard.

The old guy looked startled by Jack's question, as if he'd said too much. "Now . . . look here. Don't you be worrying about all that. I never should have mentioned it to you kids."

Jack changed the subject. "So where'd you get the parachute cord?"

"Bazooka Charlie give it to us," Ol' Henry said, looking relieved to talk about something else. "He got it from the 101st."

"How'd he get the name *Bazooka* Charlie?" Kevin asked.

"Now, lookie-here. That's a story for another day, on account of I gotta get back to work. But I think you two ought to thank this here Scrounger Charlie for scrounging up your bridge-building material," he said, giving a nod to Charlie.

"He's certainly earned the name," said Black Squirrel Jack.

The total bill came to sixty cents. Each boy coughed up his twenty cents. The new owners loaded the long screws and a whole spool of parachute cord into the Radio-Flyer, and then Ol' Henry helped them balance the big metal skid on top. They said their good-byes.

Ol' Henry watched the boys struggle with their load as they tried to maneuver over the ruts in his Property Disposal kingdom. Charlie was pulling the wagon while Kevin was pushing from behind and Jack held the skid so it wouldn't fall off.

Jack looked back and saw a small smile on Ol' Henry's face. Jack wondered if he suspected they would not be earning a merit badge.

It took them almost an hour and a half to reach The Glass House. They collapsed on the ground behind the building, exhausted. But tired as they were, it dawned on Jack that they could never leave their hard-earned supplies there. They might attract questions, especially if one of the Sevens discovered them. So he persuaded the others to push on. Their final objective for the day became the Nazi pillbox.

"Ahhhh, my back is killing me," groaned Kevin. It was his turn to be bent over the wagon, trying to balance the skid as the wagon rolled slowly over the soft forest floor.

"Mine, too," Charlie moaned, breathing heavily. "I feel like one of those guys from 4th Armored, marching to Bastogne to rescue the 101st. How did they keep going?" But at that point, he saw the pillbox. "Breakthrough!"

A hundred yards more and Charlie was sprawled on the ground.

Kevin prodded him with a toe, as if making sure he hadn't died of exhaustion. "Can't rest yet. Gotta get home for dinner."

Charlie moaned, but got to his feet to cover the supplies with leaves. After all the trouble to scrounge the materials, he wasn't gonna have them stolen by someone else.

Jack was eighteen minutes late when he finally made it back to his quarters. He tried to slip in undetected, but Queenie spotted him, and said with classic superiority, "You're late again. And what have you been up to? You're filthy." Naturally she said it just loud enough for Mrs. McMasters to overhear.

"Stop trying to cause a problem, Laura. And you, Jack McMasters, better be washed up and looking sharp in the next ninety seconds, or you're going to get it."

Jack bolted for his room to get out of his rust-stained, muddy clothes. He smiled to himself. *Materials in place to accomplish the mission.*

29

Black Squirrel Crossing

Jayla and Sam were darting from tree to tree in stealth mode. They'd agreed to help build Black Squirrel Crossing after Jack read them in on the mission. The two girls scouted ahead for Sevens while the three boys laboriously wheeled the building materials from the Nazi pillbox to the construction site. Sam and Jayla followed the most direct path possible. The boys didn't want to drag the overloaded Radio Flyer even one foot out of the way.

"I'd hate a rematch with the Sevens, but it *looks* clear," Sam whispered nervously.

Jayla nodded. "I'll signal them to keep coming."

The boy's construction plan might have sounded perfectly logical back at the Nazi pillbox, but not when they got to the ravine.

"Are you *nuts*, Jack McMasters!" declared Sam, staring up at the tree. She couldn't even tell where the crossover point would be, but it was obviously going to be way up over the creek. "Impossible!"

"Don't flip your wig, Sam. It might be impossible, but you remember me telling you about my Navy friend, Alex Knox? The guy I met crossing the Atlantic?"

"Jack, is this gonna be one of your long stories?"

"Nope. Short," he said, winking at Charlie and Kevin. "It's just that Alex told me the Seabees, the Navy combat engineers, have this saying for the times they have to build stuff that nobody thinks can be done.

Kinda like you and Jayla think this little bridge-building project of ours is impossible. Anyway, the Seabees say, 'The difficult we do at once. The impossible takes a little longer.' Okay, so there's no way we're gonna get this done, right? That means it's the impossible, so it'll take us a bit longer."

The boys grinned at Sam and Jayla, and started unloading.

Jack said, "So here's how we're going to run this operation: Kevin, Sam, and Jayla are our ground crew."

Charlie handed them each a pair of leather work gloves.

"Charlie and I climb."

"Oh, joy," said Charlie.

Jack ignored this. "I need your muscle to maneuver the metal sheet."

He started up the tree with the tool bag Scrounger Charlie had packed. "Holy cow, Charlie. What do you have in this bag? It weighs more than the skid."

Charlie caught the end of the parachute cord Kevin tossed him. "Only essentials."

As Charlie followed Jack up the tree, Kevin began feeding him more cord off the huge spool. Jack quickly reached the crossover point, wedged the canvas bag in the crook of a large branch, and hurried back down to help with the unwieldy cord. Jack did a bit of acrobatic climbing to get the cord beyond the remaining limbs. At the crossover point, he temporarily tied it to a branch. Charlie climbed up to meet him. The hardest part had been ignoring the girls' involuntary shrieks whenever Jack got overly acrobatic.

At last, Jayla threw caution to the wind when it came to the Sevens and shouted, "Jack McMasters, you get back down here right now. What's so damned important about getting across this stupid ravine anyway?"

Then it dawned on Jack: The girls didn't know the real objective for Black Squirrel Crossing. "Come on, Charlie. Time for a break."

Once Charlie scrambled down, Jack followed. "Unless you guys have told them, the girls don't know why we need this crossing. Kevin, could you give 'em the sitrep?"

"Sure," said Kevin. "Jayla, we know you're desperate to prove we can overcome every obstacle and get to the Hohenstaufen. Well, if we can get over this ravine, we might make it there and back all within a single day."

Jayla's eyes widened. "You can get over the barbed-wire perimeter fence?"

Kevin said, "Not yet. We're facing one challenge at a time. I expect Jack to come up with something; he got us this far."

"Sounds good," said Sam. "We just need to get across this stupid ravine."

But Jayla didn't budge.

Kevin tried again. "Mrs. Campbell said we'd never be able to do all the things those Russian kids did. Well, I say piss on that! We *are* going to prove we're as tough as those Russian kids. So help me uncoil a lot more cord."

Jayla nodded imperceptibly and started pulling cord off the spool. Jack gave Kevin a nod of thanks before scrambling back up the tree to be ready to receive it.

Jack and Charlie hauled it up and flipped it over the tree, letting it drop back down to Sam and Jayla. The girls grabbed on. With them in position, Kevin pulled out his pocket knife, cut the cord off the spool, and knotted his end to the skid.

"Okay, pull," he yelled to Jayla and Sam. As they did, he pushed the skid into a standing position. Sam and Jayla pulled until the rope went taut, and continued to heave, but the skid was so heavy, they couldn't budge it.

Kevin let go of the skid and sprinted to where the girls were, pulling on his gloves so he could grab hold of the cord to help them pull.

Ever so slowly, the skid began to rise. "Don't try pulling with your arms," Kevin coached them. "Use your body weight as a lever and ease yourselves down into the ravine."

The skid rose steadily higher.

"Wow," said Jack and Charlie together. It's one thing to make a plan, quite another to see it work.

Somehow, the ground crew kept moving. Grunting and straining, with cramping hands, the three made their way toward the bottom of the ravine, without ever letting go. When the skid was halfway to Jack and Charlie, the parachute cord was as taut as a bow string and looked like it might snap at any second.

"Come on, Airborne, don't fail me now!" whispered Charlie from his perch.

The cord kept holding. Jayla, Sam, and Kevin were hanging on for dear life, working their way away from the tree. The skid continued to rise.

Jack's radar suddenly went off. He sensed movement. About seventy-five yards upstream, Sevens were coming directly toward them. He froze. *If we kept hoisting the skid, they'll see us for sure. Our whole operation will fail, and they'll know exactly what we're up to.*

Charlie, just below him, hadn't seen them yet. Jack tapped him on the shoulder, signaling for him to remain silent, and then pointed to the approaching Sevens.

Getting the ground crew's attention was another story. Jack desperately tried to signal them, but they were hunched over in their struggle to pull the cord.

If I yell out, the Sevens will hear me, and the jig's up. Jack glanced back. The Sevens were no more than thirty yards away. *We're outta time!*

He drew his KA-BAR knife from its sheath and placed its razor-sharp blade against the parachute cord. With one swift stroke, Jack cut the cord. The skid sliced the air like a guillotine blade. With a loud thud, it stuck straight up in the ravine.

Sam, Jayla, and Kevin whipped around to stare at Jack. He pointed toward the Sevens. Realizing there was no time to hide, the ground crew hit the dirt and then didn't move a muscle.

"I heard something," yelled Snot-Nose. "Came from over there."

Jack and Charlie froze, watching the whole scene unfold. Jayla, Sam, and Kevin were clearly visible, lying face down in the ravine.

A bunch of the Sevens scanned the woods and then the ravine.

"What'd it sound like?" asked a blond-haired kid.

"I dunno, just some big thud," said Snot-Nose.

Jack could hardly swallow when they focused directly on the skid. *Damn. They see it!*

"Maybe it was just a falling branch," said B-Ball, sounding impatient.

Jack watched as Snot-Nose's gaze shifted. For a brief second Jack was relieved, thinking they had somehow missed it. But Snot-Nose's line of sight halted right where Kevin and the girls were lying motionless. *Crap, he sees them.*

"Okay, maybe it was a bird or something." Snot-Nose was clearly disappointed. "Let's get outta here."

And to Jack and Charlie's amazement, they moved on, disappearing into the woods.

Eventually, Charlie whispered, "How was that even *possible*?"

"I have no idea," said Jack very softly. "Let's get down there and check on the others."

Charlie whistled the all clear, and they descended.

"I heard them talking," said Kevin. "I can't believe they didn't see us."

"Me, neither," said Charlie.

"Chalk it up to a miracle," said Jayla, whose mood was changing from relief to giddiness.

"Maybe a miracle, maybe not," Kevin said, "I remember my dad once telling me, 'The eye sees what it expects to see.' At the time I didn't really get what he meant. But maybe a perfectly rectangular skid standing straight up in the middle of nowhere is such an unlikely object that their brains didn't register it."

"Did the parachute cord break?" asked Sam. When Jack explained that he'd cut the cord on purpose, she shuddered. "Are you wacked? If one of us had been in the spot where it came down, we'd have been cut in half."

"But you weren't," said Jack very calmly. "And I made sure before I cut it."

"Whoa," was all she said.

"So we gonna get this thing done, or what?" asked Kevin mischievously.

"You gotta be kidding me," said Sam. "After all that? Are you crazy?"

"Yup," Kevin said, "we're crazy, and we're gonna get Jayla to that mountain." He headed for the bottom of the ravine to try to get the skid unstuck.

Jayla turned to Sam. "You *know* we aren't quitting till it's done. So you might as well help." And she followed Kevin.

When the skid was finally hauled all the way up, just above Jack and Charlie, it was four stories above the creek.

"We gotta get this beast in place," said Charlie. "They can't hang on to it much longer."

That's when Jack really went nuts. Grabbing a nearby branch, he swung out into the open air and kicked the bottom of the skid. His kick caused the huge iron plank to swing back and forth over the open gap between the trees.

"Yank on the rope," he yelled to his troops below.

The more they tugged, the more the skid swung. Jack climbed back up into the tree and positioned himself next to Charlie. The bottom of the skid came swinging toward them. Each boy hung on to the tree with one arm, and with the other hand, grabbed the skid coming toward them. They held on with all their might, its weight almost ripping them out of the tree.

Struggling to keep the skid from getting away, Jack grunted between clinched teeth, "Ground crew, move toward me two steps."

With hands strangled by the cord and arms about to break, Sam, Jayla, and Kevin somehow managed it. The bottom of the skid came thumping down, right onto the boys' tree trunk, and stuck there. And, as good fortune would have it, the top of the skid angled back toward the other tree.

"Okay, quick! Come toward me three more steps."

The three eased forward. The top of the skid came down to where it hung just two feet above the other tree.

"Two more steps toward me."

The next thing any of them knew, that great, iron plank had positioned itself between the two trees.

"Okay, let go!"

The three on the ground collapsed. The skid stayed in place. Charlie and Jack beamed down at them.

While Sam, Jayla, and Kevin lay on their backs looking up at the crossing, they saw Jack do his famous Black Squirrel leap for the last time. He came crashing down onto the far tree.

Sam said, "You're nuts, Jack McMasters."

Charlie got a saw out of the tool bag and cut off a large limb to create a small stump. He and Jack jockeyed the skid onto it. The stump held the skid flat and steady against the massive tree trunk.

Jack made the maiden walk over Black Squirrel Crossing. The skid never budged as he came across. Smiling, the boys pulled the large screws out of the bag and secured the bridge permanently to the trees.

Charlie surprised Jack by pulling a thick rope out of his tool bag. He climbed up ten feet to a limb that hung out over the open air. He tied the big rope to it so that it hung down onto the bridge. "Now kids can hang on to the rope when crossing the bridge," said Charlie.

"Clever," said Jack.

Using the rope, they walked over Black Squirrel Crossing and climbed down the other tree to the far bank of the ravine.

Jack yelled to the other three, "Okay, your turn. Give it a go."

Sam went first, Jayla close behind, with Kevin bringing up the rear. Halfway up the tree, Sam looked down and started to lose it, but Jack and

Charlie kept telling her not to look down. It took a bit, but she finally made it, as did the others.

Five kids found themselves on the far bank of the great ravine. All with dry shoes. All smiling. All the proud builders of Black Squirrel Crossing.

Mission accomplished.

30

German/American Friendship Week

German/American Friendship Week had been *the* main topic of conversation at the McMasterses' dinner table for at least two weeks. The commanding general was opening the base for a week to Germans who wanted to visit, in order to promote friendship between the American military and the local community. The whole base was busy preparing, and all the dads had been assigned some responsibility for the event.

One day, word got out that a bunch of GIs were putting up a giant, white tent next to the runway. Every brat in the neighborhood gathered along the cliff to get a bird's-eye view. They watched as an impressive display of American military power was assembled down on the *Flugplatz*. First came the tanks, tank-recovery vehicles, and self-propelled howitzers—big cannons mounted on tracked vehicles. Then they brought in the wheeled vehicles: tank transporters, jeeps, three-quarter tons that looked like heavy-duty pickup trucks, and the world-famous deuce-and-a-halfs, those big Army trucks with two benches running along each side that soldiers sit on. The backs of those trucks were covered with large, OD-green canvas tops. The one thing all the vehicles had in common? OD green.

Jack and crew had grown up around all this Army equipment and firepower. But they knew the German kids hadn't and would probably be crawling all over it.

Mrs. McMasters lined up her children up for inspection before they left for the opening day of German/American Friendship Week. Jack was sent back to clean under his fingernails, and Rabbit had to change her dress. Her first one had gotten dirty even before leaving the apartment. Only Rabbit could have achieved that. Queenie, of course, was perfect.

Once they passed inspection, Mrs. McMasters looked each of them in the eye, and with a tone that clearly communicated "Cross me and you're dead," she read them the riot act.

"Remember, make me proud of you. Look sharp, act sharp, be sharp. You all know exactly what I expect from you—don't you?"

"Yes, ma'am," they said.

"And, there is one thing I want you to remember in *particular*. You are not just a bunch of kids. You represent the United States of America. You are the children of a distinguished United States Army officer. You will *act* like it! Do I make myself clear?"

"Yes, ma'am."

The ceremony opened with a huge parade, including the 4th Armored Division Marching Band. It looked like every American on the base had turned out for the event. But what surprised Jack was that over fifteen thousand German men, women, and children showed up. Among them were local dignitaries, politicians like the mayor of Göppingen, as well as the press. The whole thing was being broadcast on German radio and television—even on Armed Forces Radio-Stuttgart. That was the radio station Queenie, all her girlfriends, and Ingrid listened to for the latest rock-and-roll songs.

Once the parade ended, people made their way to the white tent to stake a claim to a table. That became the McMasterses' base camp. Once it was established, the kids were free to go off with their friends. Jack and Sam quickly found each other and went about rounding up the others. When they were all together, they headed off to check out the display of American military power. As they'd figured, there were tons of German kids crawling all over the vehicles.

As they stood watching, Charlie leaned over to Jack and nodded at a group of German men standing nearby. "What do ya bet some of them were Nazis during the war?"

Jack whispered back, "I think that's a pretty good bet. And I'm sure a few of them were gung-ho Nazis. But I'm also pretty sure most of them

weren't. A lot of them didn't have much choice. Ingrid told us that if you didn't support the Nazis, you could get fired from your job, and all kinds of other bad stuff."

"Still, it's kinda strange," said Kevin. "A few years ago those same guys were probably shooting at our dads."

"And, of course, our dads were shooting back at *them*," said Sam.

Jack looked at all the German kids. "Must be kinda scary or creepy for those kids, knowing we came into their country with our guns blazing—and we're still here with all this firepower."

Jayla nodded solemnly. "Yeah, and it must be hard for them, knowing their dads were Nazis and that they lost the war."

Kevin's brows furrowed. "Gotta be kinda strange."

Looking over at the group of German men, Jayla asked, "Do you think one of them could be The Watcher?"

Now that's *something actually worth worrying about,* Jack thought. And for the first time, he wondered if Jayla might worry about it just as much as he did. "Probably only one in a thousand Germans is a spy, but I sure wish there was an easier way to identify which ones *are*."

"Enough, you guys," said Charlie. "Any horrible, no good, slippery, sneaky spies are just gonna have to wait until after lunch, 'cause I am positively starving to death."

"You poor thing," Jayla said with exaggerated sympathy. "You're starting to sound like Jack, starving child of America."

The sight of the endless tables of food in the tent made Jack almost giddy. But as he headed for the chow line, his brat-radar went off. Cautiously, he glanced over at the McMasters table. Sure enough, his dad was giving him "the eye." Lt. Col. McMasters motioned for Jack to come over and bring the others with him.

"Hold up, guys. My dad wants to talk to us," he said, sounding miserable.

"Remember your ABC's, Jack," whispered Jayla. "Always Be Cool."

Sam directed a smile toward Lt. Col. McMasters. "Clever girl, Jayla. Always the clever girl."

Jack noted a bunch of strangers at their table, some obviously German. Lt. Col. McMasters introduced everyone. One was Herr Ehrlichmann, the *Bürgermeister* of Göppingen. Jack knew that meant the guy was the mayor. That made him important. Herr Ehrlichmann stood to greet them. Only then did the brats realize just how large the red-faced man was. Jack's hand was swallowed in his crushing grip.

Lt. Col. McMasters said, "Jack, this is Hans, the *Bürgermeister's* son, and his friend, Günther. They're about your age. Why don't you have lunch with them and show them around this afternoon?"

The colonel's words might not have sounded like a direct order to the Germans, but to Jack and his friends, they weren't a suggestion, and certainly not a request. Their marching orders were clear.

Because Jack's German was better than that of his friends, and not wanting to give his father any more time to dream up restrictions on what they could and couldn't do, he quickly said to the two boys, *"Willst du mitkommen und mit uns essen?"*

The two German boys jumped up from the table. It was clear they were as anxious to get away from the adults as Jack and crew.

Jack nodded at the mayor and said in German, "It was very nice to meet you."

The kids darted for the food. The first part of the chow line was all salad stuff. Hans and Günther, obviously trying to be polite, started to take some, but Charlie immediately sorted them out.

"You don't want that, guys," he said, using a bunch of hand signals and gagging sounds to communicate. "You'll die eating that rabbit food. Come down to this end where we can get cheeseburgers and fries. That's the good stuff."

Charlie put in a massive order and then led them over to a table that contained all the extras: catsup, mustard, pickles, onions, tomatoes, lettuce, etc. Everyone tried to teach Hans and Günther the fine art of making a cheeseburger. And, of course, there was a big debate about what to add or not add. For example, Kevin was a catsup-only kinda guy. Jack was an everything guy. The others were somewhere in between. It became a bit like a Three Stooges routine.

When they finally sat down at a table, Hans and Günther picked up their forks and knives.

"Whoa! Time out, guys," yelled Charlie. "Lose the silverware."

"Yeah, do it like this," said Kevin, picking his burger up with two hands and taking a giant chomp out of it.

Hans and Günther leaned back, a pained look on their faces. Jack could tell they thought this savage, caveman style of eating was a joke. They thought they were being messed with. But when they saw Sam and Jayla do it, too, they reached for their burgers. After two bites, their faces expressed true rapture. There were two new believers in that most American of inventions, the cheeseburger—and in the only way to eat it. Adding fries, a milkshake, and no parents, those two kids were pretty close to heaven.

Everyone began talking in a mishmash of German, English, and sign language. But one way or another, they communicated. Hans lived in downtown Göppingen because his father was the *Bürgermeister*. Günther's father was a farmer, and their farm was actually pretty close to the base. The two boys were school friends.

Once finished with lunch, the group headed for the tanks and trucks. Because Hans and Günther were with them, even the American kids got up on the vehicles to show them everything. Charlie pointed to where a .50-caliber machine gun could be mounted. Hans and Günther loved that. Jack told them in German that their dads were Army officers, and tankers, in 4th Armored Division.

As they climbed all over a tank, Hans said, "Jack, how is it you speak so much German? That's not something we expect Americans to do."

Jack smiled. "My nanny—*Kindermädchen*—only speaks German so I had to learn in order to survive."

Charlie cut in. "We're outta here! I want us to get a good spot."

Jayla explained that this afternoon there was a big event, and they had to get a move on.

Even the brats were impressed when an M-48 tank came roaring up in front of the crowd. The voice booming over a loudspeaker explained that they were about to show everyone how 4th Armored Division repaired a tank—right on the battlefield. Hans and Günther definitely thought the whole thing was great.

A team of mechanics jumped from a deuce-and-a-half as it rolled up to the tank. They immediately got to work loosening nuts, bolts, and the hydraulic and electrical connections of the tank's engine. The announcer kept up a steady explanation in English and German, until he was drowned out by the deafening approach of a huge Sikorsky H04S-3 helicopter. In a matter of minutes, without ever landing, the hovering helicopter lifted the six-ton engine out of the tank and hauled it on board.

Moments later her crew lowered a replacement engine back into the tank. The mechanics immediately connected up the new engine. That fifty-ton M-48 tank, with its 90-millimeter gun and its new 690-horsepower engine, roared back to life and drove away. It was definitely an impressive demonstration of the US Army's efficiency and skills. Hans and Günther were left astounded.

"Incredible," said Kevin.

"I am absolutely, positively going to become a helicopter pilot," said Jayla, eyes full of passion.

Sam explained to their new friends that her dad was responsible for getting all the parts they used in the tank repairs. Hans and Günther said that was a lot more exciting than being a farmer or a mayor.

"I don't know about that," said Sam. "I wouldn't mind checking out your farm."

"And I wouldn't mind checking out the mayor's office," said Jack.

Hans said he'd see if he could arrange a visit to the mayor's office in Göppingen, and Günther said he'd try to get them invited to his farm.

Jack thought, *These two are okay.*

Jayla whispered to him, "Maybe Günther knows how to get from his farm to the Hohenstaufen."

Jack gave a slight nod. "Pretty soon we'll ask." *Meeting these two might actually become part of the plan.*

The chopper they liked best was *Little-Bird*, pretty much a large glass bubble that flew two people. *Little-Bird*'s pilot called it a flying seat, since you could see out in all directions. When he began explaining how it was flown, they didn't understand half of what he said. But it didn't take a genius to figure out it was pretty complicated.

Well, that's not completely accurate. One of them was getting a whole lot out of the talk. Anyone could see that Jayla's brain was fully engaged and lit up to megawatt level.

At first that pilot hadn't said all that much. But when Jayla started in on the questions. . . .

Charlie leaned over to Jack and Kevin. "Jayla's gonna get that guy to teach her the entire nine-month 'copter training manual from flight school if we don't drag her outta here."

"And she'll probably think she can fly it," Kevin whispered back.

"No, it's much worse than that," Jack said. "She probably *will* be able to fly it."

His friends might not have noticed, but Jack was half serious.

That night there was a huge dinner in the white tent. Several long tables had been pushed end to end, and Jack's, Jayla's, and Sam's parents, other officers, and a whole group of Germans were seated around them. Hans's and Günther's parents were part of the gathering. Jack and his friends, along with Hans and Günther, were told to sit with Ingrid and Queenie and her friends at a nearby table. Rabbit and her buddies were at another table full of little kids. It did not escape Jack that his mother had clear line of sight to both tables.

Hans went over to talk to his parents about his new American friends coming for a visit to Göppingen. He came back smiling. "My mother said something is already being arranged. We will see you guys again!"

Once dinner was finished, the band came on stage, and people began heading for the dance floor. Their parents motioned for the kids to dance, but Jack and his crew didn't look inclined to leave the safety of their table. And the German guys didn't seem any more anxious to dance than their American counterparts. Queenie and her friends, on the other hand, wanted to get out on the dance floor, but no one asked them.

Their parents got up to dance, and the only one left behind at the adult table was a young officer named Captain Saunders. Saunders was the general's aide-de-camp. He was single and didn't have a date that night, so he had no one to dance with. That is, until he came over to their table and started talking to Queenie and her girlfriends. But it didn't take long for the girls to figure out that he was a lot more interested in talking to Ingrid than to them. The next thing the girls knew, Ingrid and Captain Saunders were out on the dance floor. After that, Captain Saunders seemed to forget to go back to his own table.

Queenie and the girls continued to chat, but didn't miss a trick. They remained glued to the whole Captain Saunders and Ingrid situation.

"Do you think she likes him?" asked Camila.

"It certainly looks like it to me," said Liz. "See how close they're dancing?"

"And they aren't just dancing," chimed in Queenie. "They even seem to be talking to each other. *How* I have no clue, but maybe the captain knows a little German."

"I saw her smile at him," said Karen.

"Yeah, that boy can't take his eyes off her," smirked Camila.

"True. But you can never really tell with Ingrid," said Queenie. "She's a good chameleon. She'd make it look good, even if she didn't like him."

"Well, I think she does. But what do *we* think about *him*?" asked Liz.

"He's certainly cute," said Camila.

"He'd better be, 'cause she could be in *Seventeen* magazine," said Queenie, protective and proud of Ingrid at the same time.

"My dad says the general really likes Captain Saunders," Karen said.

"I don't care *who* he is. He'd better just watch himself," said Queenie. "We need to keep a close eye on this."

∞🜍∞

While Queenie and her friends remained focused on Ingrid and the captain, Jack and his crew felt free to share with Hans and Günther their plans to explore the German countryside beyond the base. Charlie happened to mention Black Squirrel Crossing.

"*Ach*! Wait a minute," Hans said. "You guys can get over the big ravine? How is that *possible*? We've never been able to get across."

Jack grinned. "American ingenuity. That means we Americans find a way to do things. What we did is top secret, but we'll tell you."

Charlie explained Black Squirrel Crossing.

Günther's eyes were huge. "If you can get over the big ravine, then you can get all the way to my farm. It is by the northeast part of the base." He described a spot where they could all meet along the Cooke Barracks perimeter fence.

Charlie held up a hand. "Whoa! We can't get over that fence. Believe me, we've tried."

Günther flashed a conspirator's grin that needed no translation. "Do not worry, Charlie. You just go to *your* side of the fence. We will go to *our* side. Then we will get you over. We Germans are also quite clever."

"I will see if I can go to Günther's house tomorrow so we can show you," said Hans, flashing a mischievous grin of his own.

Jack grinned right back. "Let's do it." *I wish all the things Dad made me do were as cool as meeting Hans and Günther.*

31

German Ingenuity

As promised, Jack and crew headed out the next morning to meet up with the Germans. Jayla and Charlie were on wide flanking patrol, providing an early warning system. However, once over Black Squirrel Crossing, the mood lightened and they dispensed with security. This was their turf.

They made their way to the perimeter fence and headed north. As they looked through the barbed wire for the water trough and hand pump that Hans had described as the meeting point, they saw magnificent rolling fields and orchards. Far in the distance they could just make out the Hohenstaufen.

"From what Hans said, we should be close now," said Jack.

Coming over a rise, they saw Hans and Günther sitting on the edge of the trough.

"Ya gotta love it when a plan comes together," said Jack.

Everyone started talking at once.

"So, how do we get over the fence?" Sam asked.

Grinning, Günther said, "*Einfach!*"

Sam looked at him, confused.

"It means *simple*," Jack translated.

Günther signaled for them to follow him along the fence. About a quarter mile farther, Hans walked up to a huge, old oak tree by the fence and started climbing. Günther followed. Within seconds the boys were crawling out on a big limb that reached over the barbed wire. Once on the American side, they grabbed a couple of smaller branches so they could hang down and drop to the ground. The brats gave them a round of applause, making Hans and Günther beam.

Kevin tried jumping for the limb in an attempt to reverse the trick, but no matter how high he jumped, he couldn't grasp it.

"So how do you get back over?" asked Sam.

"*Einfach!*" Günther gestured for them to follow him once more. A bit farther down, they walked up to a tree with a strong limb reaching over the fence onto the German side.

Günther said, "We call this tree *Die Einbahnstraße nach Deutschland*, and we call the other tree *Die Einbahnstraße nach Amerika.*"

Jack burst out laughing. "This one they call *The One-Way Street to Germany*, and they call the other tree *The One-Way Street to America.*"

Now they all were laughing.

Kevin looked like he was ready to hug the tree. "I call this *Highway to Freedom.*"

Nothing could stop the brats from scrambling up and over.

Jack thought, *No wonder they were excited when they heard about Black Squirrel Crossing. They get it.*

The next two hours were dedicated to exploring the farm, which seemed like something out of a picture book: lush fields, sheep grazing on hillsides, a brilliant sky, and fluffy clouds. Perfect.

They first explored the barn, where Günther's family milked their sheep twice a day and sheared off the wool twice a year. Then they peeked in the windows of a separate stone building where his family made cheese from the sheep's milk. His family made their living selling wool and cheese. His dad hired shepherds to take their sheep grazing at different locations in the valley.

Günther laughed. "My dad has a great arrangement with the American Army so our sheep can graze on the base. Our sheep are the lawn mowers along *der Flugplatz* runways. The Army gets the grass cut for free, and the sheep get to graze for free. Everyone gets something."

The German boys could understand some English, but spoke very little, so most of what they said was in German. Jack did his best to translate for his crew. When he didn't understand them, Hans and Günther kept saying it in different ways until he finally caught on. It was pretty obvious to everyone that with Hans and Günther around, Jack's German was going to get challenged, pushed, and improved.

After a while, Günther provided lunch, though his mother never knew they had guests. He brought the kids to an apple orchard, where they picked all the apples they wanted. Günther unearthed a basket holding loaves of bread and some cheese from the farm to eat with the apples.

Jack, starving as usual, was surprised how good the sheep's-milk cheese was.

After lunch, they roamed around the German countryside, exploring.

From a high point on a hill, Jayla showed Jack at least two likely ways a person could hike to the Hohenstaufen. "Now that we can get off base, nothing stands between us and that mountain."

"You're right," Jack said. "Looks like we just might be able to get there and back all in the same day. But don't get in a big rush; we still have a lot of planning to bring this thing off without a hitch."

Jack called everyone over. "We have something to tell Hans and Günther."

Everyone sat, and Jayla explained Mission Mountaintop, starting with Mrs. Campbell and *Sputnik*. Jack translated as best he could.

Hans cocked his head to one side, considering. "We have only been there by car, and adults always knew. This will be tough."

Günther cut in, "In this case, *tough* means *German ingenuity*. That means we Germans find a way to do things. You might not know this, but we want to do better than Russian kids even more than you do!"

Hans and Günther voted to join the Americans on their quest.

Done with lunch, they had entered an old storage shed.

Jack spied two canteens. They looked military. "Wow!" he said, tapping Hans's shoulder. "Are those Nazi canteens?"

Hans's face lost all color. So did Günther's.

What did I just do? I said Nazis! He'd been warned not to bring up the Nazis, that it might upset people. That clearly was an understatement. Everyone had gone silent—and not in a good way.

"I'm sorry," Jack said, truly apologetic. "I forgot I'm not supposed to mention the Nazis. We don't need to talk about it. Please forgive me."

Finally Hans cleared his throat. He seemed to be having trouble finding words, even in German. "It wasn't our fault, you know. We were born after the war ended. We're very sorry about everything that happened." Even before Jack translated, the kids knew Hans felt helpless and regretful.

Jayla looked at him with genuine concern. "We know it's not your fault. No one thinks it was."

"We don't have to talk about this," Sam rushed to say.

"Yeah," said Charlie. "We really like you guys. We won't bring it up again."

"But you don't understand," Günther said, ever so quietly. "We *need* to talk about it. No one ever lets us talk about the war or the Nazis. It is *verboten.* How do you say? Forbidden."

"You guys never talk about it?" Jayla was incredulous.

Hans shook his head. "Never."

"Impossible," agreed Günther, emphatically.

The brats were stunned.

Sam spoke up. "If you want to tell us, that's okay. We'll listen. We can sit by that tree and listen." She cocked her head beyond the shed door to a spot in the shade.

They all walked outside and sat in the grass, the German boys sitting side by side.

Hans said, "You can't imagine how it really is. Since the war no one even says the word *Nazi* or talks about the war at all. No one dares—not even our parents, our teachers, or the priests. They are all embarrassed about what Hitler did—and what they did. It's like they think if they pretend it never happened, everyone else will forget it happened, too."

Günther blurted out, "We think that . . . that it's true . . . that you hate us. Hans slept at my house last night. When no one was awake to hear us, we talked about the great time we had playing with you on the American base. But we think you only acted nice to us because your fathers forced you to. How could you possibly like us when we are Germans and Germans tried to destroy you?"

Jack sat there studying his shoes, too shocked even to look at Günther.

Günther concluded, "We were pretty sure you wouldn't come today. We went to the trough this morning hoping you'd come but expecting you wouldn't."

"Why *did* you come, Jack?" Hans's voice was barely a whisper.

"We came because we like you. That's the truth," said Jack. "Our parents aren't making us be your friends."

"But that is not true!" insisted Hans. "At the table in the tent, your father ordered you to take us to lunch. Am I not correct? He said it like it was only a suggestion, but we could tell it was an order." Hans gave Jack a hard look. "We're not stupid, Jack. We always watch carefully what is going on around us—especially with adults. Your father ordered you to play with us."

Instead of looking defensive, Jack couldn't help grinning. "You're very sharp. Just one reason I like you. You've got what we have—brat-radar. That means you notice everything about adults. And you're right. We were ordered to play with you. But I didn't even remember that. We're used to getting orders that we have to obey instantly. For us, if you don't obey, they kill you. Well, not exactly kill you, but you know what I mean. Our fathers are military officers first, and fathers second."

"Or third," said Kevin, with a grin.

"Or fourth," Jayla chimed in.

Everyone cracked up, even Hans and Günther. It was astonishing how just that little bit of laughter broke the tension.

"So, you're right that my dad did order us to play with you. But you're wrong about it, too. It was his way to get rid of all kids at the table or to look good for the commanding general. You know, all that

German/American Friendship stuff. Our kids are playing with your kids, blah, blah, blah . . ."

"What is *blahblahblah*?" asked Hans, instantly confused.

That got another laugh, before Sam explained it.

"Anyway, spending the whole day with you was our own idea. And our parents certainly don't know we're here today. We came because we wanted to. We like you and trust you enough to have you be part of our secret mission."

Kevin added, "American parents don't tell us important things either—or want us to talk about some stuff. We can talk about the Nazis all we want, but what no one ever mentions are the Communists. It sounds like your parents are just as bad as ours."

"This is all good to hear, but we are still confused why you would want to be friends with Germans," said Hans. "Germans killed so many people they thought were inferior. Germans wanted to rule the world. It's embarrassing for us. It's hard for us to live with. Even we wouldn't want to be friends with us."

"Look, it was really bad, Hans, but it's the past," said Jack. "I didn't cause it and neither did you."

"Yeah, so you're just gonna have to get over that," said Jayla. "Because we *do* like you."

"And to prove it, we told you about Mission Mountaintop."

For a bit, no one said more. Until Jack, being Jack, said, "Can we ask some more questions about the Nazis?"

"Please do," Hans said, obviously relieved to move on. "And surely, one thing you want to know is if our parents were Nazis. Correct?"

"Well, yes. Were they?"

"My father was a pretty important Nazi in Göppingen."

"My father was one, too," Günther said.

"Were they in the military?"

Hans said, "My father was a colonel in the German Army during the war."

"No wonder you have solid brat-radar!" said Jack, grinning. "You're a brat just like us." Hans definitely looked confused by the comment, so Jack did his best to explain what military brats were, and about their brat-radar.

"Maybe I *am* a bit of a brat, even if I wasn't born when my father was in the army."

"My father wasn't in the military," said Günther, "but he tried to be. The *Wehrmacht* told him that his war job was being a farmer and producing food for the military."

"So then why did he become a Nazi?"

"I'm not sure. He never talks about it. But I do know he had a big contract to supply food to the Luftwaffe on the *Fliegerhorst Kaserne*, before it was your military base. I'm pretty sure only good Nazis got contracts like that."

"What?" said Charlie. "Our base was used by the German Air Force during the war?"

"Sure."

"Tell us everything you know," demanded Charlie.

Günther said, "Well, *Fliegerhorst* means military airfield and *Kaserne* means barracks. It was a base devoted to aircraft. One night my grandfather had a little too much *Schnapps* to drink, and he did say some things about it."

All eyes locked on him.

"In ancient times the whole area was nothing but meadows, farmland, and woods. But around 1930, when airplanes became popular, a civilian *Flugplatz* was built there. Then in 1935 the Luftwaffe took over the airfield and rebuilt the whole thing. When the war started, it was used to train Luftwaffe pilots to fly lots of different kinds of aircraft. Mostly to be fighter pilots."

"We've found big Nazi shells. And of course there are bunkers and pillboxes on the base. What were they for?" asked Charlie, fascinated.

"Most of that was from the *Soldaten der Flakabteilung*, an anti-aircraft unit."

Charlie and Jack gave each other a knowing glance.

"Their job was to protect the Luftwaffe from getting destroyed by the American and British bombers." Günther, looking a little embarrassed, said, "Sorry to say, their job was to shoot down your bombers."

"Don't feel bad," Sam piped up, "our guys were trying to bomb your planes."

"Did our bombers ever actually hit the airfield?" Jack asked.

Günther's eyes lit up. "This is what my grandfather talked about that night: The base wasn't hit for most of the war. By the end, it was one of the last airfields still open in the south part of Germany. But then it was bombed, and my father got blamed."

"What?" Jayla demanded. "Your father was a farmer!"

"Well, there was a way they could flood the *Flugplatz* during daylight and then take away the water at night so the pilots could use the airfield. Sounds crazy, right? But during the daytime it looked like a lake so the bombers left it alone."

"Cool," Kevin said.

"Yes, cool until a few of my dad's sheep wandered out into the middle of the lake one day. An American or British flyer spotted them just standing there in a few inches of water and knew something was wrong. That's when they bombed the place. My dad got blamed."

"What did they do to him?" Jack asked.

"He was terrified the Gestapo would take him off to prison. But the war ended and nothing happened to him."

"Good thing!" Jack said, "So, they had a way to flood the whole airfield and then unflood it . . ."

"That's what my grandfather said."

Jack leaned toward Charlie. "One of these days we need to gather intel on that little engineering feat."

The look on Charlie's face told Jack that Scrounger Charlie was already scrounging for a solution.

Jack said to everyone, "Now that Hans and Günther have signed on, we can follow through with Mission Mountaintop. We have Black Squirrel Crossing, The One-Way Street to Germany, and two friends to lead us through the German countryside. We're almost there."

Sam might have seemed apprehensive, but Jayla was smiling.

32

Meeting the Threat

Jack was writing an equipment checklist for Mission Mountaintop when Queenie popped her head through the door. "Mom wants us. Family meeting."

Mrs. McMasters sat on the couch, five blue suitcases lined up by her feet. "Your father needs a vacation. If we depart in two days, we can squeeze in two weeks of leave before school starts again."

"What about Ingrid?" asked Queenie.

"She needs a break, too. Her friend Lena has managed to get vacation time, so they'll be going off together."

"Where we going?" bounced Rabbit.

"We'll drive to Italy." Their mom glanced at the suitcases. "I bought us new suitcases that fit better in the car. So each of you take one. Your first job is to pack your best play clothes and one nice outfit. Then we have cleaning to do so we come home to a quarters that is spick-and-span."

Rabbit grabbed her suitcase and bounded toward her room. Queenie and Jack each grabbed one. As they walked to their rooms, he said, "These look about the same size as the packed ones. The ones *supposed* to be packed for quick trips."

Queenie smirked. "She just doesn't want to tamper with the emergency evacuation suitcases."

✺

Jack barely had time to talk to his crew before he left for Italy. For once, he wasn't thrilled about the idea of heading off to a different country—nor were Jayla and the others.

During the drive through the Alps and down to Venice, of course Rabbit was in the middle of the back seat, bouncing hour after hour. During her hundredth run-through of "Row, Row, Row Your Boat," Jack decided any planning during the trip would be impossible. At least wandering the tiny passageways of Venice and gliding on a gondola through its canals became its own adventure. Once he got to Rome and saw the walls covered in human skulls in the Capuchin Crypt and played hide-and-seek with his sisters in the Coliseum, he was enjoying himself too much to be frustrated.

✺

Jack and company were at Kevin's house, fortifying themselves with peanut butter and jelly on white bread straight out of the toaster.

"The trick is to spread the peanut butter on the toast as soon as it comes out," Jack said.

"That way, it melts. And speaking of great food, now I understand why your mom is so

fantastic at pasta, Charlie. She's Italian! And they are some of the greatest cooks in the whole—"

"Good. You're here," interrupted Karen, as she barged through the back door into the Duncan kitchen. "Jack, Queenie wants you *right now.*"

Karen kept her voice quiet, but Jack could tell it took effort—probably so the Buddha wouldn't overhear from her usual chair in the living room. Jack was all too familiar with Queenie's demands, but they were rarely delivered in such a desperate tone of voice. He followed Karen outside. Kevin, Charlie, Jayla, and Sam went, too. They found Queenie pacing next to Camila and Liz on the driveway.

Queenie looked crazed. "Jack, we've got to *do* something! Karen, did you tell him what you heard?"

Kevin's sister said, "I was down at the post library a little while ago, and I heard a girl say that Kerrigan's planning to kick Rabbit's ass."

Jack said, "What? That makes no sense."

Jayla moved a step forward. "Rabbit's just a little kid. Why would Kerrigan mess with her?"

Karen shrugged. "At first I didn't believe it either. But the girl said something about him being sick and tired of her big mouth."

"Jack, we've gotta do something to stop him once and for all," said Queenie. "It was one thing when he pounded you or Charlie—but not Rabbit!"

Jack's eyelids were half closed, but he wasn't shutting down. His brain was cranking.

"Are you listening to me, Jack McMasters? We've gotta do something, and we've gotta do it right now!"

"Oh, I'm listening," said Jack, "and we'll do something. But we are not going off halfcocked. We need to plan this carefully."

"Plan, nothin'. We just need to go kick his ass."

All eyes turned to Jack.

"Wrong. *We* are not." His voice was deathly calm. "*I'm* the one who needs to kick his ass. But *we* can't afford to lose this one. I need to ensure he is stopped for good. But that might involve all of us."

"What are you talking about?" demanded Queenie.

"Look, let's hope it comes down to just Ryan and me. But the odds of that aren't good. Times have changed. At first it was just Ryan. Then it was Ryan and his gang. Now he's also hooked up with the Sevens. In case you haven't noticed, Ryan Kerrigan is rarely alone these days. I might not get to deal with him one-on-one. If I'm going to stop him, we might end up in a situation where we need to deal with all of them. And for that we'll need a solid plan."

"Jack, we can't take on all of them," said Sam. "They aren't just stronger than we are, they also outnumber us."

"I know," Jack agreed. "But I've been thinking about this for some time. Here's what I've concluded: We don't have to beat them. We just need to make sure they can't beat us."

"How are we going to manage that?" Jayla said.

"Say that I end up challenging Ryan, but I have to do it in front of a bunch of others. I'll still challenge him to a one-on-one. And he probably won't be able to back down. And, hopefully, the Sevens will let the two of us go at it. But if I win, they might take revenge on *all* of us. We need to be prepared to defend ourselves if that happens. And that's where Kevin's story about the Spartans comes in. We need to modify the Spartan phalanx."

"Jack, this is no time for your stupid stories and military mumbo jumbo!" Queenie looked ready to wring his neck.

Kevin smoothly took over. "It's not just military talk, Laura. I got some advice from my dad on how to fight a bigger force, without exactly telling him why I needed to know. But it's going to take all of us to make it work."

"I'm listening," Queenie said grudgingly.

His sister nodded her approval, too. So did Camila and Liz.

"I'm with you," said Jayla.

Jack nodded a silent thank-you her way. He knew her support was costing her a lot. It meant postponing Mission Mountaintop. School would start next week. Pretty soon, the days would get noticeably shorter and the weather worse. Every passing day brought them closer to now or never.

Kevin explained that the traditional Spartan phalanx was a square formation, normally ten men in a row and ten rows deep, fighting shoulder-to-shoulder and moving as one.

Jack took over, "There are nine of us—not enough for the square formation, but six kids could form a tight circle with three inside."

He could tell none of them was sure where he was going with this. He was glad they kept listening.

"It's pretty obvious that Kevin and Jayla are our best fighters. We'll place them and Laura in the middle of the circle."

"Why put them in the *middle*?" ask Karen. "If they're the best fighters, shouldn't they be up front?"

"The thing is, Karen, there *is* no front. We form a circle so that no matter which direction the Sevens come at us from, we are protected. We have to give up the idea of fighting as individuals. Like the Spartans, we fight as a single unit. For the Sevens to beat us, they'll have to break through our tight formation—something that we want to make very difficult for them to do."

"So, say, someone attacks Karen," said Queenie. "What does she do?"

"She fights them off. But if the attacker is bigger and stronger than Karen, alone she might get clobbered. With the phalanx, there will be two others—let's say, Camila and Charlie—pressed tightly next to her. So they can help her fight."

"Okay . . ." said Queenie.

"Look," Jack said, "the Sevens will try and break up our circle so they can fight us individually. And we all know where *that* will lead. So we can't let that happen. We have to remain a single unit. A single fighting force."

"What do we do if the person attacking Karen is winning? Fall back?" asked Charlie.

"Nope. We do the exact opposite."

"What?" Karen gasped. "Why?"

"If you're losing, you'll most likely be getting shoved backwards, right?" asked Jack.

"Yeah," said Karen, not liking this.

"But I will yell out, 'On Karen.' And, when I do, we all move forward as a single unit toward her and swarm around both Karen and her attacker. We reclose the circle with them inside. Once they're swallowed up, our best fighters (who are in the center) take on that attacker, but now it will be Karen, Kevin, Jayla, and Queenie all fighting him. Four on one."

"Jack, *I* don't know how to fight," said Queenie. "Why am *I* in the center?"

"The whole point of the phalanx, or at least ours, is that it has nothing to do with how good an individual fighter is. It's about using what we have to best defend ourselves. For example, I know you can't box, Laura, but you're taller than most of us. So, your job will be to grab the guy and try to hold him by an arm, by the legs, by his shirt. Whatever. Just make it harder for him to fight. Then Kevin and Jayla will do what they can to stop him."

Queenie's smile was devilish. "I can do that."

Jack smiled back. "Oh, I *know* you can. The two rules are, always stay together forming a ring. And if we let in an attacker, we stop him."

Kevin was raring to go. "Let's meet behind the post gym and give it a try."

Everyone went in the house. Kevin and his friends finished their snack and cleaned up their mess. Karen, Queenie, Camila, and Liz made their own snack. Then they all walked down to the post gym.

On the way, Jack thought up a hand signal they could use. He joined his two index fingers and his two thumbs together, forming a square like the traditional phalanx. It would alert everyone to form their tight, round phalanx.

Once they were at the site of Jack's previous fight with Kerrigan behind the gym, he showed them the hand signal. To his relief, everyone accepted it and was ready to work.

They repeated the process until forming the phalanx became second nature. Then Jack had them practice moving as a single unit on his command, "On Karen . . . On Charlie . . . On me."

For the next two days they met to practice forming their modified Spartan phalanx and to fight as a phalanx, with Kevin, Queenie, and Jayla as the core of their defense.

Things were going great, until Private Finnegan came out one afternoon for a smoke break.

Something in the way they were scrapping made him stomp over to them. "I haven't helped you kids learn to box so you can go out and pick fights, or beat up other kids. I did it so you could protect yourselves and learn self-discipline."

Jayla said, "This isn't how we wanted to spend our last days of freedom, believe me, Private Finnegan. Remember that fight you broke up between Jack and that other kid? That was Ryan Kerrigan. He's out to take revenge on Jack's little sister, Rabbit. Jack has to stop Ryan, and we're getting ready to back him up in case Ryan's gang won't stand for it."

Private Finnegan studied them, and then glanced at his watch. "I'm covering for someone today. I'm here a couple more hours. Come with me."

They all filed through the back door.

Finnegan had Jack and Kevin spar in the ring while he coached them. Queenie and her crew listened closely to pick up pointers

Jack attempted to sidestep one of Kevin's punches but almost tripped.

"Footwork, Jack! Watch your footwork," said Finnegan. He turned toward the girls. "Half the fight is about your footwork. You have to be able to lightly dance out of the way, and still stay solidly enough on your feet to throw a serious punch."

The girls started watching Jack's feet as well as his arms.

At one point, Jack was sure he had Kevin. He unloaded a huge roundhouse punch, only to have Kevin sidestep it.

Camila giggled.

"Okay, hold up, you two," said Finnegan. "Come over here. We need to talk."

Panting hard, both boys hung on the ropes of the boxing ring, staring down at him.

Private Finnegan looked at the fighters, but more pointedly at Camila. "Kids, the main thing isn't how you punch. The main thing is your fight strategy. Know this: Fights are rarely ever won by a single, giant punch, or a single, lucky punch. The only way you are going to win is by wearing your opponent down. You have to tire him out. Most of all, you have to get your opponent frustrated. Do you hear me?" His eyes rested on Camila.

"Yes, coach," she said.

"More fights are won with *patience*. And more are lost because of *frustration*. Does that make sense?"

Everyone nodded.

"So watch for that one moment when your opponent gets frustrated and does something stupid. That's when you unload on him. That's when you bring it all home."

Private Finnegan focused on Jack. "You're tough enough. You've certainly shown me you can take a punch. Now if you can just keep your head, you can win."

Meaning, if I don't shut down, I can win, thought Jack. *Jayla and Kevin may be able to keep cool in the middle of a fight, but not me.*

The next day they were down by the *Flugplatz*, walking home from the post gym, when Charlie grabbed Jack's arm. "Look over by that maintenance shed. Those are some of Kerrigan's guys."

Jack changed direction. "Maybe he's with them."

"Now is probably not the time or place," said Sam.

"We can set another time and another place. But we gotta find him before he finds Rabbit."

They walked toward the shed.

"Where's Kerrigan?" Jack demanded.

Tony Keach's head bobbed as he counted heads. Jack had eight friends with him.

He said, "We don't want any trouble, Jack."

Jack glared back. "I asked you where Kerrigan was."

"He's not here," one of the others said. "His parents wouldn't let him come out."

"Likely story," said Kevin.

"But it's true," said Tony. "Like I said, we don't want any trouble."

Kevin gave him a hard eye. "Ah! So without Kerrigan you got no fight in you?"

"Just let us pass," said Tony.

"You tell Kerrigan I'm lookin' for him," said Jack. "Got it?"

"Yeah, we got it," said Tony, and he and his friends walked away.

Three more days passed and still Kerrigan hadn't been sighted.

Jack and his crew were down by the snack bar. Kevin had just finished getting his weekly haircut. Jack had come along, hoping to spot Kerrigan. The others had come as backup.

Kevin walked out of the PX with his week's stash of Bazooka. "Any word?"

"Nowhere to be seen," said Charlie.

"Time to turn up the pressure," said Jack. "I need each of you to go tell everyone in our class that I'm looking for Kerrigan. Tell them to spread the word."

"Well, that'll certainly get the pot stirred," said Jayla. "He won't be able to duck that."

"We can hope," said Jack, grimly. Then the irony of it all struck him. Since he'd first arrived, as much as Jack had tried to avoid Kerrigan, the guy had always been right there, tormenting him. Now that Jack was the one looking for a confrontation, Kerrigan was nowhere to be found.

33

Mission Mountaintop

Jayla was the first one to stop by Jack's quarters the next morning.

"How's it going?" he asked. Then he really looked at her. He remembered seeing that same look on his mom once when she fingered a fancy coat with a fur collar, then examined the price tag and walked away. Now he was seeing it in Jayla's eyes. She was giving up the mountain.

That dented him.

But so much was coming at him. It was like he was the only one left in a dodgeball game and everyone around the circle had started hurling balls. *Have to protect Rabbit. Have to deal with Kerrigan. Have to help Jayla get to the mountain. Have to help* all *of us get to the mountain before time runs out.*

I couldn't help my mom get that fur coat, but I can *help Jayla.*

In his mind, he ran toward the most important ball and caught it.

"Okay," Jack said to her, "Kerrigan or no Kerrigan, we pull the trigger on Mission Mountaintop. We notify Hans and Günther now. We make final plans and go."

"What?" said Jayla. "Really?" Her eyes danced.

Late that afternoon everyone had gathered in his bedroom to go over the mission one more time.

"Mission Mountaintop launches at oh-eight-thirty tomorrow from behind The Glass House."

"Roger that," Charlie said, grinning. His smile spread throughout the room.

Only Commander Jack's face remained serious. "Be very clear, we either leave on time, or we abort the mission. Otherwise we won't make it back by dinner."

"Did you get hold of Hans and Günther?" Jayla asked.

"Close enough. I talked my mom into letting me call Hans. He was okay with tomorrow. We'll just have to trust he works it out with Günther. We rendezvous at *Die Einbahnstraße nach Deutschland* at ten hundred hours."

"Do you each have your food supplies?" Scrounger Charlie asked.

"I have half a loaf of bread, a jar of peanut butter, and a jar of strawberry jam," Jack said as he pulled out the equipment checklist. Despite their groans, he forced them, once again, to go through it item by item.

"Okay, I'll see each of you standing tall at oh-eight-thirty," he concluded.

"Be there or be square," Sam said.

"Or as Charlie says, 'If you're on time, you're late,'" Kevin chimed in.

Charlie arrived at Jack's half an hour early, so they went to his room.

As Queenie passed by, she eyed their bulging rucksacks. "So today's the day?"

Jack didn't miss a beat. "Today's always the day. Buzz off."

"Jack, don't be lame. What makes you think you can pull off that mission without me?"

"Mission? What mission?"

"Please don't play the fool. You can't smoke me out. You're planning a hike to the Hohenstaufen. I overheard your little powwow yesterday. In fact, my girlfriends and I are coming along."

"Wrong!"

"Right."

"Not a chance, dorf."

Queenie leaned her head out his bedroom door and yelled, "Hey, Mom, Jack's—"

Fast as lightning, he was off the bed and yanking her back in the room. "Don't you dare!"

Inside he screamed, *You're messing with a plan we spent months and months making. You can't cut in on our operation and make it yours. This is freakin' baloney.*

She smiled serenely. "It's a simple decision, Jack. Either we go, or you *don't* go. Got it?" She had him, and she knew it.

He glanced at Charlie, desperate for a lifeline. But Charlie just shrugged his shoulders as if to say, "She's got your number, buddy."

"Okay! But we won't be back till dinner so bring your own food, water, and money, 'cause I'm not sharing. And we're out of here in exactly twenty-two minutes. If you and your friends aren't ready to go, too bad!"

She smiled with pure delight. "You'll wait no matter how long it takes us, because I'll tell Mom if you bug out before we get there."

At oh-eight-thirty-seven, Jack, Charlie, Sam, and Jayla were behind The Glass House. Jayla was pacing up and down. "Where's Kevin? We're already late."

Queenie, Camila, and Liz finally strolled around the building, talking about Ingrid on some special date.

Jack barked, "Where are Karen and Kevin?"

Queenie's glare said, "How dare you interrupt our very important conversation."

Camila said, "You might as well write them off. Their mom won't let them out until they've cleaned their quarters from top to bottom. Karen said it will take hours."

"What are we gonna do, Jack?" demanded Sam. "Do we postpone the mission?"

"Are you kidding?" Jayla exclaimed. "This took months, and we might not get another shot. School starts in three days." She whirled toward Jack. "We'll have to leave without Kevin"

Everyone studied him.

Jack said, "We are not leaving Kevin behind."

Jayla stammered, "But we can't abort."

"Look, I know it's critical to you, but Kevin has worked as hard on this mission as any of us. He either comes with us, or we don't go."

"Jack!" Jayla pleaded.

"You're right. It has to be today. Saddle up, everyone." He started running toward The Circle. "I need to deal with his mom."

As the others brought up the rear, Charlie sprinted to catch him. "And I suppose you have a plan for dealing with the Buddha?"

"Not exactly, but I'm working on it."

"What are you gonna tell her?"

Jack swallowed hard. "The truth, I guess."

"What?"

"Have a little faith, Charlie."

Karen wouldn't let him in, but Jack pushed past her.

A voice growled out of the darkness. "What is so important that you need to disturb me, Jack McMasters?"

Jack couldn't remember a dicier situation. "I'm sorry to intrude, Mrs. Duncan, but . . . well . . . we all have plans to meet up with our German friends and go on a hike today. And . . . it's our last chance to do it before school starts."

"Unlike you, *my* children have responsibilities this morning."

"I understand completely, ma'am," he said, making sure his voice held no hint of frustration or desperation. "But, we were hoping you'd let us all pitch in and help them. That way the tasks will all get completed, but quickly enough so they can still join us."

"Jack—"

"Please, Mrs. Duncan. You might not know this, but my mother is a master of the white glove. My sister and I are exceptionally well trained. I promise. Everything will be done to your complete satisfaction."

She slumped back in the chair, fading into thought.

Jack remained silent. He had made his case.

"Hmm," she finally moaned. Her stern eyes rose once more, focusing on him. "You know I will be expecting everyone's best work."

Karen and Kevin looked amazed when the small army invaded their quarters and went to work. Jack even volunteered for toothbrush duty cleaning the downstairs bathroom. Before he got on it, he glanced back at the Buddha. He thought he saw a smile flit across her face when Kevin said, "Liz, you can use this sponge to wipe the counters. Please make sure to shine the toaster."

Forty-seven minutes later, they were all assembled behind The Glass House.

Queenie looked at her brother and then her girlfriends. "So how's this going to work?" She was clearly trying to assume control.

Jack stepped toward her. "*I'll* tell *you* how it's going to work. We are now seriously behind schedule for our meetup with Hans and Günther. So we don't just hoof it, we double-time it. Let's move out, everyone."

Queenie said, "Hans and Günther? How did you work that out?"

"Laura, just shut it and follow. You're not in charge here. You're just along for the ride." He turned and, before she could react, started jogging through the woods.

As they ran, their web belts, canteens, ammo pouches, and small rucksacks joggled. It was all needed equipment; Jack's rucksack had eight peanut butter sandwiches, his KA-BAR knife, and his binoculars.

He sent Kevin out on point, and figured as long as Queenie and her girlfriends were tagging along, he might as well get something out of them. He assigned his sister and Karen flanking duty; they should keep their eyes peeled for trouble.

Good thing he had, too. They were hardly deployed when Jack saw Karen take a knee and signal them to hit the dirt. Within seconds, nine kids were down and motionless.

Jack wondered if the threat was real or just Karen's way of messing around with his mind.

Eventually, she got to her feet and sprinted over.

"What?" Charlie demanded.

"The Sevens," Karen said, still a bit shaken. "Kinda hairy, 'cause there were more of them than us. Fortunately they were going in the opposite direction. We just needed to stay outta sight till they passed by."

"You're sure they're gone?" Jack asked.

She nodded. "I'm headed back out on the flank, but you can move out." After another ten minutes, they made it to Black Squirrel Crossing.

Queenie and her girlfriends watched as Jayla and Sam scrambled up the tree. They were completely confused until they spotted the bridge.

Karen said, "When did you stumble on this?"

Kevin said smugly, "Stumble? How about *design*? How about *build*?"

Queenie was rocked so far back on her heels, Jack knew he could push her over with a finger. Seeing her bulging eyes was the first fun he'd had all day. He nonchalantly got on with the mission—a mission she would no longer try to take over.

As usual, once over Black Squirrel Crossing and out of sight of the ravine, the fear of a Sevens ambush lifted. Kevin started calling cadence with a chant that was the best known Airborne Ranger jody. He sang a line, everyone responded, and they kept jogging.

"One, two."

"Three, four."

"Two old ladies were lyin' in bed."

"One turned over to the other and said,"

"I wanna be an Airborne Ranger!"

"I wanna live a life of danger."

"Airborne Ranger,"

"Life of danger."

That jody led to another, as they covered the mile to the perimeter fence in record time. When they got to the trough, Hans and Günther were waiting.

"*Was ist los, Jungs?*" Jack called in greeting.

Queenie leaned over to Camila and Liz, who looked confused. "All he said was, 'What's happenin', boys.'"

Hans blurted out. "Why are you so late?" He gave Jack a look that said, *Why is your sister here?*

"It's a long story," said Jack. "I'll explain when we get over."

As if she couldn't help it, Queenie spoke up. "How are we gonna get over the barbed wire fence?"

"Just watch and learn," said Jack.

Karen said to Kevin, "*You* know how?"

"Certainly. We're going to take *Die Einbahnstraße nach Deutschland.*"

"The *what*?"

"Oh please, don't you know any German?"

"Like you're the grand master of the German language," she shot back.

"It means *The One-Way Street to Germany.*"

When they got to the tree, Jack went first. He wanted to fill Hans and Günther in quietly about Kevin's mom holding them up and how Queenie threatened to expose them if she and her friends couldn't tag along.

They both agreed sisters could be very painful; Jack had had no choice.

Hans said, "We had better not use roads if we can help it. There are so many kids it will call attention. Someone could see us and tell our parents."

The band of eleven kids made their way through the green, rolling sheep pastures, down into Günther's apple orchard, where they each picked a snack. While they munched, Günther led them across large fields and down into a woods. He knew all its paths, and when they encountered a stream, he showed them where the rocks were best for crossing. Next they came to a farm that belonged to a family Günther knew. Unfortunately, halfway across a huge field, they spotted the father on a tractor.

As Camila said, "Should we run?" Günther signaled for them to hit the dirt.

He hissed, "We wait till the tractor turns around and heads back in the other direction. Then we run."

Jack dropped his head to the ground, almost choking on the churned-up dirt. Ingrid had said she could still smell the plowed earth and sugar beets from the night she escaped. Was he in a beet field now?

Finally, Günther started to slink away, and the others followed. When they reached a fenced-in pasture of grazing livestock, Günther led them to a set of wooden stairs with three steps up one side and three down the other. "Perfect for humans, worthless if you're a seven-hundred-kilo cow," he said.

But fifteen yards into the field, Sam lost her nerve as she saw just how huge seven hundred kilos could be. "Is it safe to cross this field? I mean, are they gonna charge us?"

Jack translated with a straight face, but Günther cracked up. He confirmed to Jack they were dairy cows, not bulls.

Jack turned to Sam. "We won't have to be matadors. He says they're cows thinking, *Look at all those kids. Will they hurt us? Should we run away?*"

That got a laugh from everyone—even Sam.

The next farm brought another challenge. Hans and Günther didn't like Frederik, the kid who lived there. The more stories they told about him, the more he sounded like Ryan Kerrigan. The kid was obviously mental.

Queenie said, "Let's deal with Mr. Pain-in-the-Ass right now."

Hans shook his head, "Frederik isn't just a bully. He's also sneaky and he can count. He will avoid us but figure out we're up to something and try to spoil it."

Kevin nodded, "If he rats us out to any adults, there's no more Mission Mountaintop."

"The situation calls for stealth," Jack said. "The best solution is to avoid contact with this Frederik guy. Let's climb into those hills and go around the farm."

Hans and Günther okayed the plan.

The trek up wasn't easy. The path narrowed, forcing them to walk in single file. To everyone's relief, when they neared the top, things opened up.

But Jack called a halt. "We can't walk here. We need to go back down the hill about twenty yards and cut through the brush."

"Why should we leave the path?" demanded Queenie. "That's ridiculous. I'm hot, I'm tired, and I'm not going to fight my way through that stuff."

"Actually it's *not* ridiculous, dink!" he exploded. He'd had enough of his sister for one day.

"So what's the score, Jack?" asked Sam, obviously trying to calm the situation.

"If we walk along the top of this hill, anyone can see us for miles. Just look back down. If we can see Frederik's house, he'll be able to see us against the skyline. We need to keep off that ridge line. I don't like it any more than you do, Queenie, but we can't risk getting busted."

"You call me Queenie one more time today, you little cretin, and I'm gonna clean your clock!" But without another word, she was the first to plunge into the thick brush.

Once beyond Frederik's farm, they found an easier path through the hills and finally took a break on a grassy hillside with a clear view of the Hohenstaufen. They still had about three miles to go, but it was time for lunch.

Jack dug through his rucksack to unearth seven of the PBJs, only slightly smashed. He tossed one to each of his friends. Hans and Günther looked at theirs with polite skepticism.

Hans gingerly touched the brown-and-purple glop oozing from a worn spot in the wax-paper wrapper. "What is this?"

Charlie looked puzzled. "Peanut butter."

Günther's jaw dropped open. "You milk peanuts?"

That pretty much got all the American kids rolling in the grass.

"Sorry," said Jack. "That sounded funny. No, we just smash peanuts up and somehow that makes them spread like butter."

Sam added, "Peanuts and grape jelly are great together."

Hans and Günther each took a bite and were instant fans.

As the kids dug more food out of their rucksacks to eat or trade, Charlie noticed the canteen Günther was drinking from.

The German boy smiled. "You want to trade us your American canteens for our Nazi canteens?"

"Heck, yes," said Charlie.

And that's how he and Jack each ended up owning Nazi canteens. And how Hans and Günther became the proud owners of US Army canteens. Each kid knew he got the better deal.

"Okay, troops. Enough chitchat," said Jack. "It's time to get on with the last leg of this journey."

They moved out.

"Wow, look at that!" Charlie pointed into a huge pit the size of three football fields.

As Jack approached, he realized this was the stone quarry Ingrid had described on their first trip to the train store.

He didn't see any workers below, but he carefully studied the bulldozer, front-end loader, and huge dump truck just in case. It looked like no one was in the quarry. No better time to explore!

The kids scrambled down into the quarry, swarming over the big equipment. When Karen climbed into the huge scoop of the front-end loader, she found a large chunk of sparkling rock.

"Diamonds!" she shouted.

Everyone rushed over.

Hans said, "We call this *Quarzkristall*."

Jack smiled. "So do we—quartz crystal."

"What's quartz?" Karen asked. "Is it a jewel?"

Hans shrugged. "They crush it and then melt it."

Günther winked. "Like peanut butter."

"And a *Glasbläser* puts it on the end of a tube to blow it into glasses and bowls."

Queenie said, "Glass blower? I've seen one."

Hans nodded. "We Germans are some of the greatest *Glasbläsers* in the world."

The others quickly joined the Great Quartz Crystal Hunt. They found samples that were white, dark gold, and clear.

Jack found a two-and-a-half-pound chunk with a beautiful golden color. He took off his web gear and put it in his rucksack. Even if it somehow smashed the PBJ he was saving for the trip home, sacrifices had to be made. He added the smaller crystals he'd found. Now, more than ever, he wanted the rock quarry model at the train store. He could surround it with the quartz he'd found. Next objectives: Earn enough money, and make Ingrid take him to Göppingen.

Queenie found a nice piece, too. She eased up to Jack and said, "It's probably starting to get late. Should we head up the mountain?"

"Yeah. Good idea."

"It's been a good day, Jack," she said, smiling. "You know I won't say anything to Mom. Right?"

"Yeah, I know."

"Hey, Jack, I don't have a backpack. Will you carry my rock?"

"Nope! It's been a great day, but you carry your own rock."

"I'll pay you."

Jack needed money now more than ever. "How much?"

"Twenty-five cents," she suggested.

"Seventy-five."

"Not good enough."

"Fifty. Twenty-five to haul it up the mountain, and twenty-five to haul it all the way home."

"That's a lot." But she held out the rock.

"Money first."

"I only have twenty-five cents with me."

Jack thought about it. "Okay, gimme that much now. You can have the rock back when you pay me the other twenty-five."

"Deal." She dug the quarter out of her jeans pocket and handed it over with her rock.

Jack smiled at his shrewd bargain. But his back would be in serious pain by the time he got home.

As Queenie walked away, he noticed Jayla was looking like the one whose rucksack weighed a thousand pounds.

He walked over. "What's wrong? We made it. Mission Mountaintop is a success."

She shook her head. "Not till we reach the top of the mountain, and not till we make it home."

Jack thought, *That* Upshur *officer was right; an objective has to be remember-able.* "Jayla, getting to the top is just for fun, not part of our objective to prove we're as good as Russian kids."

"What are you saying, Jack?"

"Think back. Mrs. Campbell said there was no way we could get to the Hohenstaufen all by ourselves. Correct? She never said we had to get to the *top* of the mountain or all the way back home."

When that sunk in, everything about Jayla changed, as if the boulder in her rucksack turned to paper mache. "You're right. We've already proven her wrong. We've done it!"

"Yup," he said. "We're as tough as any Russian kid."

34

Unexpected Encounter

Hans gathered the group. "It's about two kilometers to the top. Definitely not the hardest hike in Germany. I mean, there's no rock climbing or anything. We just have to keep following the path." He made a zig-zag motion with his hand. "But toward the top it gets pretty steep."

Jack did some quick calculations. "We'll have to keep up the pace to get back in time."

Queenie sighed. "Plus there's all the way home."

Jack shrugged. "Anyone who doesn't feel like keeping up can hang out down here."

Everyone started for the path.

Serious exhaustion set in as they neared the summit. But once actually on top, the magnitude of their accomplishment filled them with energy.

"We are victorious!" Kevin shouted, dancing around, with arms pumping overhead.

"Take that, Russian kids! We're as tough as you are," Charlie yelled, his fists flying in a series of jabs.

"And more resourceful, too," said Sam, spinning like a dancer.

Queenie just stared at them. "What are you guys talking about?"

"One day in school, Mrs. Campbell said we could never climb this mountain. Of course, she never even thought we'd *try*," said Sam. "We just proved her wrong."

"Actually," Jayla piped up, with a glance at Jack, "we proved her wrong when we reached the mountain. By climbing to the top, we've exceeded her challenge."

"But, of course we have," said Sam. "Because we're with the great Jayla Jones and she always exceeds expectations!"

Everyone laughed, then collapsed on a grassy incline. Sprawling on the grass, letting the summer breeze cool them, they looked over the patchwork of fields and towns of Wunderland.

Jack had given them time to rest before they had to head back down. Queenie and her girlfriends peeled off by themselves. Jack could hear them jabbering—as usual. The German guys were talking quietly together. Plopping down by the others, Jack traced the route they'd taken to get here. Far in the distance, he could just make out the airfield on the Army base.

It brought back a memory of the first time he'd looked out over that airfield from the cliff in front of The Glass House—that first day when he trudged alone around The Circle in the snow, wondering if he'd ever find his place here and make friends. Wondering if anyone would ever follow his lead. The next day, there was Kerrigan, calling him a weenie, forcing a fight. Charlie had stood by him that day, and every day. Then Kevin had stuck his neck out for him on *his* first day of school. What had Kevin said to Mr. Reynolds? That it seemed wrong to kick a guy when he's on the ground. That was probably why Kevin had stuck by him through Little League, and covered for him with the coach when he'd deserted the team. Kevin had convinced him not to quit.

Jack felt Sam looking at him. He turned toward her triumphant grin. She'd thought he was crazy to try to build Black Squirrel Crossing, but she hadn't bailed on him. She'd hung in there. Literally! He could still see her hanging on to that parachute cord for dear life as they hoisted the skid into the air. She'd wanted to kill him for cutting the cord when the Sevens showed up. But she'd taken up the cord to begin again. Black Squirrel Crossing let them duck the Sevens, get over the ravine, and make it to the mountain.

Jayla was staring down into the valley, lost in her own thoughts. The day they first met, she'd razzed him about all his military jargon. But she always got the point of his war stories. She was smarter than he was—smarter than all of them. And fast with her fists. She'd kept Basketball Head off him in his big fight with Kerrigan. She'd always signed up, no matter his objectives. Well, he'd signed up for her mission, and they'd made it work.

Behind Jayla were Hans and Günther, now part of the gang. And they knew it. Their One-Way Street to Germany was key to Mission Mountaintop. And Jack's German was what made their friendship possible—which he owed to his mother's crazy "No English with Ingrid" rule. His mom would be mortified to know she had helped them get to the mountaintop. That made him chuckle.

Jack leaned back and closed his eyes to concentrate on the breeze against his cheeks, the hum of his friends' chatter, and the fresh smell of mountain air. This time, it wasn't just doing Mr. Reynolds's ritual to use his senses, he was truly relishing the moment. The end of a great quest with true friends.

Jack forced himself back on his feet. "Okay, guys. If we want to get home by six, we've got to get a move on."

That got everyone up, gathering their packs.

Hans suggested a steeper, but more direct, route down the mountain that led through a village. That sounded fine to Jack. In less than half an hour, they reached the village.

As they walked by a crowded, little bar, Sam came over to Jack. "My canteen is empty. Could we go inside to buy something to drink?"

Hans looked into the bar. "It might be better to keep going."

Jack followed his glaze. He noticed a few patrons looking out the open door at the mob of kids draped in army gear.

"Sorry, Sam. Let's keep moving," Jack said. "We've made it this far. No point pushing our luck."

"You're probably right," she said reluctantly, and kept moving.

Jack checked once more to see if interest in them had died down. Something caught *his* interest: a man standing at the far end of the bar, talking on the phone. Jack couldn't see his face, but even so, he could tell the guy had military bearing. He stood very erect, speaking with authority.

Probably a cop or something, thought Jack.

As if he'd sensed Jack eyeing him, the guy whirled around—and Jack recognized him. Shocked and strangely disturbed, Jack moved out of his line of sight.

He caught up with the others.

"Wait up a second," he said shakily.

After one look at him, they gathered around.

"There was a guy at the end of the bar using the phone," Jack said. "Did any of you notice him?"

No one had.

"People like that bar because they let you pay to use their phone," Günther offered. "So it's not that unusual."

"Maybe not, but I got a clear look at the guy. I'm pretty sure it was Herr Stein, our janitor from school."

"Good thing we didn't stick around," Sam said. "He might have recognized and reported us."

"True," Jack said, "but something's bothering me. Something about him being there."

"Oh, come on, Jack. We all know the guy's a dipstick," said Queenie. "Why get bent out of shape?"

"I dunno," he said. "There was just something about him. Something's off. At school, the guy always seems old, and like a nobody. Ya know what I mean?"

"Yeah. So?" said Charlie.

"Well, the guy I just saw was totally different. He seemed very serious and superior and in command. In fact, at first I thought he might be a cop or military. I don't know what to think."

"I'll go check it out," Queenie offered. "I won't be long. And don't worry. I'll be stealthy. I just want to see if it's really Herr Stein."

"I'll come along to help you fit in," said Günther.

"Thanks. I bet these blue jeans shout that I'm an American."

Günther shrugged. "All German girls want American blue jeans. It's our canteens and army stuff that will make people look."

Jack held up a hand. "Thanks for offering, Laura, but we need to do more than make sure it's Stein. We need to know what he's up to. I have to listen in on his call."

Sam's eyes said she thought things were spinning out of control. "This isn't the time to get nuts. If we're busted, even *I* will get killed for being up here."

Jack's eyes hardened. "I can feel it. Something isn't right. That guy is up to something—something bad. Something that could hurt not just us but the adults."

"I don't get it," Sam said.

"Neither do I. That's why I need to get close enough to hear him."

"Well, you can't just walk in there," Jayla said. "And you'd better be quick. His call won't last forever."

Günther's face was pinched in thought. "I'm pretty sure that place has a door off the back alley. Maybe we could use that."

"Günther, Hans, come with me," said Jack. "The rest of you head up this street, but then wait for us."

"Please don't!" Sam pleaded.

The three were already gone.

The back door was locked. Jack forcibly resisted the urge to kick it.

Hans swallowed hard. "I'm going around through the front. There's got to be a bathroom in the back. I'll ask if I can use it."

A few minutes later, the door opened and Hans came out, closing the door but not entirely. "He's still on the phone. We can hide under a counter at the end of the hall. It's pretty close to that end of the bar."

The hallway was so dark, Jack could hardly make out the *Toilette* sign over a door. Hans squatted under the counter and the others followed.

Squished underneath, Jack pressed his back against the wall. The space gave them cover from above, but anyone looking from the side would easily see three boys crouching there.

At first they only heard general noise coming from the single, large room.

Then a man said, as if on a phone, "Yes . . . um-hum . . . um-hum."

Jack could tell the other two were getting anxious. "We have to confirm it's Stein. Let's take a quick look while he's preoccupied with his call."

The caller said, "Yes. . . . Yes."

Jack and Günther peeked around the corner. The guy's back was to them, but they could both see him in the mirror that ran behind the bar. It was definitely Stein.

If they could see *him*, he could see *them*. They slowly ducked back around the corner.

Stein said, "Well, call back right away." He hung up the phone.

Jack nodded to the others, and they pressed even harder against the wall.

Günther eventually whispered, "What now?"

Very quietly Jack said, "Let's stay put and see if they call back—"

An old man rounded the corner. Seeing them, he poked his head under the counter and demanded, "What are you three up to?"

But before they could sputter an excuse, his face broke into a grin. "Scared you, didn't I?" Clearly pleased with himself, he headed for the bathroom.

Heart pounding like crazy, Jack leaned over and said, "Forget that old man. Günther, I think you and I will stay. Hans, you get outta here. Make sure the bartender sees you leave so he doesn't get suspicious."

Ring. . . . Ring. . . .

"Hello. . . . One moment, sir."

"Yes, sir. . . ." This time the voice wasn't Stein's.

Jack signaled Hans to go. But added, "Get a good look at who's on that phone."

Hans got to his feet and strolled nonchalantly through the bar.

Jack thought, *That Hans has nerve.*

The man on the phone said, "Yes, I can confirm they just received six new-model tanks. . . ." Long silence. "Yes, two new diesel tanker trucks. . . . We'll try to find out. . . . We'll let you know. Yes, you can reach us at the usual number."

Jack looked at Günther and whispered, "We're outta here."

In the alley, they talked over everything they'd heard. Jack wanted to make sure he hadn't missed anything.

"That all seems pretty strange," Günther said. "Why would that guy know so much about what is going on at the Army base? And who were they talking to?"

"No idea," said Jack. "But keep it under your hat till we can figure it out."

When they caught up with Hans, his face was unusually tight. "Sorry, Jack, I could not see his face. I do know he is much bigger than Stein."

"Hair color?" Jack asked.

"Blond or maybe gray. Very short, like Kevin's. Sorry I couldn't see more."

"You did great. First, you got us in. Second, we confirmed it was Stein. And third, we learned someone else is in on it with him."

"Let's get away from here," Jack said as they rejoined the others.

"Was it Stein?" asked Charlie.

"Definitely."

"And?" Queenie asked, her eyes narrowing.

"Something isn't right. I don't know what. But he is not like the guy we know."

"You keep thinking. I can manage this," said Queenie. In a loud voice, she yelled, "Come on, people. Time to go home."

For once Jack was glad for his bossy sister. He did need to think.

Weird. I only saw the back of the guy for a split second, but that was enough to tell me he was a cop or a military guy. How'd I know that? Then he turns around—and it's our nobody janitor. The whole thing just doesn't make sense. It was definitely Stein . . . and he wasn't alone.

The stones in his rucksack shifted, banging his lower back.

Why would those two be talking about new tanks and tanker trucks? The big one talked about the usual phone number . . . like they use it to report in all the time. It's like they're relaying intel on 4th Armored. The thought shook him. *Could they be Communist spies—like the ones Ingrid talked about? This is bad. We can't keep this to ourselves.*

He picked up his pace so he could talk to Charlie and Kevin. They were with the German guys, talking about World War II.

He listened for a minute but then cut in. "We've been over this before. The Nazis are a thing of the past. Today America and Germany need to team up against the Communists. The past hasn't kept us from being friends; it's the future that counts."

"*Ach*, I think that makes good sense," Günther said.

Jack said, "What do you know about the Communists?"

Again, Günther spoke up. "Our parents hate the Communists. The Communists want to destroy our way of life. But our country was cut in two just before we were born. Suddenly there was East Germany and West Germany. If you were in the East, you became East German and that country was run by Communists and Russians."

Hans said, "We had the good fortune to live here."

Günther nodded grimly. "We hate the Russians and the Communists, but we feel sorry for East Germans who got stuck siding with them. We know friends who have cousins and grandparents in East Germany."

Hans jumped in. "Do you see? We hate the East German Communists, but they are still Germans just like us. It's hard."

"Wow, that would be kinda tough to sort out in your brain," Charlie said.

Jack nodded. "You have your East and West. America had a war between our North and South. Even brothers were on different sides. Lucky for us, that war ended a long time ago and we're still the *United States*."

"I wish we had one Germany," said Hans, "but a free one, not Communist."

"And there are Communists who want one Germany, too. But they want you *not* to be free," said Jack. "There are over three thousand Communist tanks on the other side of the Iron Curtain. They're pointed at us both—West Germans and Americans. So if you stand with us, against them, we will have a solid friendship. But if one day you side with the East Germans against us, our friendship will be over."

Günther shot out his hand to shake Jack's. "We are with you, Jack. Just like we were with you today in that bar."

Jack shook his hand. "That's great, because I am convinced Herr Stein and his buddy are spying on our tanks to see if we're strong enough to defeat the Communist tanks. But getting anyone to believe us might be very difficult."

Kevin's shoulders hunched over. "Especially without telling them where we were today and how we found out."

"Well," said Hans, "no matter what, we are with you."

Jack could feel it; their friendship was being cemented against a common enemy. For the first time since seeing Stein, Jack felt hope.

35

Resolution

At The One-Way Street to America, Jack made sure he was the last in line to climb back on base. As he waited, he turned to Hans and Günther.

"Thanks, guys. You were a big help getting Jayla—and all of us—to the mountain."

"It became our adventure, too," said Günther.

"I'll let you know if I figure out a plan about Stein. And especially if you can help."

Hans nodded gravely. "Make an excuse to telephone my house. It's our fight, too."

When the brats came off Black Squirrel Crossing, Jack knew they were back in Sevens territory. He considered deploying security, but didn't have the heart to make his exhausted crew walk point or take up flanking positions. They all just shuffled along in a clump.

Tired as he was, Jack's brain kept circling back to the bar. *What if we hadn't run across Stein today? What if we'd never overheard their conversation? But we did! What do we do?*

Then his brain drifted. . . . He imagined that instead of dragging his body through this forced march, he was lounging in comfort with his buddy, Alex, on the *Upshur*. They were having their best conversation—the one about Jean-Sébastien. Then Alex searched Jack's face and said, "When the time comes, will you be ready?"

That shook him. *The time* has *come. My time. Jean-Sébastien met the Panzer Lehr, that elite Nazi tank group. I met Stein. Both simply happened. But once Jean-Sébastien knew what it meant, he had the guts to stay involved. I know this means trouble. I have to stay involved, too. I have to tell Dad. Is there any way to say it without explaining where and how I found out?*

Even though it was twenty minutes to six, they had to stop and rest. Within sight of the Nazi pillbox, they collapsed on the forest floor. Queenie looked more tired than Jack could ever remember, but that didn't keep her from pushing for more details about the bar. This time Jack didn't hold back. He unloaded all his worry about Stein and the other guy possibly being spies.

"They *have* to be spies," said Kevin. "Why else would they be relaying information about tanks and fuel trucks?"

Charlie lay there, looking asleep, until he piped up, "This whole thing reminds me of The Watcher."

Jack swallowed hard. "The Watcher had military bearing, just the way Stein had today on the phone. Maybe The Watcher's been cleaning up after us at school, and we just never knew it was the same guy."

"Now that you mention it, I think you could be right," said Sam.

"We have to stop them," Jayla said. "What's our next move, Jack?"

"We need to make sure Stein and this spy ring gets busted," he said. "But this is bigger than just us. For once I think we need help from our parents."

"Whoa!" Queenie said. "They'll go nuts if they find out we were up at the Hohenstaufen."

"And if they find *that* out, they'll also want to see how we got off base," said Kevin. "There's no way we can let *that* happen."

"Not to mention they might find out about Black Squirrel Crossing," said Charlie. "And they'd probably make us take it down."

"You're right. You're *all* right," Jack conceded. "But this is a matter of security. Army security. We have to let them know. I just need to come up with a way to do it without telling them all the things we *don't* want them to know."

"How's that possible?" Queenie asked.

"I'm the only one who actually overheard them. That makes me the one to talk to my dad. How, I don't know, but I'll come up with something."

They resumed the trudge home, heads down, focusing on putting one foot in front of the other. Jack's back was killing him. The rocks in his rucksack had smashed a dent near his spine. For about the tenth time, he thought, *I'm gonna stash them here and come back for—*

Out of nowhere a large group of Sevens sprang up.

Everyone froze.

Where'd they come from? There must be fifteen of 'em! Why didn't I deploy security?

B-Ball Head came sniffing around, a smirk on his face. "What you got there, Carron? Is that a Nazi canteen I see? Where'd you get it?"

"Got it from a German kid," Charlie mumbled defensively. "I traded him for it."

"BS, Carron. That's just BS," B-Ball said. "It's ours. Ya see, Carron, there's a new rule around here. Any German stuff found in these woods is *our* property."

"Yeah. Hand it over," demanded Snot-Nose.

"Consider it a tax," said B-Ball. "You hand it over, and just maybe we give you guys a pass."

Queenie leaned toward Jack and whispered, "Should we make a run for the ravine? Try to ditch 'em?"

"Or give them the canteen?" Sam asked. "He said they might let us go."

Jayla's eyes darted for a way to escape. "What do you want us to do, Jack?"

He knew they were waiting for his call. Maybe, if they were rested, they could have defended themselves. But they could barely stand, let alone fight.

Ryan Kerrigan suddenly emerged from a clump of trees.

For once, instead of shutting down, Jack filled with cold determination. His exhaustion gave way to exhilaration.

"No," he said, loudly enough for even the Sevens to hear. "This ends now! We do not run! And we do not give them anything! This is where we make our stand."

Kerrigan stopped about twenty yards away. "I hear you been looking for me, McMasters?"

"And I hear you're gonna pound my little sister. Big mistake, Kerrigan. Time for you to stop picking on people."

"You gonna make me?"

Jack said with a certainty none of them had heard before, "Right here and right now."

"Slow down," interrupted B-Ball. "Before you two scrappers have at it, gimme that Nazi canteen, Carron."

"B-Ball, shut-up about that canteen!" Jack snapped. "This isn't about stupid Nazi stuff."

Then, turning back to Kerrigan, he said, "Just you and me. None of your little friends. And none of the Sevens. Just the two of us. Understand?"

Jack didn't bother waiting for a response. He tore off his web gear and handed it to Queenie. As he stared down Kerrigan, his fingers formed a Spartan square.

Jack advanced on him while his crew slowly edged toward each other.

"Put up your dukes, Ryan," Snot-Nose shouted with delight. "Give us a good show."

Kerrigan smiled over at the Sevens. "This shouldn't take long. McMasters is a complete weenie."

The taunts didn't faze Jack. He got into a fighter's stance, his feet beginning to dance lightly as he circled Kerrigan. He reminded himself, *Patience. Let him come to you.*

It took a minute, but Kerrigan finally took the bait. He closed in with a right to Jack's face.

Jack blocked it with his left, immediately noticing Kerrigan was holding his fists high, trying to protect his own face. He was holding them a little *too* high. Jack unloaded a quick right and left into his ribs. He made solid contact.

Backing away, Kerrigan gasped for air.

"Come on, Kerrigan, show us your stuff," yelled one of the Sevens. "Take this pretty dancer out."

With lightning speed, Kerrigan came in low. Jack fought back, but in a series of punches, Kerrigan finally landed one on his right cheek, knocking him off his feet.

Kevin yelled, "Get up, Jack!"

Jack knew Kerrigan would start kicking any second. He scrambled back onto his feet. Before Kerrigan reacted, Jack attacked, landing another hit to the ribs and one to his mouth.

Jack could see it in his eyes: Kerrigan felt pain and increasing frustration. Jack was supposed to be an easy target. It wasn't working out that way.

For the next few minutes, both fighters kept giving and getting, but neither was gaining the advantage. The Sevens were growing impatient.

Someone yelled, "Come on, Kerrigan. I thought you said this guy was a weenie."

Another chimed in, "You're not makin' it look like he's much of one. In fact, I'm beginning to believe he's gonna take *you*."

"I thought you said you were good, Kerrigan," shouted Snot-Nose. "Now! Finish this guy."

With the back of his hand, Kerrigan wiped blood from his lip. A crazed look came into his eyes.

Jayla yelled, "Watch for it, Jack."

Kerrigan let out a blood-curdling yell and charged. Arms outstretched, he sprang into a flying tackle.

To Jack, Kerrigan seemed to be floating toward him through the air. Kerrigan's head was coming at him just the way a baseball did. Jack could sense the moment that head would sail over home plate. At just the right moment, Jack's feet glided sideways. Kerrigan's outstretched hands sailed past him. Jack hit Kerrigan's head with all he had.

Kerrigan went down. Kerrigan went down hard. He didn't get back up.

The fight was over.

Jack knelt down next to Kerrigan. Once he was sure the guy wasn't seriously hurt, he whispered, "You ever touch any of us again . . . you touch anyone I even *know* . . . you and I will be doing this little dance again."

Getting to his feet, he saw his friends positioned just the way they'd practiced. Jayla, Kevin, and Queenie in the middle. The others around them. Before the Sevens had time to react, Jack moved in, taking his place in the circle.

B-Ball turned away from Kerrigan, who still hadn't gotten up. He glared at Charlie. "I want that canteen *now*, Carron."

The Sevens began to advance on them.

"I don't *think* so," Jack said. "Our woods. Our stuff. *You* back off."

"Jack, Jack, Jack, you're dreaming," B-Ball sneered. "You can take Kerrigan, but you can't take all of us, now, can you?"

Jack just said, "You want the canteen? Come and get it."

It was obvious this wasn't the answer the Sevens were expecting, but at a nod from B-Ball, two Sevens immediately attacked the phalanx. Neither managed to penetrate the circle. One got his face scratched by Karen. The other was clobbering Charlie until Queenie reached through the circle and smashed the guy's foot with a quartz chunk someone had dropped. The guy fell backward, grabbing his foot and screaming in pain.

"Stand your ground," Jack commanded.

B-Ball came at Sam. He grabbed her by the arm, trying to drag her out of the circle. As she stiffened and fell forward, Jack yelled, "Advance on Sam."

The entire phalanx moved as one. The circle opened, enveloping both B-Ball and Sam.

B-Ball now found himself alone in the middle of the phalanx.

As Sam scrambled out of the way, Queenie yanked B-Ball's right arm, pulling it back. Kevin and Jayla unloaded a volley of punches into him.

The giant of a kid, knowing he was in serious trouble, and desperate to get away from them, used all his weight to break out of the circle.

The phalanx immediately closed up—ready for the next assault.

Jack spotted Snot-Nose standing back, assessing. Kerrigan would be okay, but he was still down. One Seven had scratches, another couldn't walk, and B-Ball wasn't looking too good. Snot-Nose sneered, "Enough with the stupid canteen. We're out of here."

And, amazingly enough, no one argued with him.

As the Sevens left, Jayla walked over to Jack. "You were right. We didn't have to beat them; we just had to keep the Sevens from beating us."

Victorious, but considerably worse for wear, Jack and Queenie walked into their quarters at 6:39 p.m.

Lt. Col. McMasters was pacing—obviously agitated. The minute he turned toward them, Jack saw the angry glint in his eye.

"Where the hell have you two been!" he exploded.

"Sorry," Jack said, staring down at his muddy pants.

The colonel's voice went deadly. "You look me in the eye, and you address me as *sir* when you are speaking to me, young man."

Jack's head snapped up. He straightened his shoulders and locked eyes on his father. "Sorry, sir."

"Sorry? Sorry is for losers!" the colonel snapped. "Speaking of which, just look at you two. Dirt from head to foot. You're a complete mess. And your shoes are a disgrace!" With an eagle eye, he inspected both of them for additional infractions. "I see somebody's smashed up your sorry-ass face again. Looks like once again you failed to deal with your problems."

Jack stammered, "Dad, it wasn't—"

"Don't you dare say it wasn't your fault, you miserable excuse for a boy."

Jack flinched. "I was just trying to say today wasn't about me."

"I don't give a shit who—"

"Dad, you've got to listen!" Queenie shouted in frustration. "We're late, but it could have been a lot worse. The fight today wasn't about Jack. He was protecting Rabbit. What he did was great."

"What?" demanded Mrs. McMasters, entering the living room at the mention of Rabbit. "Hold on a moment, John. What's this about Rabbit needing protection?"

At that moment Rabbit came strolling in and blurted, "Yeah. Why do I need protection? I can take care of my—"

"In your room, Rabbit," commanded Mrs. McMasters.

"What'd I do?"

"Now!"

She glanced toward her father for support, but after one look at him, she vanished.

Mrs. McMasters demanded, "Explain yourself, young lady."

"You know who Ryan Kerrigan is, right? He's the one who beats up everyone in Jack's class. He's the reason Jack got thrown out of school."

"So?" demanded Lt. Col. McMasters, still hot.

"So we found out Ryan Kerrigan was tired of Rabbit's big mouth and he was gonna pound—"

"What?" demanded Mrs. McMasters. "Someone that old was actually going to hurt her?"

"Damn it, Jack. If you'd dealt with Kerrigan the way I told you to, this never would have come up."

"Dad!" Queenie blurted. "If you'll just listen, you'll find out Jack *did* address the issue. You've heard about Kerrigan, but it involved a lot more than just him." She told them about his gang and the Sevens, and how stopping Kerrigan meant dealing with all of them.

Lt. Col. McMasters calmed down long enough to ask a real question. "So, what happened?"

Queenie said, "When we found out Kerrigan was coming after Rabbit, Jack put out the word he was looking for him."

"He what?" Mrs. McMasters gasped.

"Yup. But Kerrigan's been ducking him for the last three days. That is, until late this afternoon." Then she explained how they'd been jumped by the Sevens in the woods and that Kerrigan had been with them.

"So you were outnumbered by older kids. What did you call them? The Sevens?" By then, intrigued, Lt. Col. McMasters asked Jack, "What did you do?"

"Well . . . sir, I called Kerrigan out for a one-on-one." He briefly recapped the fight.

Queenie jumped in. "When Kerrigan finally didn't get back up, Jack told him if he ever messes with Rabbit, or any of us, he was gonna get it again."

Once more Mrs. McMasters looked shocked, but Lt. Col. McMasters actually seemed pleased.

"So how did you finally learn to handle yourself in a fight?"

"After that fight with Kerrigan, when I got kicked out of school, you told me I should stick tight to Kevin Duncan. Well, during that same incident, Mr. Reynolds told Kevin that he knew how to choose the right friends and that he should stick tight to me. So that's what we've done ever since. Kevin's the one who taught me to box. He's the one who helped me prep for Kerrigan."

"I knew I liked that kid," the colonel said. "So what did the Sevens do after the fight?"

Queenie continued. "They didn't let it go. They came after all of us."

"Outnumbered by how many?" asked a surprised Lt. Col. McMasters.

"With Ryan on the ground, they still had at least four extra." Queenie turned to Jack. "Tell Dad about the Spartan phalanx."

Jack said, "We knew that in order for me to take on Kerrigan, we might have to face the Sevens. We needed a strategy to defend ourselves. So Kevin asked his dad how a smaller, weaker force could defend itself against a stronger, larger force. That's when Col. Duncan told him about the Spartans and their phalanx formation. I just modified it for our smaller force."

Lt. Col. McMasters studied his son.

Queenie picked up the story. "Jack made us all practice our own Spartan phalanx for several days till we knew how to fight as a single unit. In fact, he drove us all crazy, making us practice so much. But I have to admit, in the end, it worked. Even all those Sevens couldn't beat our unified force."

Lt. Col. McMasters was looking at his son with new eyes. It was obvious he was seeing him as a strategic thinker. Smiling, he said, "Jack, what you did reminds me of an old drill sergeant I had in basic training. The guy used to bark at me, 'McMasters, remember the Six P's: Prior Planning Prevents Piss Poor Performance. Well, young McMasters, it seems to me you did an excellent job of prior planning when it came to dealing with your Kerrigan problem. Congratulations."

"Thanks, Dad."

"Now how about dinner for these warriors," the colonel said, turning to his wife expectantly.

"We *were* having *sole meunière*."

"Ah, one of my favorites," he said.

"Well . . . I hate to break it to you, but unlike you tough warriors, sole is a very delicate fish. And at this point it is no longer salvageable."

Queenie glanced at her dad to see if that was going to set him off again. Instead, he said, "Well, if I can't have my favorite dinner, I guess Jack has earned one of *his* favorite dinners. Let's all jump in the Roadmaster and go to that *Gästehaus* up by the Hohenstaufen for *Schnitzel mit Pommes frittes*.

How strange. Jack could feel that his father was content with him. Even if it didn't last, Jack would remember this moment. His father felt he had done okay.

Once their dinner order had been taken, Queenie leaned toward Jack. "What about Stein? You gonna tell him?"

Jack would have done almost anything not to spoil his dad's mood. But the image of Stein locking eyes on him from the end of the bar kept coming back. If the guy was a spy, he could threaten all of their lives. There might not be time to waste. *Okay, Jean-Sébastien, here goes nothing.*

"Dad, is it true that the 4th just received six new model tanks and two new fuel trucks?"

The colonel looked at him with more than a little suspicion. "Yes. How do you know about that?"

"Earlier this afternoon, before we got jumped by the Sevens, we were climbing trees in the woods. Some German men came walking along the path below us. They had no idea we were up there. They were talking about the new equipment."

Queenie gave him a look that said, "Okay, I see how you're gonna play this."

"And?"

"Dad, we're sure they've been spying on 4th Armored Division. We even know who one of them is. He's our janitor at school."

"Jack . . ." his father said, seeing where this was headed and wanting to cut it off.

"Dad, just let me finish. They said they were on their way up to the Hohenstaufen to make a phone call. They were going to tell someone about the 4th receiving that new stuff. Why would they be reporting that if they weren't spying?"

"I think you're letting your imagination run wild." But the colonel's voice held no anger or frustration. He seemed to be treating this as a grownup conversation. "I know that the 4th just announced some new job openings. They are looking for mechanics to help with that new equipment. Those guys you overheard were probably just going up there to call some of their friends and see if they'd be interested in those new jobs."

"You really think that's possible?" Jack asked, skeptical.

"Yes, I do. Lots of Germans work for us. And most of the new people we hire are friends of the Germans who already work for us. We figure that if they are good workers, their friends will be, too."

"Maybe . . ." Jack wondered if he'd read everything wrong.

"Actually, I think it's pretty likely, Jack."

Jack remembered crawling through the ventilation ducks with Alex, pretending the engine-room workers were spies or saboteurs. *Could I be pretending this time, too?*

But the moment he asked himself the question, he knew the answer. This time was different. This time something really *was* wrong.

"Dad, it didn't sound like a help-your-buddy call. It was more like they were plotting something. More serious."

"Their whole conversation was in German, right? Could you have misunderstood some of it?"

Now it was Jack's turn to flare up. "Not a chance, Dad!" *Besides, Hans and Günther had made sure of that.*

"Okay, okay, don't get offended," said Lt. Col. McMasters, letting a little smile cross his face. "I know how good your German is."

Jack settled back down. Then he thought to ask, "Why would they go all the way to the Hohenstaufen to have a private call? If it was just to their friends, why wouldn't they call them from on base?"

"They aren't supposed to call outside numbers from on base. They were probably going to use a public phone up there. There aren't many public phones available in Germany. It's not like America where there are payphones everywhere. That phone at the mountain might be one of the only publicly available phones outside of Göppingen."

"But—"

"But nothing. Quit letting your imagination get the better of you. I'm sure you just misread their intent. I'm proud of you for protecting your little sister and dealing with Kerrigan. Let's leave it at that. Okay?"

Jack glanced over at Queenie. Her answering look said, "Let it go. Dad's not buying it."

Just then their waitress appeared with food. She set a large plate of *Schnitzel mit Pommes frittes* in front of Jack, and it smelled oh, so good. He couldn't help thinking, *I guess I'll leave it for now—but just for now.* The moment his mom picked up her fork to begin eating, all Jack's concentration shifted to *Schnitzel*. He was in heaven.

And his father being okay with what he'd done. Well, that was even better than *Schnitzel*.

Jack slept badly. In his dreams, he'd spent half the night trying to get a look at the big guy in the bar. The other half, he was being chased by Stein.

By morning Jack was sure of two things: they were spies, and he needed to make the adults understand.

By habit, he sat down at his train board. *What was different? Why did Col. McHenry believe Jean-Sébastien? Why couldn't Dad believe me like that?*

Jack took the two chunks of quartz crystal out of his rucksack and placed his piece on the train board. Then he placed a sheet of paper on a flat spot on the board and, turning the rucksack upside down, he shook out a small pile of quartz shards.

He traced a question mark through the jagged stones. *Jean-Sébastien wasn't more believable than I am. It was his story that was more believable. Col. McHenry was ready to believe the Germans were preparing a sneak offensive. Dad isn't expecting spies on base.*

Jack started arranging the pebbles one by one on the board. *Col. McHenry recognized that the threat was real, so he sent Jean-Sébastien back for more intel on the Panzer Lehr. I need to get better intel on Stein so Dad will recognize that this threat is real, too.*

At breakfast, his father's place was empty. "Where's Dad?"

"Tanks rolled at zero four hundred this morning," Mrs. McMasters said.

Queenie and Jack looked at each other, startled.

Queenie said, "When's he getting back?"

"Laura McMasters, I know you're smarter than to ask such a question. None of us knows when the troops will return. So I won't have you pestering me for an answer. He'll be home when he's home, and that's all there is to it. Do I make myself clear?"

"Yes, ma'am."

"Besides, you should have known he wasn't here," said Rabbit, dripping hot cereal from her spoon back into her bowl. "We never have this crummy Cream of Wheat when Dad's around."

"Rabbit, one more smart word and you're in your bedroom."

"I'm just saying—"

"Bedroom!" pronounced Mrs. McMasters, banishing her.

That was the last word anyone said.

36

And . . .

Jack was back at his train board when Queenie walked in.

She studied his chunk of crystal. "It looks good there."

Then she handed him a quarter. Jack smiled back and handed over her rock.

She smiled, weighing it in her hand. "Thanks, Jack. I forgot how heavy it was."

He grinned. "Heavy and pointy. I think one dent in my back will never go away."

"I bet. It was some adventure. Have you really been planning the whole thing for half a year?"

"Yes . . . , I guess we have."

"I can't believe you guys built that bridge over the ravine. That had to be one of the most critical pieces."

"Yup. It makes everything easier. Not just exploring the other side, but getting away from trouble."

"And you figured out how to get off base."

"Well, Hans and Günther came up with that."

"An incredible day. Besides everything else, you finally settled the score with Kerrigan."

"*We* settled it. But you're right. I don't suppose Ryan will be an issue anymore. And if we stick together, maybe the Sevens will leave us alone."

Queenie began turning the chunk of quartz over and over in her hands. "You're right," she finally said. "Kerrigan's one problem out of the way . . . but what about Herr Stein? There's still something about that guy that doesn't sit right with me. What Dad said could be true, but—"

Jack shook his head. "He didn't hear those guys on the phone. He didn't see Stein turn into a soldier before his eyes. Stein's a much bigger problem than Kerrigan ever was."

Jack watched the turning quartz glint in the light of his lamp. "It's also pretty strange that yesterday I was talking with Hans and Günther about the Communist tanks up on the Iron Curtain and now 4th Armored Division is probably heading toward them."

Queenie thought about that for a while. "Mom seemed kinda upset at breakfast."

"Yeah, or at least distracted."

She shivered. "Do you think something bad has already happened? You know, that caused the tanks to roll?"

Jack turned off his lamp. "Remember how Dad said that 'Prior Planning Prevents Piss Poor Performance'? Well, you and I planned weeks ago. Let's see if Mom has messed with the emergency evacuation suitcases."

They slipped down the hallway. Queenie quietly opened the closet door.

The light was so dim they had to get down on their hands and knees to check. Both heads bent close to see the right latch of Queenie's pink suitcase.

The hair was gone.

Staying True to Jack's World

This is a work of fiction. The characters in the book are fiction, and the story is fiction. However, the setting and history are as real as I could make them. In fact, here are some aspects of *BRAT* that are real: the USS *Upshur*, Göppingen, Cooke Barracks, 4th Armored Division, the Iron Curtain, and the Stasi. I have gone to significant lengths to ensure that the historical setting for the story is depicted as it really was.

In addition, I have tried to make the story accurate to its time, 1957 to 1959, so I wrote it with the language, customs, and practices of those times. I wanted the reader to genuinely experience life as it was. My fabulous editor has, in fact, consistently busted my chops for trying to slip in slang terms not yet said in 1958. As such I believe I may now have the longest list of documented slang terms that were used by military brats in that time period.

But being period correct was not always comfortable. You may have noted that, by today's standards, some things in this book are not politically correct. For example, I refer to Jayla's mother as a Negro and her father, Lt. Col. Jones, as colored. Believe me when I say I struggled with that. It would have been far more comfortable to call them African American—but in 1958 the term did not exist, at least not as it is used today. I owe a lot to my dear friend **Sheila Talton** for getting me over that hump, and helping me to better understand the lives and language of black America during that time period.

Why the Dandelion and the Barbed Wire?

In Part One of the book, when the kids are on the ship, the decorative spacer is a dandelion. That might seem a bit strange, until you learn that the dandelion is the official flower of the military brat. "The dandelion puts down roots almost anywhere, and is almost impossible to destroy, and survives in a broad range of climates. Military children bloom everywhere the wind carries them. They are hardy and upright. Their roots are strong, cultivated deeply in the culture of the military. . . . They're ready to fly in the breeze that takes them to new adventures, lands, and new friends." (Author unknown) Jack, Queenie, and Rabbit are very much in the wind as they are being blown halfway around the world. In Part Two, once they reach Germany, the decorative spacer becomes a piece of barbed wire, because as the brats set down roots in the land of the Iron Curtain, that symbol overshadows much of the story.

Contributors of Photographs
That Became Illustrations in this Book

The BRAT Team

It has been an honor to write this story, but that honor is not mine alone. An amazing group of people over the last four years have grown into what I call The BRAT Team—those who have been so instrumental in bringing an idea through concept and creation all the way to you readers. I can't imagine any first-time author having a better team.

These teacher-coaches and book-production experts provided countless hours of help and value that brought this work to life. If I am the storyteller, they are everything else that made this book what it is.

Editorial

Lori Mulligan Davis, the person who most influenced, architected, and affected this book, my writing coach, my editor, and now my friend. Wow, does that woman have a lot of patience to put up with me. Believe me when I say, if the writing in this book is good, it is because of Lori—it is her doing. When I showed her the first several chapters of my first draft . . . well, anyone else would have thrown me out then and there. Why anyone would have taken me on. . . . But oh, is she sneaky. I must have had over a hundred disastrous flaws as a writer, but she only smiled and said, "Well, let me teach you two things and we'll work on that." Then she would say a week or two later, "Here is another thing. Let's work on that." She never let on what a wreck I was. And good thing for me, or I might never have stayed with it if I'd known how far I would have to come. Lori is a great teacher, a great coach, a great motivator, a great writer, and (Lord, help me!) also part of the grammar police. You are fun, you are patient, you are kind, and you are seriously disorganized. What would I do without you? When this book has success, it will be because of you.

Kristina Cowen and **Nancy Nehmer** batted cleanup, and Lord knows we needed these razer-sharp proofreaders.

Advisors

Colonel Brett Sylvia, now Commander of Strike, the 2nd Brigade Combat Team, 101st's Airborne Division, is the busy man who made time to be my military editor, ensuring the armor and infantry material in the book was correct. Brett is both an Airborne Ranger and a tanker. Besides tuning up content, he gave me detailed background explanations that improved the story.

Gavin Sylvia, Col. Sylvia's son, is a brat with a can-do attitude. All writers should be so lucky as to have a beta reader like Gavin. Talk about feedback! Gavin returned his copy plastered with over three hundred sticky notes—full of excellent comments and corrections.

Chris Faber, one of my earliest readers, first read the book when he was ten. Wow. His feedback was a mind warp. He is nothing short of wicked smart, giving me sage advice way beyond his years. He was the first to help me know my characters had actually come to life.

Simon Perutz, my wise friend, was the first adult I dared let read the book. It was through his feedback that I understood the book needed some drastic rewrite, but with his continued encouragement I began to believe the story could get legs.

Yogi Mahendra and **Dee Ott** were early encouragers that kept me going.

German Experts

Willi Hass, of Munich, carefully corrected all the German phrases in the book—more than once.

Peter and **Sibylle Sonnenberg,** originally from Stuttgart, made sure the German was in the proper Göppingen dialect.

The Advance Team

Michelle Miller, Bob Holliker, Louis Bartrand, Mimi Hayes, Misty Corrales, Chris Kyrios, Joseph Condrill, and that very talented writer, **Patty Tracy Perrin**—brats one and all—kept me straight and made sure that the unique world of us brats was accurately portrayed. **R Jamaal Downey**

and **Donna Musil** helped me think through the positioning of the book for the brat community. Also a special thanks to Donna for allowing me to use her film short, *Growing UP Army*, on my website, to help those who have never had exposure to military families get a feel for what it means to be a brat.

Production and Design

Jordan Vouga, graphic designer and brand creator in Berkeley, California, developed the clean and deceptively simple Bravur Media logo, brilliantly playing off the Spartan hoplite shield.

Lauren Tackbary, Berkley-based graphic designer, created the brat dandelion and barbed wire decorative spacers, one of my favorite elements in the book.

Mark Davis, a graphic and font designer from New York, selected the readable-but-cool period-correct style fonts used in the book. I love them.

Judy Ostarch and **Andrea Reider,** in LA, did a beautiful job with the whole book layout, getting ready for **Nick Vergoth** (x-military intelligence) to print it at Lake Book in Melrose Park, Illinois.

Christine Goulden was worth the trip to New York City just to have her photograph my author headshots. Somehow, she always manages to capture that just right moment. She and **Muhammad Salman** built my author's website.

Jivko Jelev is the talented illustrator who managed to create the "pirate map" illustrating where Jack McMasters and the brats lived and operated. It was no small undertaking to draw an accurate map of a large chunk of Cooke Barracks circa 1958. Jivko then transformed period photos from the late 1950s into the illustrations throughout the book.

Greg Samata and **Tim O'Brien** were the dream team who created the cover. I never realized just how hard it could be to create a decent book jacket. After the fourth unsuccessful attempt, I had the great good fortune to meet Greg. Among other things, Greg is a creative genius and a master at creating a brand. He said, "Scrap everything—we are going to hire some great models to represent Jack, Rabbit, and Queenie, and dress them in period-accurate clothes and do a photo shoot." I thought that was pretty outrageous, especially when the Chicago photographer, **Melissa Salvatore**, was working to get those kids into character to get just the right shot. But when it came time to find an illustrator to take those great photos of the kids and turn them into a book cover, I knew Greg was a wild man. He dropped a *TIME* magazine with an incredible cover on me, saying, "How's that for an illustration? He did the Hunger Games covers, too. Let's go get *that* guy." I should have immediately known he wasn't joking. That's just what he did. And the next thing I knew, we had one amazing book cover.

Getting the Word Out

Natalie Faye, from Paris and Morocco, greatly expanded my social media presence.

Carla King, from San Francisco, helped me put together the distribution strategy for the book. Carla definitely knows the ins and outs of book sales.

Syliva Perez, fellow brat and TV news reporter in Chicago, conducted the interviews and worked her magic to bring the book trailer to life.

The Glue

My wife, the love of my life, who holds me together.

Need I say more? I have the very best of teams. You can join us on Facebook and Goodreads. Your positive reviews will lead other readers to *Brat and the Kids of Warriors*.

I surely hope you have enjoyed the first book in this series, and that you'll be back for more. As Editor Lori says, "Book One just pushes the boulder to the top of the hill. Book Two lets it really roll."

Thank you for reading.

—Michael Joseph Lyons